CUT THROAT

Lyndon Stacey is an animal portrait artist by trade and has a love of Western-style horse riding. She lives on the outskirts of the New Forest. Her second novel, *Blindfold*, is available in Hutchinson.

'Lyndon Stacey's novel is not only set in the world of horse racing, but like Francis's books, features a clean-limbed young chap – in this case American rider Ross Wakelin, seeking to make good in England after personal problems in the US – getting entrammelled in skulduggery. However, Stacey possesses another of Francis's attributes in being able to tell a lively, absorbing . . . story of murder and horse mutilation . . . and the reader has a very good time'

Gerald Kaufman, *The Scotsman*

By the same author

Blindfold

LYNDON STACEY

CUT THROAT

arrow books

Published by Arrow Books in 2003

1 3 5 7 9 10 8 6 4 2

The right of Lyndon Stacey to be identified as the author of this
work has been asserted by her in accordance with the Copyright,
Designs and Patents Act, 1988

First published by Hutchinson in 2002

Arrow Books
The Random House Group Limited
20 Vauxhall Bridge Road, London SW1V 2SA

Random House Australia (Pty) Limited
20 Alfred Street, Milsons Point, Sydney,
New South Wales 2061, Australia

Random House New Zealand Limited
18 Poland Road, Glenfield
Auckland 10, New Zealand

Random House (Pty) Limited
Endulini, 5a Jubilee Road, Parktown 2193, South Africa

The Random House Group Limited Reg. No. 954009

www.randomhouse.co.uk

A CIP catalogue record for this book is available from the
British Library

Papers used by Random House are natural, recyclable products
made from wood grown in sustainable forests. The
manufacturing processes conform to the environmental
regulations of the country of origin

Typeset by SX Composing DTP, Rayleigh, Essex
Printed and bound in the United Kingdom by
Cox & Wyman Ltd, Reading, Berks

ISBN 0 09 942945 4

For my mother, who always believed.
And for my father and Bob Stembridge,
who would have been so very pleased.

Acknowledgements

I would like to thank Martin Peaty MRCVS, of The Barn Equine Surgery, Dorset, Mark Randle of the Wiltshire Police, and the staff at BSJA headquarters, Stoneleigh, for their patience in answering my many questions, and to make it clear that any inaccuracies are entirely my fault for not asking the right questions!

Also, thanks to Sue and James at Hutchinson, and Dorothy, my agent, for their help and encouragement.

And last, but by no means least, thanks go to Anthony McConnell and Brenda, my 'Fairy Godmother' who, between them, started the ball rolling.

1

Twelve hundred pounds of charging horseflesh hit the wooden railings chest high and somersaulted into the north stands. Faces, frozen with horror, moved in desperate slow motion to get out of the path of the crazed beast, and their screams were all that its helpless rider could hear. The slamming, sickening impact, the smell of horse sweat and newly painted wood and the taste of blood were all crowded out by those piercing, hysterical cries.

He couldn't move, couldn't breathe. Pain filled his chest. Panic rose, constricting his throat, and the animal's flailing hooves threatened to decapitate him at any moment. Still they screamed. Why couldn't they stop? The noise filled his mind, tore at his senses, on and on and on . . .

'No!'

Ross cried out, kicking at the bed covers that had twisted round his legs, and sat up gasping for breath. Sweat glistened on his face and arms, staining his grey tee-shirt, and his hair clung damply to his scalp.

He swung his legs over the side of the bed and sat, waiting for the pounding of his heart to steady. His head throbbed heavily and his mouth tasted bad. The jeans he still wore bore testimony to his nocturnal ramble along the beach. Sand grated between his toes and he felt unwashed and very sick. Considering the amount of alcohol he had consumed, he was surprised he hadn't fallen into the sea.

The delicate state of his health was not improved by the loud buzz of the doorbell, a moment later.

Ross groaned, head in hands. Perhaps whoever it was would go away.

It buzzed again, the sound reverberating inside his head, and muttering darkly, he pushed himself to his feet.

Stumbling across the room, he stubbed his toe on a chair leg and swore, as yet unfamiliar with the layout of his mother's Florida beach house. Needing a peaceful refuge and knowing it to be empty, he had flown down from Georgia the previous day, when he had finally been forced to admit to himself what the rest of the world had long ago decided: that his career as a professional rider was over.

The doorbell sounded a third time. Ross jerked the door open irritably and squinted against the sunlight.

The slight, blonde female who stood on the

doorstep surveyed him from head to toe with wide-spaced, blue-grey eyes. She tilted her shoulder-length bob to one side and pursed her lips.

'My, you have had a bad night,' she observed in aristocratic English tones.

'I've been out jogging,' Ross lied blandly. Lindsay Cresswell, friend and fellow rider, was someone he would normally have been pleased to see, but not today, and especially not in the condition he was in.

'Yes, of course.' She sounded unconvinced. 'Aren't you going to ask me in?'

'Sure, if you want to join me for breakfast.'

'I was thinking more of lunch,' Lindsay said dryly. 'It's half-past twelve. That must have been some run!'

Ross looked at his watch and grudgingly conceded the point. He stood back, allowing her to step past him and into the dim interior. Then he slammed the door irritably, immediately regretting it as his aching head protested.

'You'll have to wait while I freshen up,' he mumbled mulishly. All he really wanted was to be left alone.

Lindsay threw open the curtains to admit the sunlight of a glorious May day and righted an empty wine bottle that was lying on the coffee table.

'Fine,' she said brightly, sitting on the luxurious cream leather sofa and picking up a magazine.

Ross slammed the bathroom door for good measure.

3

Ten minutes later he emerged, having showered and changed, his dark brown hair towelled dry and combed back.

'That's better, you look almost human,' Lindsay said, coming through from the kitchen and handing him a cup of steaming coffee.

His temper in some part restored, Ross surveyed her with affection. Her thick, naturally blonde hair framed a face with almost classical bone structure and flawless, lightly tanned skin.

They had met on the show circuit some eight months before and had quickly struck up an easy companionship. She was in America for a year on a working holiday as nanny-cum-groom for a friend with a young family, and the knowledge that when she returned to England she was expected to become officially engaged to James, her childhood sweetheart, had provided the relaxed atmosphere in which their friendship had grown.

At first the existence of this distant relationship hadn't worried Ross; lately it had begun to prey on his mind.

'I guess you didn't come all this way just for coffee,' he said, collapsing on to the immaculate upholstery.

'No, I have a proposition for you.' She sat opposite him and took a sip from her cup.

'Oh?' His tone offered no encouragement.

'I was talking to my uncle about you.'

'I bet he was just fascinated.'

'As a matter of fact he was. Interested, anyway. You remember I told you he has a small

4

showjumping yard back in England? Well, two weeks ago he lost his rider.'

'Kinda careless of him,' Ross observed.

'Ha-ha,' she said with a brief, humourless smile. 'No, the young lad he had riding for him wasn't up to the job and apparently there was a big bust-up between him and one of the other owners in the yard, which ended in the rider being thrown out. So now they're stuck, and I suggested you.'

'Oh, yeah?' Ross laughed mirthlessly. 'And they're so short of riders in England that he'll jump at the chance of taking on an unknown from the States – especially one who comes complete with a reputation for unreliability.'

Lindsay ignored the sarcasm. 'It's mid-season. Most of the riders worth their salt already have enough on their plates. I mean, it's one thing to take on an extra horse or two, but not a whole yardful. He's got an ex-jockey exercising them at the moment but if he doesn't find someone soon, the other owners will take their horses elsewhere. But, understandably, Uncle John is very particular.'

'Like I said,' Ross murmured.

'Anyway, I suggested you and he's willing to give it a try.'

Ross frowned. 'Why in hell would he? He doesn't know me from Adam!'

'No. But I do,' she said patiently, 'and he trusts me. Well? What do you think?'

Ross was silent for a moment. 'I think your uncle should look someplace else,' he said then, avoiding her hopeful eyes. 'I'm through with that game. I'm sorry, you've had a wasted journey.'

'What do you mean? You can't just give up – it's your life! Horses are in your blood. That's what you told me, remember?'

'Well, I was wrong. I've changed my mind, and now I've quit. Finished. Okay?' Ross put his cup down on the table and stood up, his lithe six foot two frame towering over her briefly before he walked away towards the window.

'No, it's not okay!' Lindsay exclaimed incredulously. 'You can't let them win, just like that. It's like admitting they're right to doubt your nerve!'

'Maybe they are.' Ross watched the waves lazily lapping the sand of the deserted beach.

'My God, you *are* feeling sorry for yourself, aren't you?' She rose to her feet, banging her cup down hard on the tabletop. 'All washed up at twenty-seven. Well, don't let me interrupt your self-pity. Why don't you have another bottle of wine? Or two!' She picked up her bag and whisked out of the room.

Ross stayed motionless, sighing as he heard the door slam and her footsteps recede down the gravel path. He was disgusted with himself, but most of all he was conscious of having lost Lindsay's respect, and that hurt. She, of all people, deserved better treatment. Throughout his long hospitalisation and convalescence following the accident, she had been one of his most frequent visitors, and one of the few to continue to support him as his attempted comeback fell apart around him.

He looked across at the open liquor cabinet but made no move towards it. Before the previous night's binge, he had never used alcohol to drown his sorrows and the way he felt this morning didn't encourage him to change his habits. He ran his fingers through his hair and groaned, wondering if his mother kept any antidote to the poison she stored in such quantity.

The doorbell buzzed again. Crossing to the door, he opened it a crack and peered through.

'My car keys,' Lindsay said huffily.

Ross obligingly fetched them but kept them enclosed in his hand.

'Stay and eat?' he suggested sheepishly.

'I shouldn't have thought you'd feel like food,' she remarked, avoiding his gaze.

Ross considered this.

'Guess you're right,' he agreed, holding the keys out obediently.

Suddenly, Lindsay smiled.

'Thanks, I'd love to stay.'

He could never say for sure just how the decision was made, but the following week found Ross alighting on to the tarmac at Heathrow after a flight from Miami that had been delayed by a bomb hoax and endless security checks.

Lindsay had painted a very tempting picture of life in her uncle's small Wiltshire yard, although Ross nursed no illusions that it would be a bed of roses. But when the alcohol-induced depression wore off and his natural resilience edged back, the challenge of a completely new start began to exercise a strong attraction. He was honest enough to admit, if only to himself, that no small part of its allure lay in the knowledge that Lindsay stabled her own horse in the yard and would sooner or later return to her home just three miles away.

He phoned the Colonel before taking an airport bus to Woking, from where a train connection delivered him safely to Salisbury, albeit some seven hours late. Here he was met by a neatly dressed man of fifty or so, who announced that he had been sent to collect Ross and led the way to a gleaming, dove-grey Jaguar.

He learned that his driver went by the name of Masters and that he worked for Colonel Preston – Lindsay's Uncle John – but not a lot else. Ross settled back wearily in the sumptuous leather-covered seats and in the fading light of the early evening marvelled, as he had done on the train, at the constantly changing scenery. Houses, woods, fields and moorland, all within the space of a few miles. In the States, you would have to travel for days to see such varied terrain.

It was nearly dark when Masters turned the Jaguar off the road and on to a gravel drive set between two huge limes, the car's headlights picking out a sign that announced Oakley Manor.

'I'll take you straight to the yard,' he told Ross, breaking a long silence. 'The Colonel won't be able to see you at the moment. You were expected earlier and he's had to go out.'

'Yeah, well, nothing I could do about it,' Ross

said. 'I spent most of the night at Miami airport.'

Masters shrugged non-committally.

The car swept between two single-storey buildings into a well-lit yard and the middle of a crisis.

No sooner had they rolled to a halt than a stocky young female burst out of a nearby doorway at a run. She checked in obvious disappointment as Ross climbed out of the Jaguar.

'Oh, I thought you were the vet!' she wailed. 'I called him ages ago. What am I going to do? Sailor's dying, I'm sure he is!'

'Okay. Slow down. What's the problem here?' Ross asked, his fatigue instantly forgotten.

There was a moment's hesitation as the girl stared at him. 'Oh, you're the new rider, of course. It's Sailor – one of the two-year-olds in the bottom field – I think he's got colic. Bill's out, and when I went down to check on them after dinner, Sailor was thrashing about on the ground, covered in sweat and kind of drooling at the mouth. I tried to get him up, but I couldn't get near him. It was awful!'

'Is anyone with the horse now?'

'Yes, Leo's down there but *he* can't get him up either. Oh, thank God!' she exclaimed as a Range Rover rapidly decelerated into the yard and stopped beside the Jag. 'Here's Roger.'

The occupant of the Range Rover, a youngish man with a friendly face and a shock of curly hair, leaned across and opened the passenger door. 'Where's the patient?' he asked without preamble.

'Bottom field,' the stocky girl told him.

'Okay, Sarah, jump in. We'll go down in this. Is Bill there?'

'No, he's not here. He's gone to a tack auction with the Colonel. They should have been back by now. Oh, God! It *would* happen tonight.'

As the girl climbed in next to the vet, Ross slipped, uninvited, into the back seat and slammed the door hastily as the vehicle lurched forward. Nobody queried his right to be there and Masters, who had remained silent throughout the exchange, watched his departure with a resigned shake of his head.

They crossed the yard, swung left and bumped perhaps two hundred yards down a grassy track, with Sarah repeating her tale to the vet as they went. The track ended at a metal field gate, where the three of them scrambled out, leaving the Range Rover's headlights on to illuminate the area beyond. A few strides took them to where the stricken horse lay, convulsing weakly.

A lean, wiry figure rose to its feet at their approach and Ross could just make out the aquiline features of a young man with close-cropped dark hair and a glint of gold in one ear. Leo, he presumed.

'Hi,' Roger said. 'How is he now?'

'Quieter. He's stopped thrashing about.'

'Hmm, that's not necessarily a good sign,' the vet said as he put his bag down and knelt at the horse's head. 'How long has he been like this?'

'I found him about forty minutes ago,' Sarah told him, her voice shaking. 'He was much worse then – thrashing about and scraping at the ground with his feet. I rang you straight away, but they said you were already out.'

'Yeah, another emergency. A difficult foaling. I came as quickly as I could.'

'What d'you think's wrong with him?'

'Can't say for sure,' Roger said, shining a pocket torch into the horse's accessible eye and then moving to listen to his heart and lungs through a stethoscope. The horse moved feebly, giving a long-drawn-out, breathy groan, and he patted it, soothingly. 'His pupils are dilated and his pulse is rapid and very weak.'

'There's shit all over the place,' Leo commented. 'I nearly slipped up in it.'

'It *could* be colic,' Roger went on, moving his stethoscope to listen to Sailor's gut. 'But I think there's something else. I'm worried about the salivation. It's not usual.'

'Poisoning?' Ross suggested.

The vet looked up, noting his presence with a momentary frown. 'It's a possibility,' he admitted. 'All I can do at the moment is try and make him more comfortable.' He straightened up and headed for the Range Rover. 'I'm afraid, whatever it is, we're probably going to lose him.'

In the light from the vehicle, Sailor shuddered and kicked all four legs as a spasm took him. Beside Ross, Sarah made a small despairing sound, and without thinking, he put a hand out to squeeze her arm comfortingly.

'Diazepam,' Roger said, coming back, syringe in

hand. 'An anti-convulsant. It'll help relax his muscles.'

The horse groaned and kicked again as he knelt to inject it.

'Poor old fella,' he said softly.

Less than twenty seconds later, Sailor heaved a huge, rattling sigh and relaxed.

'Ah,' the vet said regretfully, patting the still neck. 'That's not the drug. I'm sorry, I'm afraid he's gone. Is he one of the Colonel's?'

'No. Mr Richmond's,' Sarah told him, staring wide-eyed at the corpse, and Ross recalled from Lindsay's briefing that Franklin Richmond was a wealthy businessman and one of two owners besides John Preston himself who kept horses in training at the Oakley Manor yard.

'Oh, Christ! It would be, wouldn't it?' Roger said heavily.

Sarah stifled a sob. 'I can't believe it! He was so full of life this morning. We had the digger down here, clearing the ditches, and the youngsters were all racing round together. How could it have happened?'

'This field's quite marshy, isn't it?' the vet commented thoughtfully, packing his stethoscope away.

'Yes. Why?'

'Are there any other horses still in here?' he asked, ignoring the question.

'Yes . . .'

'Right. Well, I think we should get them back to the yard where we can keep an eye on them. Just as a precaution. Come on, I'll give you a hand.'

Even though they were wearing headcollars, the operation to catch the remaining four two-year-olds and persuade them to pass the body of their erstwhile companion took nearly a quarter of an hour. Halfway back to the yard the vet received another call-out on his mobile phone, handed his charge to Leo, and departed to patch up a pony that had got hung up in a barbed-wire fence.

The remaining group were met in the yard by a wiry, taciturn little man who introduced himself to Ross as Bill Scott, stable manager, and suggested that the youngsters be put in the schooling area for the night. It seemed that Roger had given him the bad news on his way through the yard, and had promised to return first thing in the morning.

'Give them plenty of hay, Sarah,' Scott instructed as she led the way to a gate in the corner of the yard.

Ross let his two-year-old loose in the school along with the others, and turned back to the yard where Scott stood waiting.

'So, you're Ross Wakelin. You're late,' he observed.

'I phoned from the airport,' Ross said, surprised. 'The flight was delayed.'

'Yes, I know.' Scott's tone implied that this was no excuse. 'Well, I've got work to do so I'll show you your room. The Colonel said to tell you he'd see you in the morning.'

Ross wasn't sorry. He had slept very little at the airport the previous night, and at that moment desired nothing more than a bite to eat and a bed to black out in. He certainly felt in no fit state to confront his future boss.

Scott led the way across the yard to a door set between two stables. Automatic security flood-lights came on at their approach and horses peered out at them, wisps of hay trailing from their muzzles.

'This used to be a coachhouse. The Colonel had it converted,' Scott told him, opening the door to reveal a flight of wooden steps leading steeply upwards. 'Now it's two bedsits. Your room is on the left; the other belongs to Leo. Bathroom's straight ahead. You'll eat with me and the missus in the cottage. Dinner's normally at seven-thirty but she'll have saved you something, so come over when you're ready.'

Without further ado he turned and ambled away with that rolling, slightly bow-legged gait peculiar to seasoned horsemen. Ross wondered with momentary amusement if *he* would end up walking like that, given time.

He found his room to be quaint and surprisingly comfortable. Long and low, it had cream-painted walls and masses of dark beams. The floor was of uneven boards liberally scattered with bright rugs, and against one wall sagged a huge sofa that had seen better days but was preserving its dignity under a striped horse blanket. A wood-effect electric fire promised warmth if needed, and entertainment came in the shape of three rather discoloured Stubbs prints and a portable TV.

14

Seated smugly on top of this was a polished mahogany Buddha, a souvenir of some far-off land, and on top of the fire an ancient Bakelite-cased clock ticked loudly. At the far end of the room, underneath the sharply sloping ceiling and partly obscured by a half-drawn partitioning curtain, was the bed.

Ross' last meal was a distant memory, so pushing the recent tragedy determinedly to the back of his mind, he dumped his bags, combed his hair and went in search of Bill Scott's 'missus' and something to eat.

The door of the Scotts' cottage stood open, spilling a column of light into the yard. Ross found himself in a large room that obviously served as kitchen, dining room and lounge, and bore signs of once having been three smaller rooms. Directly in front of him was a scrubbed pine table round which you could comfortably have accommodated a baseball team, and beyond it, sprawled in an armchair and watching a game show on the television, was Bill Scott. He didn't look up as his wife bustled forward to greet Ross, and beyond telling him to come in and shut the door behind him took little notice of the American. Ross wondered what he could have done to antagonise the older man; after all, they had barely exchanged a dozen words.

'I'll do it, Ross. You sit down,' Mrs Scott said, pulling a chair out for him. 'Your dinner's just on ready.'

A pie with melt-in-the-mouth pastry and boiled potatoes appeared before him almost before he had settled into his chair, followed shortly by a large wedge of something she called Dundee cake and a mug of steaming coffee. Whatever else might befall him in his new job, Ross reflected, he wouldn't starve.

It seemed Bill hadn't eaten either. He came to sit at the table but his attention was clearly still on the television quiz and it was left to his wife to initiate conversation, which she did with a shocked reference to the fate of poor Sailor.

'Poison!' she said, shaking her head in disbelief. 'Whatever next? Poor Mr Richmond is *so* unlucky.'

'In what way?' Ross asked.

'Oh, don't let's go raking all that up,' Bill said wearily. 'What we've got to do now is make sure the others are all right.'

His wife ignored him.

'His best horse was killed in a knife attack last year,' she told Ross. 'It was horrible. We had the police here and reporters hanging around for days. Poor Sarah was that upset, she had to go on tranquillisers.' Her eyes shone, recalling the drama of it all.

'Oh yeah. I remember now,' Ross said. 'Lindsay told me about it when it happened. Didn't he win the Hickstead Derby?'

'Yes, and it's history now, so just let it be,' Bill cut in.

Ross would have liked to know more but felt that provoking an argument would probably not be the best way to begin his association with the Scotts.

In the mellow light inside the cottage, the couple

16

appeared to be in their mid-forties: he tanned, with receding salt-and-pepper hair and a deeply lined face; she a comfortably rounded, attractive brunette.

'Have you been to England before, Ross?' she asked, as the meal wound to a close.

'Once when I was a kid,' he said. 'My father brought me with him on a business trip and we saw the Christmas show at Olympia. It was pure magic. I think that's when I decided I wanted to be a rider.'

'It's a lovely show,' she agreed, getting to her feet. 'More pie? Or cake?'

Ross declined, sitting back in his chair and looking about him. The cottage was attractive in a homey sort of way, furnished and upholstered with quality but not extravagance. Assorted mementoes of foreign holidays sat incongruously amongst more traditional English pieces, reminding Ross of the Buddha in his own room.

He would have liked to have questioned Bill Scott about the horses and the other staff, but as soon as the meal was over, the stable manager retired to his armchair once more and appeared to have his attention firmly fixed on the flickering screen before him. Ross thought that perhaps he didn't like to bring his work home, as it were.

'Do the others eat here?' he finally asked Mrs Scott, obediently lifting his elbows as she wiped the table before bearing his plate away to the washing-up bowl.

'During the day,' she replied. 'Then young

17

Sarah usually goes home for her dinner and Leo goes out, as often as not. They stayed on this evening, of course, because Bill was out. Are you sure you've eaten enough?'

'Yes, thank you, ma'am. That was lovely.'

Mrs Scott laughed out loud. 'The only person we call ma'am in this country is the Queen,' she told him. 'You call me Maggie, like everyone else does.'

Ross smiled and nodded, liking her a lot more than he did her husband.

Soon, pleading exhaustion, he excused himself and made for his bed.

2

Apart from Leo banging the bathroom door when he came in at some ungodly hour, nothing disturbed Ross' sleep that night. He rose early from habit and spent ten minutes going through the exercises his physiotherapist had set him, adding one or two of his own for good measure.

On a table opposite the foot of his bed he had found a kettle, two mugs, and jars containing instant coffee, tea and dried milk. He filled the kettle from the tap in the bathroom and made himself coffee, drinking it black while standing at the window overlooking the yard.

From this vantage point the set-up looked neat and well-ordered. The buildings surrounding the yard were of red brick, and appeared old but immaculately maintained. All the paintwork gleamed and no stray buckets or abandoned tools were to be seen. It seemed that the Colonel liked his yard run with military precision.

In the centre of the open space a huge stone trough held water that reflected the sky. To his left as he looked from his window was a row of loose-boxes that opened directly on to the yard; opposite was a long wall with windows and two archways which he guessed led into a corridor with more stables. To his right were a barn, the driveway to the main house and, out of sight, the Scotts' cottage and the gravel drive leading to the road. In the far right-hand corner of the yard, between a large foaling box and the barn, the grassy track they had followed the night before led to a five-bar gate and a field bounded by woodland. From a second window at the other end of his room he had a view of the large sand arena where they had put the two-year-olds, and a steeply rising field that obscured the road beyond. Thankfully, the youngsters all looked fit and well.

It was a far cry from the vast dusty expanses and barn stabling that Ross was used to in America, but it was a glorious morning and a second chance beckoned. Whistling softly, he began to dress.

He heard Leo come out of his room, go down-stairs and out into the yard, and then caught sight of him crossing to the stables on the other side.

When Ross made his appearance in the yard shortly afterwards, feeding had been completed and mucking out was well under way. Bill, Leo and Sarah, bustling about with wheelbarrows, muck-sacks and buckets of water, greeted him with two 'good mornings' and a 'hi'.

Unsure what was immediately expected of him

and anxious not to get in the way, Ross drifted into the tackroom. There, amongst the smell of leather, soap and metal polish, he immediately felt at home. Neat rows of gleaming saddles and bridles hung above wooden blanket chests, each bearing a different name: King, Simone, Clown, Cragside ... He paused. Cragside was a big strong horse judging by the severity of his bridle. Fly, Butterworth, Bishop ... Ross inspected each set of tack carefully, learning something about each horse from the tools of his trade. All the leather was supple and clean, the bits and stirrups shone. He was impressed.

'Time for breakfast.' Bill Scott spoke from the doorway. 'The Colonel wants to see you ride after you've eaten.'

As they crossed the yard towards the cottage, Scott gave Ross a sidelong glance.

'You're lame,' he remarked, his tone faintly accusing.

'A little,' Ross agreed. 'It doesn't affect my riding.'

Considering that after his accident he had been told he would be lucky if he ever walked without a stick again, he had always felt it would be churlish to resent the slight limp he'd been left with.

Scott grunted. 'I hope not.'

Breakfast would have been a solemn affair without Maggie's chatter. Bill Scott was clearly not disposed to talk and Leo Jackson proved to be reserved to the point of surliness. Ross wasn't sure whether it was the result of a heavy night, but when formally introduced, he acknowledged the new-comer's presence with only a brief nod and then returned his attention to his eggs and bacon. Wearing black jeans and a khaki tee-shirt, he looked in the daylight to be something over thirty, with dark hair and eyes, and a faintly olive complexion.

Sarah Owen appeared to be little more than a teenager and was painfully shy. She turned pink whenever Ross spoke to her and never once met his gaze during the entire meal. He sighed to himself. His workmates promised to be a laugh a minute.

Breakfast was barely over when Roger arrived, collected Bill and drove on down to the scene of the previous night's tragedy. They had been gone some twenty minutes when a white Mercedes pulled into the yard, and Sarah, who had at Ross' request been putting names to the horses' faces, paused and said unhappily, 'That's Mr Richmond.'

Going across to meet the expensively dressed, middle-aged man who was climbing out of the car, Ross found him to be slightly overweight but good-looking, with dark hair going grey at the temples and brown eyes that clearly reflected his sadness at his horse's death.

Ross was mildly surprised by this. Youngstock turned out in a field to mature generally represented promise rather than an emotional bond.

'Mr Richmond? I'm Ross Wakelin. Bill's with the vet. I shouldn't think they'd be much longer,' he said as they shook hands.

'Have they said how it happened? What did Roger say?' Richmond was plainly agitated.

'From what he said last night, I gather some kind of poison is a possibility,' Ross told him.

'Bastards!' Richmond said bitterly. 'Why now?'

'I'm sorry?' Ross replied, bewildered.

'Oh, no, *I'm* sorry.' Richmond almost visibly pulled himself together. 'What a way to welcome you!' He turned as they heard the Range Rover returning. 'Ah, here's Roger.'

The vehicle drew up beside them and the vet erupted from it in what Ross was coming to recognise as his typically energetic way. 'Franklin, what a bloody shame. It would have to be one of yours!'

'Was it poison?' Richmond demanded.

'It was,' Roger confirmed, his good-natured face registering regret. 'Hemlock. Hemlock Water Dropwort, to be precise.'

'But . . .' Richmond appeared to be struggling to process the information. 'When I got the message last night, I thought . . . Are you saying that this was something he found in the field?'

The vet nodded. 'In a manner of speaking. I had my suspicions when Sarah told me there'd been a digger in, clearing the ditches. You see, the whole plant is poisonous but the root is by far the worst part and it's the only bit that's really palatable. It's supposed to be sweetish but I wouldn't recommend trying it. You'd probably be dead within minutes.'

'You're saying that the digger exposed some of the roots and Sailor helped himself?'

'I'm afraid so.' Roger held up a polythene bag that contained several creamy-white, elongated roots, three to four inches long, and a small quantity of muddy water. '*Oenanthe Crocata.* Otherwise known as "dead men's fingers". You can see why. Easy to overlook when it's growing – it looks a bit like cow parsley.' He stepped back towards the Range Rover. 'Look, I must go. I'll do a gut sample when the hunt stables collect him and let you know for sure. But it all fits. Bloody shame!'

'Surely they won't feed a poisoned horse to the hounds?' Ross was surprised.

'They don't feed much horsemeat to the hounds at all,' Bill Scott told him dourly. 'Apparently it's too rich. Most of it's incinerated these days.'

Colonel Preston arrived in the yard five minutes later at nine o'clock prompt, and was standing talking to Franklin Richmond when Ross came down from his room having swiftly exchanged jeans for grey cord breeches and leather boots.

The epitome of the retired Army officer, from the tips of his carefully tended moustache to the toes of his gleaming brown shoes, the Colonel had greying hair under a flat cap and blue-grey eyes that missed nothing. He greeted his new employee politely with a handshake and a brief smile, subjecting him to a long searching look that Ross felt laid bare all his doubts and insecurities.

'I've heard a lot about you, young man,' he said, genially enough. 'Lindsay would have it that you're a pretty hot property. I shall expect great things.'

'I'll do my best, sir,' he promised, returning the smile.

Behind them, Leo led a big brown gelding out of the covered stables.

'Ah, King,' the Colonel said. 'King's Defender. Let's see what you make of him.'

'Sure.' Ross nodded. He greeted the animal with a pat and a Polo mint and then tightened the girth. The horse stood like a gentleman as Leo gave Ross an efficient leg-up into the saddle, and he rode into the school adjusting his stirrup leathers as he went.

Richmond and the Colonel made their way along the outside of the arena and leaned on the fence, the Colonel's tweed-suited frame propped upon a shooting stick. Bill Scott stood beside his employer and Leo and Sarah stood at the gate to the yard. The two-year-olds had been checked over and moved to another field, and half a dozen show-jumps of varying sizes had been erected for Ross' use.

He put his intensely interested audience out of his mind and concentrated on the job in hand. King felt mature, calm and confident, but Ross guessed he was going to have to work for his jumps. Nobody had told him anything about any of the horses as yet and he hadn't asked. He knew this was a test of his ability to read and adapt to his equine partners.

After ten minutes or so of suppling exercises – circles, serpentines and changes of speed – Ross put King's Defender at one of the easy training fences. The horse flicked his ears back and forth as he approached, waiting for Ross' command. Sensing what the horse wanted, he sat deep into the saddle and drove him hard at the jump. With a swish of his tail King responded and the coloured poles flashed safely by beneath his neatly folded legs.

Ridden decisively, the horse didn't put a foot wrong and Ross relaxed and began to enjoy himself. It had been nearly a month since he had last been on a horse, and the satisfaction of settling into a smooth partnership again was immense.

Leo led a second horse through the gate as Ross slowed up, and without stopping to speak to the Colonel, he changed horses.

The difference was absolute. This mare was smaller, much younger and bubbling with nervous energy. Ross rode her with gentle hands, playing with the bit in her mouth, asking her to listen. Gradually she settled. He turned her towards a small jump and she exploded into action. Caught momentarily off guard, Ross had to use much skill and not a little strength to bring her under control again.

Rebelling, she threw her head up, legs ramrod stiff, and stopped with her nose touching the poles. He swore at himself under his breath for being caught out like a novice. Swinging the mare away, he circled a time or two, then put her at it again.

This time he was ready. He kept her on a short bouncy stride and urged her on from three strides out.

Success.

She bounced over the fences like a rubber ball, legs in all directions, head high, but touching nothing. As he slowed the mare down, Ross caught sight of the Colonel and Richmond nodding and smiling as they turned away from the fence, and knew he had passed the first test.

As Ross dismounted in the yard, the Colonel came over and gave the little mare a carrot. 'Not bad,' he commented. 'She's not the easiest ride.'

'Thank you, sir.' Ross could see that praise would be hard earned.

'Come up to the house tonight and we'll have a chat, all right?'

'Sure.'

Franklin Richmond lingered a little longer.

'He's taking a big chance on you, you know,' he said, studying Ross' face keenly. 'We all are. If it hadn't been for young Lindsay's recommendation you wouldn't be here, because I have to say you don't exactly come with impeccable references.'

Ross was surprised to hear he came with any references at all. 'I've made one or two mistakes,' he admitted. 'But then, who hasn't?'

Richmond smiled ruefully. 'Who indeed?'

He had started to turn away when Ross said impulsively, 'Do you mind if I ask you something?'

He paused. 'Fire away.'

'Why did you assume someone poisoned your horse deliberately?'

Richmond looked up at the cloudless sky and sighed. 'Ah. I thought you must have noticed that. The thing is, I had a horse die last year, too, and that most definitely wasn't an accident. I suppose you've heard about Bellboy?'

'Sure, but I didn't realise he was yours until yesterday. He was found dead with his throat cut, wasn't he? There was quite a buzz on the circuit for a while.'

Richmond nodded. 'So you see, when I found a message on my answering service, telling me one of my horses had suddenly died, I thought it was happening all over again.'

'But didn't they ever find out who killed him?'

'No.' Richmond sighed again. 'I think the general consensus was that I had it done.'

'For the insurance?'

'Yes. Well, to be honest, I'd probably have thought the same if it was somebody else's horse,' Richmond said. 'After all, he *was* seventeen – a fair age for a competition horse, by anyone's standards – and we *were* thinking of retiring him at the end of the year. So you can see how people put two and two together. The value of the current Hickstead champion, still in training, would be far greater than that of a retired one, however good he'd been.'

'But that's not how it was,' Ross stated slowly, watching the businessman's face.

'I loved that horse, Ross,' Richmond said simply, and the remembered anguish showed clearly in his eyes.

The day passed quickly. There were horses to exercise, to rub down, and to feed. Lunch. Then more exercising, grooming and feeding, tack to clean, and finally the yard to be washed down and

28

swept. At six-thirty in the evening, contented horses munched hay, knee-deep in dry straw beds, and the four weary workers were free to go their separate ways for the evening.

Ross was exhausted. There were ten horses in the yard, in various stages of training, and he had ridden six of them at one time or another during the day. In addition to that, he had done his share of the routine stablework once he had learned where everything was. It was the hardest day's work he'd done since leaving hospital four months previously and a dull but persistent ache in his left knee reminded him of that.

Sarah had climbed on her bicycle and departed for her home in the village, and as Ross lay where he had collapsed on the sofa in his room, he heard Leo go down the wooden stairs and, a few moments later, the roar of his motorbike as he left the yard.

After the evening meal, Ross combed his hair, pulled on clean boots and jeans and made his way to the main house as the Colonel had suggested.

At the end of the drive the large grey-stone building looked centuries old as it sat basking in the last of the evening sunshine. Masters, who presumably doubled as chauffeur and butler, opened the impressive, stone-arched, oak front door and with a stiffly polite bow, showed Ross into the study.

Colonel John Preston turned away from the darkening window at the rear of the room as Ross entered. His gaze travelled up over cowboy boots, faded Levis and blue cotton shirt to Ross' face and then beyond. 'Thank you, Masters,' he said, and the other man withdrew.

'So,' the Colonel said, after offering his visitor a leather-upholstered chair and a glass of sherry, 'you're a Yank.'

Ross didn't rise to the bait, merely inclining his head. He sipped the sherry, which was horribly sweet.

'I don't like Yanks,' his employer stated uncompromisingly. 'We could have won the war without them and we don't need them now.'

'Then why hire me?' Ross asked evenly.

The Colonel snorted. 'I didn't have much choice with that niece of mine pestering me. Robbie Fergusson, who owns King's Defender, was threatening to take his horses away if I didn't find someone soon. Franklin offered to put up the airfare, so what had I got to lose?' He paused, observing Ross thoughtfully over his glass. 'Lindsay says you're good. Are you?'

'Yes,' Ross said, returning his gaze steadily.

'A big-headed Yank.'

'Did you want me to say no?'

The Colonel harrumphed.

'I've made enquiries about you,' he said after a moment. 'Rumour has it you've lost your nerve.'

'But you don't listen to rumour.'

'You think not?'

'I'm here, aren't I?' Ross observed with indisputable logic.

The Colonel chuckled suddenly. 'You don't

beat about the bush, do you, Mr Wakelin?'

'You're not exactly pussyfooting around yourself,' Ross said, deciding the gloves were off.

'No, it's not my way.' The Colonel regarded him thoughtfully. 'Tell me, how do you like the place? Do you think you'll fit in?'

Ross relaxed a little, sensing another hurdle safely negotiated. He was faintly surprised at the degree of relief he felt, realising that now he was here, he wanted to stay.

'I like it. You've got some promising young horses, I'd say.'

The Colonel nodded, pleased. 'They're a mixed bunch, I suppose, but yes, I'd agree there's a fair bit of talent there. All they need is the right jockey.'

They sat in silence for a moment, sipping sherry. Somewhere a dog scratched at a door and Ross heard Masters' voice as he let it out.

'I think you'll find the grooms are good workers,' the Colonel said then. 'Leo is new, of course, barely a month here, but he's had experience – worked in racing stables in Ireland – and he's a competent rider. He had good references. Sarah is a local girl. She's young but immensely dedicated.' He took a long sip of his sherry. 'Bill's a real gem. Came to us ten years ago but he's been around stables all his life. He's probably forgotten more about horses than you'll ever know.'

Ross had always felt that to be a rather dubious recommendation, but he nodded nevertheless.

'He was a very good steeplechase jockey in his day, until injury put him out of the game,' the

Colonel went on. 'Never be too proud to ask for his advice.'

Ross took another sip of sherry, trying not to grimace.

'Who's in charge in the yard?'

The Colonel looked at him keenly. 'You are, if you want to be. But I had hoped you would work as a team.'

'Sure. *I* hope we will, too, but I like to know where I stand.'

Colonel Preston grunted and poured himself another sherry, offering Ross a top-up that was politely declined. For a moment there was silence.

Ross looked around appreciatively at the Colonel's comfortable study. Worn leather armchairs, an untidy desk, bookshelves from floor to ceiling on one wall, and family photographs everywhere, including some of the Colonel in his army days. One caught his eye particularly.

'My late wife,' the Colonel said, seeing the American's interest. 'Lindsay's aunt. There is quite a family resemblance, isn't there? I see Caroline every time Lindsay smiles. It's almost as though she lives on in her.'

'I see what you mean.' Ross leaned forward to look more closely. 'She's very beautiful. You must miss her.'

'Her car was forced off the road by a drunk driver playing chicken. Our twelve-year-old daughter was in the passenger seat. They were both killed instantly.'

'I'm sorry.' There didn't seem to be anything else to say.

The Colonel looked bleak for a moment then pulled himself together.

'So, tell me about yourself. I'd not heard of you until Lindsay spoke of you, although I believe she may have mentioned you in her letters. How long have you been riding?'

'About fifteen years. I started when I was twelve, when I went away to school and spent the holidays with my uncle who was a dealer with a small spread in Indiana. It wasn't – ah – convenient for me to go home at that time.' No need to mention his overworked lawyer father, and his flighty socialite mother who had begun to see the disadvantages of having a teenage son around to remind people of her encroaching years.

'Uncle Walter taught me to ride. It was a baptism of fire, I guess you'd say,' Ross related with a boyish grin. 'He believed falling off was the best way to learn how to stay on. There were times, when I was spitting out teeth and mouthfuls of dirt, I disagreed with him. But now, I think he was right. It sure taught me to sit tight. Gradually it got so I'd be the one who sorted out the awkward horses, and as I grew older I got a name for it. People would send my uncle their problem horses for retraining, and then one or two of them wanted me to continue riding for them. It was only a seasonal thing because by then I was at college, but I guess I was hooked already. When I graduated I went on to law school – Dad wanted me to join him in partnership – but I couldn't settle to it. I took a year out, started riding for a yard near my uncle's, and never went back.'

'So you're quite well known in the States, are you?' the Colonel enquired.

'In Indiana, maybe.' Ross laughed. 'I'm afraid I got caught in a rut, with a name for being a rough-rider, a sort of trouble-shooter, and that was all I was given to do. Then, a couple of years ago, I went to ride for a trainer-cum-dealer with some really promising horses and began to have some success. The trouble was that every time I got a horse up to top level he would sell it on for a handsome profit and I'd be back to square one again. Good for his business, not so good for my career. Last year I toured the circuit with a string of horses, including one permanent ride owned by a friend of the boss. Vixen. A mare with a great deal of talent and, unfortunately for me, a brain tumour.'

'Hence the accident,' the Colonel observed.

'That's right.' Ross had no wish to talk about the horror of that day.

'You were out of action for . . . how long?'

'Nearly six months all told,' Ross said. 'They said it would be longer, but I was lucky. I heal fast.'

'But you didn't go back to riding?' the Colonel probed.

'Sure I did, but not to the same place. I had time to think while I was laid up and decided I was through with building somebody else's career. I wanted to become a full-time showjumper and maybe one day try for the national team. I told my former boss I quit and struck out on my own.'

'And?'

'I couldn't get the rides. Somehow word had gotten round that I'd lost my nerve; that I'd been fired because I wasn't fit after the accident, physically or mentally.' The American looked bleak, the wounds too raw, too recent.

'Sour grapes?'

Ross nodded. 'I guess so. He took it pretty bad when I left, but it wasn't as if he'd been paying me while I was laid up or anything. I got a couple of rides from people I'd ridden for in the past, but one way or another they didn't work out and pretty soon I found I was on a kind of unofficial blacklist.'

'I've done a little checking up on you – newspapers and such. You were pretty smashed up, by all accounts,' the Colonel stated bluntly. 'It must have affected you to some degree. How do I know those people weren't right? How do I know you *won't* let me down when the going gets tough?'

'You don't.' Ross remembered those press reports well. He had laughed over them with Lindsay, in hospital.

> Ross Wakelin, the showjumping rider who was injured in a spectacular fall at a show in Detroit at the weekend, is now recovering in hospital. His promising career has suffered an unfortunate setback after the accident, in which he sustained severe concussion, broken ribs, collarbone and left

ankle, and multiple fractures to his left knee. Mr Wakelin's condition is said by a hospital spokesman to be comfortable.

There are believed to have been other casualties when Mr Wakelin's horse left the arena and crashed into the crowds but their injuries are not thought to be severe.

Comfortable! What the hell did *they* know? And it was strange how his career had never been described as promising when he was actively engaged upon it. By that time he was aware there had been other casualties among the spectators, but luckily, due to the extreme heat, the open north stand had been largely abandoned in favour of the cooler south and west ones and a far greater tragedy averted.

'Then tell me why I should take a chance on you.' The Colonel broke in on his reflections, bringing him back abruptly to the present. 'Sell yourself.'

'I'm confident I can make a go of it,' Ross said, meeting the Colonel's gaze steadily. 'But I can promise you this: if at any time I think I can't, you'll be the first to know. All I ask is that you give me the same assurance. I've had enough of backstabbers.'

The Colonel nodded. 'That's fair enough. Is there anything you want to ask me?'

'Uh . . . Lindsay said your last rider fell out with one of the owners. What was that about?'

'Ah, that was unfortunate,' the Colonel said.

'Stephen Douglas. He was a young lad with an ambitious father. He wasn't really experienced enough for a responsibility of this magnitude and eventually Robbie Fergusson became so unhappy with the way his horses were going he wouldn't let Stephen ride them any more. The situation was untenable so he had to go. Before that we had Perry Wilson. You may have heard of him? Damn' fine rider! He retired shortly after Bellboy was killed. His heart just didn't seem to be in it after that. You've heard about that business, I suppose?'

'Lindsay told me about it,' Ross confirmed. 'It's hard to believe someone would do something like that.'

The Colonel sighed. 'There seems to be very little humankind is not capable of,' he said heavily. 'But it's all in the past now and we have to move on. And so, to that end, it seems we have a Yank.'

A slow smile curved the American's lips. 'I've never worked for a Limey before, either,' he said. Then added, after a carefully judged pause, 'Sir.'

The Colonel smiled in return.

'*Touché*,' he said.

3

The days took on a certain pattern. As Ross settled into the rhythm of the yard he voluntarily took on the care of two of the horses.

His two, the bouncy mare Flowergirl that he had ridden on his first morning, and Black Bishop, a big German-bred novice who was owned by Robbie Fergusson, were stabled in two of the larger loose boxes that opened directly on to the yard – Flo because she fretted if she could not see the outside world and Bishop because of his sheer size.

Early-morning feeding and mucking out were followed by breakfast in the Scotts' cottage, over which the timetable for the day was discussed and set. Then such horses as were not being schooled that day were taken out for exercise along the roads and in the neighbouring fields and woods. Afterwards they were rubbed down and the next batch started. Leo proved to be a capable rider but with little finesse, and Sarah rode with sensitivity but lacked confidence, so Ross had to plan their rides with care. Occasionally Bill Scott would join them, but more often he chose to stay behind.

When Ross schooled any of the horses in the sand arena behind the stables, Scott would lean on the gate and watch, but he seldom commented.

After feeding the horses and themselves at mid-day, the whole process would begin again, until eventually each horse that was in training had had either riding-out exercise, or a schooling session, or both. All the horses then had to be strapped – the horseman's term for a complete and thorough grooming – which took at least half an hour per animal. Tack had to be cleaned, beds replenished with straw or wood-shavings and then the horses fed for a third time before the human population of the yard was free for the evening.

They made a good working team, each pulling their weight, but in between times, where there should have been companionship and a growing camaraderie, they remained just four separate people. Bill Scott was always civil but not disposed to be friendly. Sarah reddened and became tongue-tied if Ross spoke to her at all, and Leo ignored him unless spoken to directly.

Towards the end of his first week, Ross was busy working a big grey horse called Woodsmoke in the arena when he noticed that Franklin Richmond had come to watch with Bill. He completed his intended workout and then reined in and let the horse stretch his neck on the way back to the gate.

'He's working well, Ross.' Franklin patted the horse as Ross dismounted, clearly pleased. 'I'd say things are looking up, wouldn't you, Bill?' he asked, turning to the stable manager.

'Maybe,' he replied without enthusiasm. 'But schooling's one thing, competing's quite another.'

'Ah well, with your support he's halfway there,' Franklin observed warmly.

Bill looked at him suspiciously as he reached to take the horse's reins.

'That was a double-edged remark, if ever I heard one,' Ross said with amusement, as Woody was led away towards the stables. 'What is it with that guy? It can't be anything I've said or done 'cos he's been acting like that from day one.'

'No, it's just Bill,' Franklin said, shaking his head. 'The horses and the success of the yard mean everything to him, and after the fiasco with poor Stephen Douglas, I suppose it'll take a while to convince him that you're equal to the job. I shouldn't let it worry you.'

'If you say so.' Ross was unconvinced.

'Actually,' Franklin went on, as they walked towards his car, 'the one you've got to watch – though I shouldn't say it – is old Fergusson. He can be a mean devil, that one, if you get on the wrong side of him. I don't know why he has horses, really. Must be some kind of unfulfilled personal ambition. He used to ride as a youngster, I believe.'

'And why do *you* have horses?' Ross asked,

interested. 'It's obviously not for the money.'

'That's for sure!' Franklin laughed. 'No. It's because I love them, and because I love the whole bright colourful circus of showjumping and shows.'

'It doesn't look so glamorous from this side,' Ross remarked with a rueful grin.

'That's why I'm paying and you're doing,' Franklin pointed out with an answering smile.

The afternoon ride that day was a disaster.

Ross was riding one of Franklin's horses, which was young, unpredictable and went by the name of Fly – short, apparently, for Barfly. Leo had been allocated Simone, an excitable mare whose speciality was speed classes. Sarah brought up the rear on Red Queen, a generally biddable chestnut mare nicknamed Ginger that, like Black Bishop and King's Defender, belonged to Robbie Fergusson. Fergusson himself, Ross had discovered, was an international chess player of some standing, which explained the names.

Ross was trying unsuccessfully to get the energetic Fly to stop spooking at imaginary horrors in the hedges and pay attention to him, and because of this was unaware of trouble brewing behind him.

Eventually, glancing back to check on the others, he could see at once that Sarah was unhappy. Ginger was jogging restlessly, making evil faces at Simone, and Leo's innocent expression wasn't entirely convincing to Ross' eyes.

41

'What's going on?' he asked, reining Fly in and dropping back. 'Sarah?'

She turned a predictable pink and mumbled a negative.

Ross stifled his exasperation. There was no point in asking him, but Ross could make a fair guess that, bored with the steady pace that was being set, Leo was bent on having a little sport with Sarah. Whatever he was doing was clearly upsetting the chestnut mare and he was obviously revelling in Sarah's growing nervousness.

'There's no need to ride on top of one another,' Ross observed testily. 'Move Simone over and give Ginger some space. Come on, give Sarah a break!'

Leo did as he was told with no appearance of resentment but Ross was not fooled. Leo had not so far been openly insolent but Ross often had the feeling, as now, that offensive gestures were being made – even if only metaphorically – at his back. Was it something in his own character, he wondered, that provoked such a reaction in his workmates?

This unproductive train of thought was broken into by a sudden clatter of hooves on the tarmac surface of the lane and a fleeting glimpse of Sarah's terrified face as Ginger torpedoed by and disappeared round the bend ahead. Fly nearly turned himself inside out in his efforts to emulate the chestnut's rapid departure and when Ross did calm him sufficiently to follow Ginger, progress was only made sideways in stiff-legged, jarring leaps.

Ross darted a venomous look at Leo and surprised an expression of unholy glee on the other man's face.

Rounding the bend he was met by Sarah, unhorsed and in tears but on her feet. Ahead, the road forked.

'Ginger?' he shouted at the unfortunate girl.

Sarah pointed right.

Ross steered Fly off the slippery road surface and on to the verge before putting him into a canter. Half a mile further on, he met Ginger coming back. Pulling up, he braced himself to try and catch her flying reins as she careered past, but at the sight of her stable companion she slithered to a halt and waited, head high and sides heaving.

Steadying his own excited mount, Ross edged alongside the chestnut and took her rein. The mare jerked back from the contact, eyes wild, and then a great shudder shook her frame and she drooped visibly, becoming tractable again.

Progress back to the yard was necessarily slow. Sarah could not be persuaded to remount Ginger and she was not really competent enough to ride either Fly or Simone. When questioned, neither she nor Leo seemed able to give any sensible explanation of what had caused the mare's sudden flight. Ross kept his temper only with difficulty.

Later in the day, recalling the expression on Leo's face when Ginger had bolted, Ross decided to search out Sarah and uncover the truth of the matter.

He found her in the haybarn but she was not alone.

'What the hell do you think you're doing?'

Leo whirled about at the sound of Ross' voice, removing his hands from their position on the wall to either side of Sarah and holding them out, palms upward, in a gesture of innocence.

'Me? I was just having a friendly chat with the little lady,' he said, smiling sweetly. 'Ain't that so?' he added over his shoulder to Sarah, who cast him a frightened glance and, without looking at Ross, bolted past him and out of the door.

'Women!' Leo said, with pursed lips and an exaggerated shrug. 'You never know what they're going to do next.' He laughed and made to move past Ross but a firm hand on his shoulder detained him.

'You can be pretty sure what *I'm* going to do next, if ever I catch you messing with her again,' Ross promised softly.

For a moment Leo's face became taut with anger and his dark eyes narrowed. Then he laughed.

'Take it easy, Yank. I don't want the little mouse, you have her. She's probably more your type.' He twisted away from Ross' grip and went out into the yard, whistling cheerfully.

Ross was eating a solitary meal that evening when the telephone rang in the cottage. Bill had taken Maggie to a nearby village for a bingo night, something he apparently did every Thursday.

After a moment's hesitation Ross answered it.

'Ross, it's Franklin. Are you free tonight?'

'As in . . .?'

'As in free to come and see a couple of horses with me? An old dealer friend rang me and said he had a couple I might like to look at.'

'Tonight?'

'Well, he said to come soon, and I'm tied up for a couple of days now.'

'Sure, but the thing is, I'm not sure Bill can make it. He's taken Maggie to bingo and I gather he has to pick her up again in a couple of hours.'

'Well, it's just a preliminary look. We won't be making any decisions tonight. You can borrow the Land-Rover, I imagine?'

'Yeah, I guess so. Where do I have to get to?'

'It's a place near Blandford but it's not easy to find. Best thing would be if I met you on the way and we went on together.'

'Sure, that's fine. Where and when?'

'Right. Go to Salisbury, take the Blandford road, and I'll meet you at the Dog and Crook – it's a pub about fifteen miles along on the right-hand side. Eight-thirty all right?'

'Sure.' Ross looked at his watch. 'I'll be there.'

The Dog and Crook was a big square whitewashed building, standing on a high point of the lonely road. Window boxes stuffed with geraniums did their best to liven up the plain walls and carefully tended bedding surrounded the gravel car park.

There was no sign of Franklin's white Mercedes when Ross pulled up at 8.26, so he switched off the

Land-Rover's engine and sat watching the activity behind the lighted windows of the pub.

Bill Scott had been a bit put out when told of Franklin's call. As Ross had thought, Bill was committed to picking Maggie up at half past ten, and as there was no guarantee that they would be back from seeing the horses by then, he agreed with rather bad grace that Ross had better take the yard's Land-Rover and go on his own. Although he had no wish to make his relationship with the stable manager any worse than it was, Ross could not help but be glad that he wasn't coming.

'Ross Wakelin?' A cultured voice spoke through the open window of the Land-Rover, right next to Ross' ear.

He turned his head and came face to face with a complete stranger.

'Who wants to know?'

The man straightened up and fished in an inner pocket. In the fading light, Ross could see exquisite tailoring, a fiftyish fine-boned face and neatly cut, steel-grey hair.

'My name is Edward McKinnon.' The man offered him a business card. 'Franklin Richmond asked me to meet you here.'

Ross glanced at the card but didn't take it.

'Where *is* Franklin?' he asked, bewildered. 'We were supposed to be looking at some horses.'

'Ah, yes. The horses. A little subterfuge, I'm afraid. I'm sorry about that.' McKinnon withdrew the card, unabashed. 'Shall we talk out here, or would you like to go inside?'

'Why should I want to talk to you at all?' Ross demanded. 'I don't know who the hell you are . . . Oh, sure, I know you told me your name,' he said, waving his hand as McKinnon offered his card once more. 'But I mean *who* are you? *What* are you?'

'Of course. Forgive me. I run a company that specialises in industrial security, safeguarding everything from buildings to information. Industrial espionage is big business these days, you know.'

Ross had never really thought about it.

'And?'

'And also, on a smaller scale, and mostly for existing clients, we perform a private investigative service. All strictly above board, no spying or anything of that sort.'

'Of course not,' Ross murmured.

McKinnon looked at him sharply.

'Okay,' Ross said, sighing, 'so you work for Franklin Richmond. Why would you want to talk to me? I only just met the guy.'

'Exactly,' McKinnon said with some satisfaction. 'Look, why don't we go inside? I'm getting a crick in my neck standing here . . .'

Ross hesitated and McKinnon held out a tiny, flip-top mobile phone. 'Would you be happier if you checked with Franklin?'

'No, it's all right. I've come all this way. Tell you what – you buy me a beer and I'll give you ten minutes to get my attention. If not, I'm outta here. Is it a deal?'

'Thank you,' the older man said, inclining his

head graciously and stepping back to let Ross open the door.

Five minutes later, at a quiet corner table, the American faced McKinnon over a half-pint of what seemed to pass for beer in England.

'Okay. The clock's running.'

McKinnon ran his forefinger slowly around the rim of his wineglass, apparently deep in thought.

'If I told you that my company is investigating the killing of a horse called Bellboy, would that get your attention?' he asked at last.

Ross' eyes narrowed. 'It might,' he acknowledged cautiously.

McKinnon took a deep breath as if preparing for the plunge.

'What I'm about to tell you is in the strictest confidence.' He paused and looked calculatingly at Ross, as if trying to assess the risk. Apparently he had an honest face for McKinnon continued. 'It's something only two or three people know and it's imperative that it goes no further.'

'Basically – it's a secret,' Ross put in, amused. He looked at his watch pointedly.

'It's not our policy to enlist outside help but Franklin was keen that you should know. You seem to have made quite an impression on him.'

'But how can *I* help? The horse was killed nearly a year ago. Hasn't the trail gone a little cold?'

'It might have, if that was all there was to it,' McKinnon agreed. 'Look, I need to fill you in on a little background information. Will you give me the time?'

'Okay.' Ross was interested in spite of himself. 'Shoot.'

'Franklin Richmond, as you may know, is a successful and extremely wealthy businessman. He inherited a small but thriving financial consultancy and has built it up to international proportions. In common with many other wealthy men, he indulges a passion for horses. Racehorses at first, but more recently showjumpers. In fact, he devotes every spare minute that he has, outside business and family commitments, to his horses. I'm told his interest in them borders on the obsessive. You'd probably know more about that than me.'

'I doubt it. I've only met the man twice.'

'Of course, I was forgetting. Well, anyway, you can imagine how he felt when at approximately eleven o'clock one Sunday evening last October he received a phone call telling him that Bellboy, his internationally successful jumper and personal favourite, was at that moment breathing his last.'

'That's really sick!' Ross said, disgust showing in his face. He remembered how *he* had felt when at fifteen he had found his pet dog dead at the side of a quiet road. Filled with useless anger, the injustice of it had haunted him for weeks. How much worse to know that somebody had intentionally killed the animal you cared for.

'So what did he do?'

'First he called the yard and then the vet, but by the time anybody got to the horse it was already too late. They found him lying in the straw with his throat cut.'

49

'But it had only just happened?'

'Within the last hour.' McKinnon nodded. 'Bill Scott did his rounds at ten o'clock as usual. He checked every horse and all was quiet.'

'So, what then? Did you trace the call?'

'Yes. A phone box on a lonely stretch of road near Blandford. Not a chance of anyone having seen anything at that time of night, and the telephone had been wiped clean. Not a single print.'

'Sick but clever,' Ross observed.

'If he hadn't been, we would have caught him by now,' McKinnon assured him stiffly.

'Sure. Sorry.' Ross paused. 'Wasn't there some stuff a few years back where other horses were being attacked with knives? I don't know if it's still going on.'

'It is, I'm sorry to say,' McKinnon said with distaste. 'But I'm told that in the main the motive for those attacks is sexual perversion and in consequence it is nearly always mares that are attacked. Also, although those poor animals are often badly maimed, they are not usually killed outright.'

'And you're absolutely sure Richmond didn't do it himself for the insurance?'

'You've met him. What do you think?'

'I'd say no. But I'm no detective,' Ross pointed out.

'Well, I'd stake my life on it,' McKinnon stated firmly, then added a little sheepishly, 'besides, we checked. His alibi was watertight. Admittedly he could have employed a third party, but in reality the sums involved would be as chicken-feed to a man like Franklin.'

Ross half-smiled at this flawed avowal of trust. He supposed a lack of faith came with the job.

'Obviously he didn't recognise the voice?'

'He said it sounded Irish. But no, he didn't recognise it.'

Ross frowned. 'Nothing to do with the IRA, I suppose. It's just – I was thinking of Shergar . . .'

'Nothing we can discover. And highly unlikely, I would think. Although Bellboy was well known within the showjumping world, the general public is far more keyed-in to racing. The impact on the media was short-lived.'

'And he has no obvious enemies,' the American mused. 'Or if he had, you would have checked them all out by now.'

'No, we don't think so.' McKinnon gave Ross a speculative, sideways look. 'In general, Franklin Richmond is honest and fair, both in business and in his personal life. As a result he seems to be almost universally well liked.'

'So,' Ross said slowly, 'I guess that makes it extortion. A demand for money. Pay up or we'll do worse.'

McKinnon inclined his head, a faint smile playing about his lips. 'Impressive, Mr Wakelin. Franklin said you were sharp.

'Yes, a message was left exactly a week later, when the immediate brouhaha had died down. And again from a remote telephone kiosk, though not the same one. Richmond was to make regular, specified payments into a numbered account in the Cayman Islands or another of his horses would meet with a sticky end – the extortionist's phrase, not mine,' he added quickly. 'The horses were not to change yards or be sold, and no third parties were to be involved. Most especially not the police.'

No wonder Franklin was edgy when he was told Sailor had been poisoned, Ross thought. He swallowed the last of his beer. 'And now, I guess, we get to the reason why you're telling me all this.'

McKinnon reverted to fingering the rim of his glass. 'To be honest, as I said, it was Franklin's idea, not mine. I wasn't keen,' he admitted. 'I insisted that I meet you first. But now I have – well, I think it might be worth enlisting your help.'

Ross shook his head. 'But *I* don't!' he stated unequivocally. 'I'm a rider, not a private investigator, and the way things are panning out, I'm likely to have quite enough on my hands just doing that.'

'That's a shame,' McKinnon observed calmly. 'In spite of my reservations, I was beginning to think you might be of real help.'

'Thanks,' Ross said ironically, 'but no thanks. Surely you've got manpower enough already?'

'Men, yes. But no one who could be as close to all this as you are. You will be closer than anyone except Franklin himself. Look, I'm not asking you to change profession, merely to keep your eyes and ears open for anything that might seem out of place or unusual.'

'You figure it's someone in the Colonel's yard, then. In effect you're asking me to spy on the people I'm going to be working with?'

McKinnon shrugged. 'We don't know who it is. But it is logical to assume that there may be some connection between the yard and the extortionist. He seems aware of the horses' every movement. But as far as spying goes – if you must use that word – you wouldn't be troubled about it if you'd seen Bellboy as Franklin Richmond was forced to see him.' He paused, his lip curling in distaste at the memory. 'The police took photographs. It was horrific. Do you know how much blood a horse has?'

'That size? About fifty – maybe fifty-five pints,' Ross said absent-mindedly. 'But what about the police? And the insurance company? What did they make of it?'

'They investigated, of course. The insurance company had Franklin bring in a security firm to guard his remaining horses day and night. But after a couple of months they were convinced that it was a one-off. We obviously couldn't tell them what was really going on. For one thing they would probably have withdrawn their cover in a flash. Most policies cover malicious damage but the expectation of it is not high. Insuring all Mr Richmond's horses in such circumstances would almost certainly constitute too great a risk. After all, I'm sure I don't need to tell you how impossible it would be to guard just one competition horse every minute of the day without badly disrupting its training. Who knows where the danger might lie? Poison . . . a sniper in the woods . . . or a knife in the stable, as in this instance. There was one case, some years ago now, where one of Britain's leading lady riders had half her horses poisoned by a madman or someone with a grudge. As far as I know, they never found out who was responsible.'

Ross was thoughtful. 'If I agreed to report anything unusual, that's all I would do – no snooping around or asking questions.'

'Just keep your eyes and ears open,' McKinnon agreed, taking care not to exhibit any sign of triumph. He took a sip of his wine.

'So, do I get to know who the others are?' Ross asked casually.

McKinnon looked sharply at the American over the rim of his glass. He took another slow sip. 'Others?'

'Oh, come on! You must have other people working on this thing.'

'Of course,' McKinnon agreed. 'But to date we've made no significant progress. It's a tricky business. A question asked in the wrong place could make matters very much worse. It's not like investigating a *fait accompli*. We lacked the inside angle. Until now, that is.'

'But you're not going to tell me who the others are?'

'It's better that I don't,' McKinnon said, shaking his head judiciously. 'What you don't know, you can't give away, accidentally or otherwise.'

'Jeez! I'm not going to be tortured, am I?' Ross exclaimed in mock alarm.

McKinnon wisely decided to ignore that. He handed Ross a slip of paper. 'If you need to contact me, you can ring that number,' he said patiently. 'It's my private line, not the main office. Keep it somewhere safe. Better still, learn and destroy it.'

'Real undercover stuff,' Ross said, amused. 'Shall I swallow it? Or shall I burn it and flush the ashes down the john?'

'I really don't care if you make a bloody omelette with it,' McKinnon said, his careful control slipping for a moment. He was rewarded by an appreciative grin from the American. 'So you will help?'

Ross sighed, still unconvinced. 'I guess so,' he said at last. 'Just eyes and ears, though, nothing more.'

McKinnon nodded. 'That's all we ask.'

Ross got to his feet and the Englishman followed suit, extending his hand. His clasp was, as Ross would have expected, cool and firm.

'Thank you for your time,' he said in his courteous way.

'A pleasure,' Ross returned ironically. 'Besides, there was nothing on TV.'

Ross had little opportunity to think over what McKinnon had told him, for that weekend saw his first show in England. It was a big agricultural show not far from Basingstoke and the horses had been entered before Stephen Douglas had left the yard. The Colonel had consulted Ross and Bill and decided to let the entries stand.

Leo had spent Friday afternoon washing and polishing the Oakley Manor horsebox, and by seven o'clock the following morning the three competing horses were loaded and the box was rocking gently down the gravel drive to the road.

Ross drove, glad of the distraction. To keep them clean, he wore leather chaps over his white breeches and behind him in the cab hung his black jacket, brushed and sheathed in polythene.

For perhaps the first time since he started riding in shows, twelve years before, he was nervous. So many people were going to be watching him closely, assessing his ability not only to ride but also to compete, and there were a hundred and one things that could go wrong.

And that's if I'm lucky, he thought wryly.

His stomach had tied itself into knots and he had had to force himself to eat a reasonable breakfast, knowing he would need the energy later. A supportive team would have been a great plus, but Ross had the uneasy feeling that neither Leo nor Bill would be too devastated if he made a fool of himself. At present, Leo sat beside him in unfriendly silence.

'What's the time?' Ross asked as they slowly began to gain speed on the main road, ears attuned to the muffled thuds in the back as the horses shifted to maintain balance, and one eye on the video monitor that allowed him to see in black and white miniature how they were travelling.

'Haven't you got a watch?' Leo returned cockily.

'Sure, but I can't find it . . .' Ross' voice tailed off and he glanced sideways at Leo, who wore what could only be described as a smirk.

'Have *you* got it?' he demanded.

'What would I want with your watch, Yank? I've got one of my own.' He pushed up his sleeve to reveal an extremely expensive-looking timepiece.

Ross wasn't sure what to think. He had taken the watch off while he washed the stable stains from Cragside's pale grey coat and could have sworn he'd put it on the shelf above the sink in the tackroom but it wasn't there when he went back. It hadn't occurred to him before that anyone might have taken it, but now . . .

If it had indeed been Leo, then it seemed that that one act of revenge had satisfied the groom, at least for the time being, for when they reached the showground he became a model of efficiency. He unloaded and tacked up the horses as they were needed, folding and tidying rugs and leg protectors ready for reuse, and even warmed up King while Ross walked the course.

Once in the saddle, Ross' nerves evaporated. This was his job. He knew exactly what had to be done and he would do it. Lifted by Ross' confidence, King's Defender took his first class easily and added a fourth place later in the day.

Cragside, the Colonel's big, solid grey, jumped a slow but careful clear in both his classes but lost to far faster animals, and Simone rounded the day off with a first and a third in her speed classes.

Colonel Preston had arrived shortly after ten o'clock, driven by Masters, and watched the proceedings with every appearance of satisfaction. Even Bill Scott looked a little less sour as the day wore on.

The Colonel appeared in the horsebox park as the horses were being loaded for the return journey.

'All well?' he asked.

'Sure.' Ross heaved up the spring-loaded ramp with Leo's help and secured it in place. 'Simone's nicked the inside of her knee somehow but it's nothing much. I'm pleased with them – they all did well.'

The Colonel nodded. 'You didn't do so badly yourself,' he said. 'For a Yank.'

'Thank you, sir.' Ross smiled, well satisfied.

The next day the ground began to crumble under his feet.

4

It was Monday, officially the yard's day off. Leo and
Sarah were free to do what they pleased and Bill
looked after the horses with help from a local
farmer's daughter, mucking out and feeding, then
turning the resting horses out to grass to relax for
the day. Bill's rest day was supposed to be Tuesday,
but according to Sarah, he seldom took it.

Ross rose later than normal, but out of habit
went down to the yard to help, unable to remain
idle. The day stretched ahead of him uninvitingly,
and over breakfast he voiced his intention to ride
some of the horses that had missed out on
exercise the day before. He wondered aloud
whether Bill fancied joining him but the older
man muttered something about having work to
do and disappeared into the stable office, shutting
the door firmly behind him. Shaking his head,
Ross turned to collect the first saddle and bridle.

After working Bishop in the arena for an hour, he saddled Ginger and set off to explore the countryside, thankful to be free for once from Sarah's nervous awkwardness and Leo's sullen presence.

He made his way down the lane behind the Manor and past some farm cottages. When a heavily built German Shepherd came leaping and snarling to the end of its chain as he passed, Ross instinctively tightened his grip on Ginger, remembering her sudden panic with Sarah. But nothing seemed further from her mind today. She remained docile, almost lazy, her long ears flopping back and forth with the movement of her stride. This was how she normally behaved. Even when jumping she was scarcely more animated, clicking her toes over each fence, often bringing a light pole down as she skimmed over.

Ross relaxed and turned his attention to the beauty of the Wiltshire countryside. It was early summer and the leaves still looked fresh and new. Birds sang and the sun was warm. After the vast unchanging tracts of land in parts of his native America, impressive as they were, England's leafy lanes, copses and green fields enchanted Ross. They seemed somehow intimate; they narrowed life down to more manageable proportions. Lindsay had often said that America made her feel insignificant, like looking up into the night sky. With a surprising twinge of loneliness, Ross realised how much he was missing her and wondered how soon she would return to England.

She still had three months of the planned year to run, but had mentioned the possibility of cutting her visit short.

As he rode down a narrow bridleway and into the shelter of a valley the sun became quite hot and flies began to buzz around both horse and rider. Ross broke a whippy branch from a willow tree and used it to fan his face. Ginger swished her tail and shook her head.

'The flies bothering you too, girl?' he asked, and leaned forward to flick the leafy branch round her ears.

She stopped dead, her body taut and quivering.

'What the . . .?' Ross laughed. 'Come on, girl. Stop messing me about.'

Ross didn't normally carry a whip out hacking, he didn't find it necessary, but now he wished he had one. In spite of his urging her with legs and voice, the chestnut mare refused to budge. Exasperated, he stung her with the twig in his hand.

With a high-pitched squeal the mare bolted.

When a horse is hell-bent on running there is little any rider, however strong, can do to stop it. Ginger was no exception. Catching him unprepared, she ripped the reins through his fingers and ran. The bottom of the valley was reached in no time and she floundered in the boggy stream that ran through it, almost pitching Ross over her head. He threw his weight back and she leapt clear of the soft ground, heading at top speed for a copse halfway up the valley side. Ross searched ahead desperately for a gap in the trees large enough to admit a horse and rider at speed, and found none. Ginger showed no sign of stopping.

Ross contemplated baling out, but thoughts of several thousand pounds' worth of showjumper charging riderless through the countryside and his own aversion to walking home kept him in the saddle. He abandoned attempts to slow the mare, throwing all his weight on to one rein instead, in an effort to turn her. Gradually she came round, and without slackening speed tore down the valley side again, through two gorse bushes without seeming to see them, and plunged into the bog once more.

At this point, lower down the valley, the bog was deeper and wider and as her forefeet sank into the mud, her momentum carried her body up and over to land heavily on her back. Ross was catapulted clear, hitting the soft ground with his shoulder and rolling to his feet, the reins, from long practice, still gripped firmly in his left hand.

Ginger regained her feet swiftly and lunged clear of the marshy ground, dragging Ross with her for a few feet before stopping. Her ears were flicking back and forth in agitation and her whole body was coated with a mixture of foaming sweat and peaty mud. Her lungs worked like bellows driving air through scarlet-lined nostrils, and she shook with the violence of her heartbeats.

'Steady, girl. Easy does it.' Ross kept his voice low and steady, trying to convey a calmness he was far from feeling.

Ginger stared past him with white rimmed eyes,

her attention apparently focused on some terror he could not comprehend. Then, suddenly, she heaved a shuddering sigh and was quiet.

Ross stepped closer and patted her. She seemed relaxed now and very tired.

He automatically straightened the saddle and picked bits of moss out of her muddy mane, then leaned weakly against her neck with his eyes closed and began to shake uncontrollably.

Ross suffered no physical ill effects as a result of his fall and neither, as far as he could tell, did the mare.

The yard was deserted when he returned and he was able to clean up Ginger and her tack, as well as changing his own grass-stained clothing, before Bill appeared to do the midday feeds. He apparently noticed nothing amiss and Ross did not mention the incident, feeling that admitting the mare had bolted with him would do little to enhance the stable manager's already doubtful opinion of him. He would make sure, though, that Sarah didn't ride the mare out again.

That night the nightmares returned with a vengeance.

Tuesday dawned clear and sunny. Ross trudged downstairs and out into the yard feeling as though he hadn't slept for a week. He paused at the water trough halfway to the stables and sloshed ice-cold water over his head, gasping as it ran down his back, inside his shirt. He knew he would have to ride Ginger again, later, but worked mechanically through the usual tasks, trying not to dwell on the fact until gradually his natural resilience began to reassert itself.

After breakfast he rode Flowergirl out in the fields with the others and survived a spirited attempt to buck him off when he gave her a pipe-opening gallop. He rode back to the yard still buoyed up by the exhilaration of their headlong charge and half-believing he had imagined his fears of the day before. If only he could get the picture of Ginger's wild, unfocused stare out of his mind . . .

He passed the brown mare's reins to Sarah and went to get a beer from the refrigerator in the stable office next to the tackroom. When he returned, Bill was leading Ginger out into the sunshine. The mare was due for a schooling session as she was entered in an evening show the following day, and Ross wasn't sure whether to be pleased that he was riding her within the confines of the arena or unhappy that Bill would almost certainly be watching him.

Once aboard, any apprehension he may have had vanished. She was just a horse, like many others he had ridden; no more or less dangerous than King or Bishop. It was just an unfortunate coincidence that she was a chestnut mare, as Vixen had been. Vixen had had a brain tumour; a once-in-a-lifetime chance. Ginger was just a little moody, as redheads often are.

The schooling session went smoothly. Ginger did all that was asked of her obediently, if not exactly eagerly. Bill seemed pleased, which was unusual for him.

'Perry Wilson used to say that mare would be good one day,' he told Ross. 'Douglas didn't like her, but she seems to go well for you.'

Ross thrust his doubts aside. 'She can certainly jump when she feels like it,' he agreed. 'Let's hope she feels like it tomorrow.'

Bill nodded. 'Mr Richmond has just arrived. He's brought Peter with him. He's got a day off school. I think he's hoping to see you ride Clown.'

Peter, Ross had learned, was Franklin Richmond's twelve-year-old son, whose developing passion for horses had been rewarded by the birthday gift, some months before, of Clown, an extravagantly marked skewbald. Stephen Douglas had apparently made no headway at all with this exuberant youngster, who, at six, was just being introduced to serious training.

Leo had brought Clown out and as Ross relinquished Ginger to Sarah, he could see Franklin running knowledgeable hands over the horse, watched by Bill and a slim, fair-haired boy. Clown was an eye-catching animal, which was probably why Peter had chosen him, with irregular splodges of white on a shiny brown coat. He was tall and a little narrow with bright, eager eyes. Ross liked him.

'Morning, Ross.' Franklin turned to meet him with a smile. 'Shame about that horse on Thursday, wasn't it?'

'Yeah. Good-looking but devious,' he agreed,

straight-faced. 'I told Bill he didn't miss much. Not his sort at all.'

'Anyway, this is my son Peter, who's got a day off school today,' Richmond said, putting his hand on the boy's head. 'Peter owns Clown.'

The boy glowed with pleasure and held out his hand to Ross, a touch of shyness in his serious grey eyes.

'Hi, Peter. That's a fine animal you have there.' Ross shook the small hand solemnly.

'He's out of a Grade-A jumping mare, by the son of a Grand National winner, so he should jump.' Pride echoed in every syllable of Peter's voice.

'Oh, he will,' Ross assured him. 'Once we get him settled and his mind on the job.'

The schooling session went well, on the whole, although it was Ross' third ride in quick succession and his knee was beginning its familiar dull ache of protest. Clown put on a rodeo act to the delight of his youthful owner. Ross stuck with him, a little embarrassed at his inability to get him settled, but eventually the skewbald had worked off his high spirits and began to work quite sensibly.

It was clear, as he rode up to the gate at the end of the session, that Clown's exhibition had done Ross no harm in Richmond Junior's eyes. He regarded Ross with something akin to hero worship as the American leapt down and offered the boy a ride back into the yard.

Ross was dog tired that night and rolled into his bed and a deep slumber that neither unpleasant dreams nor the discomfort in his knee could disturb.

Ross encountered Stephen Douglas for the first time at the Lea Farm indoor show the next evening. The Oakley Manor horses were in sparkling form. Ross was accompanied once more by Leo, who was in an uncharacteristically cheerful mood. He managed the horses with his usual rough-edged efficiency and Ross found himself wishing, for the umpteenth time, that the groom was a little easier to get along with. They could have made a good team.

As Ross warmed up Butterworth in the practice area for his first class, he watched Stephen Douglas jump a lucky clear round on an impetuous grey gelding that threatened to get away from him on every corner. He knew Douglas would recognise the Colonel's horse as one he had ridden, and so smiled in a friendly fashion as the boy came out of the ring. Douglas looked hard at Ross as he passed and then deliberately turned away.

Ross was mildly disappointed; it was inevitable that their paths would cross fairly regularly and he hadn't wanted there to be any hard feelings.

The course was large but fair, and Butterworth pulled like a train, jumping high and clear and beating his nearest rival by almost three seconds in the timed jump-off that followed. Douglas' grey finally succeeded in getting away from him and swept him past the last wall before he could regain control. Ross sympathised. He had ridden his share of difficult horses.

Simone pulled out all the stops and jumped to a brilliant second in a very hotly contested speed class, and then had a fence down in a Qualifier. Ginger, to Ross' surprise and relief, behaved impeccably and came away with fourth in the same class.

At the end of the evening, as the less experienced horses and riders were loading up and driving away, Ross changed back wearily on to Butterworth to pull off a marvellous win in the Open class, the biggest of the show.

He felt that the gods were smiling on him at last and his satisfaction was unaffected by the look of intense dislike angled at him by Douglas as they lined up to receive their prizes. If the guy wanted to be petty, then let him. Ross felt he had made the offer of friendship.

Back at the lorry, Leo had the other horses loaded and soon Butterworth was untacked and decked in the multitude of protective pads and boots necessary for the journey.

While Leo loaded the horse, Ross eased his tired feet out of his close-fitting boots and hung his jacket in the purpose-built cupboard in the forward compartment. He looked forward to the day when success would buy him a fully equipped horsebox with living quarters, and he could stretch out after a show on a soft couch and let someone else wrestle the heavy lorry through England's maze of narrow streets and lanes.

Sighing deeply with weary content, he transferred himself to the cab and began the homeward journey.

*

Ross' contentment was unhappily short-lived, for as Butterworth left his stable the next morning, bound for the fields and a day's rest, it was clear that something was very wrong. The big gelding walked stiffly into the yard with his back hunched and head held low.

Sarah looked round at him doubtfully and then across at Ross with a question in her eyes. With a cold, sinking feeling, he signalled to her to stop and walked over to inspect his most promising partner more closely.

Soothing the horse with a stream of low-voiced, nonsensical words, Ross ran his hands along Butterworth's spine and down his hind legs. He repeated the action, pressing more firmly, and was rewarded by a distinct flinch and a flattening of chestnut ears.

Bill came up behind the American.

'Back?' he asked, in a voice that suggested he already knew the answer.

'Yeah. He's in a fair amount of pain.'

'I'll call Roger,' Bill said, turning away. 'I was meaning to ring him about that Sailor business anyway.'

Ross sighed, motioning Sarah to put Butterworth back in the box. Back problems were often depressingly slow to improve and had a tendency to be recurrent.

The vet came just as Ross was sponging Bishop down after a hard schooling session. He bounced out of his dust-covered Range Rover, wearing baggy corduroy trousers and engaging, boyish grin.

'Hello again,' he called cheerfully. 'Right, where's the patient?'

In spite of the occasion, Ross felt his spirits rise a notch. A smiling face had become a distant memory.

Roger West's examination was swift but efficient.

'There is definitely some tightness there. Just about here.' He indicated an area midway along the horse's spine. 'It may be a strained muscle or he may have put it right out. It could have been done rolling in his box.'

'Can you do anything?' Bill asked, at Butterworth's head. 'Or shall we call Annie?'

'She'd be your best bet,' Roger agreed, nodding his mop of tousled brown hair. 'If she can't do anything we'll have to make arrangements to get the old fellow X-rayed. And that'll cost you.'

'Who's Annie?' Ross wanted to know.

'A kind of equine chiropractor,' the vet told him. 'She's quite amazing. Sometimes you can see a ninety-nine per cent improvement straight away. I wish *I* could get such immediate results.'

'Sort of "Take up thy bed and walk"?' Ross observed.

Roger laughed. 'Well, almost. But seriously, she's well worth watching. Don't you have people like her in America?'

'Sure. I've heard of them, but I've never seen one at work. And you never know quite how much to believe.'

'That's true enough. Still,' Roger said soberly,

'whatever the outcome, it'll be rest and a gradual return to work for this one, I'm afraid. No more jumping for a bit.'

Ross nodded in resignation.

Annie Hayward arrived at noon the following day in a Land-Rover that looked as though it had seen service in both World Wars. Somewhere between thirty and fifty, she was a huge woman with an ageless, weather-beaten face, arms like a shot-putter and a voice that would have put a foghorn to shame.

Although she dressed like a farmer, in jeans and a checked shirt, her long, honey-gold hair was plaited and secured with an incongruous pink ribbon.

Butterworth behaved like an angel for her. Annie pushed, pulled and prodded, instructing Ross to hold up various of the horse's feet in turn, and finally slammed the heel of her palm into the side of the chestnut's spine with a force that made him stagger.

'Now lead him out,' she boomed.

Bill led Butterworth into the yard. The horse moved gingerly at first, as though waiting for the pain, but then gradually grew in confidence and relaxed.

Ross was impressed.

Annie wiped her hands on her torn jeans and nodded. 'Turn him out to grass for six weeks or so then I'll come again. Unless he looks uncomfortable in the meantime,' she added. 'In that case, give me a call.' She mopped her brow with something that looked suspiciously like a dishcloth, conjured from somewhere about her person. 'Any beer in the fridge?' she enquired.

'Sure.' Ross smiled and went to fetch some.

The stable office door was closed and the blind down. When Ross went in there was a slithering crash to his right. As his eyes adjusted to the gloom, he could see Leo standing by the refrigerator, just reaching for the handle. Behind him on the floor lay a jumble of pens and papers and an upturned tray.

'What in hell are you doing?' Ross demanded.

'Just getting a beer, Yank. What are you doing?' Leo returned insolently.

'You don't need to turn the office upside down to find the fridge.'

'I knocked it. It slipped,' Leo said dismissively.

'Why didn't you put the light on so you could see what you were doing?' Ross sighed. 'Okay, forget it. But bring a fourpack while you're there.'

'Anything you say, Yank.'

Ross swallowed his irritation, picking up the fallen tray and its contents before following him out. To rise to the bait would only give Leo satisfaction.

With Butterworth potentially out of action for the best part of the season, Ross had to put his disappointment behind him and concentrate on bringing the others up to his standard.

He had high hopes of King's Defender, who was

already an experienced campaigner and with improving fitness was a definite prospect for the international shows at Hickstead or Birmingham.

King's Defender, at fourteen, could not however have many more seasons in him, nor could Woodsmoke, a ponderous old warrior of sixteen who belonged to Franklin Richmond.

Simone was essentially a speed horse, jumping the smaller, twisty courses with swift precision but without the scope needed for the bigger tracks. Of the younger novice horses, Ross' greatest expectations lay with the big German-bred Black Bishop and bouncy, eager Flowergirl.

In the copse behind the home meadow, somebody had at some time built a small cross-country course of rustic jumps, and Ross and Bill had spent one busy evening repairing broken fences and clearing encroaching undergrowth to make it useable once more.

On the day following Annie Hayward's visit to Butterworth, Ross saddled Bishop and with a wealth of protective 'boots' on the horse's valuable black legs, took him out into the copse for a training session.

The value of the low rustic fences was in their rigid construction – the poles being bolted to the uprights – which encouraged the horses to pick their feet up, and the undulating terrain that promoted surefootedness and good balance.

Bishop worked like a dream. He skimmed through the wood, giving all the jumps at least a foot's clearance, enjoyment evident in every stride.

Ross walked him back to the yard on a loose rein, letting him blow and dreaming of the places he could go with this exceptional young horse. This was a once-in-a-lifetime talent, he felt sure.

A sudden rustling in the hedge caused Bishop to shy and Ross, instantly alert, turned to see a long black snout and forepaws pushing through the quickthorn. Bishop swung round, snorting nervously as the newcomer scrambled out and proved to be the German Shepherd from the local farm.

'You're trespassing,' Ross told it with mock severity. 'Come on. Better come with me.'

The dog watched him warily but when he rode on it followed at a discreet distance, and when he reached the yard it flopped down in the shade of the overhang and appeared happy to stay there.

No horse is perfect, and if Black Bishop came close to perfection to ride, he was the devil's own job to handle in the stable. The giant horse's pet hate was having his legs touched, which made him the bane of the farrier's life.

The safest way to apply or remove leg guards or bandages was for one person to hold the horse's head while the other tackled the task.

On this occasion when Ross dismounted in the yard there was not a soul in sight. With a resigned sigh he led Bishop into his stable and, having removed the saddle and exchanged the bridle for a headcollar, tied him up short to the ring in the wall. This done, he began to remove the boots, thanking God that Velcro and sprung clips had long replaced the fiddly straps and buckles of old. Even so, the job was a tricky one and the only way to remove the boots from the hind legs was first to grasp and hold tightly the hamstring tendon above the horse's hock joint and, by so doing, incapacitate the lower leg temporarily.

Ross talked soothingly to the horse all the while, although his words seemed to have little effect. With great relief he was reaching down for the last straps when he felt something shove him forcibly between the shoulder-blades and was sent sprawling into the straw by Bishop's hind legs.

With a grunt of outraged surprise the black jumped forward and lashed out with both back legs. Massive, steel-shod limbs that could power the horse over six foot of timber with ease slammed into the kickboards with a deafening crash, missing Ross' head by a whisker.

He scrabbled on the slippery straw to get out of the way as Bishop regained his balance and lashed out again. For a few moments his world was a confusion of pistoning black limbs and cracking, splintering wood as he rolled like a jockey to avoid being trampled, and then he was on his feet and lunging instinctively for the horse's head to try and restore control.

He released the slip-knot and hung on grimly as Bishop spun round one hundred and eighty degrees to see what had attacked him, and then threw his arms round the horse's neck just behind the ears and let his weight bear the animal down until he was still.

As Bishop gradually calmed, Ross stood up

straight again and looked towards the door. There was nobody there, although he could hear footsteps hurrying across the yard in his direction and after a moment Bill appeared.

'Is the horse all right?' he asked anxiously, seeing Ross on his feet and apparently in one piece.

Ross took a deep breath to steady himself. He patted the sweaty black neck and nodded. 'I think so. I'll have a look in a minute if you'll hold him.'

'Looks like he caught you,' Bill observed. 'What happened?'

Ross looked down, surprised. His hand was gashed and bleeding freely but there was, as yet, little pain.

'I . . . um . . . overbalanced. You know what he's like with his back legs.'

Bill clicked his tongue contemptuously. His expression plainly said it was Ross' own fault he had been kicked. Ross ignored him.

'Let's get him settled,' the stable manager said. 'Then we'd better look at that hand.'

With Bill's help Bishop was soon rubbed down and munching contentedly at a full haynet, his flash of temper forgotten.

The two men made their way to the tackroom with the saddle, bridle and troublesome boots, discussing Bishop's touchiness. Ross said nothing to Bill about how the incident had happened. In fact, now it was over he wasn't at all sure himself. Perhaps he *had* overbalanced.

'Where are the others?' he asked casually.

'Oh, I don't know. Somewhere around. No – that's not right. Sarah's got a dentist's appointment and I sent Leo to feed the youngsters. He's taking his time, though.' He stopped short. 'What's that bloody dog doing here?'

'I found him in Home Meadow. I'll take him back later.'

Bill grunted. 'Shooting him'd be kinder, poor sod! Old Trenchard keeps him chained up day and night. He oughtn't to have a dog, that man. Now, let's have a look at that hand.'

Ross obediently held out his left hand.

Bill unwound the handkerchief Ross had hastily wrapped around it and hissed through his teeth. He looked up under his brows at the American. 'You'd best let Maggie have a look at that. It might need stitching. She used to be a nurse, patched me up when I was still racing.'

With the wound deftly bathed and dressed, Ross abandoned plans to school Clown, taking him out instead for exercise on the roads. Sarah, back from the dentist, came with him on Cragside. He had fed the dog on scraps from the cottage kitchen before setting out and now it trotted at a discreet distance from Clown's heels as if it had been doing so all its life.

Ross called in at the farm on his way past and discovered 'Old Trenchard' mending a fence in his back garden.

'Brought the bugger back, have yer?' he grunted. 'Thought it might have got run under this time. More trouble than it's worth.'

'I'll take him off your hands if you don't want him,' Ross offered.

Trenchard straightened up from his hammering. 'Well now, I don't know about that. Cost a fortune, German Shepherds do.'

'Then I'm surprised you don't take more care of him,' Ross observed. 'I'll give you fifty pounds for him.'

Trenchard rubbed his chin with a grubby paw. 'Well now, he's worth a lot more . . .'

'Not to me, he's not.' Ross turned away.

'Cash?' Trenchard said hurriedly.

'Cash,' Ross agreed, taking his wallet from his back pocket.

By the time Ross had eaten lunch and taken Flowergirl into the arena for a schooling session his hand was swollen and throbbing. If it hadn't been for the fact that there was a big show the next day, he would have passed up the exuberant little mare in favour of a quieter ride, but she had been having trouble with spread fences and he wanted to get her sorted out if he could.

The day was humid and windless, and at the end of an hour both horse and rider were weary and damp with sweat. Flo was a rewarding pupil, though, and Ross was well content with her progress as he turned her loose and watched her roll in the sand.

'Nice work.'

Ross turned to see Franklin Richmond leaning on the gate. For once, Bill Scott wasn't beside him.

'Thank you, sir.'

'Oh, please, Ross! Not "sir". Call me Franklin. "Sir" makes me feel like a schoolmaster.'

'Okay.' Ross came to stand with his back to the gate, leaning on it.

For a moment there was silence.

'Are you still mad at me for Thursday?' Franklin asked.

'No, not really. McKinnon explained your reasons.' He paused, fiddling with the bridle, hunting for a way to say what he wanted to. 'Look, I appreciate the difficulty you're in and I'd like to help, but I don't see what good I can possibly do . . .'

'And you came over here to ride horses, not get involved in somebody else's problems? It's okay, I understand.' Franklin held up a hand to forestall Ross' protest. 'I'd feel the same way, I'm sure. But – well – I thought it couldn't do any harm, your knowing. We've come to a dead end and you might just stumble on to something. By the way, what have you done to your hand?'

'Oh, it's nothing. Just Bishop getting antsy about me touching his legs.' Ross watched Flo mooching round the arena. 'You seem very cool about this blackmail thing.' He squinted sideways through the sunshine at Richmond. 'I'd be tearing my hair out.'

'I did at first,' Franklin Richmond told him with a resigned smile. 'But it's been nearly eight months now. You can only live in fear so long. Then the threat becomes part of your life. Normal. Until

79

something like the other night happens, and then you start jumping at shadows again.'

Or in my case, something like Ginger, Ross thought, wryly.

'How long can you sustain the payments?' he asked. 'Isn't this ruining you?'

'No. I'm in no danger of bankruptcy just yet, but I've had to tighten my belt quite a few holes. Whoever it is has gauged it about right.'

'Not enough to starve the golden goose?' Ross mused.

'That's about it.'

'But surely this guy doesn't imagine you're going to go on paying him forever? He must know you'll try to catch him.'

'Oh, yes, he knows. And to help us along he lays shoals of red herrings and laughs as we run round trying to net them.'

'He knows about McKinnon?' Ross asked sharply.

'Oh, I shouldn't think so. At least, not specifically. Although I haven't told the police, he must know I'd hire someone. But he gives no sign that he knows who, and usually he likes to show off what he's learned about my actions. He's left several messages on my answerphone, all of them from call boxes and seldom the same one twice. "Good to see Woodsmoke going so well"; "Had a puncture today, did you, Richmond?" That sort of thing. I feel like nothing I do is private, but McKinnon doesn't think I'm being followed. At least, not all the time. This guy is playing with me.

He's got me on his hook and he's enjoying watching me wriggle.'

'You think it's someone you know personally, then?'

'I suppose so.' Richmond ran his fingers through his greying hair. 'It smacks of personal spite. But I can't conceive who would do such a thing and in such a way. It's frightening to think someone hates me that much.'

Flo came back to the gate, nuzzling at Ross' sleeve. She tried an experimental nip and he pushed her away, slapping her on the rump as she went.

'Your marriage . . . ?' Ross let the implied question tail off, wondering if it would be considered impertinent. After all, he hardly knew the man.

'Over,' Richmond said, shortly but without rancour.

'Divorce?'

'Yes.'

'Does she hold a grudge?'

'Marsha? She wouldn't even know how to spell it. She certainly couldn't put together anything like this. Besides, the courts made sure she'd never lack for money.' Richmond spoke without bitterness but in the tone of one who has learned his lesson the hard way.

Ross slipped the bridle reins round Flo's neck and opened the gate to lead her into the yard.

'Does she have a boyfriend?' he asked.

'Dozens.' Richmond shook his head at Ross' enquiring glance. 'No, nothing there, I wouldn't have thought. All lightweights. Flotsam and jetsam; pretty boys attracted by her sweet face and the even sweeter smell of her money.'

'You don't think very highly of your ex-wife,' Ross observed.

'I married for all the wrong reasons. She was very beautiful. It gave me a buzz to turn up at social functions with a blonde bombshell on my arm. But in between the parties – well, you know the saying. "Marry in haste . . ."'

Ross laughed. 'I think my father would sympathise.'

'Yes, I'm not the first and I won't be the last. I don't regret it though, it brought me Peter.' Richmond's eyes shone with fatherly pride. 'He makes up for everything.'

'And your wife . . .?' Ross hesitated again. 'There was no trouble over custody or anything?'

Richmond glanced at him, amused. 'McKinnon said you were a born investigator and I can see what he meant. You've asked me almost exactly the same questions he did when I first approached him.'

'I'm sorry. I guess it's in my blood. My father's a lawyer.'

'Don't be sorry. If you don't ask, you don't find out. You'll find I'm not easily offended, and if I am, I'll tell you so. In answer to your question: no, Marsha's mercenary instincts are far stronger than her maternal ones. Peter visits her about once a month and she never gives me the impression that parting from him is any great wrench. A small boy

82

would cramp her style pretty much, I imagine.' He paused, then changed track as Bill appeared in the tackroom doorway. 'Well, I have to be going. I'll see you at the show tomorrow. I'm bringing Peter along to see Clown's debut. He's very excited.'

With a wave of his hand and a nod to the stable manager, Richmond turned away and headed for his car.

Ross walked Flowergirl on across the yard.

'You had a long talk with Mr Richmond,' Bill observed as the American passed.

'Didn't I, though?' Ross agreed, with no intention of satisfying the little man's curiosity.

Bill scowled.

'He's coming to see Clown tomorrow and bringing Peter,' Ross said, relenting a little.

That didn't please Bill either. He was of the opinion that the skewbald was not ready to appear in public, but the unfortunate hitch in Butterworth's career had left an empty space in the horsebox and Clown's entry had gone in with the others to cover just such an eventuality.

As Ross rubbed the sweat and sand out of Flo's coat with a wisp of twisted hay, he pondered his conversation with Richmond. Whatever McKinnon's alleged opinion of him as an investigator, he thought it highly unlikely his supposed aptitude would be put to the test.

With far more immediate concerns to attend to, such as preparing four horses and their equipment for the following day, Ross comfortably relegated the whole matter to the back of his mind.

5

When Ross and Leo set off for the South Midlands show at six-thirty that Sunday morning, they took with them an extra pair of hands in the person of Danny Scott, Bill's fifteen-year-old son. Ross had met him fleetingly the previous weekend, but during the week the boy lived with his aunt in order to be nearer his school in Salisbury.

Danny was a slim youth, a little taller than his father, with dark hair and a thin, intense face. Horses were his passion and before they had left the winding Wiltshire lanes behind them, Ross had discovered that the boy had a burning ambition to follow in his father's footsteps and become a steeplechase jockey. Unfortunately it seemed that Bill was equally as determined that he shouldn't.

Chatting to the lad helped pass the time a lot faster than travelling alone with the unresponsive Leo, and took Ross' mind off the impending challenge. This was by far the biggest of his first three shows in England and he knew his performance here would be closely watched.

They arrived at the showground soon after eight o'clock and the sun was already promising discomfort in the hours to come. Leo swung into action with his usual sullen efficiency, helped more willingly by Danny, who proved to be every bit as capable.

Clown came out of the horsebox looking like a kid at Disneyland: bright, eager eyes darting every which way at once. Ross tacked the horse up, sprang into the saddle while Clown was still wondering how to react, and rode off to a quiet corner of the field to try and work the kinks out of him in private.

By the time he was called for his first class, Clown had settled far better than Ross had dared to hope, but after crossing the showground to the outside ring where he was due to jump, the horse's eyes were almost starting from his head. There was as yet no sign of Franklin Richmond and his son, for which Ross was grateful, as the skewbald charged into the ring and then stopped dead, seemingly rooted to the spot by the sight of the announcer's caravan.

The round, when Ross finally managed to get Clown's attention, was patchy. While he concentrated, Clown jumped very well, but every corner was taken with his brown and white face turned rigidly to the outside, staring goggle-eyed at all the sights of the showground. Subsequently, he missed seeing many of the fences altogether and a fair few poles adorned the turf when they left the ring.

There was little time for reflection as Leo was waiting with Flowergirl, and they exchanged mounts in the collecting ring so Ross could ready the little mare for her first class.

The day wore on.

The Colonel arrived mid-morning, just in time to see Flowergirl win her novice class, after which Ross changed back on to Clown and rode him to and fro round the showground, hoping to familiarise him with all the sights and sounds. A few people smiled to see the showy skewbald but Ross saw nobody he knew except Stephen Douglas, by whom he was studiously ignored. For a fleeting moment he found himself missing all the friends he had had on the circuit in the States but only until he reminded himself how fair-weather many of them had turned out to be. Not many had cared to risk being associated with a failure.

Around midday, when the bigger classes began in the main ring, Ross jumped an immaculate round on King's Defender and followed it with an unlucky four faults for a fence down on Flo, who jumped brilliantly round a more difficult course than she was used to. When he returned to the ring on King for the jump-off against the clock, the competition was warming up well. Two horses had already gone clear and the time to beat was fairly tight. Since Ross' earlier round, the commentary team had changed and the new voice behind the microphone sounded smooth, practised and extremely professional.

When his number was called, Ross rode King into the ring at a steady canter. The horse champed excitedly at his bit, snatching at Ross' hands, and pints of froth cascaded from his open mouth. The height of the jumps had been increased since the first round and in particular the second to last fence, a triple bar, looked huge. As Ross circled the ring to settle his mount, the public address system crackled into life.

'Next to jump we have number three five six, Ross Wakelin on Mr R. Fergusson's King's Defender. Ross has recently come over from America where he had a particularly disastrous last season, and has taken over the ride on this horse from one of our own young riders.'

Normally the voice of the commentator merged into insignificance with the other background noises, but Ross was surprised into listening to this rather unflattering description of his recent history. The bell went for the start of his round and, all else forgotten, he set to work.

King pulled out all the stops that afternoon and Ross rode him on a fluent, time-efficient line, turning tightly, but not so tightly as to interrupt his rhythm. As they turned to the last line of fences, Ross knew they had a chance. He pushed King for every ounce of effort, lifting him with hands and heels at each jump. They flew the triple bar, King's toes just clicking on the top pole as they went over, and steadied for the upright to finish. The crowd cheered and clapped as horse and rider shot between the timing beacons to stop the clock. Ross patted King's sleek bay neck as they pulled up and praised him quietly, his blood still racing with the familiar thrill of competition.

'A lucky clear round there for Ross Wakelin on King's Defender,' the commentator remarked over the loudspeaker. 'Mr Wakelin goes into the lead with a time of forty-two-point-eight-five seconds.'

Ross stared at the commentary box, dumbfounded, as he rode past. What was lucky about it? King had jumped beautifully. He shook his head in bewilderment.

Colonel Preston was waiting outside the collecting ring accompanied by a tall wiry man with a shock of red hair and piercing blue eyes that were almost hidden by low bushy brows.

Ross jumped down and patted King again.

'Ross, this is Robbie Fergusson,' the Colonel announced.

Ross had guessed as much. He held out his hand with a smile.

'Hi. How d'you do? This is one hell of a horse, you know.'

Fergusson's clasp was strong and brief.

'It's the first time he's been ridden properly for months,' he said, somehow making the compliment sound more like a complaint. 'That Douglas boy couldn't ride a seaside donkey!'

Ross didn't feel it was his place to comment. From what he had seen and heard, there was little wrong with Douglas' riding that wouldn't be put right by a little more experience.

'I'm not too good on donkeys myself,' Ross admitted with a grin.

Apparently humour wasn't the Scotsman's strong point. He fixed Ross with a bright blue gaze. 'I'll expect significant improvement from all my horses this summer,' he told him. 'I pay a fortune to keep them with the Colonel and lately I've seen sod-all in return. I've had a mind to give it all up.'

'I'll do my best,' Ross promised soberly.

Fergusson maintained his visual probe for a moment longer, then nodded and turned to the Colonel, effectively presenting his back to the American.

'I hope you're right about him,' he remarked, not troubling to lower his voice.

'Oh, I think so,' the Colonel replied as they turned away, and Ross took a deep breath to quell rising irritation.

Over King's saddle he caught sight of Leo approaching, riding Clown who was now considerably quieter and flanked by Franklin and Peter Richmond.

'They're calling you for your other class,' Leo told Ross as he jumped off the skewbald and held out the reins to the American. 'I left Danny looking after the box.'

'Lead King up and down for me, will you? I might need him again if we've won anything.' Ross vaulted on to Clown's back and turned towards the novice ring.

'How's he going, Ross?' Peter asked excitedly as he hurried alongside.

'Oh, fine,' Ross lied cheerfully. 'But you must remember it's all very new to him and not expect too much.'

Clown's class, though still novice, was somewhat more testing than his earlier, disastrous one had been and Ross didn't hold out much hope of completing the course, but he could but try.

The skewbald surprised them all. After an experimental buck as he began to canter, he settled down and actually started to concentrate on the job in hand. They left the ring with eight faults and a feeling of satisfaction on Ross' part. What the horse felt he couldn't say for sure, but Ross had a suspicion it was smugness.

Peter was thrilled with Clown's progress, showing a maturity of understanding far beyond his years. Together with Franklin, they made their way back to the main ring.

'How many more to go?' Ross asked one of the other riders.

'This is the last and you're still the fastest clear.' Then as a pole dropped to the turf for four faults, 'That's it! You've done it! Well done!'

Ross tightened the girth and mounted, accepting congratulations from his fellow competitors. He wondered what Fergusson would have to say about it. Probably not much. He rode into the ring to receive his rosette and prize and once again was aware of Stephen Douglas scowling at him from lower down the line. He didn't let it bother him.

When he left the ring after a lap of honour, the Colonel was waiting to congratulate him. Of the Scotsman there was no sign.

'Want to ride King back to the box?' Ross asked Peter.

'Can I? Brilliant?' Ross tossed him into the saddle where he looked tiny, like a toddler on a Harley-Davidson. Peter's face was radiant. King's Defender plodded good-naturedly, switching off like a pro after the job was done.

Ross' last classes of the day were for Black Bishop. He left the other three horses being settled for the journey home and took the big black to warm up.

Both Bishop's classes went well. The horse proved to have the perfect competitive temperament. Completely unruffled by the occasion, he jumped everything high and wide with intense concentration, never looking like hitting anything. Ross forgave him unreservedly for his recent bad-tempered behaviour and his own sore hand.

Their second class was in the main ring and the big German-bred animal attracted not a little attention from Ross' fellow riders.

'Come up in the world, haven't we?' a husky female voice commented from slightly behind Ross.

He turned. 'Danielle!' he exclaimed delightedly. A petite, pretty brunette, Danielle Moreaux was a successful international rider from Belgium and a girl he had dated a time or two before his accident.

'Ross, it's nice to see you again,' she said

warmly. 'Back on the winning track I see, too. I was told in America you had given up.'

'I had.' Ross grinned.

'But now you've come out of retirement?'

'For one last try.'

'You have some nice horses this time, I think,' she said, running her eye over Bishop approvingly.

Ross nodded. 'This fella's one of the best I've ever ridden,' he agreed. 'But he's young yet. I don't want to rush him.'

'Well, it's time you had some luck. You deserve it, you really do! Oh, number thirty-five, that's me! Come on, Bosun. Wake up, you lazy lump!'

She gathered up her reins and Ross watched appreciatively as she rode away towards the ring entrance, a neat figure in black jacket and cream breeches astride a grey thoroughbred.

In due course, Bishop jumped an immaculate clear and followed it with another in the jump-off, half an hour later. Ross didn't push him for a fast time, unwilling to do anything to upset the young horse's wonderful rhythm and balance at this early stage. He was well satisfied with the horse's performance.

'A clear round,' the commentator confirmed. 'But a slow time of fifty-eight seconds. You'll have to try a bit harder than that, Ross. Put some heart into it!'

He was furious.

'What's with that guy?' he demanded of Danielle as they passed in the collecting ring. 'Why can't he keep his smart-ass comments to himself?'

'Well, I suppose you can't expect him to be your biggest fan,' Danielle said matter-of-factly.

Ross looked blankly at her.

'You mean, you don't know who he is?' she asked, swinging her horse round to come alongside.

'Should I?'

'Oh!' the Belgian girl exclaimed, exasperated. 'Where have you been all these years? That's Harry Douglas. Everybody knows him! He does the commentary on TV and at all the big shows over here.'

'Okay. But why pick on . . .? Ah.' The light dawned. 'Douglas, as in *Stephen* Douglas?'

'Exactly.' Danielle nodded. 'In his eyes you're riding the horses his son should be riding. The fact that Stephen made a mess of the job is presumably beside the point to daddy's way of thinking.'

Her number was called and she rode away, leaving Ross to reflect that with opposition in such influential places, gaining recognition in England could prove to be just as hard as it had been in the States.

The next morning, Ross was busy schooling Barfly in the arena when the Colonel appeared and stood watching with Bill at the gate.

Fly was an unrewarding pupil. He had the ability, but his attitude left a lot to be desired. Ross had started early with the young horse, before the sun made any exertion uncomfortable, and when his employer appeared he was about ready to stop.

93

He did another ten minutes or so and then rode over to the gate where the Colonel waited, alone now.

'He's a bit of a bugger, isn't he?' he observed as Ross dismounted.

'You're not kidding,' Ross agreed. 'It's not that he can't, he just doesn't try.'

'Mmm. We could see he was being stubborn. I thought you were remarkably patient, considering.'

'Well, he's young yet,' Ross said, setting Barfly free to roll and wondering if there was a purpose to the Colonel's apparently casual visit.

'You're good with the youngsters,' the older man went on. 'Even Robbie Fergusson was impressed. He rang me this morning.'

'Just to tell you that?' Ross was sceptical and wary. Something in the Colonel's body language told him this was perhaps sugar to sweeten a bitter pill.

'Well, no, as a matter of fact,' he admitted. 'Ross, I'm afraid Fergusson has decided to sell King. He had a good offer yesterday and sees it as a way to cover some of his expenses. I think perhaps things are a bit tight at the moment.'

Ross' face hardened against the familiar disappointment.

'I see,' he said tonelessly.

'I'm sorry.' The Colonel sounded genuinely so. 'The thing is, King is in good health and the form of his life but at fourteen, as you know, his value can realistically only go down. He'll only have two or three more years at the top, however careful we are.'

'Sure, I understand,' Ross said with resignation. 'You know he qualified for Birmingham yesterday?'

'Yes, I know,' the Colonel said quietly. 'That clinched the deal.'

'Instant success. Bought, not worked for,' Ross said wryly but without bitterness. It was a familiar scenario. 'When will he go?'

'Probably at the end of the week. Look, I've got to go now. Come up to the house later, for a sherry.'

When he had gone, Ross tacked up Ginger and, coming across Danny in the yard, invited the boy to accompany him on Simone. Danny, who had a day off school due to something called a 'teacher training day', was a very able rider; a talent which his father did little to encourage.

'Did *you* go to college, Ross?' he asked as they clattered along the country lanes with the dog at their heels. 'Dad wants me to go to college but I don't want to. I don't need A-levels to be a jockey.'

'Sure I went,' Ross said. 'And I went on to law school too. My father wanted me to be a lawyer and join the family firm.'

'But you didn't, did you?' Danny said eagerly. 'You went your own way. Why can't Dad see I've got a right to live my own life?'

'I guess he only wants what he thinks is best for you,' Ross said, cringing inwardly as he heard himself echoing generations of parents with his words. 'And it never hurts to have some academic qualifications too. Horses are a risky business – look at me, I almost had to go back to studying law.'

Danny was not convinced. 'I could always turn to training if I couldn't ride any more,' he said with the easy optimism of youth. 'And anyway, Dad doesn't want me ever to be a jockey. Not now. Not in two years' time. Not ever!'

The American suppressed a smile at his boyish despair. 'In a year or two he won't have any say in the matter, as far as I can see,' he observed. Then, as they turned off the tarmac surface on to a grassy woodland track, 'Come on, let's get some practice in now, anyway.'

He hitched up his stirrups five or six holes and waited while Danny did the same, then, crouched jockey-like over their horses' necks, they put them into a gallop and thundered down the track between the trees. It wasn't until they pulled up, legs aching from the unaccustomed position and faces glowing with exhilaration, that Ross remembered it was Ginger he was riding.

Ross spent the afternoon cleaning tack. It being Monday, Bill was on his own and it didn't seem fair to leave extra work for him. As he worked amongst the smells of leather, saddle soap and metal polish, Ross pondered his own, so far unrewarded attempts to befriend the man. Scott might, as the Colonel alleged, have an exhaustive fund of equine knowledge locked away in his head but to date that was where it had stayed. Apart from when it was absolutely necessary, he had shown no inclination whatever to talk to Ross.

He had a strange feeling that Bill regarded him as a failure just waiting to happen, and although the horses' recent successes had undoubtedly pleased the man, his cold reserve where Ross was concerned had not noticeably warmed.

As though summoned by Ross' thoughts, the stable manager appeared in the doorway.

'I could have done that,' he observed dourly.

'That's okay. I don't mind.'

Bill grunted. He wandered around the tack-room, looking at a bridle here, tidying a blanket box there, whistling tunelessly through his teeth all the while, until Ross could cheerfully have strangled him.

'I'd rather you didn't encourage Danny in this stupid idea of becoming a jockey,' Bill said suddenly from behind him. 'It's really none of your business.'

Ross caught his breath at the unfairness of this unexpected attack. He turned slowly to find Bill glaring belligerently at him.

'I've done no such thing,' he said evenly. 'But I'll not *discourage* him either, and if you've got any sense, you'll hold off too. It's his life, after all, and if he's got any spirit, opposition will only make him more determined. Believe me, I know.'

'It's none of your bloody business!' Bill repeated with tight-lipped fury. 'Just stay out of it. He thinks you're some kind of hero. Can't see you for what you really are. When he does, he'll despise you as he despises me.'

Ross shook his head emphatically. 'No. You're wrong there. He doesn't despise you. If he did he wouldn't be aching to follow in your footsteps, would he? You should be proud of him. He'll do it, you know. Without your support if he has to, but he'd much rather do it with.'

'What makes you think you've the right to tell me how to bring up my son?' Bill hissed furiously. 'You're a fine bloody role model, aren't you? Don't think I don't know the *real* reason you lost your job in America! You might fool the Colonel and Mr Richmond but I know better, and it's only a matter of time before they find out for themselves. So why don't you get out while you can still go with dignity?'

With this, Bill turned abruptly on his heel and left the tackroom. Ross stared after him in bemused silence.

Obviously Bill had somehow come to hear of the rumours that had surrounded his 'retirement' in the States, but quite what that had to do with Danny's ambition to be a jockey, Ross couldn't see. Somehow, too, it failed to account for the violence of the outburst.

Just before noon the following day, a red MG Roadster drew up in the yard and Lindsay climbed out, looking slim and tanned in cotton hipsters and a cropped top.

Ross had just finished hosing Bishop down after a hard but rewarding session in the school. He turned the tap off and went towards her, drying his hands on his unbuttoned denim shirt and smiling widely.

'Hi! When did you get back? And why didn't you tell me?' He took advantage of the occasion to give her a welcoming kiss on the cheek.

'Yesterday morning, early. It was a spur-of-the-moment decision. I've been longing to see how you're getting on and suddenly I couldn't wait any longer, so I rang the airport and they had a cancellation – so here I am! I was going to ring but then I thought I'd surprise you all.'

Bill and Sarah had appeared from the tackroom and joined in greeting Lindsay. Leo stood watching from a doorway until he was introduced and then turned on a hitherto undemonstrated charm.

'You're just in time for coffee,' Ross told her. 'Let me put Bishop away and we'll go and find Maggie.'

'Do you know, that's one of the things I've missed most about England. Maggie's baking.' Lindsay laughed. 'That and Gypsy. I'm longing to ride her again.'

Ross knew from their long conversations in the hospital that the Colonel's yard was barely three miles from the sizeable Georgian manor where Lindsay's family lived, and which was managed as a venue for conferences and up-market functions. She had told him that throughout her childhood, her ponies, and then horses, had been stabled at Oakley Manor to prevent her becoming, as her mother put it, 'one of those abominable little horsey girls who always smell of stables'. As the

99

only child of the Cresswells of Cresswell Hall, she was expected to make a suitable marriage and in due course take over the running of the Hall.

Seated at the table in the Scotts' cottage, Lindsay munched on one of Maggie's rock cakes and demanded to hear, in detail, about all Ross' successes to date.

'And what happened to your hand?' she asked, after commiserating with him over the loss of the ride on King.

Ross hesitated. 'I . . . uh . . . got kicked,' he said. 'Bishop is a tad grouchy about having his legs handled, but it's nothing much.' He flexed the fingers of his bandaged hand to prove it was still operational.

'"The patient is said to be comfortable",' Lindsay quoted, grinning.

Ross smiled back. 'Yeah, that sort of thing,' he agreed, noting that Leo was regarding him with a sullen stare, and wondering, not for the first time, if somebody really had pushed him under Bishop's feet. He shrugged the thought off. They had had their differences, but Leo had never given him any reason to think he wished him actual harm. For the most part they worked together well.

'Whose is the dog?' Lindsay asked, seeing the German Shepherd lying half under Ross' chair.

'Mine,' he said, reaching a hand down to stroke its head.

'My, we have settled in, haven't we?'

'Actually, it was more a case of the dog adopting me,' he told her.

Lindsay snapped her fingers, bending down to look at the animal. 'Come on. Come and see me. What's his name?' she asked.

'I don't know,' Ross said, realising that he'd never even thought about it. 'I just call him "lad", or "boy".'

Lindsay looked heavenwards.

'Honestly, men!' she said, heavily. 'We'll have to think of one for you,' she told the dog, who flopped his tail but made no move towards her.

Maggie got up to clear away empty mugs and offer refills, and Ross remembered that he had another horse to ride before lunch.

'Come on, back to work,' he said, standing up. 'Sarah, will you saddle Clown for me in a minute? Leo, the poles in the jumping lane need picking up. Put them at two foot six, will you?'

Lindsay finished her coffee. 'Thanks, Maggie, that was lovely. I must go and see Uncle John, but first I want to see my darling Gypsy. Is she here or out in the field?'

'She's in the paddock behind the barn. I'll come with you,' Ross suggested.

As they walked, Lindsay glanced appraisingly at him. 'So how're things, really?'

'Good,' he stated. 'I'm glad I came. Thanks.'

'Oh, don't be silly! I must say you look a lot better than last time I saw you. You've lost that haunted look. England must suit you.'

'Wow! Was I that bad?' Ross joked, uncomfortably.

Lindsay nodded. 'Awful. You had me worried

for a bit.' They had reached Gypsy's field and she called the mare over.

'Yeah, well, I'm not especially proud of that little episode,' he admitted on a sigh.

'You had good reason.' Lindsay reached out to pat her horse. 'Anyway, it's all in the past. Now you can show them what you're really made of!'

'Sure,' he agreed, pushing all thoughts of Ginger firmly to the back of his mind.

Shortly after that Lindsay departed with a cheery wave to visit 'Uncle John', and Ross was left with mixed emotions. Seeing her again had lifted his spirits even more than he had expected, but his pleasure was tempered by the knowledge that somewhere in the wings lurked the man she was to marry.

'James? Oh, he's still in Hong Kong at the moment,' she had said in answer to his casual query. 'I spoke to him two days ago but he wasn't sure how soon he'd be back.'

Ross banished the absent James to the dim recesses of his mind, along with Ginger. He was getting quite good at it.

6

Lindsay's return acted like a breath of fresh air blowing through the yard at Oakley Manor. Leo exerted himself to be the classic romantic and affected deep hurt when she refused to take him seriously; Sarah came out of her shell and could be heard chatting quite animatedly to the older girl; even Bill was a shade more cheerful.

Lindsay spent at least part of most days at the yard, exercising Gypsy and sometimes one of the other horses. As far as Ross could tell, she seemed unaware of the growing strength of feeling he had for her and he took care to keep it that way. For her part, she gave no hint that she regarded Ross as anything more than a friend and he wasn't prepared to risk losing the companionship they shared by suggesting anything more.

A few days after her return he raided his savings and bought a battered jeep to run around in,

Although he had been told he could borrow the yard's Land-Rover, Ross didn't like to use it on other than yard business in case there was an emergency. Besides, it was in his nature to be independent.

He also took Lindsay's less than subtle hint and went into Salisbury to get his hair cut, using the opportunity to fill out his sparse wardrobe and equip himself with a mobile phone and a new watch at the same time.

King was collected at the end of the week, and after consultation with the Colonel, Cragside was turned out to grass, Ross feeling that the solid grey had neither the ability nor the temperament to progress any further. Come autumn he would be sold as a hunter.

With Butterworth invalided indefinitely, the yard was down to seven horses in full work, not counting Gypsy, and with Lindsay around and Danny soon home for the holidays it seemed ridiculously overstaffed.

Ross' dog had settled in well, lying around in shady corners while Ross was in the yard or the school, padding softly out to follow the horses when he rode out to exercise and following him into his room at night. In the cottage or up at the main house he sat quietly behind Ross' chair as if he had been trained to do so and in general avoided everybody but Ross, whom he worshipped, and Sarah, whom he tolerated. He took to the jeep at once, jumping into the back as soon as Ross started the engine and travelling with his black muzzle resting on his master's shoulder.

The horses travelled to a couple more shows; Bishop and Flo building on their promising beginnings, and Franklin's old horse, Woodsmoke, pulling off a surprise win over a huge course at Lea Farm one evening.

Simone was proving hard to beat in speed classes, and although Ross still mistrusted Ginger, she didn't put a foot wrong at any of her shows and was even placed once.

Gradually the horses were beginning to accumulate the placings and amounts of prize-money that would move them up the grades and qualify for the bigger shows at Hickstead, Birmingham and Olympia. Regular attendance at county shows and smaller venues like Lea Farm was an inescapable part of the process.

Franklin Richmond's problem, never again spoken of by the man himself, began to fade into the back of Ross' mind.

Then the spell was broken.

It was a Tuesday. Lindsay's MG swept into the yard as usual, just after breakfast, but in place of the habitual jeans and jodhpur boots, she wore a smart skirt and blouse, with pearls gleaming at her throat.

'Sorry, folks,' she said with a rueful smile. 'James is coming home at the end of the week and I've got to go shopping for something to wear at our engagement do. I'm meeting a girlfriend in half an hour. London will be hell in this heat.'

Ross promised to exercise Gypsy for her and

with a cheery wave she was gone, leaving him feeling more depressed than he cared to admit.

Bill and Sarah had gone out to do road work on Flo and Woody, and Leo was in the jump store repairing broken wings, when Ross brought Ginger into the school.

His mind was not entirely on the job in hand, he admitted to himself afterwards. He had been moodily wondering what kind of a man James Roberts was, that Lindsay should choose to spend the rest of her life with him: but that didn't in any way excuse or account for Ginger's subsequent behaviour.

It began in the way it had before, though Ross didn't notice the signs at first. Her ears began to flick to and fro nervously and she tossed her head a time or two. Her back hunched and stiffened, and her stride became choppy and uncomfortable.

Now fully alert, Ross guessed that the hammering noises emanating from the jump store were probably at the root of her unease and called out to Leo to stop working for the moment.

At first he thought Leo had not heard or was pretending he hadn't, but then the door opened and with a reverberating crash, he tossed several planks out on to the concrete apron.

Ginger exploded.

Quicker than thought, she whipped round and tore across the arena, heading blindly for the rails. Ross put all his weight on to one rein and pulled her head round until her muzzle was almost touching his knee and then, when a collision with the fence seemed inevitable, she lost her footing in the soft sand and fell heavily on to her side. Ross rolled off and tried to hang on to the reins as she scrambled furiously to her feet, but she ripped them through his fingers and whirled away.

The first thing she did was run into the rails on the other side of the school but they held and she rebounded and began to circle the arena at top speed. She careered past Ross five times before she started to slow up.

The first time, he moved towards her as she passed but could see by the look in her eyes that she would run him down if he got in her way, so he stood still and waited for her to calm down in her own time.

Eventually she stopped by the gate, head high and flanks heaving. Ross steeled himself to walk quietly up and take hold of her broken rein.

She didn't move; didn't even seem to notice him. Then she shuddered and her body drooped with released tension.

Ross patted her sweaty neck and then looked round.

Leo was leaning on the fence, watching with evident enjoyment. 'Did I frighten her?' he asked innocently. 'I'm so sorry.'

Ross didn't trust himself to answer. He knew he should climb back on the chestnut mare straightaway. It was the first thing he had been taught by his uncle, all those years ago. It was the first thing anyone was taught. Normally, it was the obvious, if sometimes painful, thing to do. Just now, though,

Ross didn't care if he never rode the mare again.

But Leo was watching.

Ross put the broken ends of the rein together over Ginger's neck and raised his foot to the stirrup. The hand that reached for the back of the saddle was not as steady as he would have liked, but Leo was too far away to see. He swung aboard once more.

Ginger didn't move a muscle.

Ross knew, as he went through the motions of a schooling session, that he hadn't only remounted to prove his nerve to the watching groom or to show the mare that she couldn't get away with such behaviour. He had done it to satisfy himself; and it bothered him that he should have needed to.

Ross did the rounds with Bill that night, as usual. Topping up water buckets and haynets, straightening rugs where worn, and tidying beds. He always enjoyed this part of the routine, setting everything right for the night and leaving the horses munching contentedly or dozing, sleepy-eyed, on their feet.

The night was warm and humid. Grasshoppers chirped in the long grass behind the stables, and bats swooped and dived overhead. The last animal seen to, Ross said goodnight to Bill and stiffly climbed the stairs to his room. His troublesome knee had borne the brunt of his fall from Ginger and was protesting.

Leo's room was quiet. He was still out, and would be until the pubs closed, Ross guessed. The dog padded to its customary corner and collapsed with a gusty sigh as Ross made coffee and switched on the TV. Two depressing current affairs programmes; a soap opera; a comedy show with canned laughter; and a Japanese film with subtitles. He switched it off and listened to Woody moving about down below.

Almost inevitably his thoughts turned to Lindsay and how great she had looked that morning, and he wondered again what the absent James was like. In his mind he pictured him as plump and serious, bespectacled and suited, but deep down he knew that, parental pressure or not, Lindsay would not settle for a wimp.

His knee was determinedly aching now and he got up to find some paracetamol, knowing that it wouldn't be the whole answer but hoping it might help.

Bloody Ginger! If it weren't for Bishop, he would tell Fergusson just what he could do with his horse.

His brief meeting with the man had certainly not endeared him to Ross. It seemed that Fergusson regarded his horses in the same light as the chess pieces he had made his name with: as non-sentient beings to be manipulated at will. Any failings they might show he automatically attributed to their rider. Ross was thankful that tournaments and masterclasses kept Robbie Fergusson away from Oakley Manor for much of the time.

Just before midnight, he heard Leo come in, making no attempt to disguise his noisy progress.

Half an hour later Ross was still awake, tossing and turning in the too-warm darkness, naggingly aware of his throbbing leg.

At some point he must have slept, for the dreams came again; the familiar nightmare of the screaming crowd, the struggling horse and the suffocating weight on his chest. With a gasp he awoke, sitting bolt upright.

The night was quiet. No breath of wind disturbed the curtains at the open window. Across the room the dog was padding around restlessly. Ross wondered if he had disturbed it.

He sat up, eyes heavy with tiredness but reluctant to sleep again lest the nightmare return. Despite the warmth of the night he found he was shivering and his thoughts turned involuntarily to an unopened bottle of Scotch that nestled amongst his winter sweaters in his suitcase under the bed. He had used whisky in the past to dull the pain in his leg and help him sleep, but not for months now.

The very fact that he hadn't unpacked his winter clothes, Ross knew, was a measure of his insecurity. He had felt in a way that it would be inviting fate to slap him down. Now, just as he had begun to feel that things were going right at last, Ginger had reawakened the old self-doubt.

Whisky.

Temptation.

So easy to give in.

Ross gave himself a thorough mental shaking. He swung out of bed, reached for his jeans and pulled them on. If he couldn't sleep he would go for a walk.

The dog seemed pleased to be out, running round him in tight circles, wagging its tail. The moon was about three-quarters full and gave just enough light through the high cloud for the American to see when he left the lamplit yard and moved out into the home field.

The tranquillity of the night restored some sense of perspective and after ten minutes or so he headed back towards his room in a much better frame of mind than when he had left it.

Then the dog growled.

Ross put a hand on its head to quieten it and stopped, eyes searching the shadows. Just as he was about to move on, convinced that the dog had heard a cat or a fox, he saw a pool of light moving along the ground behind the horsebox. His heart thumping heavily, he moved forward quietly on the concrete apron in front of the stables. This part of the yard was in deep shadow, the lamplight obscured by the bulk of the lorry.

The torchlight flashed higher once or twice, as if searching at the stable doors for a particular head, then disappeared. It occurred to Ross that the prowler might be making for the covered corridor where the other horses were housed.

They found the horse lying in the straw with its throat cut. It was horrific. McKinnon's words echoed like a warning in Ross' mind, and throwing caution to the winds he sprinted down the concrete apron and round the back of the horsebox. The

111

dog shot past him and into the darkness of the doorway before he could stop it. Ross cursed and made to follow. Then a flicker of movement at the edge of his field of vision halted him in his tracks. The prowler was still outside. He shrank into the shadows and watched.

Somewhere at the other end of the yard he could hear the dog barking, but the sound gradually receded. He had obviously come out of the other doorway at the far end of the corridor and was now running aimlessly round the home field. Stupid bloody mutt! Ross thought. No help at all.

After a minute or two had passed, Ross, scarcely daring to breathe, heard a whisper of movement and a shadow detached itself from the cover of the building, just a few feet away from where he stood.

He stepped out after it.

'Stop right there!' he said sharply. The words sounded unnaturally loud after the strained silence and the question *Or else?* seemed to hang in the air between them.

To Ross' surprise, the shadowy figure obeyed. The prowler was of similar height and build to Ross himself and as such presumably male, but as he turned, his face was in darkness. He raised his hands shoulder high in apparent surrender.

What light there was shone into Ross' face and he paused, one arm uplifted to shield his eyes, trying to see, unsure of himself. Prowlers were supposed to run, not give themselves up to obviously unarmed challengers. Surely it wasn't anyone he knew?

'Who are you?' he demanded, wishing there were a shovel or pitchfork within reach. He was very aware of the night wind blowing through his open shirtfront. It made him feel uncomfortably vulnerable.

What if the prowler had a hidden knife?

The trespasser waited calmly; a silent, black silhouette with hands empty and still.

His very immobility unnerved Ross. He took a step closer and to one side, moving his head to try and see the man's features.

Suddenly the intruder moved. Before Ross could react, his wrist was grasped, a hand hooked under his armpit bearing him back and down, and the man stepped past and threw him neatly across his hip.

Helpless, Ross had no sensation of falling but found himself sprawling on the gravel, gasping for air like a landed fish. He rolled instinctively to protect himself from further attack but it seemed the intruder was no longer interested in him for he sprinted away and as Ross regained his feet he could hear footsteps receding on the gravel of the drive.

Ross reached for the stable wall and leant against it, deeply winded, as the dog belatedly returned and swept past him growling, apparently on the trail of the intruder at last. Seconds later Ross heard the snarl of a powerful engine coming to life and the squeal of a car's tyres as it pulled away. He leaned back against the brickwork, waiting for his breathing to become less painful, and after a moment a cold wet nose pushed itself into his hand.

'Stupid mutt,' Ross chided the dog, ruffling its coat affectionately. 'Where were you when I needed you?'

He pushed away from the wall and made his way round the stables. Everything seemed in order. All doors were locked that should be. Most of the horses were wide awake, alerted by the commotion, though some were already settling down again and blinked sleepily at him as he turned on their light. None lay with their throat slit, as he'd at first feared. He patted the necks of those that approached him and spoke to them quietly, then turned off the lights.

For perhaps half an hour he waited quietly in the shadows with a pitchfork to hand, then calling softly to the dog, he made his way back to his room. He was not surprised that Leo hadn't woken after an evening at the local, though he had half-expected Bill to appear.

He knew he should probably have woken Bill when he first saw the torchlight but at the time preventative action had seemed all-important and now there seemed little point. Bill would probably feel it his duty to inform the police and, quite apart from his reluctance to spend the rest of the night answering questions, Ross wasn't entirely sure whether Franklin Richmond wouldn't rather leave the police out of it, if it had anything to do with Bellboy and the extortionist.

He decided, as he lowered himself thankfully

into bed, that his best course of action was to contact Richmond as soon as he could and let him do what he wished about the affair. Then it occurred to him that if the prowler was anything to do with the extortionist and he had, as McKinnon suspected, a contact within the yard, Ross' own silence would seem somewhat suspicious.

His mind thoroughly bogged down with bluff and counter-bluff, he slipped into an uneasy slumber.

7

When Ross awakened the next morning, the first thing he thought of was the torch. It had been the light of a torch which had alerted him but when the prowler had turned to face him he'd held nothing in his hands. So, he had either put it in a pocket – unlikely, as his silhouette had shown he was wearing nothing bulky – or he had dropped it or put it down somewhere.

Perhaps it was still there.

Only Sarah was in the yard when Ross emerged into the chill of the early morning. He smiled absent-mindedly at her, noting with mild irritation that even that made her redden, and went about his search.

He found nothing.

Later, when the team was settling down to breakfast, he casually mentioned his nocturnal excursion.

'The dog got me up last night,' he said over toast and marmalade. 'I took him out and when I came back from the field, I thought I saw someone in the yard, over by the horsebox. The dog barked and ran at him, and he made off.'

This potted version, he had decided, would satisfy the innocent and ungodly alike. Failing to mention his pathetic attempt to restrain the intruder could easily be construed as a matter of bruised pride.

'Why didn't you wake me?' Bill demanded sharply, and beside him, Sarah stared with wide, frightened eyes.

Ross shrugged. 'I heard a car start up out in the lane. Figured whoever it was would be long gone.'

'It'd take an earthquake to wake you anyway, dear,' Maggie said, filling coffee cups. 'And I sleep with cotton wool in my ears to drown his snoring,' she told Ross, who smothered a smile.

Bill glowered at his wife as she passed his coffee.

'It was probably one of those hippies,' she went on, ignoring him. 'Been hanging round the local villages ever since they were turned away from Stonehenge. Looking for somewhere to camp, I suppose. Old Trenchard was saying he's padlocked all his gates. He swears the blighters had a chicken off him the other night, but then, he would.'

'Well, I don't suppose they'll be back if they've had a taste of the dog,' Bill observed grudgingly. 'But another time, call me anyway. After what happened last year we can't be too careful.'

Ross silently blessed Maggie for providing an

instant and plausible explanation for the prowler. In fact, he reflected, it might well have been the right one, if it hadn't been for the powerful and well-tuned sound of the car's engine. However, he had covertly watched the faces of his companions and if any of them knew anything more about last night's events than he did, they were taking care not to show it.

Lindsay arrived while the exercise rota was being set and the day settled into a familiar routine. Ross rode out with Leo and the two girls; light exercise because the horses were going to an evening show. When they clattered back into the yard an hour or so later, the Colonel was waiting, talking to Bill and another, younger man whom Ross didn't know.

Lindsay clearly did. 'Roland!' she cried delightedly, slipping off Gypsy and running forward to meet him.

In the long days in hospital, Roland had figured frequently in Lindsay's conversation. He was her cousin, Ross remembered, the Colonel's son, and from the way she had spoken of him, Ross knew she adored him. He jumped off Woody and followed in a more leisurely fashion, taking time to observe the newcomer.

Roland Preston was straight out of a fashion plate, a vision in a pale cream, 1930s-style suit; one of the kind that looked as though it had been made for someone two sizes larger. His sandy hair was short and brushed back from an aristocratic brow. A pair of tinted spectacles hid his eyes and, despite the heat, a silk paisley scarf was knotted loosely about his neck. The whole effect was very P.G. Wodehouse.

He received Lindsay with open arms and swept her off her feet as one might a toddler, swinging her round in a full circle before putting her down. Lindsay hugged him.

'When did you get back? It's been so long,' she said, her eyes shining. 'How long has it been? Ten months? A year?'

'Surely not?' Roland said in mock dismay. 'Besides, you're forever on the telephone. I've got a few days off and drove up from London last night, if you want to know, but it's surely a case of when *you* got back. You're the one who's been careering around America '

'Ross,' Lindsay said, drawing away from Roland, 'meet my absurd cousin Roland. Roland, this is Ross.'

The fashion plate held out a lean, tanned and perfectly manicured hand.

'Delighted, dear boy,' he drawled, smiling amiably. 'Delighted. Lindsay's told me so much about you.'

'Don't believe a word of it.' Ross obliged with the expected response.

'No?' Roland queried thoughtfully, one eyebrow raised. 'A shame. I was quite impressed.'

Lindsay punched her cousin playfully on the arm. 'Don't listen to him, Ross,' she advised. 'He'll tie you in knots.'

'You're probably right,' Ross agreed good-

119

naturedly. 'After all, English *is* only my second language.'

The Colonel laughed out loud. 'Oh, I think the Yank can take care of himself, Lindsay,' he said. 'I wouldn't be at all surprised if Roland has met his match at last.'

His son smiled politely.

When Ross telephoned Franklin Richmond later on his mobile, he seemed philosophical about the night-time intruder.

'Thanks for doing what you did,' he said, 'but be careful. I don't want anybody getting hurt over this. After all, I don't think for one moment that we could stop this madman getting to the horses if he put his mind to it. We couldn't maintain a guard indefinitely, twenty-four-seven, as they say. The thing is, if it *was* our man, I can't imagine what he was up to. I mean, I'm paying up as it is. Why do anything further and risk upsetting everything? It doesn't make sense. It's almost as though he wants more than just the money. As if he wants to keep me on edge.'

Ross went over this conversation in his mind on the way to Lea Farm that evening. He had immense admiration for Richmond's strength of character. He supposed a man who daily thought and dealt in millions became used to pressure. When he had told Ross that it was safe to call him on his private line at the office because the building was regularly checked for 'bugs', Ross had revised his first, clichéd, impression of what top-flight financial consultancy involved.

'You're quiet, Yank,' Leo remarked suddenly. 'Thinking about blondie?'

Ross swallowed his irritation. He was damned if he'd give Leo the satisfaction of seeing his reaction. Poker-faced, he said blankly, 'Who?'

'Oh, very good, Yank,' Leo said. 'Very good. "*Who?*"' he repeated, mimicking Ross.

Ross kept his eyes on the road ahead. He didn't know why Leo had chosen this moment to pick a quarrel, maybe it was just boredom, but he did know it had gone far enough.

'You do know I have the power to fire you?' he remarked conversationally.

'I was hired by Scott,' Leo stated, defiantly. 'I'll answer to him.'

'And he answers to me, if need be.'

Leo was silent for a moment, his face sullen. Then: 'If you do, you'll regret it, Yank,' he promised softly.

'I doubt it,' Ross said, swinging the lorry through the gates of Lea Farm in a slow, smooth curve.

The evening went well enough for the most part. Once the horses were unloaded and the rush was on, Leo seemed to put aside his animosity and concentrate on his work, as usual.

Ross' time passed in an endless stream of warming up, walking courses and competing, then changing mounts and starting all over again.

If anything, he found walking the courses the

most tiring part of the business. Trudging round the arena, measuring the distances between fences, rehearsing the turns and assessing the viability of short-cuts was an integral part of the game, but with his troublesome leg it was exercise Ross could have happily done without.

He had a full lorry, Simone, Clown, Flo and Woody, and until Bill turned up in the Land-Rover, only Leo to assist him.

The horses jumped well but without the spark of brilliance needed to win classes against stiff opposition. Apart from a fourth for Simone in a speed class, Ross was out of the money all evening, so when both Woody and Flo qualified for the jump-off in the big class of the night he was determined that at least one of them should be placed.

One thing that especially caught the American's eye at Lea Farm that evening was the appearance of Stephen Douglas, pale and grim-faced, striving to control an extremely powerful dark chestnut, whose sole ambition seemed to be to proceed as fast as possible in whatever direction he happened to be headed.

Douglas had tried to combat the animal's natural inclination with a bewildering array of gadgets which were quite plainly never intended to be used simultaneously. The horse, far from being subdued by the multitude of straps and curbs, fought all the harder.

Ross shook his head in wonderment.

'That boy hasn't a hope of holding him,' Bill

said, coming alongside. 'He's just too much horse. Should have been gelded years ago but some pop star owns him and won't hear of it. I ask you, who'd want to breed a foal with that temperament? He's a failed racehorse, you know. Mr Richmond told me about him. Used to run away going down to the start and wouldn't go in the starting stalls when he got there. Useless animal. Might as well be shot.'

'That's kinda hard,' Ross said. 'You gotta admire his spirit, don't you?'

Bill snorted and walked away.

While Ross warmed up Flo in the collecting ring, he watched Douglas trying to qualify the chestnut for the same jump-off.

From the start it was clear to even the most uninformed observer that if any of the fences were left standing at the end of the round, it would be due more to luck than judgement. The chestnut stallion proceeded in a series of short, jarring leaps with his head tied down until it nearly touched his chest, and had no chance of seeing, let alone clearing, the fences. Douglas looked desperately unhappy as he fought to stay in control and they left the ring with all but three fences down and both horse and rider perspiring freely.

Ross was first to go in the jump-off on Flower-girl, and although the fences were somewhat bigger than the little mare was used to, she jumped a cracking round, only dropping a pole at the very last. Ross patted her dark, sweating neck as he rode out into the collecting ring where Leo was walking

Woody round quietly. He changed horses and warmed the big gelding up again in the whirling mass of horses that inhabited the small area where the practice fence had been set up.

In due course his number was called and Ross turned Woody towards the ring entrance. Leo patted the horse as it passed and said, 'Go for it!'

Ross blinked, surprised at his uncharacteristic enthusiasm.

Woody was a grand old horse, at sixteen finding the biggest spreads a little beyond him but still pulling like a train. Ross entered the ring keeping him on a tight rein. He circled, the bell went and he was away.

The first four fences were fairly simple, then he had to take a pull to collect the veteran for a double of planks and push on for the triple bar that followed. Woody responded gamely and the red-and-white poles flashed by a good six inches beneath his neatly tucked-up hooves.

'Steady, steady,' Ross murmured as they swung round the bottom of the arena, kicking tanbark up against the wooden boards, and turned into the last line of jumps.

Woody wouldn't be steadied. He plunged forward, flying the first and, adjusting his strategy, Ross drove him on to take the next on a long stride. His heart was singing. He could win this!

The old horse bunched his hindquarters and leapt high and wide but his momentum tipped him forward on landing and he stumbled, ploughing a furrow in the loose footing with his nose. Ross sat back to assist his recovery and with a sickening jolt the girth snapped.

The American hadn't a hope of saving himself. As the saddle slipped beneath him he saw the tanbark rushing up to meet him, tucked his chin in and rolled like a steeplechase jockey.

Horse and rider came to their feet unharmed but on Ross' part, at least, annoyed and disappointed. The saddle lay tumbled in the tan at his feet and he scooped it up and trudged towards the exit to a smattering of sympathetic applause. Woody had been captured near the exit barrier and stood watching his approach with anxious eyes.

'That was number twenty-one, Ross Wakelin and Woodsmoke,' the commentator reported. 'It can happen to the best of us, but a shame that, he was well up on the clock. Next we have number three-three-oh, Mr S. Harding on his own Gregory.'

Ross left the bright lights behind him as he walked out into the dusk, leading the big gelding.

Bill came hurrying up.

'What the hell happened there?'

'Girth snapped,' Ross said shortly.

'Bad luck,' he commiserated.

Ross said nothing. He hadn't had time to inspect the broken girth closely but he had an idea that luck had little or nothing to do with it.

Ross was more than usually thoughtful as he drove home that night. The girth, when examined, was found to be sound. What *had* given way were the leather straps that the girth buckled on to. These, three on each side, were sewn on to two strips of canvas webbing that passed over, and were fastened to, the main inner structure or tree of the saddle. What made the incident odd was that to prevent this very failure, one strap was always sewn on to one piece of webbing and the other two on to the second. Both lots of stitching had apparently given way at the same time.

This suggested two possibilities: either the person in charge of Woodsmoke, and therefore his tack, was guilty of extreme negligence in not noticing that the stitching was badly worn; or, worse, somebody had deliberately cut or frayed the stitching just before Ross was due to ride.

In spite of his immediate suspicion, Ross instinctively shied away from this second notion, though it had to be said that the first was highly unlikely. Bill looked after Woody and it was unthinkable that someone with his almost obsessive attention to detail would miss such an obviously dangerous sign of wear. Unless, of course, he chose to.

Ross dismissed this idea. Too many people rode Woody in the course of a week for this to be a viable form of sabotage. Which meant that the damage was recent, and in view of their discord on the way to the show, suspicion fell heavily on one person.

Ross braked gently at some traffic lights and rolled his head from side to side, trying to ease a stiffening neck. He looked across at Leo.

The groom was looking away from him, out of the side window. The red light reflected on the hard line of his jaw and haloed his black hair. Even from that angle his expression was unfriendly.

Bill had gone on ahead and when they reached the yard was waiting with rugs and stables ready for the returning horses, feeds in mangers and haynets hung. Even so, it was close to an hour before they retired to the cottage for a late supper. Ross' neck had stiffened still further, and he was glad to follow Maggie's suggestion that he soak in a hot bath for a while. When he eventually reached his bed, sleep came swift and deep.

Around dawn the dog woke him, standing at the door and whining. Ross murmured heartlessly that he would have to wait, turned over and was instantly asleep once more.

Sleep was tenacious in its grip on him and he was only just emerging from under the duvet when he heard the chorus of whinnies and banging that habitually greeted Sarah's arrival in the yard. He pulled his jeans on and padded on bare feet out into the bathroom he shared with Leo. Cold water restored some form of semi-intelligent consciousness and he was on his way back to his room when he heard the scream.

He was down the stairs and out of the door before its echoes had died away, and Leo was right behind him. He sprinted across the yard, heedless of the sharp stones under his unprotected feet. Bill appeared from the direction of the cottage, hopping as he pulled on his boots. Ross burst

127

through the doorway into the covered section and staggered as Sarah collided with him, on her way out at top speed.

'Hold up! Steady now. What is it?' he demanded, grasping her arms.

The girl raised wide, frightened eyes to his. 'It . . . it's Clown!' she sobbed. 'Oh, God, it's happened again!'

Ross pushed her away, his blood suddenly running cold. 'No. Please, no,' he begged under his breath as he raced along the corridor to Clown's stable.

The skewbald stood in the corner of his box, head up and eyes rolling wildly, his whole body trembling with violent muscular spasms. What stopped Ross in his tracks, however, was the blood. Clown's white throat was drenched with it; it was smeared and splattered all over his gaily marked coat and in places it had splashed and run down the whitewashed brick walls of his stable. It seemed inconceivable that a horse could have lost so much blood and still be standing.

'Jesus!' Leo had caught up and was peering over Ross' shoulder.

'Go and call the vet,' Ross urged. 'Quickly!'

For once Leo obeyed instantly and without question, collecting the office key from Bill as he passed him in the corridor.

Ross unhooked Clown's headcollar from its place outside the door and advanced slowly into the stable, murmuring soothing nonsense to the distressed animal all the while. Clown backed further into his corner, his rump bunching as he hit the wall.

'Steady, little fella,' Ross told him. 'Easy now. Nobody's gonna hurt you. You'll be all right now. Steady, fella.'

The horse raised his head still higher and Ross frowned as he got a closer look at his injuries. Feeling trapped, Clown made to rear. Ross stood still and the horse eyed him anxiously.

Slowly, very slowly, Ross reached out a hand to Clown's neck and rubbed the wet coat. The horse trembled violently and jumped as though Ross' hand was hot. Still moving slowly, he slid the headcollar rope over Clown's stiffly held neck and quietly reached under to grasp the end. After a minute or two, and a lot more soothing, he was able to slip the headcollar on. He looked across to the door where Bill stood watching silently.

'Poor fella,' he said. 'He's in a terrible state.'

'West is coming straightaway,' Leo reported, appearing abruptly behind the stable manager.

Clown jumped nervously.

'Quietly,' Ross warned softly. 'Bring me some warm water, a sponge and a blanket.'

'What do you think, Ross?' Bill asked softly. 'How bad is he?'

'I may be wrong,' Ross said, looking the horse over, 'but at the moment I can't see any major wounds.'

Bill looked puzzled. 'What are you saying? There must be. There's so much blood.'

Ross nodded. 'There's a hell of a lot, but I can't

see where it's coming from. I know this sounds crazy but I don't think it's his.'

'What?' Bill struggled to take in Ross' words. 'What d'you mean? I don't understand.'

'Me neither.' A combination of shock and the early-morning chill on his bare skin were having their effect on Ross and he shivered. 'Best make up another box for him, don't you think?'

Bill hurried off and Ross stroked Clown gently. The smell of blood was sweet and sickening. He willed Leo to hurry with the water.

When Roger West arrived fifteen minutes later, Clown had been washed down, covered with a warm blanket and moved to a different stable. They had offered him a bran mash but he was still too strung-up to eat and stood trembling in a corner.

The perennially cheerful young vet examined Clown in total bewilderment, eventually pronouncing him free from injury but deeply traumatised. He gave him a sedative injection and, after taking samples of the blood from the walls of his stable, left with instructions to keep the skewbald warm and quiet.

'What now?' Ross asked, as he and Bill watched West's Range Rover depart. Sarah had been calmed and comforted by Maggie and a cup of hot, sweet tea, and was now helping Leo with the routine mucking out. The sun was climbing steadily into a deep blue sky and a tractor made its noisy way down the road at the end of the drive.

'You look as though you need another bath,' Bill

observed, casting a disdainful look at Ross' bloodstained person.

Maggie had handed Ross a jumper while he waited with Clown for the vet. Now it was liberally doused in bloody water and the rough wool was irritating his bare skin.

'I guess I'll take one,' he said. 'But shouldn't we call the police or something?'

Bill shook his head. 'I rang the Colonel while we were waiting for Roger. He said no. Wanted to speak to Mr Richmond first.'

'But don't the police have to be told?' Ross asked with what he hoped seemed like natural curiosity. In fact he knew that Franklin wouldn't want the police involved if it were possible to avoid it. 'I would have thought this sort of thing had to be reported. Especially after what happened last year?'

'And a fat lot of good they were then,' Bill said bitterly. 'Said it was local yobbos going home drunk or some such thing. Then they would've had us believe Mr Richmond did it hisself for the insurance. Bloody fools, the lot of them! As if someone who felt the way he feels about his horses could even think about doing something like that. Bellboy was a legend, he was, with a heart as big as a lion's.'

Ross stared into the middle distance, at the clouds of dust that were all that told of the recent passage of the Range Rover.

'Did they never find out who killed the horse?'

Bill shook his head, sighing 'No, never. And

now this. I thought when I first saw him . . . Well, you know. That's why Sarah was so upset, of course. She used to look after Bellboy. It's criminal, but to the police it's only an animal. They click their tongues and take notes but you can see they think they're wasting valuable time. There are some funny laws where animal deaths are concerned. Did you know you don't legally have to report running over a cat? Never mind that it's somebody's pride and joy . . . part of their family.'

Ross shook his head, thinking again of the death of his dog. Nobody had reported that either. He would never know how long it had taken Rebel to die.

When Ross emerged from the bathroom, he found the rest of the team sitting down to breakfast.

'The Colonel just rang,' Bill told him. 'Mr Richmond is coming at ten and he wants us both up at the house.'

Ross nodded. He had remembered, while he bathed, how the dog had asked to be let out early that morning and wished desperately that he had done so.

Who would he have surprised?

Ross couldn't imagine anybody he had yet met doing such a thing. Except perhaps Leo. But he would have laid odds that Leo had been genuinely taken aback by what they had seen this morning, and he was honest enough to admit that his suspicion of the man stemmed mainly from their mutual dislike.

132

And where would anyone get that much blood? A slaughterhouse, perhaps?

He wondered, also, if his encounter with the prowler the night before had provoked the attack. The person he had attempted to waylay then had certainly not been carrying anything that could have contained blood, so it hadn't been a first attempt, foiled. Unless . . .

What if there had been two prowlers?

Guiltily, he remembered accusing the dog of stupidity in running the wrong way.

What if he hadn't? What if the man Ross had challenged had merely been a lookout?

He gave up then, his thoughts leading nowhere.

Maggie Scott was full of the morning's events. As kind-hearted as they came, she nevertheless thrived on any kind of gossip and the more shocking the better.

'What kind of sick mind can have dreamt up a thing like that?' she asked of nobody in particular. 'They ought to be locked away. Poor Mr Richmond, he's so unlucky! Somebody must have it in for him. Still, it's not as bad as last time, thank the Lord. God forbid that that should ever happen again! But why Mr Richmond's horses, do you suppose? Do you think it's just a coincidence?'

Bill grunted something unintelligible through his eggs and bacon and shook his head. Sarah sniffed loudly, prompting Maggie to hurry to her side, and when Ross glanced up he noticed that Leo had a very thoughtful expression on his face.

He became aware of the American's scrutiny. 'How are the bruises, Yank?' he asked with a smile that was anything but concerned.

'Oh, you'll find I don't bruise easily.' Ross returned the smile. 'But it's kind of you to ask. By the way, the school wants raking, it's very uneven. Perhaps you'd do that this morning?'

He knew he shouldn't antagonise the man, but seeing a sulky scowl replace Leo's sly grin more than made up for any guilt he might have felt. Raking the school was an arduous and tedious job even on a cool day.

Today was not going to be a cool day.

Ross and the stable manager walked up to the house with the German Shepherd at their heels. The dog co-existed quite happily with the Colonel's spaniels, each party affecting not to notice the other. As the two men approached the door, Bill looked at his watch.

'It's about ten, isn't it?' he asked Ross. 'This old watch is slow and I've lost my other one.'

'What, your gold one?' the American exclaimed. 'I thought that was on a chain.'

'It was. Bloody thing broke,' Bill said disgustedly. 'Had it fifteen years, never looked like breaking. My first anniversary present, that was.'

'That's a shame! Well, you might find it yet, I suppose, though I never found mine. Yours is bigger, of course. Have you any idea where you might have lost it?'

Bill shook his head. 'Could be anywhere,' he

said hopelessly. 'In one of the boxes. In the school . . . out in the fields, even.'

'Maybe Leo will turn it up while he's raking,' Ross suggested with an optimism he didn't feel. He secretly thought it more likely that the groom already knew where the watch was, but he could hardly say so.

'Yeah, and maybe he won't.'

Bill sounded sour and Ross glanced at him speculatively as the door opened to his knock.

The Colonel and Richmond were awaiting them in the Colonel's study, as usual. Ross wondered idly if the rest of the house had been consigned to dust sheets. On every occasion he had visited he had found his boss in his study, no matter what the time of day.

'Thank you, Masters. We'll have coffee now,' the Colonel said as Ross and Scott were shown in. The four men rearranged chairs and other articles of furniture until they could all be seated comfortably, and as Ross sank into the depths of a worn leather armchair, his dog padded round behind it and lay down with a deep sigh.

'You've got a faithful companion there,' Franklin observed.

'Yeah, and if I'd taken a little more notice of Fido here this morning, I might have caught our joker red-handed. Literally!' he added.

Bill looked sharply at him, obviously considering this to be in poor taste.

The American ignored him. He knew the older man disapproved of his informal manner with their employer. Bill's own demeanour was deferential to the point of servility. No matter what he might feel, or even say at a later date, he never queried an order or suggestion made by the Colonel or one of the owners. Ross had a fair idea that this unquestioning obedience sometimes exasperated Preston greatly.

'Franklin and I have been discussing this deplorable business,' the Colonel began. 'And we feel that in view of last year's tragedy, and without knowing if there is any connection, we should take steps towards better security, at night at least.' He paused, smoothing his moustache in a manner that Ross had come to recognise as a sign of thoughtfulness. 'Having said that, and for the same reasons as last time, we have decided that intensive and complicated security measures are both undesirable and impractical. We cannot and would not wish to turn Oakley Manor into a sort of Fort Knox for horseflesh.'

The others variously nodded or voiced their agreement.

'After all,' Richmond added, 'it's been nine months since Bellboy was killed. At the time, I hired men with dogs and walkie-talkies but they were here for months and all they did was dent my bank balance and keep the horses awake. How long was I supposed to continue? It may never have happened again.'

Ross cleared his throat. He already knew what Richmond would say but it would seem odd not to question him. 'It seems to me somebody went to a great deal of trouble last night, but for what? Just to scare the hell out of us? Surely there must be some deeper motive behind these attacks? This sort of thing doesn't happen to the same person twice by accident. Is there something you're not telling us?'

'Ross, I don't think . . .' The Colonel sounded uncomfortable but Franklin Richmond put up his hand and shook his head.

'No, John. It's all right,' he said gently. 'I understand his suspicion. It's only natural. After all, he hasn't known me as long as you have. No, I've no idea why I'm being targeted. I only wish I did.'

A light tap at the door heralded the return of Masters bearing a tray laden with coffeepot and cups. He was followed closely by Roland, immaculately attired in the kind of expensive country casuals that might grace the models in *Country Life*, and by Lindsay, in jeans and jodhpur boots as usual. She was laughing up at her cousin in response to something he had said, and Ross' spirits lifted instantly.

'Oh, I say!' Roland exclaimed. 'Are we interrupting something?' And he advanced unhesitatingly into the room in a manner that suggested he had no intention of letting the possibility deter him. He greeted Franklin with easy familiarity and nodded to Ross and Bill.

'Franklin, I'm so sorry about Clown,' Lindsay said with ready sympathy. 'What a horrible thing to have happened! Horses absolutely hate the smell of blood, don't they? I can't imagine who could do such a thing.'

137

Coffee was served and conversation became general.

Roland, Ross discovered, had a positive genius for making sudden and complete changes of direction in his conversation, quite often in response to some remark which he appeared to have misheard. At one point, when Ross and the Colonel were discussing the way horses sleep on their feet and Ross was saying that he had never yet seen Flowergirl lying down, Roland broke in, quite uninvited, with a little-known fact concerning sheep.

Ross watched him carefully, but try as he might could not decide whether the Colonel's son was really as flakey as he appeared or whether he was privately amusing himself at their expense. If he was trying to annoy his father he was certainly doing a good job of it. The Colonel had very little patience with his recently returned offspring.

'I hear you had a spot of bad luck with Woodsmoke last night,' he remarked to Ross.

'Er . . . yes,' he agreed. 'The girth snapped. One of those things, I guess.'

Bill bristled. 'It should never have happened. I'd swear that stitching was sound.'

Franklin sent Ross a searching look from across the room, but the Colonel appeared unconcerned. 'As Ross said, these things do happen. It's not necessarily anyone's fault.'

'Dangerous sport, showjumping,' Roland observed, apparently to his coffee cup. 'Don't fancy it, myself.'

'You wouldn't fancy anything that might soil your hands or spoil the look of your favourite suit,' the Colonel said with undisguised contempt.

His son appeared to consider this. 'No, I shouldn't think I would,' he agreed, finally. 'I'll leave that sort of thing to our all-American action boy.' He observed Ross from under his brows with a fleeting glint of amusement in his grey eyes.

'Roland! Don't be wicked!' Lindsay exclaimed, laughing. Then, to Ross, 'Don't let him fool you. You are looking at the hardest rider to hounds Wiltshire has ever seen. Roland was tipped to become Master a few years ago.'

'So, what happened?' Ross enquired.

'I saw sense,' Roland told him.

'He went to Sandhurst,' Lindsay informed him.

'Sandhurst?' Ross was lost.

'Army officer training,' the Colonel supplied. 'Like West Point. They were wasting their time, though.'

'You didn't stay?'

Roland made a face. 'Up at dawn, square-bashing, assault courses, mud, bossy sergeant-majors . . . and guns! I never could get used to those guns.' He shuddered dramatically.

'Oh, shut up,' Lindsay said, exasperated. 'He was in the army for eight years, Ross. He was very good at it.'

The Colonel stood up, heading for his desk. 'He threw away a promising career,' he grunted. 'Works in a bloody china shop now.'

'Antiques,' Roland said, mildly. 'Import and export.'

'Whatever,' his father said dismissively. 'Look, I didn't ask Ross and Franklin here to discuss your failings. We have business to get on with.'

'Don't let me stop you,' Roland said obligingly, making no move to leave.

The Colonel made a visible effort to keep his temper, turning his back on his son and handing a sheaf of colourful brochures to Ross and Bill. 'Have a look at those.'

'We've decided the time has come to think about getting a bigger horsebox,' Franklin explained from his chair. 'I've marked the two I favour. See what you think.'

After the merits of the various vehicles had been discussed at length, the meeting broke up with Lindsay saying she wanted to take Gypsy out for exercise before lunch because she had to meet James at the station that afternoon. In the event, Sarah and Leo accompanied her on her ride and Bill went to the saddler's with Woody's saddle and a number of other items that needed repairing.

Ross took advantage of the period of quiet this afforded to school Ginger again. She was due to jump at a fairly important show at the weekend and he knew that she needed at least one intensive session before then. He'd ridden the mare out the previous day, returning to the site of her previous panic attack, but she hadn't put a foot wrong. He was finding her increasingly difficult to understand.

On this occasion as he worked her in the newly raked school she was willing, if not exactly eager. Her flatwork was supple and obedient and she jumped with good style. Still Ross was not happy with her. She felt to him like an automaton, characterless and uninspiring.

Towards the end of the hour he had allotted the mare he noticed Franklin Richmond leaning on the gate and rode over. As was his habit, he untacked the steaming mare and let her cool off and roll in the sand if she chose.

'That mare's coming on nicely,' Richmond said, by way of greeting.

'Mmm.' The doubt sounded in Ross' voice.

'You don't think so?'

He shrugged, non-committally. 'She's a touch unpredictable.'

'So is life,' the businessman observed.

'True.' Ross squinted at him against the bright sunlight. 'What did you make of this morning's demonstration?'

'He goes to a lot of trouble, doesn't he? I'm awaiting the message that will undoubtedly follow.'

'More money?' Ross suggested.

'I suppose so,' Richmond said. 'But somehow I don't think that's the reason for all this. As I said before, it's as though he's playing with us and I think he felt the game was becoming a little too tame.'

Ross frowned. 'A dangerous sort of game.'

'Some people thrive on danger. It becomes an addiction. In your own way, you obviously do.'

'That's not the same,' Ross protested. 'I don't do it just for kicks.'

'Don't you?'

Ross found he couldn't answer. After all, why did he ride? For the elusive glory? For the money? Hardly! He rode because it was a continual challenge. Because it was difficult and testing, and because of the incredible high he felt when it all came right. Sure he did it for kicks.

He and Richmond watched Ginger flirting and squealing with the horses in the field beyond the school.

'I shan't pay him any more, you know,' Franklin said suddenly. 'I've had enough. If he wants a confrontation he'll have it sooner or later, and I'll be damned if I'm going to give him even more money in the meantime. I'm having the yard watched again, secretly. Nobody else will be told. McKinnon will arrange it.'

'Do you think that'll work?'

'I don't know. I hope so. I've got to do something. McKinnon is convinced we must make a stand if we're going to bring this bastard out into the open. I'm prepared to trust his judgement. It's what I pay him for, after all.' He ran his fingers through his hair and smiled at Ross. 'You attacked me very convincingly this morning.'

Ross grinned. 'Thought I'd better act in character. The Colonel would have expected it.' He paused. 'What do you know about Roland?'

Franklin laughed. 'Got your detective's hat on again? No, seriously, I've known Roland as long as

I've known John. Not intimately, I admit, he hasn't spent much time here lately, but he went to school with my nephew Darcy. His relationship with his father is somewhat strained, but he's harmless. I'd describe him as a determined eccentric.'

Ross nodded. 'Lindsay seems very fond of him, anyway, and she's usually a fairly good judge of character.'

'Though you say it yourself,' Richmond observed, amused.

Ross grinned and shook his head. 'Hell, no. That's not what I meant.'

'I know,' Richmond acknowledged, smiling. 'Look, I've got to go. Work to do. Look out for yourself, okay?'

'Sure,' Ross said, liking the big, easy going businessman more with each encounter. 'You too.'

The riders returned as Ross finished hosing Ginger down and led her to her stable. Sarah looked unhappy and Lindsay harassed. Leo was whistling cheerfully.

'Trouble?' Ross enquired, following Lindsay into Gypsy's box.

She sighed. 'Oh, I don't know. No, not really. It's just that Leo will keep teasing Sarah and she can't defend herself. She's like a mouse. Honestly, I don't know how you stay sane working with those two. Leo's so insolent to you. I've heard some of the things he says and I wonder you don't clobber him.'

'I wouldn't give him the satisfaction.'

'Yes, but think of the satisfaction it would give *you*!' Lindsay countered, laughing.

'There is that,' he agreed. 'I guess I'd better have a word with him. We don't want to lose Sarah, do we?'

Lindsay departed soon afterwards, saying that she didn't expect to have time to exercise Gypsy the next day, Friday, but that she had begged a space in the horsebox for the second day of the Gloucester show on Sunday.

Ross watched her go with regret, supposing that with her boyfriend on the scene she would be a less frequent visitor to Oakley Manor. She had already confided that her mother wasn't happy with the amount of time she had been spending with the horses.

8

The show at Gloucester ran over the weekend. Although stabling was provided for competitors who were travelling a long way, Ross and Bill had decided to travel up on both days so that they could enter the maximum number of horses and, at the same time, cut down on stabling fees.

The Oakley Manor contingent set out in thick fog at six-thirty in the morning. The journey was about eighty miles and, what with the fog and an unscheduled stop just before Swindon, they needed every minute of the time they had estimated it would take.

The hold-up was due to Fly getting an attack of claustrophobia in the crowded lorry, and Ross asked Danny if he'd mind travelling with the horses to keep an eye on them. Although he would far rather have had the boy's company in the cab, Danny had a quiet, sympathetic way with the horses and, additionally, could be absolutely relied upon not to doctor the equipment.

Once on the showground, Leo and Danny unloaded the four horses and let them stretch their legs and graze while Ross went in search of the secretary's tent and a timetable. He saw several familiar faces on his way, including Danielle, who greeted him with obvious pleasure, and Stephen Douglas, who didn't.

The last of the fog was thinning fast now, beaten back by the growing strength of the sun. As Ross strolled back to the lorry he felt that overall, life was pretty good.

The day started well, improved steadily and ended with triumph.

Franklin Richmond arrived at ten o'clock with Peter and a fair-haired, smartly dressed young man of about Ross' age whom he introduced as his nephew, Darcy. They were just in time to see Barfly jump to an unexpected fourth place in Ross' first class of the day. Ross was as surprised as anyone and could only surmise that the flighty creature had fretted his fidgets away on the journey up and was now prepared to concentrate.

When Clown followed his stablemate's performance with a clear round in his class and an unlucky four faults in the jump-off, Franklin was beaming and Peter was over the moon. Darcy confided in Ross that he didn't really understand the finer details of the game, but he knew his uncle thought Ross was doing a great job.

While Ross was walking Flo round the collecting

ring prior to her first class, he watched Stephen Douglas jump a neat clear on a breedy bay mare who went by the name of China Lily. In spite of her performance, Douglas passed the American looking tense and unhappy. The reason, it transpired, was his second ride in the class, the headstrong chestnut he had ridden at Lea Farm.

He returned to the practice area on the stallion and Ross watched the ensuing struggle with a large measure of pity. Both horse and rider were confused and frustrated, and up to the time when Ross was called into the ring, Douglas hadn't managed to get his mount's attention for long enough to attempt the practice fence once.

On entering the ring, Ross' attention switched immediately and completely to the job in hand. He circled the mare, the starting buzzer sounded, and they swept smoothly through the timing beacons and up to the first fence.

Flo felt fresh and fit. Her brown ears flicked back and forth for signals and Ross obliged by talking quietly to her. 'Steady girl, steady. Good girl Steady. Wait. Wait. Good girl!'

She jumped like a stag, making the course look easy, which to be honest, it was. The course designer had set few traps, aiming to encourage rather than to trick. Ross rode out with a satisfying clear behind him.

Stephen Douglas was next but one and catapulted into the ring as though the horse had a tiger on its tail. The stallion had his head tied down, as before, until he could hardly see where he was going, and consequently made matchwood of three of the first five fences. Then, with a mammoth effort at the sixth, the leather strap snapped, the stallion got his head up and was away.

Douglas made a creditable attempt to control the horse, keeping him on line for the next two jumps, which they took at racing speed with a good foot to spare, but thereafter the initiative belonged with the horse. They circled the ring three times, Stephen Douglas red-faced and wholly impotent, before the chestnut slowed enough for his rider to jump off and drag him to an untidy halt.

The crowd, silenced by impending tragedy, now burst into weak applause, precipitated by relief as much as anything. The voice of the commentator commiserated and announced that Stephen Douglas and Telamon had retired, and the next competitor cantered out into the ring.

Douglas trudged past Ross just outside the collecting ring, his horse quieter now but dark with sweat and obviously upset.

'Bad luck,' the American said from force of habit but nevertheless meaning it.

'Piss off!' Douglas hissed venomously.

Ross shrugged philosophically.

'Did you expect anything else?' Danielle rode alongside Ross.

'I guess not,' he admitted, ruefully. 'To tell the truth, I'd forgotten.'

She smiled provocatively at him. 'You're just a naturally nice guy.'

'Tell me more,' he invited.

'I'll tell you over dinner tonight, if you like.'

'Sorry,' Ross said, feeling mildly so. 'I'm not staying over. We're bringing another lot up tomorrow.'

'Oh, well.' Danielle made a face. 'A girl's got to try.'

Flowergirl won her class, with China Lily a close second, and went on to a third place later in the day. Ross wished the Colonel had made the trip up to see her. He lunched with the Richmond clan in the members' enclosure and emerged, having repeatedly refused large helpings of strawberries and cream, to find Leo and Danny quarrelling furiously.

Leo, it appeared, had gone in search of a 'quick beer' and hadn't returned for the best part of three-quarters of an hour. Danny, left with four horses and only one pair of hands, was incensed; especially as Clown, with impeccable timing, had chosen that moment to untie himself from the side of the lorry and go in search of greener pastures. Danny had had to enlist the help of a groom from a neighbouring horsebox to watch the remaining horses while he went in pursuit.

Leo, in his own defence, swore that he had not been gone more than ten minutes and said that the boy was trying to make trouble.

Ross gave him a withering look and told him to tack Simone up for the next class, and then spent the next five minutes trying to calm Danny down. He had obviously expected Ross to tear a strip off Leo and in spite of promising to deal with him later, Ross was left with the notion that Danny had joined Lindsay in thinking him a soft touch.

The truth was that he had no wish to start what could turn into a flaming row, in public and eighty miles from home, with four horses to cope with. He wouldn't entirely put it past Leo just to down tools and walk. The right time would come but it definitely wasn't now.

Simone was in sparkling form, narrowly beaten by Danielle's experienced gelding in her first class and turning the tables convincingly in the second.

'Ross Wakelin, you're no gentleman,' she chided him laughingly as they lined up to receive their rosettes and prize money.

Ross grinned back, enjoying the flirtation.

Franklin Richmond and his family were waiting to congratulate him as he left the ring.

'I should say that has successfully laid the ghosts, hasn't it?' Franklin asked Ross quietly.

He nodded. 'I hope so.'

Day two of the show was a little less hectic. The lorry was full again, with Woodsmoke, Bishop and Ginger taking their turn. Also travelling with them was Gypsy, although Lindsay herself was making the journey in her boyfriend's car.

Without even the distraction of navigating, Ross found the journey tedious in the extreme. Danny had elected to travel with the horses again, mainly, Ross suspected, to avoid Leo's surly company. Leo, for his part, passed the journey in silence, watching the scenery slide by with a set expression on his thin face.

Ross wondered what it was that made him so grouchy. Something in his childhood, perhaps, had given him that 'bite before you are bitten' mentality. Ross supposed he should pity the man but in all honesty felt only irritated dislike.

Turning his thoughts away from his companion's character defects, he began instead to dwell on his other problem. He was uncomfortably aware of Ginger's presence in the lorry. She had not misbehaved since her outburst of temperament in the school earlier that week and gave him no reason to suppose she would do so again, but the possibility was there. He had awakened in the night, shaking and drenched with sweat after the nightmare had struck again, and this morning felt edgy and tired.

The showground reached, lorry parked and engine rattling to silence, Ross leaned his head back and closed his eyes, wishing fervently for a couple of hours' peace and quiet in which to catch up on his lost sleep.

Voices outside. Lindsay had arrived.

'Hi, Ross. Good journey? Fit and raring to go?'

'Fine,' he lied. 'You?'

'Oh, it was lovely to be chauffeur-driven for a change,' she said. 'James, come and meet Ross Wakelin, the John Whitaker of Wiltshire.'

The young man who stepped forward as Ross jumped down from the cab was tall, well built, pleasantly good-looking and instantly likeable.

Ross smiled and held out his hand. 'So you're the lucky guy. Pleased to meet you.'

'I've heard a lot about you,' James said. 'In fact, Lindsay talked of little else the whole way here.'

It was said completely without rancour but she protested: 'That's not true! We talked about a lot of things. The thing is, I feel sort of responsible for Ross' being here, as it was my idea. And anyway, you asked about him in the first place!' she finished, returning her attack to James.

He held his hands up, grinning good-naturedly. 'Okay, okay! Keep your hair on, girl!'

'Well, I guess that sorted you out, fella,' Ross observed.

'Didn't it just?' James acknowledged, and departed to explore the showground with Lindsay on his arm.

The morning started fairly well.

Ginger completed her first class efficiently but without flair. Bishop had an unlucky pole down in the same class and it was eventually won by a jubilant Stephen Douglas on his useful new ride, China Lily. Ross congratulated him but might as well have addressed the horse for all the response he got.

Lindsay was placed second in her first class of the day, and when Woody exerted himself and won a topscore competition, the Oakley Manor crew paused for a picnic lunch feeling fairly pleased with themselves.

The Colonel arrived soon after, with Bill. The

stable manager looked unfamiliar in cavalry twills and a tweed jacket, his thinning hair carefully combed and a new cloth cap perched on top. They looked over the horses, collected the latest news and results, and then took themselves off to the grandstand to meet Robbie Fergusson who had once again made time in his hectic schedule to come and see his horses jump.

Ross wished he hadn't bothered. The man was never satisfied.

Bishop was Ross' first ride after lunch and he mounted up in good time in order to give the horse a chance to settle. He rode round the outside of the main ring a couple of times, giving the horse plenty of rein and allowing him to look around at his leisure. His own thoughts drifted to Lindsay and James Roberts.

The guy was pleasant enough, with no obvious inclination to flaunt what Ross knew to be his considerable wealth. He seemed to have a conventional sense of humour and respect for the views of others. A paragon, in fact, but married to Lindsay . . . Ross couldn't see it. Or perhaps he just didn't want to.

Idly, he wondered if she had ever slept with James. He supposed that she must have but they didn't behave like lovers, more like old friends. Ross shrugged mentally. It was none of his business, after all.

'Mr Wakelin! Could I have a word?' A confident, well-spoken voice, one of many in the British horse world. The speaker was middle-aged, bespectacled and going a little thin on top. It was amazing what you could see from the back of a seventeen-hand horse. The guy probably didn't even know he was going bald, himself.

'Sure.' Ross reined in and dismounted.

'I'm a journalist.' The man flashed his press card. 'I write a column for the *Sportsman* and I'm doing a feature on the county showjumping scene. You know, "The testing ground for the international horses and riders of the future" – that sort of thing.' He smiled at Ross.

'Yes?' Ross said politely, and waited.

'Well, I'm interested in what *you*, as a newcomer to the English circuit, think of the standard at these shows.' He reached into an inside pocket and produced a mini tape-recorder. 'Do you mind?' he asked, holding it up.

'No, I guess not. But I can't say I've thought much about it at all,' Ross said, playfully cuffing Bishop's nose as the horse tried to nip him. 'I suppose, if anything, there's a wider range of abilities represented at these shows than at similar events back home. You know, people who obviously keep one horse in their backyard and manage on a shoestring, whereas in the States you have to haul several hundred miles between shows and maybe spend the season on the road. You have to be pretty well heeled to do that. I think it's good that everybody can have a go.'

'How do the English horses compare with those in America, then?'

Ross laughed. 'What *is* an English horse these

days?' he asked. 'Thoroughbreds are pretty much the same the world over and a lot of the horses in showjumping nowadays seem to be German- or Dutch-bred. There are good horses on both sides of the Atlantic. It's just a question of getting the best out of them.'

'You've come to England to take over the ride on Colonel Preston's horses . . .'

'Among others,' Ross interposed.

'What makes you suppose you can improve on his previous rider's performance, and where do you see yourself going from here?'

Bishop was becoming fractious as the riders gathered in the vicinity of the main ring for the start of the afternoon's bigger classes.

'Well, I can't guarantee that I will but I've had a fair bit of experience with young horses,' Ross said, fending off a more determined lunge by the black horse and hearing teeth snap within inches of his arm. 'Look, I really must get on. I'm sorry, you'll have to excuse me.'

'Of course,' the man said. 'Thank you for your time.' And without further ado, he melted into the crowd.

Relieved at having got rid of him so easily, Ross vaulted into the saddle and concentrated on regaining Bishop's attention.

Lindsay rode alongside. 'I wondered where you'd got to,' she said. 'You'll have to walk the course in a minute. What did old Douglas want? I was surprised to see you two acting so chummy.'

'Douglas? Not Harry Douglas?' Ross groaned

'He said he was a journalist. He didn't give his name.'

'He *is* a journalist,' Lindsay said. 'He's commentating here too. Why? What did you say to him?'

'Nothing. At least, nothing important.' Ross frowned, trying to remember if he'd said anything that could be deliberately misconstrued. 'He just asked me for my views on showjumping in this country. He seemed okay . . .'

Lindsay grimaced. 'The smile of the crocodile! He's well liked in general and very popular as a commentator on TV. He writes his column under a pseudonym, though, and he's "anonymously" torn several careers to shreds.'

'Thanks a lot! You've really put my mind at rest.' Feeling decidedly uneasy, Ross rode away to concentrate on Bishop's preparation for the next class.

In the event, the black surpassed himself. The track was straightforward but big, and he jumped it like a Grand Prix horse. Ross felt unstoppable and even Harry Douglas, now back behind the microphone, had to admit that the horse had jumped well.

In the timed jump-off, Ross had the advantage of going last and watched while the standard was set by King's Defender and his new jockey, Mick Colby. Lindsay's Gypsy did her best but was not quite fast enough; neither were Douglas Junior and China Lily. Half a dozen others tried and failed before Ross rode in on Bishop.

As he circled, waiting for the buzzer, Ross rode past the jumps at the far end of the course, mentally rehearsing the line he would take. The crowd hushed expectantly but Ross was not aware of anything but the smooth rhythm of the horse beneath him and the job to be done.

The buzzer went, the first fence loomed and flashed by well beneath Bishop's black belly, and the race was on. Everything went to plan. Bishop didn't put a foot wrong. He was maturing fast and when Ross asked him to jump off an angle, he responded without fluster. Only when the final upright was landed perfectly and Ross steadied the horse after the dash for the timing beacons did he become aware of the roar of applause.

'Well, that was a winning time of thirty-seven-point-oh-four seconds,' Harry Douglas announced. 'Thirty-seven-point-oh-four, for Ross Wakelin and Black Bishop. A horse to watch in the future.'

Lindsay was waiting in the collecting ring when Ross rode out and dismounted. She threw her arms round his neck and hugged him. 'Oh, Ross, that was brilliant! I always knew you could do it,' she cried.

Over her shoulder, he spied James beyond the collecting ring ropes and raised his hands in an expression of helplessness.

James grinned good-naturedly and mouthed, 'Congratulations!'

Several of the other riders, including Mick Colby, slapped Ross on the back and Danielle, not to be outdone, hugged and kissed him soundly. He accepted and enjoyed the success philosophically. Another day it would no doubt be a different story.

The prize-giving over, Ross handed Bishop to Danny and changed on to Woody, who jumped a moderate round and wasn't placed.

'Oh, well, you can't expect to win them all,' the voice from the loudspeakers observed annoyingly. 'Ross had a bit of a tumble from this horse last time out, so it's not surprising if their confidence is a little shaky.'

Ross took a deep breath and quelled his rising irritation. He needed all his wits about him to ride Ginger in the last class.

Leo appeared to take charge of Woody, smiling at the expression on the American's face. Ross ignored him, too weary to care. 'Tell Danny to put the dropped noseband on Ginger,' he said, and went in search of a long, cool drink.

'Buy you one?' a husky, feminine voice suggested as he headed for the refreshment tent.

'Shouldn't it be the other way round?' Ross enquired, turning to smile at Danielle.

'Only if you're old-fashioned. We Europeans are very modern,' she added archly. 'Besides, I'd probably have died of thirst waiting for you to ask!'

'But I didn't even know you were there,' he protested. 'Well, I *am* old-fashioned. What'll it be?'

The area around the beer tent and its attendant clutch of umbrella-shaded tables was home to thousands of alcoholic wasps and Ross and Danielle elected to take their drinks on the move.

'Harry has really got his knife into you,' Danielle

commented as they wove their way through the crowds.

'Mmm,' Ross agreed.

'You don't sound too worried.'

'It's only words. Actions speak louder, they say.'

Danielle looked doubtful. 'Mr Douglas has a very loud voice.'

Ross shrugged. 'I don't have to listen.'

'No, but others will. He's a popular man.'

'Well, there's damn-all I can do about it,' Ross observed. 'Maybe he'll grow tired of bad-mouthing me and pick on someone else.'

They wandered in comfortable companionship among the trade stands until it was announced that competitors for the last class could now walk the course. This they did together and then Ross thanked Danielle for her company and went in search of Danny and Ginger.

He headed for the horsebox and met Ginger coming in the opposite direction, but instead of being led by Danny, Lindsay was riding her.

'Hi, I thought you'd be about ready for her.' Lindsay smiled and swung down, her blonde hair, unconfined by a crash hat, bobbing on her shoulders.

'I'd rather you didn't ride Ginger,' Ross said, his tone a little sharper than usual from the mild shock of seeing her playing unconsciously in the lion's jaws.

'Why ever not?' Lindsay asked, taken aback. 'I was only walking her. She's a dozy old creature,'

159

'She can be difficult if anything upsets her,' Ross warned.

'You're joking!' Lindsay quizzed him, laughing.

'I'm not.' Ross was exasperated. Why couldn't she just accept it? He didn't want to draw attention to his unease over Ginger because of the inevitable comparisons people would make with events in the States. So easy to conclude that he was influenced purely by fear.

'Well, well. Old Ginger has hidden depths, have you, old girl?' Lindsay patted the chestnut neck, still not convinced.

'She's only eight,' Ross reminded her.

'Yes, I know.' Lindsay wrinkled her nose at him. 'But she always acts old.'

'Damn Danny!' Ross exclaimed. 'I particularly said I wanted her in a dropped noseband.'

'Shall I fetch it?' Lindsay offered. 'I don't think it was his fault. Leo was tacking her up.'

'No, never mind. I don't suppose it'll make much odds. She does look half-asleep.' With Leo in mind, he swiftly went through the checks that were becoming second nature to him lately.

Lindsay watched him; half-frowning, half-amused. 'My, we *are* safety-conscious these days, aren't we?' she observed. 'This isn't the Ross I used to know.'

The Ross you used to know didn't have a budding saboteur for a groom, he thought darkly.

'Maybe I'm getting old,' he joked.

Lindsay laughed, but as she watched Ross mount the chestnut mare, her expression grew thoughtful.

By now, he had other things on his mind.

Ginger was in a mood.

He could sense it at once. Whereas that morning she had been unenthusiastic but obedient, now he felt open resentment radiating from her. She had never felt quite like this before. On the two previous occasions she had thrown a tantrum there had been no warning and Ross didn't know whether this unwillingness presaged another irrational fit or whether it was just a sulk. He did know that his own mouth was dry and he was aware of a growing tension in his muscles. That wouldn't help. Horses are quick to sense the mood of their rider. He concentrated on relaxing.

As he rode round the collecting ring he saw Lindsay watching him intently from the ropes with James at her side. He smiled brightly at them as he went by, projecting a confidence he was far from feeling. They both smiled back.

The collecting ring was filling up with competitors wanting to make use of the practice jump before they went into the ring and Ginger was flattening her ears at any who passed too close. Ross put her at the single-pole fence once and she clicked her toes over it with the minimum possible effort. He found a corner and let her stand.

Fourth to go in the class, Ross didn't have long to wait. He rode into the ring acutely aware of Robbie Fergusson's piercing, analytical eyes watching him from the grandstand.

Ginger felt mulish.

'Next to jump we have number one hundred and

fifty-four, Ross Wakelin on Mr R. Fergusson's Red Queen.' The loudspeaker whined and popped and Ginger jumped nervously.

Ross wondered if Harry Douglas had finished tormenting him for the day. He shortened his reins, and with seat and heels bullied the mare into an unwilling canter. As soon as the buzzer sounded he headed her for the first fence, intending to give her no time to think. It was an undemanding rustic pole over brushwood, but she proceeded on stiff legs and barely slithered over it, clicking her toes on the top as she did so. The second fence followed quickly and Ginger was bustled over it before she knew where she was.

Two down, nine to go, Ross thought to himself as he swung Ginger round the bottom of the ring to the third.

She would have none of it.

As she passed the entrance to the collecting ring she slowed dramatically and Ross knew all the way to the third that he was fighting a losing battle. Her head came up, her stride grew shorter and shorter, and she stopped abruptly at the base of the fence.

Ross swore under his breath. He knew from her demeanour that she had made up her mind and he hadn't a hope of changing it, but he also knew that he had to give the appearance of trying. He turned the mare away to get a second run at it, and she bolted.

Furious, he put both hands on one rein and pulled her round. After two or three tight circles she stopped, head high and eyes showing white.

Ross considered slapping her with the end of the reins – he never now carried a crop on the mare – but almost immediately decided against it. She was just a hair's breadth away from berserking and the memory of those screams, those terrified faces moving too slowly, flashed across his inner eye.

It couldn't happen again. It must not.

Ross touched the brim of his crash hat, glancing at the commentary box, and turned Ginger back to the collecting ring, hating to give in but fearing the consequences of the alternative. The audience produced a smattering of applause and lost interest, looking to see who would be next in. Ross wished he could forget it as easily but he doubted if he would be allowed to.

'Ross Wakelin and Red Queen have retired,' the loudspeaker announced. 'Back to the drawing board with that one, I feel. Better luck next time, Ross.

'Next we have number ninety-six, Mick Colby on Mrs Colby's very good mare . . .'

Ross reached the collecting ring on a still-twitchy Ginger and dismounted, keeping his face averted so that nobody could see the fury he felt sure must show. Fury at the patronising tones behind the public-address system; at fate for having put him in this impossible situation; and irrational fury at himself for having failed to keep the mare going, even though he didn't know what else he could have done.

He ran the stirrups up and loosened the girth, preparing to lead her back to the lorry.

'She *has* got a stubborn streak, hasn't she?' Lindsay appeared at the mare's head. 'I've never seen her like that before.'

'She's dangerous,' he muttered, darkly. 'Completely crazy.'

Lindsay came round to Ross' side, catching sight of his expression for the first time. 'Wow! She's really got to you.'

'It wouldn't have mattered so much if Fergusson hadn't been here,' he said. 'She *would* choose today.' He glanced across to the grandstand and saw Ginger's owner pushing his way through the crowds in the members' enclosure below.

'Let's get out of here,' he suggested. 'I'd prefer to be bawled out in a less public place.'

The horses were loaded and ready to travel by the time the Colonel and Bill finally reached the lorry. Somewhere along the way they had shed Fergusson, for which Ross was deeply grateful.

'All ready to go?' the Colonel asked.

Ross nodded, searching his employer's face for some clue as to his mood. The Colonel gave nothing away. Bill was looking rather less than ecstatic, though. Lindsay had already left, swept off by James in his powerful Mercedes some twenty minutes earlier, having been assured that there was nothing further she could do.

'Are you all right, Ross?' the Colonel asked suddenly. 'You could change places with Bill, if you wanted. He wouldn't mind taking the lorry home.'

164

Ross hesitated, tempted. His leg ached dully and his head had begun to throb in sympathy but he didn't particularly want to spend the lengthy journey home hearing what Fergusson had had to say about his performance that afternoon.

He hesitated too long. The Colonel made the decision for him and within moments Ross was sinking into the passenger seat of Preston's Jaguar. Any fears that he'd had were laid to rest when the Colonel remarked that it had been a very encouraging weekend and he proposed having Ross and Bill up to the house the following evening to discuss plans for the future careers of the horses currently in training. Relieved, Ross leaned back against the headrest and closed his eyes, letting the waves of fatigue wash over him.

He woke with a start as the car turned into the gravel drive of the Oakley Manor yard.

'It would seem to be a good thing you didn't drive the box,' Colonel Preston remarked dryly.

Ross apologised, feeling even more exhausted and heavy-eyed than he had before.

Sarah emerged from the tackroom followed, Ross was surprised to see, by Darcy Richmond. As news of the day was exchanged and congratulations given and received for Bishop's win, Ross noticed that the shy teenager was far more animated in Darcy's company than she had ever been in his. He could see that he was going to have to do something about the deplorable flaws in his own character.

Presently Darcy excused himself, reminding

Sarah as he did so that he would pick her up at half-past eight. The girl positively glowed.

Understanding dawned.

The Colonel departed for his evening meal and Ross went in search of a cup of coffee before the horsebox and its attendant workload arrived.

It was two o'clock in the morning when Ross jerked awake from his familiar nightmare and sat up in bed. He was sweating freely in the warm night air, despite having kicked the covers off the bed, and his muscles were trembling.

As so often in the dark hours, his spirits were low and he hadn't the energy or the willpower to raise them. The dog slept on at the foot of the bed, apparently unaware that he had woken.

Ross found it hard to believe that a dream of such violence and noise could be enacted entirely within his head. The screams, his own desperate cries of warning, how could they be silent? And the chestnut mare that crashed through the rails night after night . . . it had become impossible to tell any more whether it was the American horse or Ginger.

Ross rubbed his eyes and slid off the bed, trying to banish the images from his mind. He wandered across the wooden boards and paused, looking out of the window. Then froze.

In the middle of the yard, with his back to Ross and lit from all sides by the security lighting, stood a man.

Shit! Ross' heart missed a beat. What to do for the best?

He had his mobile phone but who should he ring? Who could come in time? Should he let the dog out? The man must be mad, standing there in full view.

Then the figure turned.

Ross let out breath he hadn't been aware of holding in a deep sigh of relief. The 'intruder' was Roland.

Looking up suddenly, as if aware of being watched, the Colonel's son saw Ross at the open window and bowed extravagantly, sweeping off an imaginary hat.

Ross touched his forehead in a mock salute and turned back into the room. He couldn't imagine what Roland was doing there but standing in the fully lit yard as he had been, it was ridiculous to suppose he had intended any harm to the horses.

Ross returned to his bed, hoping for deep, untroubled sleep.

9

UK NEWCOMER UNIMPRESSED WITH BRITISH TALENT.

Ross groaned aloud at the headline on page five of the *Sportsman*. Bill had passed the paper over wordlessly as they sat down to breakfast on Monday morning.

The *Sportsman* was a weekly publication covering a wide range of sports and offering a comprehensive run-down of the previous week's results. It prided itself on being first with the news of the weekend's events and indeed, its staff obviously worked throughout Sunday night to produce the paper in time for a Monday distribution. A copy was regularly delivered to the Oakley Manor yard. It lay open now at the start of the equine section, which contained news and reports from all the biggest shows, along with other articles of interest.

Ross poured himself some coffee and read on.

The article started as it meant to go on, with a misquote:

'I don't think much of the standard at county shows,' British showjumping newcomer Ross Wakelin told me at the Gloucester Agricultural Show at the weekend. Ross, who came to England two months ago after losing his job in America for reasons he was not prepared to discuss, now rides for Colonel Preston's yard at Oakley in Wiltshire.

Asked how he rated the English horses in comparison with those in the USA, he laughed and said, 'What is an English horse these days?' It seemed to be his opinion that, in general, British riders are a lot less professional than their American cousins, and tend to keep their horses on a shoestring in their back gardens.

When asked how he intended to improve on the performance of the young rider he had replaced, Mr Wakelin, 27, implied that he had a great deal more experience – although yours truly has as yet failed to uncover any evidence of significant success in the States.

Quizzed further, Wakelin declined to continue the conversation and, displaying a very firm hand with ace chess player Robbie Fergusson's promising Black Bishop, he turned on his heel and walked away.

The article went on to discuss the performancess and merits of various other horses and riders at the show, before giving a round-up of results.

Ross smarted at the injustice of the piece. Even if he had known to whom he was talking, he doubted he could have escaped Douglas' vindictive distortions.

Bill was watching him over a forkful of bacon and fried bread.

'Not too clever, I guess,' Ross admitted, ruefully. 'If I'd known who he was . . .'

'Bloody stupid, I'd say!' Bill said without bothering to finish his mouthful first. 'Why on earth did you have to say all that? If you want to put people's backs up, you're going the right way about it.'

'I didn't say it,' Ross protested. 'At least, not the way he's reported it. But, like I said, I didn't know who he was. I've never seen the guy before. I can't just ignore him, could I?'

Bill grunted, non-committally.

'I think it's very unfair,' Maggie remarked, placing a well-filled plate in front of Ross. 'He can't persecute Ross just because Stephen wasn't up to the job.'

Bill snorted. 'He can and he will.'

'Well, I think it's very unfair,' she repeated, as if that redressed the balance.

Leo sauntered in, yawning. He often didn't rise until mid-morning on his day off, usually going out after breakfast and not reappearing before midnight. He immediately spotted the paper and read it with ill-concealed relish.

170

'You won't be too popular if you say things like that,' he observed gleefully.

Ross ignored him and with a chuckle Leo tucked into his breakfast.

'Roger West rang earlier,' Bill announced. 'He'd got the results of Sailor's gut sample. It *was* that hemlock plant that poisoned him. And apparently the blood he took from Clown's stable was ox blood. I suppose it came from an abattoir.'

Ross frowned. 'Why would anyone want to do that? That's what gets me. And what excuse would you give for wanting a bucket of ox blood or whatever?'

'And do you take your own bucket?' Leo put in, earning withering looks from the others.

As they were finishing their meal, a vehicle decelerated into the yard with a wrenching of gears and rolled to a stop outside the tackroom.

'It's that Annie woman,' Maggie remarked in a disapproving voice from the window. 'What does she want?'

'Come to check on Butterworth, I expect,' Ross said. 'I'll go.'

Annie Hayward it was. Attired in jeans held up by braces, and a khaki tee-shirt, her two beribboned plaits were topped off by a flat cap.

'Hi, Ross!' she boomed. 'How you doing?'

'Oh, I'm okay. How 'bout you?'

'You're a damn poor liar. Harry Douglas has it in for you, your leg's giving you trouble and you're not sleeping well.'

He grinned. 'What are you? Telepathic?'

'I read papers and I use my eyes. You look bloody awful.'

'Well, thanks for that,' he said with quiet irony. 'You ought to get a job with the terminally ill. You'd go down a storm.'

Annie chuckled and together they began to walk across the school towards the field gate. Butterworth and his young companions materialised at Ross' piercing whistle, jostling and bickering for pole position at the gate.

'He's looking a lot happier. Have you worked him at all?' Annie asked.

'You said not to.'

'Yes, I know I did. But you'd be surprised how many people think they know better. Once the horse is sound they ignore everything I've told them.'

Ross caught the big chestnut, rubbing his velvety muzzle with a forefinger. 'No point calling the doctor if you don't take his advice,' he remarked.

Annie squinted at him against the morning sun.

'It's do as I say, not do as I do with you then, is it?'

'Meaning?'

'Your leg.'

'Ah, but the doctor didn't actually say I couldn't ride,' Ross pointed out.

'Did you actually *ask* him?' she countered acutely.

Ross laughed. 'My point exactly.'

Annie shook her head, acknowledging defeat. She felt along Butterworth's spine, pressing hard. The horse didn't flinch.

'You'll do,' she said, slapping the chestnut rump. 'Give him another couple of weeks just to be on the safe side, then ease him back into work. No jumping yet, though. Now, what about you?'

'What *about* me?' Ross was caught off balance by her abrupt change of direction.

Annie waited, saying nothing, her eyes on his face. Ross met her gaze for a fleeting moment then shifted his to focus on some far-distant point.

'Looks like it's going to be another hot day,' he remarked conversationally.

Annie sighed. 'All right, all right. I can take a hint. But do me a favour, Ross. Don't let them get to you.'

'I don't intend to.'

'Good. Now, if we can get this fellow right, there'll be no stopping you.'

Roland strolled into the tackroom while Ross was up to his elbows in warm water and saddle soap. The dog looked up from its blanket in the corner and thumped its tail on the stone floor a time or two, which was unusual for him.

'All alone?' Roland asked somewhat un-necessarily.

Ross gestured round the otherwise empty room.

'I thought it was your day off, old boy.'

'It is.' Ross wondered if the Colonel's son had come hoping to find the place deserted.

Roland cleared a space by the old stone sink and rested his immaculate beige corduroys against it.

'You had a successful show, I hear.'

'Not bad.'

'So, things are looking rosy on the showjumping front?'

'Could be worse,' Ross said, wishing he could see behind the mask he felt sure Roland wore. 'How are things in antiques?'

'Oh, fine, fine,' Roland said, with the air of one delighted to be asked. 'I didn't realise you were interested.'

'I'm not,' he replied sweetly. 'I'm just making conversation.'

Roland grinned. To Ross' mind, the first truly spontaneous action he had seen from him.

'What's the dog's name?' he asked with the abrupt change of subject Ross was beginning to recognise as characteristic.

'He doesn't have one.' Ross abandoned sponge and soap and began to reassemble the bridle he had been cleaning.

'I'm surprised he didn't bark at me last night.'

Ah, now we come to the real reason for your visit, Ross thought.

'You obviously didn't make any noise,' he said.

'My army training, I expect. Actually, I came to survey Father's security arrangements.'

'You live here,' Ross observed. 'You don't have to account for your actions to me.'

Roland picked a dripping stirrup iron out of the sink and dried it absent-mindedly on a cloth. 'That's true,' he agreed. 'As a matter of fact, I was surprised to see you awake.'

'I was hot. Got up to open the window,' Ross lied unashamedly.

'It is hot, isn't it? Fancy a beer?'

Ross did and fetched two from the stable office. They drank companionably enough, exchanging platitudes. At times Ross felt as though he were being gently and subtly milked for views and opinions. He answered vaguely, and often with a question, amused to notice that Roland, for all his upper-class-idiot act, gave little or nothing away in return.

'Lindsay isn't here today?' Roland asked presently.

'No.'

'I thought she was a frequent visitor, these days. Can't seem to stay away.'

'She comes to ride Gypsy.'

'James seems a nice fellow. Jolly good sort.'

'Mmm.'

'Rich as Croesus, of course.' Roland studied Ross under lazily drooping eyelids.

'Bully for him,' Ross murmured, aware that for some reason Roland was probing for a reaction. 'I must get some more dog food,' he said thoughtfully, with a switch of topic worthy of his companion.

Roland smiled faintly, crushing his beer can in one lean, brown hand. 'Big appetites, dogs,' he observed, sauntering out of the door.

Ross watched him leave with narrowed eyes and a slight shake of the head. He had never before met anybody so completely inscrutable.

Ross and Bill were just finishing evening stables when a silver Nissan sports car swept into the yard and Darcy Richmond eased himself smoothly out. Looking round, he caught sight of Ross by the tackroom door. 'Sarah still here?' he asked.

'It's her day off.' He was surprised that Darcy hadn't known that. After all, they had presumably been out together the previous evening. 'I think she's gone to London with her parents for the day. She said something about it to Maggie.'

Darcy looked briefly put out and then apparently remembered that she had mentioned the trip. He brightened. 'I was going to suggest going for a drink. I suppose you wouldn't like to come?'

Ross' lips curved ironically. 'I'd make a poor substitute.'

Darcy laughed. 'Still, how about it? Just beer and a game of pool or something.'

'Sure, why not?' The Colonel had called at lunchtime to postpone the usual Monday evening 'debriefing' and Ross felt that anything would make a change from the endless procession of soap operas and quiz shows on the television. He arranged to meet Darcy at the end of the drive, around eight.

The pub that Darcy drove them to, later that evening, was genuinely 'Olde Worlde', its beams adorned with a bewildering number of horse brasses, corn dollies and long-defunct tools of obscure rural trades. It was dimly lit, slightly smoky, and peopled with a number of local farm workers as well as one or two romantic couples tucked cosily into pew seats in dark corners. It was Englishness at its most attractive; unselfconscious and largely uncontrived. The sort of look striven for by designers but never quite attained. It couldn't be. It was the product of sheer age, evolved over centuries.

The promised pool table was conspicuous by its absence, a fact either that Darcy didn't notice or for which he felt no need to apologise. Ross didn't mind.

Franklin's nephew was a pleasant companion. It was the first time Ross had really had a chance to speak to him. He looked pretty much as Franklin might have done twenty years ago, although Franklin was dark and Darcy fair, like Peter. Light hazel eyes looked out candidly from a face that was just beginning to thicken around the jawline.

Ross learned that Darcy worked in his uncle's company in a position of some responsibility and that Richmond Senior had provided for him ever since his father – Franklin's brother – had died in a car accident when Darcy was eleven.

'My father wasn't well off when he died,' Darcy explained, carefully wiping the condensation off his beer glass with a forefinger. 'His business partner absconded with their secretary and the contents of the bank account. My father was altogether too trusting.' Darcy smiled sadly. 'He was a very unlucky man, one way and another. Uncle Frank's been great, though. He's treated me like a son. The best schools, university, vocational training and a position in his company. My own father couldn't have done more.' Darcy paused, eyes glittering strangely in the half-light as he regarded his glass intently.

'And you get on well with Peter?' Ross remarked. He judged Darcy to be about his own age or maybe a year or two older, and wondered when Franklin's wife had come upon the scene. Jealousy would have been understandable.

'Yes.' Darcy smiled warmly. 'He's a terrific kid. We're very close.' A distracted look came over his face and he glanced at the wall clock behind the bar. 'He's gone out tonight, I believe. A school friend's birthday party. Local cinema and on to McDonald's or somewhere, you know the sort of thing.'

Ross nodded.

'Uncle Frank married Marsha when I was fifteen,' Darcy continued, remembering. 'She was some lady.'

Ross regarded his companion speculatively. 'But they weren't happy?'

'Not for long. She was unfaithful, you know. Franklin was mad to think he could pin her down. She was like a butterfly, beautiful but flighty. She could never have settled for long.'

Ross digested this. Franklin hadn't admitted in so many words that his wife had been unfaithful, though Ross had guessed it.

'I suppose Peter will inherit the company in due course,' he said. 'It's kind of a strange situation for you, I guess.'

'It's never seemed strange to me.' D.. his head, looking surprised. 'Besides, I s.. necessarily work for Richmond Finance for ever. I have it in mind to be independent one day.'

They drank in silence for a moment, then Darcy looked at Ross. 'So, what's the story of *your* life then?'

'No story, really.' The American shrugged. 'Just a crazy ambition and one long battle against the odds.'

'Uncle Frank says you could have been a lawyer. What changed your mind?'

'A dislike of being pigeon-holed, perhaps?' Ross suggested. 'I really don't know. I was probably a bit of a rebel. Everybody expected me to follow my dad into law, and at that age you want to prove you can make your own choices. Horses were there. I loved them and, I guess, I loved the challenge, so I took it.'

'Well, it seems to have been the right move. I know Uncle Frank thinks you're a hot property.' Darcy smiled, getting to his feet and reaching for Ross' glass. 'Another drink?'

Ross nodded and thanked him.

'I don't suppose he'll find another Bellboy in a hurry, more's the pity,' Darcy said, returning a few moments later with the drinks. 'In fact, he only got *him* after practically pinching him from under old Fergusson's nose. He wasn't best pleased, I can tell you. "I've a mind tae take ye tae court over the matter." ' Darcy did a fair, if exaggerated, imitation of Fergusson's Scottish tones. 'Uncle Frank had him six years or so before he was killed. That was a crying shame. You've heard about it, of course?'

'Sure, Lindsay told me,' Ross agreed, cautiously. 'And Bill was talking about it the other day. Were you around when it happened?'

'No, I wasn't. I had a long weekend off work and went sailing. I went out on my boat on the Friday and didn't get back until the Monday afternoon. I wish I'd been here. My uncle was devastated. He really loved that horse.' Darcy shook his head, sadly. 'They never did catch the bastard responsible. Uncle Frank just says it was a one-off. He can't believe anyone would do that sort of thing to get at him. He's so good-natured, sees the best in everyone, but he's trodden on a few toes in his time, I can tell you. When you're in business you can't help it. And now, I hear, someone is threatening Peter's horse.' He looked disgusted. 'Honestly, how low can you go?'

Ross shook his head, not caring to speculate.

'Tell me something, though,' Darcy said after a moment. 'Why do you suppose whoever it was used real blood? Surely red paint or for that matter tomato ketchup would have done? I mean, where would anyone get that much blood? It's bizarre.'

'Horses hate the smell of blood,' Ross explained. 'To them it means death. As herd animals, they'd naturally run from it. Horses are animals of very primitive instincts, you know. That's why, when they first feel a man on their back, their natural reaction is to buck and then run. To them it's reminiscent of having a mountain lion drop on them from a tree. Of course, they don't think of it like that. They just react without knowing why.'

'I see. So Clown would have wanted to run from the smell, but not been able to. No wonder the poor creature was in a state.' He took a long swallow of his beer and shook his head. 'There must be some sick, sadistic bastard out there somewhere.'

Ross nodded. 'You can say that again.'

Darcy laughed. 'Not if I have too many more beers,' he said, and the conversation turned to more pleasant topics.

'Am I keeping you from something?' Ross asked after a while, amusement in his eyes. His companion had glanced at his watch at least three times in the last ten minutes.

'No, not at all,' Darcy exclaimed. 'It's just that – well, to tell the truth, there's a big football match on TV tonight, England versus Argentina, a replay, and I've just remembered that I didn't set the video.'

'Well, let's go then,' Ross said, getting up.

Darcy made a show of protest but gave in with only scant argument.

So much for my scintillating company, Ross thought, unoffended.

The journey was only six or seven miles and, far from hurrying, Darcy drove, if anything, more carefully than he had on the outward trip. Wary of traffic cops, Ross suspected.

Five minutes or so into the journey, Darcy's phone chirruped from the dashboard. He picked it up, glancing apologetically at Ross. He looked politely away out of the window and watched the roadside trees materialising in the powerful head-lights and sliding swiftly past into oblivion.

'What!'

Darcy applied the Nissan's brakes as though a yawning void had opened up before them. The car slid to a halt, slewing a little sideways in response to Darcy's one hand on the wheel.

'When? How did it happen? Oh, God! . . . Yes, I'll be there right away. Oh, God!'

He replaced the phone with a shaking hand and sat back in his seat with apparently no thought of moving the car from its rather hazardous position, parked diagonally across the road. He looked blankly ahead.

Wherever he was going to be 'right away', he was not in any hurry, Ross reflected.

'Would you like me to drive?' he offered, after a moment.

'What? No. Yes, perhaps you'd better.' Darcy seemed to have momentarily forgotten the American's presence. 'Thanks.'

He turned to look at Ross with wide, shocked eyes. 'Peter's been knocked down by a car,' he said in a tone that suggested he was finding it difficult to take the news in. 'He's been rushed to hospital. They won't say how badly he's been hurt. Oh, God! It's all my fault . . .'

Ross got out of the car and went round to the driver's side. 'Move over,' he said briskly. 'You'll have to give me directions. Is it far?'

'No. Only about ten minutes. Odstock, near Salisbury.'

'Okay.' Ross put the seat back to accommodate his longer legs and they set off. He raced the silver car along the country lanes, enjoying its power and handling in spite of the occasion. He considered Darcy's earlier remark. 'How can you say it's *your* fault?' he asked, bewildered. 'You weren't there. You couldn't have stopped it.'

Darcy was silent for a moment. 'It *is* my fault,' he reiterated. 'Uncle Frank wasn't keen on Peter going. He has to be so careful, because of kidnappers. I persuaded him. Peter desperately wanted to go and I took his side. So it's all my fault.'

'It was an accident,' Ross said, joining the main road and heading for Salisbury. 'It was nobody's fault. You can't keep people wrapped up in cotton wool. You mustn't blame yourself.'

Franklin Richmond was pacing the bustling hospital corridors like a caged lion when Darcy and Ross arrived. He and his nephew embraced, clinging to each other momentarily for comfort.

'How is he?' Darcy asked breathlessly. 'Is he going to be all right?'

Franklin shrugged and shook his head. He had arrived, he explained, twenty minutes before, to be told that his son was in the operating theatre and he would have to wait to speak with the doctor. A nurse had assured him, however, that Peter was not on the critical list. A deeply furrowed brow in an ashen face was evidence of how distressed Franklin was.

Ross, feeling surplus to requirements at this moment of family crisis, wandered off and returned with two disposable cups of hot, sweet tea. Darcy accepted his gratefully but Franklin looked blankly at Ross as though he couldn't quite place him.

'Drink this,' Ross urged. 'It'll do you good. Ease the shakes.'

Franklin took the cup obediently and began to sip, his thoughts obviously elsewhere.

'I don't take sugar,' he protested mildly, after a moment.

'Tonight you do. It's good for shock.'

Franklin walked away and back again.

'How did you come to be here?' he asked as he drew level with Ross once more.

'I drove Darcy. We were out for a drink.'

Franklin walked away again, giving no sign of having heard. He drained the cup and put it on a windowsill.

A door opened and a nurse bustled out, holding a clipboard to her chest like a shield against emotional involvement. Franklin stepped forward. 'Please, nurse . . .?'

'I'm sorry. The doctor will be with you shortly.' She smiled sympathetically, side-stepped and continued briskly on her way.

The doctor, when he did come, looked exhausted. He took off his glasses and rubbed his eyes with his knuckles as he explained to the

Richmonds that Peter had suffered two broken legs and extensive bruising and was presently being prepared for surgery. The fractures appeared to be clean and should heal without complication. There was no sign of internal injury and he was conscious. His father could see him briefly if he wished.

In the event, both Franklin and Darcy followed the doctor through the door and Ross kicked his heels until they returned a bare two minutes later, then took his leave.

Franklin, reassured that his son was in no immediate danger, had progressed beyond anxiety to all-consuming fury.

'I'll get him, Ross!' he promised. 'I'll get the bastard who did this! They say it was a hit and run but someone must have seen him. It's a busy town, for God's sake!'

Hearing the raw emotion in Franklin's voice, Ross remembered what he'd said about living with fear. He had seemed then to have impenetrable armour, but it appeared he had an Achilles heel in Peter.

Ross restored the keys of the Nissan to Darcy, telephoned for a taxi and made his way home.

It was only as he paid the driver and walked down the gravel drive to the yard that it occurred to him that somebody else might also have recognised that Peter was Franklin's Achilles heel, and that thought made his blood run cold.

Not wanting to be overheard, Ross made an excuse to drive into the village just after breakfast the next morning and telephoned Franklin on his mobile from the side of a leafy lane. Having been prepared to leave a message, he was a little surprised to find him at his office as usual. Peter, he was told, was progressing satisfactorily although still very shocked and upset. The hospital couldn't say for sure how long he would have to stay in, possibly only ten days or so, maybe as much as a month.

'*Both legs*, Ross,' Franklin said with anguish. '*Both legs* broken. He's only twelve and he's in so much pain.'

'Poor kid.' It wasn't enough, but what could he say? Ross hesitated, reluctant to voice his suspicions. 'Do we know exactly what happened yet?'

'Yes, I spoke to Amanda Medway, the mother of the birthday boy, last night at the hospital. She came on after she had seen the other children home. They'd been to see the film and were crossing the road on one of those automatic crossings . . . you know, the ones with the traffic lights and bleepers? Apparently Peter dropped his pullover as he was going across and stopped to pick it up. She says he was only a fraction behind the others and the lights were still red, but the car came from nowhere, accelerating, she said, with no intention of stopping. The driver can't have been looking where he was going. The police think it was probably joyriders. Peter didn't stand a chance.'

'Accelerating, you say?'

'Yes, I think that's what she said,' Richmond replied slowly. 'Yes, she did, because she said none of them had heard it approaching and then suddenly it was there . . .' He paused, his voice trailing off. 'Why do you ask? You're not thinking . . .?'

'I honestly don't know,' Ross said, unhappily. 'But I think you'll have to consider it. Your Mr X must know how much Peter means to you and we've made it more difficult for him to get at the horses. What if he's trying a change of tactics?'

'But, Ross!' Franklin was clearly devastated. 'Peter could have been killed! Surely he'd know the police would have to be involved if there were any suspicion of foul play? Besides, if Peter *had* died I would never have paid him another penny. I would have hunted him down. If he knows me, he would have known that. If it *was* him he took a terrible risk. Ross, you don't seriously think . . .?'

'I don't know. I've thought all round it. It just seems too much of a coincidence, you making a stand over payments and this happening. But I agree, he would have been taking one hell of a risk. Perhaps he felt he had nothing to lose. Has he left any messages since last night?'

'I don't know. I haven't been home. Oh, God, Ross! This is getting out of hand. I never thought . . . I mean, horses are one thing, but this? Surely not?'

Ross was silent. He really didn't know what to say. But the more he thought about Peter's accident, the less likely it seemed to him that that was what it was.

'I'll have to pay.' Franklin's voice deepened with defeat. 'I won't risk my son. Nothing's worth that.'

'Don't give in yet,' Ross said impulsively. 'If somebody can keep an eye on him, Peter is surely in the safest possible place for the time being. That should give us two clear weeks to flush this bastard out. What d'you say?'

Richmond sounded tired. 'What can we do in two weeks? It's been months.'

Ross wished he knew.

'We'll call his bluff,' he said. 'Take the fight to him. Force him to make a mistake.'

'If it *was* him last night, he's already made his biggest mistake,' Franklin said, anger overcoming despondency. 'I'll get on to McKinnon. See what he says.'

'Do the police have anything on the car?'

'Only that it was stolen. Taken from a pub car park. They found it half an hour or so after the – after it hit Peter. It was on its roof in a field just outside Salisbury, blazing merrily. They're satisfied that it was joyriders. They don't expect to catch the culprits.'

'Who knew that Peter was going on the trip? Darcy said it was a last-minute decision.'

'Poor Darcy. He's very cut up over this,' Richmond said. 'He's convinced he persuaded me to let Peter go, but to tell the truth, I probably would've given in anyway. Either way, if you're right and it *wasn't* an accident, it wouldn't have made any difference, would it? I mean, they would just have chosen another time and place.' He paused, thinking. 'I don't know who else could have known about the outing, except perhaps the parents of the other children. Oh, this is crazy, Ross! If someone hates me this much, you'd think I'd know about it! It just doesn't make any sense.'

It made some kind of sense to someone, Ross thought, but to whom?

'I really wish I could help,' he said. 'I suppose McKinnon has checked your telephones?'

'He does it every few weeks,' Franklin confirmed. 'He's about due to do it again now.'

'See if he'll do it right away, like this morning,' Ross advised. 'I can't see how else anyone could have known about Peter's outing, unless they were watching the house. And . . . er . . . do you have smoke alarms?'

'Some.' Franklin was appalled. 'You don't think . . .?'

'I don't know what to think,' Ross admitted. 'But we'd be stupid to take any chances. The battlefield has been extended. You've got to try and second-guess the bastard.'

Franklin sighed, reluctantly agreeing, and after promising to visit Peter that evening, Ross rang off.

A combination of the sticky heat and Leo in one of his more than averagely annoying moods had Ross feeling scratchy and bad-tempered before the day was very far advanced, and he was glad when Lindsay's familiar red MG turned into the yard.

She hadn't come, it transpired, with the intention of riding but fell in quickly enough with Ross' idea of hacking the horses to the river and letting them splash around in the shallows.

She exchanged a flowery cotton skirt for Sarah's

'emergency' jeans, which were kept in the tack-room in case of torrential rain or some other disaster. A string of pearls and matching earrings were taken off for safety and she joined the others in the yard, flashing a reproving look at Ross who was plainly amused at the sight of her in jeans two sizes too big.

Turning the trouser bottoms up a time or two, she mounted Gypsy, and with Leo, Danny, Sarah and Ross all suitably mounted, it was quite a procession that wound its way through the shady lanes to the copse that bounded the river.

Here they passed a pleasant half-hour letting the horses play in the water. Ross was aboard Bishop, whose taste ran no further than to pushing his nose about in the shallows. Gypsy, on the other hand, pounded the surface of the water vigorously with a playful foreleg, showering her rider and all those within six feet with river water.

Ross watched Lindsay laughing, the sun shining through her fair hair and the thin cotton blouse that she wore, and found the knowledge that she was forbidden fruit increasingly difficult to accept.

'You look very serious,' she teased as they turned for home. 'Is life so very hard?'

'I was thinking about Peter Richmond,' Ross said, only half truthfully, and then felt guilty as the laughter died out of her face.

'I heard about that,' she said, frowning. 'What an awful thing to happen. Have they traced the driver yet?'

'It was a stolen car,' Ross told her. 'Joyriders, the police say.'

'Prison's too good for them,' Lindsay declared vehemently. 'Like drink-drivers, they should be publicly flogged.'

'If they can catch them,' Ross agreed, glancing sideways at her fine-boned, determined face, and liking it just as much in anger as in laughter. He realised that he had loved the girl for quite a while.

Roland was waiting when they arrived back in the yard. He ambled out of the cool darkness of the tackroom, a beer in his hand, and smiled up at the riders in his lazy fashion.

'Nice day,' he observed, looking infuriatingly cool himself, in a white linen suit.

Nice day for doing nothing, Ross thought, mildly irritated.

'You're looking damned attractive as usual, cousin,' Roland said to Lindsay. 'You would appear to have lost a little weight, though,' he added thoughtfully, eyeing the jeans.

'Idiot,' she said affectionately, laughing at him. 'If you want to do something useful, you could always bring out a few more of those beers.'

'Is it the butler's day off?' Roland asked. 'Well, I suppose I could do it, just this once. Do you know, I think I shouldn't mind being a butler. Shouldn't be surprised if I made a very good one.'

As he wandered off into the tackroom once more, apparently considering this notion, Lindsay laughed out loud. 'He's nuts,' she said, shaking her head. 'Anyone would think he hadn't two brain cells to rub together but he's really very bright. He only started acting the fool to annoy Uncle John, I think. It certainly does that.'

Ross was puzzled. 'Why should he want to? Did they fall out or something?'

'In a way. Uncle John had Roland's life all mapped out. He wanted him to follow in his own illustrious footsteps. He was made up to Colonel very young, you know. A natural soldier. For a while it looked as though Roland was going to be the same but then he lost interest and resigned his commission. My uncle was very disappointed, though I must say I rather admired Roland for it. It can't have been an easy decision to make. Uncle John is very strong-willed and made no secret of his feelings.'

'Like father, like son.'

Lindsay squinted into the sun, looking over Gypsy's back at Ross. 'You're right. Most people don't think they're at all alike,' she said, 'but they are, you know, though they'd be the last to see it.'

Roland reappeared at this point with a four-pack of cold beers held aloft, balanced on an imaginary tray. 'Last pack,' he announced. 'You'll have to draw lots.'

'There are plenty more in the cottage,' Danny said, coming out of Simone's stable. 'Anyway, Sarah doesn't drink beer.'

'You don't?' Roland bent a lofty, inquisitive eye on the girl. 'A female of some delicacy, I perceive.'

Sarah flushed darkly at finding general attention

focused upon her and glanced suspiciously at Roland, unsure if he was laughing at her.

'Don't take any notice of him, Sarah,' Lindsay advised. 'He's a wretch. I expect Maggie has some lemonade in the fridge. Actually, I think I'd prefer that too.'

Lindsay departed fairly soon afterwards, and after visiting Maggie and charming a slice of apple pie out of her, so did Roland.

Ross waited until after the evening meal, when the fiercest heat had abated, before working Bishop in the school, practising speed turns and angled take-offs. He returned the big horse to his box after three-quarters of an hour, well pleased with his performance.

After a quick change of clothes and a clean-up, he was about to set off to visit Peter when Bill hailed him. He was wanted on the telephone.

'Hi, Ross, it's me,' Lindsay's cheerful tones greeted him. 'Look, I'm sorry to bother you, but I wanted to catch you while it's still light. You see, I can't find my pearls.'

'*Your pearls?*'

'My necklace and my earrings. You remember, I took them off this morning when I came out riding? I put them in my skirt pocket when I took it off and by the time I changed back, quite frankly I'd forgotten about them. I thought perhaps I'd dropped them in the office, but you obviously haven't found them. I suppose they could be in the yard . . .' Her voice trailed off, sounding doubtful.

'Well, I'll certainly have a look,' Ross assured her. 'But I'm sure somebody would have found the necklace by now if it had been out in the open. Have you looked in your car?'

'Yes, straight away. Oh, what a nuisance! It's typical of me. I'm sorry to be such a pain.'

'Nonsense. We all lose things.' But Ross was struck by an unwelcome thought. This wasn't by any means the first time things had gone missing. 'Look, I'll go and have a look right now, before I go out. I'll give you a ring if I find anything.'

He rang off with an idea already forming in his mind and an inner voice warning him at the same instant that he'd do better to forget it. He gave the yard and tackroom a sketchy search and climbed into the jeep, still uncertain as to whether or not he would put his plan into action.

He drove towards Salisbury with the warm evening wind in his hair and the dog's head resting on his shoulder. He tried to concentrate on Franklin Richmond's troubles but other thoughts intruded: riding Ginger at the weekly Lea Farm show the next evening; the loss of Lindsay's jewellery and his suspicions about Leo.

Peter Richmond was not alone when Ross was shown into his room at the hospital; both his father and Darcy were at his bedside. But lying back on his pillows, with both legs raised in traction, Peter's pale and strained face, in which the eyes were dark smudges, was the one that caught and held Ross' attention. He smiled and walked forward as Darcy made way for him.

'Hiyah, soldier! How ya doin'?' Ross asked cheerfully.

Peter mustered an answering smile. 'Hello. I'm okay, thank you. But it does hurt.' Peter's good manners didn't desert him, even in these unhappy circumstances. 'Doctor Trent says I'll be up and about in no time.'

Ross pulled up a chair, admiring the young boy's courage.

'Sure you will,' he said. 'Look, I asked your dad and he said he's fitted you up with a VCR, so I've brought a couple of our training videos along with me. The first one's Clown, so you can see what kind of progress he's making. And you're not to laugh at the bit where I fall off!'

Ross saw instantly that he'd struck gold. Peter's eyes lit up eagerly as he took the cassettes. He thanked Ross profusely and looked hopefully at his father.

'All right,' Franklin said, with the air of one reluctantly granting a favour. 'I'll put one on for you. I can see visitors will be just so much excess baggage from now on.'

Peter grinned, confident of the affection behind the assumed tone.

Ross saw Darcy smiling at the invalid with shared enjoyment of the moment and thought that though the boy might be lacking a mother's love, he certainly didn't miss out on family feeling.

He stayed a while, commentating at Peter's request on the first of the videos, before a nurse came to turn them all out and give the boy some medication.

The dog was waiting for him in the jeep and jumped up, tail waving.

'Okay, Fido,' Ross said, cuffing it playfully. 'Are you gonna drive, or shall I?'

He drove home steadily, his mind on his proposed plan of action. The yard was deserted. A light showed in the cottage but the windows of the two bedsits above the stables were dark and Leo's motorbike wasn't in the shed.

He had no excuse for backing out now. Leo rarely returned before closing time and Ross could usually hear his bike's powerful roar as it decelerated in the lane outside. There would be no better time for taking an unauthorised snoop around his room.

The dog padded up the stairs at his master's heels and he unlocked the door to his own room and let it in. Pausing only to collect a torch, he went out again, turning off the light and closing the door behind him.

Pulse rate accelerating, he stepped across the narrow landing to Leo's door and paused, listening intently. Below, one of the horses pulled at the hay in its rack and snorted as dust tickled its nostrils. Nothing else stirred.

Ross took the key to his own door from his pocket and slotted it into Leo's. It wouldn't turn. For an instant, Ross experienced a strange mixture of disappointment and relief. Then he tried the handle and the door opened smoothly. It hadn't been locked.

With his circulation doing overtime, Ross took one last look down the darkened stairs then slipped into the room, closing the door behind him.

The curtains were open and a glimmer of light from the yard lit part of the ceiling but it was not enough to search by. Ross cupped the torch in his hand and, forcing himself to take his time and be methodical, began to go through Leo's things.

With the light shaded he could only see a small part of the room at any one time and it occurred to him with a sudden flash of amusement that it would be just his luck to work his way round the room and then find Leo already in residence, asleep on the bed, or worse still, waiting for and watching him.

Once the picture had formed in his mind, it wouldn't be banished and Ross couldn't settle again to his task without risking a quick unmasking of the light to scan the whole room.

No one lurked in the shadows. He shaded the light once more and continued his search.

He wasn't surprised to find the groom's room untidy and disorganised, for although Leo was an efficient worker, neatness was definitely not his forte. Discarded shoes and items of clothing littered the floor and hung from every chairback and open cupboard door.

A place for everything and everything out of its place, Ross thought wryly as he picked his way round the room.

It resembled a church jumble sale that had been hit by a particularly vicious tornado. And, what

197

was more, the room smelled faintly of tobacco smoke, which definitely contravened yard rules. Ross wondered that Maggie hadn't complained about that when she came to clean up once a week. On the floor at the head of the bed were a couple of bottles of spirits and judging by the labels, Leo had expensive tastes.

Ross worked his way briskly through the bedsit, which was an exact mirror image of his own, finding that the wardrobe and the chest of drawers were the only places that were tidy. These held a collection of designer garments and two or three leather jackets that would have cost the best part of two weeks' wages and appeared not to have been worn.

Ross frowned. It began to look as though his suspicions concerning Leo were justified and it seemed his thievery was not restricted to his working environment.

The minutes ticked by and Ross' nerves didn't improve. The longer he searched, the more he wanted to finish and get out of the room and, conversely, the less inclined he felt to leave without finding anything.

What he expected to find he couldn't really have said. A string of pearls would have been nice. But Leo, if he *was* guilty, was not only an opportunist, he obviously also knew where he could pass on his stolen items fairly smartly.

Disappointed, Ross finally gave up and moved to the door. Hanging on a hook on the back of it was the denim jacket Leo often wore in the early mornings.

Having searched all the other pockets he had come across, Ross quickly went through these. A pack of chewing gum, a folded pen knife and a tube of Polo mints, which the horses were very fond of, in the left, and in the right an oily rag, a few coins and two dog-eared business cards.

Ross casually turned them over: M. A. Kendall – Wholesale Butcher, and Simmonds-Fox & Son – Bespoke Tailors. With a sigh, he returned the objects to their respective pockets and turned to give a last quick flash of the torch round the garment-littered interior.

Suddenly a light came on in the yard, and before the full significance of this had penetrated Ross' consciousness, he heard the door at the foot of the stairs open and the sound of someone's carefree whistling floated up to his horrified ears.

For an instant he froze. Then the cogs started turning again. There was nowhere to hide so he would have to bluff his way out.

As the door banged shut, he nipped across the room, grabbed and uncapped a half-full bottle of spirits and gulped a hasty mouthful, sloshing a little down his shirtfront for good measure.

Letting himself out on to the landing, he slammed the door behind him, then turned and gave a theatrical 'Shhh!'.

Leo sprang up the last few steps, clearly furious, to be met with a smile of pure innocence.

'Whoops! Wrong door,' he said, slurring his speech and leaning forward confidingly toward him.

He patted Leo's arm and, with the extreme care of the somewhat less than sober, made his way past him and started across the landing.

He almost made it.

Leo, frowning intently, watched him for a moment or two, then with sudden fury lashed out and caught Ross' shoulder as he passed by, spinning him round again.

'What were you doing in my room?' he demanded, eyes glittering dangerously.

Ross forced himself to relax. 'Wrong door,' he repeated stupidly, looking at Leo through half-closed eyes. 'Not my room at all.'

Leo caught hold of the American's shirtfront with both hands and, bearing him backwards, slammed him with vicious force into the doorpost. It caught Ross squarely between the shoulder blades, shocking the air from his lungs and cracking painfully against the back of his head. He gasped involuntarily and through the momentary haze of pain, heard the dog whine and growl on the other side of the door.

Leo's face was only inches from his own and as Ross' vision sorted itself out he saw the groom's fury relax into an equally unpleasant smirk.

'Been drinking, have you, Yank?' he said slowly, and then sniffed close to Ross. 'Maybe you have at that.' His grin widened. 'Perhaps the Yankee wonder boy is having a little trouble with his nerves.'

You can say that again, Ross thought.

He felt Leo's grip loosen slightly then and seized

his chance. Swinging his left hand sideways to find the door handle, he twisted it open before his captor realised what he was doing.

With a rush the German Shepherd filled the doorway, hackles up and lips bristling with a warning that was backed up by two rows of gleaming white teeth.

Leo's hands dropped away from Ross as if he had suddenly become too hot to touch.

The dog growled and licked its lips ominously.

'Okay, Yank. You win this time,' Leo conceded as he backed away, eyes never wavering from the dog. 'But if I were you I'd be careful. You may not always have your pooch around to look after you.'

Ross felt he should say something but didn't know what and hadn't completely recovered his breath, so he caught hold of the dog's collar to prevent it from following Leo and smiled in what he hoped was an intensely irritating manner.

As Leo reached the relative safety of his own door, he paused, his confidence returning a little.

'I heard your nerves were shot,' he said, transferring his black gaze to Ross once more. 'Now I see it's true.'

With a deft movement he retreated into his room and the door closed behind him.

Ross swung away from the support of the doorpost with a painful sigh. His sleuthing effort had shown him that Leo quite possibly had something to hide – his reaction had been extreme even for someone with his quick temper – and demonstrated how close beneath the surface violence lay.

It had also, Ross thought despondently, done little for their future working relationship.

He wondered what twist of fate had brought the other man back so early, and why he hadn't heard him arrive.

'C'mon, boy.' Ruffling the dog's fur affectionately, Ross went into his room and shut the door, resting his aching head against the cool paintwork for a moment.

All in all, he was beginning to wish he *was* drunk.

10

It was Wednesday and Ross wasn't having a good day. Bishop had trodden on his toe at feeding time; he had spilled a cup of coffee at breakfast; Leo was smirking at him in an infuriating manner every time they passed; and he had a headache.

It was now mid-morning. The day was cloudy but stickily hot and Ginger seemed to be in a state of nervous tension.

When Ross went to her stable to collect her she was already tacked up and as he put out his hand to take her rein she flinched away as if he made a habit of hitting her. Concerned, he patted her, reassuring her with his voice, but she remained edgy, ears flicking back and forth agitatedly.

Still talking quietly to her, he led her out into the yard. As they reached the doorway, Leo strolled by with a bucket and haynet. Ginger started nervously, throwing her head up, and the nearside rein pulled off the bit ring and came away in Ross' hand.

He cursed, caught hold of the mare's bridle and then looked closely at the stud billet fastening. It appeared undamaged. Whoever had cleaned it last had obviously not fastened it properly. If that had come undone while he was riding ... And on Ginger, of all horses!

He re-attached the rein, checking the other one and making a mental note to have a word with Sarah, under whose care Ginger came.

He rode the chestnut mare into the school, trying to be patient and calm with her. Much to his annoyance, Bill came and stood leaning on the gate, watching. After twenty minutes or so of suppling exercises, during which Ginger contrived to remain totally stiff and uncompromising, Ross turned his attention to the scattering of low training fences in the centre of the arena. Both he and the mare were soaked with sweat and equally determined not to let the other dominate.

Ginger approached the smallest of the obstacles at a grudging and uncomfortable canter. Six feet away she dug her toes in and came to a ragged halt. Ross circled the mare away and back to the fence, coaxing a fraction more speed from her. She flattened her ears crossly and refused again, her body rock-hard with tension.

Ross sat still, regarding the fidgety, foxy ears, his legs moving with the rhythm of her breathing, and tried to puzzle out her odd behaviour. There was nothing to be gained from trying to bully her when she was like this. After a moment he patted her sweaty neck and she flinched away from his hand. She had been badly frightened at some point, that was for sure, but why was she so moody?

Suddenly, Ginger threw up her head and ran back a few paces, jerking Ross rudely to attention. Bill was halfway across the school towards him, a lunge whip in his hand. The mare snorted, regarding the whip with horror.

'Stay back!' Ross called, urgently.

Bill appeared not to hear. 'Thought I'd get behind her with this. That'll make her think,' he suggested, indicating the whip with its six-foot thong.

'No!' Ross said sharply. He could feel Ginger's rising panic. 'Just leave her to me.'

'You don't seem to be making much of a job of it,' Bill grunted but he stopped, nonetheless.

Ross ignored him.

'One good crack'd soon get her going,' the ex-jockey persisted. 'I wouldn't touch her with it.'

'She has a phobia about whips,' Ross explained with fragile patience. 'Believe me, it would do far more harm than good.'

'You're too soft on her. She needs a firm hand.'

'She's completely spaced out! She needs to go back to square one and be brought on slowly,' Ross argued. 'And even then I don't think she'll ever make the top. She hasn't got the temperament for this game.'

'Well, one of you hasn't, that's for sure,' Bill agreed, turning away.

'What in hell do you mean by that?' Ross demanded of his departing back.

The little man didn't answer. He didn't have to and they both knew it.

Ross seethed inwardly, annoyed at himself for rising to the bait and knowing as he did so that Bill's words had only hit home because his self-confidence was already badly dented where Ginger was concerned.

Stiffly, he dismounted, aware for the first time that his back was bruised. Memories of the previous night nagged at him for the umpteenth time that morning. It was worse than physical pain to have given Leo a feeling of power over him, however false its basis. With his already shaky reputation, the rumour that he had hit the bottle could spell death to his career. It had been a spur-of-the-moment decision but one that with hindsight he bitterly regretted. Better by far to have faced Leo on equal terms and taken the consequences there and then.

Easy to be wise now.

He went to work on Ginger again, leading her over a pole on the ground, then walking her over a raised pole. She relaxed slowly and by the end of half an hour he was riding her over crossed poles at two foot six. He called it a day, supposing he had achieved something, though it gave him little satisfaction to finish up where he'd intended starting.

'She'll have to do better than that tonight,' Bill observed as Ross led the weary horse back into the yard.

'I'm not taking her tonight,' he said shortly. 'She needs more work. I'll take Clown instead.'

'More work, huh?' The stable manager gave Ross a long, hard look. 'If you say so.'

Ross ignored him. It was becoming easier. 'Sarah,' he called. 'Ginger needs sponging down.'

She looked up from filling water buckets. 'I don't do her any more. Leo does. He said he'd cleared it with you.'

'Did he now?' Ross said under his breath.

Leo appeared to take Ginger's rein, smirking unpleasantly. The chestnut drew back nervously and her unsettled state suddenly made sense, as did the unfastened rein of earlier.

'Leave her!' Ross said sharply. He turned to Bill. 'Did you know anything about this?'

'No, nothing. And I don't appreciate being kept in the dark.'

'How was I to know it was such a big deal?' Leo demanded. 'Sarah wanted to look after Woody, so I said I'd swap, that's all.'

'I – I didn't,' she protested, round-eyed.

'Well, you'll go back to doing her from now on,' Ross told Sarah. 'And you'll ask me personally before you make any such changes in future, do you understand?'

Sarah flushed fiery red and stammered in confusion.

Ross waved a dismissive hand and turned away, running his fingers through his damp hair. Life seemed to be becoming very complicated.

*

Ross arrived at the Lea Farm evening show in a mood of increasing irritation. He had offered to take Danny along, as a treat for the younger boy, and to give Leo the evening off, as a treat for himself. Unfortunately, Bill turned down the offer on Danny's behalf and he was stuck with Leo, who now had the added encouragement of knowing that he was beginning to get to Ross.

On the way to the show they had been followed for a stretch by a police car going about its duty and Leo took great delight in advising Ross to drive carefully. 'You wouldn't want to be breathalysed,' he remarked slyly.

Ross ignored him and Leo chuckled about it for a lot longer than was necessary.

The crowd at Lea Farm was the usual bunch. Many of them acknowledged Ross with a nod or a wave as he arrived, and later, as he warmed Clown up in the exercise ring, a friendly voice hailed him.

'Hi, Mick!' Ross said, with pleasure, reining Clown in. 'Haven't seen you here before.'

'It is rather on the edge of my range,' Mick Colby agreed. 'But I heard that all the big names were coming here now . . .' He gave the American a sideways glance.

'. . . and you thought you might learn something from watching them,' Ross finished smoothly.

Colby made a face and swung his horse away, laughing.

Clown was on his toes. He hadn't jumped in an indoor arena before and entered the ring with eyes on stalks, ogling the crowd, the jumps and the timing apparatus as though he suspected an ambush. When Ross asked him for a steady canter round the top of the arena prior to starting, the skewbald leapt into a short bouncy stride that made his teeth rattle. Expecting the worst, Ross put him at the first fence.

More by luck than judgement they safely negotiated the first three before flattening a gate which descended with a 'whoomph' that excited the young horse still further. He cleared one more fence, then took three foot six of planks out by the roots, stumbled, and bucked in annoyance. Ross pulled him up sharply, touched the brim of his crash hat to signify retirement and rode Clown, jiggling and sweating, from the arena. Nothing would be gained by persevering in that manner.

The voice behind the microphone was sympathetic and Ross was thankful that he hadn't got Harry Douglas' barbed comments to put up with.

'Is that what I'm supposed to watch and learn from?' Colby asked, pausing on his way into the ring.

'Son of a bitch! Did you see him?' Ross demanded, disgustedly. 'Still, it'll give you new boys a chance.'

He dismounted and patted Clown's brown and white neck as the crowd applauded Colby's entry into the arena.

'Problems?' Franklin Richmond came up behind him.

'No, thanks, I've got plenty of my own,' Ross responded glibly, then remembered to whom he was speaking. 'Oh, Lord, I'm sorry. That wasn't funny,' he said quickly.

'That's okay.' Franklin was unoffended. 'I expect you have. I've just seen that groom of yours sitting on the horsebox ramp, smoking.'

Ross looked heavenwards. 'I'll talk to him,' he promised. 'But to be honest, I've about had it with him. He's got a serious attitude problem and if he's not careful, he'll be out on his ear.'

When he reached the lorry, Leo had finished his cigarette and was tacking up Flowergirl. Ross decided to let sleeping dogs lie for the time being.

Back at the exercise ring he discovered the Colonel, Lindsay and James Roberts leaning on the rails. He slipped off the mare and went to greet them, his eyes on Lindsay's cotton-clad figure. She had twisted her hair into a knot on top of her head in a cool, sophisticated style. Ross thought she looked wonderful and experienced a sharp stab of jealousy seeing James standing with one arm casually circling her waist.

He greeted his boss politely, then turned to Lindsay.

'No luck with the necklace, I'm afraid.'

She looked stricken. 'Oh, Ross, I'm so sorry! I should have rung you. James found it this morning, *and* one of the earrings. They'd fallen under the seat in the MG but he had to take it out to get at them. I forgot you might be looking for them. Sorry.'

'I'm just glad you found them,' he replied.

'Me too. Mother would have killed me. She gave them to me on my eighteenth.'

'So, did she drag you along again?' Ross commiserated with James. 'You'll have to get her interested in a lady-like pursuit, like flower-arranging or knitting.'

Lindsay scowled at him. 'It was James' idea to come, not mine,' she said defensively.

'Well, I knew she wanted to come really and you know what women are,' James said, looking over her head at Ross. 'If they can't do what they want to, they sulk for days.'

'Tell me about it!' he agreed.

'Oh! You're insufferable, both of you,' Lindsay gasped, torn between annoyance and reluctant amusement. 'Come on, Uncle John, you're a gentleman. Take me away from these two chauvinistic louts! Ross, I hope you fall off!'

The Colonel obligingly tucked her hand through his arm and together they turned away.

James grinned, shrugged expressively to Ross and followed.

Ross mounted and began to work at suppling the brown mare, thinking that he liked Lindsay's fiancé very much and at the same time wishing him on the other side of the world.

Mick Colby appeared, having changed from his novice ride on to King's Defender. Ross thought the old horse looked happy and well.

Gradually, the exercise ring filled up again. Stephen Douglas rode by on China Lily and later Ross saw the big chestnut, Telamon, being ridden by a hefty, florid-faced rider he didn't know. The horse looked even leaner than he remembered and just as unhappy.

Flowergirl jumped a typically energetic round but tipped a pole into the tanbark for four faults. It was one of those evenings. The class was eventually won by Douglas, whose mare was in cracking form, with Colby taking second place. Ross didn't see what happened to the chestnut and his new jockey, save that the horse preceded the rider from the arena by the best part of a minute.

As Ross was walking Flo back to the horsebox, Leo appeared unexpectedly, riding Woodsmoke. A neighbouring groom was keeping an eye on the lorry, he said, in answer to Ross' query. He wore a cat-with-the-cream smile that made Ross distinctly uneasy and he checked Woody's tack closely before mounting.

Franklin's horse jumped carefully into the jump-off in the last class but Flo dropped another unlucky pole. Douglas also had a fence down and glared murderously at Ross as if daring him to find it funny. Ross just turned away.

In the jump-off, the competition was fierce and although Woodsmoke did his best, he couldn't find the speed to beat his younger rivals.

Leo had disappeared in the direction of the horsebox with Flo and Ross was preparing to follow when Colby jumped off King beside him.

'Bad luck,' he said. 'Not your evening, was it?'

'Can't win 'em all,' Ross observed, philosophically.

'Don't I know it? Hey, sorry to hear about Black Bishop. Damn shame!'

Ross stopped in his tracks. 'What about him?'

'I . . . I'm sorry.' Colby looked confused. 'I heard you'd lost the ride . . .'

'Says who?'

'I don't know, mate. Fella on the grey told me. I don't know who told him. It's not true then?'

'If it is, nobody's told *me*,' Ross assured him. 'And I can do without that kind of rumour.'

'Hey, I'm sorry. I'll do what I can to scotch it.'

'Obliged.' Ross returned to the lorry, recalling Leo's smugness and deciding not to give him the satisfaction of mentioning the matter.

They drove home in heavy silence. As they turned off the main road into Wiltshire's rabbit warren of lanes, Leo reached inside his denim jacket and produced a hip flask.

'Here you are. This'll steady your nerves and drown your sorrows, Yank,' he said, offering it to Ross.

Ross gritted his teeth, his knuckles white on the wheel.

'Don't push your luck, fella,' he warned softly. 'You're flying very close to the flame.'

Leo chuckled most of the way home.

Ross lay awake for quite a while that night, once again regretting the mischance that had brought Leo down on him the night before. He had told Bill that the motorbike had a flat tyre, which explained the silence of his approach but not his early return

Ross felt that the whole episode and its consequences would have been more bearable if his search had yielded something useful. As it was, it looked as though it had all been for nothing.

Even without the excuse of Lindsay's missing pearls, he'd been tempted to search Leo's room. Too many little things went missing around the yard. But if Leo *was* responsible, then he obviously knew where he could pass them on without delay. Ross had looked everywhere. In fact, if he hadn't been so thorough, he would have been out of the danger zone before Leo had returned. He supposed he should be thankful he had not been caught actually going through the man's pockets.

Suddenly, as if someone had turned a light on in his mind, he remembered the business card he had found and glanced at dismissively, and its significance was all at once blindingly obvious.

Clown had been soaked in ox blood. And where better to obtain a large quantity of blood than a slaughterhouse?

What excuse one would give for wanting it was a debatable point but of little importance. What mattered was that somebody *had* got it. And it could surely be no coincidence that Leo was carrying the card of one 'M. A. Kendall – Wholesale Butcher' in his pocket.

Had Leo, then, been the prowler Ross had challenged that night in the yard?

Ross didn't think so. *His* man had been tall and fairly broad, not of wiry build like the groom.

Who then? *Had* there been two of them? And

what of the other card? Anyone less likely to have used the services of a bespoke tailor than Leo, it would be hard to imagine.

He sighed and turned over, trying to sleep. The problem would still, unfortunately, be there in the morning.

The next day, Ross telephoned Edward McKinnon for the first time. He had ridden Fly out on his own and made the call from a lonely hilltop. A machine answered. Ross told it his name and said he would ring back later.

The machine clicked and McKinnon cut in. 'Ross? I'm here. What can I do for you?'

As briefly as he could, he told McKinnon his suspicions about Leo's thieving and of the consequent search of his room. He told him about the business card and also mentioned the prowler he had encountered the night before Clown was daubed with blood. He said he didn't think his assailant had been Leo, but that the dog had chased someone else who could possibly have been.

McKinnon had heard about the prowler from Richmond. 'We checked on Leo Jackson when he was first employed by the Colonel,' he told Ross. 'At least, in so far as to establish his whereabouts at the time of the Bellboy incident. At that time he was working in a racing stable in Ireland. So if he was responsible for this second incident, then it was probably on the instruction of another party.'

'From what you've told me about the extortionist,' Ross said thoughtfully, 'he doesn't sound the sort of character to get involved with a two-bit sneak thief like Leo. I mean, Leo is so blatantly aggressive. There's nothing subtle about him. It seems more likely to me that Leo stole that business card along with something else – a wallet, perhaps – from somebody's pocket or car. Besides, I would swear he was as surprised as the rest of us at finding Clown in that state.'

'Maybe.' McKinnon paused, apparently to digest this information. 'Yes, I think you're probably right. Though I don't see why he should have kept the card. Unless he just forgot that he had it. Anyway, I'll put somebody on to this Kendall – see if we can get some kind of a description from him. After all, it can't be every day that they have a customer asking for a couple of gallons of ox blood.'

'And what about Peter's accident? Has anything more turned up on that?' Ross asked.

'There was a message on Franklin's answerphone yesterday,' McKinnon said. 'Remote callbox, as before. The caller advised Franklin to toe the line and said "It could have been worse." '

'So it *wasn't* an accident?'

'Well, possibly not.' McKinnon was cautious. 'The thing is, it was widely reported – the papers, local TV, you know the sort of thing. Easy enough to claim responsibility after the event.'

'I suppose so.' Hearing muffled hoofbeats, Ross cast a quick look around him. 'Look, I'd better go now. Somebody's coming. Shall I call back tomorrow and see what you've come up with?'

'If you like, or I can let you know through Franklin.' McKinnon sounded amused. 'What happened to the man at the pub who didn't want to get involved?'

'I *am* involved, damn you! Just as you knew I would be. So don't bother to say "I told you so".'

'I wouldn't dream of it,' McKinnon protested, the amusement very evident. 'Well anyway, thanks for the information. But don't stick your neck out, *please*. I've got people who are employed to take risks. If there is anything else you think we should look into, let one of them do it. It wouldn't be so catastrophic if they got caught.'

'What *would* you do if one of your people got caught snooping?' Ross asked curiously.

'Disown them,' McKinnon said shortly. 'But they know that. It's one of the conditions of the job. We'll pay for the best legal aid, but we won't come forward ourselves. But that's beside the point. They are trained not to get caught.'

'Cyanide pills?' Ross murmured, amused in his turn.

'No, Mr Wakelin,' McKinnon said heavily. 'They fall on their swords.'

There was a click as he disconnected and Ross smiled. The man was really quite human.

His ride completed and Fly returned to his stable, Ross crossed the yard carrying the saddle and bridle to hear raised voices from the tackroom. In the doorway he all but collided with Darcy Richmond, who pushed past him with a muttered

217

apology and made for his car. Ross watched him go, puzzled, then went on in.

Leo was inside, half-heartedly soaping a bridle and wearing a self-satisfied smirk.

'What now?' Ross asked, heavily.

'Now?' Leo was all innocence.

'You know what I mean. What have you said to upset Darcy?'

Leo curled his lip. 'Mind your own business, Yank.'

'Anything you have to say, in this yard, to one of the owners or their family, *is* my business,' Ross said forcefully. 'And if you want to continue to work here, you had better remember that!'

Leo continued to sneer. 'He warned me to stay away from his girl,' he said. 'He needn't have bothered. I don't want the little mouse anyway. I prefer the other one – the classy blonde.' He glanced sideways at Ross to gauge his reaction.

'You wouldn't know class if it kicked your butt,' he said mildly, dumping his saddle down beside the one Leo was about to clean. 'When you've finished that, you can do this one,' he added with the air of one bestowing a great favour and turned away, heading for the cottage and a cool drink.

Out of the corner of his eye he caught Leo's black scowl and for once the satisfaction was all his.

Ross had to go into Salisbury the next morning and rang McKinnon from the jeep when he got there.

'I'm not going to leave my name and number, so

you might as well pick up the damn' phone if you're listening,' he told the answering machine.

McKinnon picked it up.

'And good morning to you too, Ross,' he said politely. 'I do love your particularly American brand of charm.'

Ross smiled to himself. 'What news?' he asked.

'Well, we tracked down Kendall the butcher and paid him a visit,' McKinnon reported. 'I think we gave him the fright of his life. He was convinced that we were from Public Health or MAFF and insisted that he had not and would never sell ox blood to anyone under any circumstances. However, when we offered a little – shall we say – financial inducement he remembered that he *had* had an enquiry but of course had refused to deal with the man. As far as he could remember it was a fairly young man, late-twenties to early-thirties he thought, dressed like a countryman and wearing a flat cap and sunglasses. He couldn't remember what kind of car the man drove but what *was* interesting was that Kendall thought he might have been Irish. Which tells us . . .?' McKinnon finished.

Ross thought for a moment.

'Which tells us the ox-blood man is almost certainly our original Mr X, and that he is young. It also tells us what we already know: that he's careful enough to cover his tracks even when he doesn't expect us to be close behind.' He paused. 'What excuse did he give for wanting the blood?' he asked curiously.

McKinnon laughed. 'Our friend, Mr X as you call him, is nothing if not inventive. He said he was a member of a Civil War re-enactment group. Said they wanted to do Marston Moor and it had to be as realistic as possible. You know how fanatical some of these groups are. Kendall said the man was very enthusiastic, wanted to tell him all about the group. I gather he had quite a job to get rid of him. He certainly plays his part well.'

'Would've served him right if Kendall had wanted to join,' Ross observed. 'He certainly covers his tracks.'

'If he didn't, we would have caught him by now,' McKinnon assured him. 'We had already tried all the local slaughterhouses and butchers. This one was in Buckinghamshire.'

'Sure,' Ross said, placatingly. 'No offence meant. Any other news?'

'We de-bugged Richmond's house again.'

'And?'

'We found a rather clumsy device, on the phone-lines outside. Suspiciously clumsy, I'd say.'

'You mean, he wanted it found,' Ross said. 'So again, that presupposes that he knew you'd be looking?'

'Oh, I'm sure he did,' McKinnon said. 'He must know Franklin would have somebody working to catch him. We have always accepted that. He knows, and he's quite confident that we aren't going to uncover him. We made another complete search of the house, in case that one was a decoy, but we didn't find anything else.'

'But, clumsy or not, that bug could have told Mr X where Peter was going to be last Monday, right?'

'It could,' McKinnon said slowly, 'though I'm still not one hundred per cent sure that that was anything but an accident. It just doesn't feel right to me.'

'Well, you're the expert,' Ross conceded. 'Look, I better go. There's a guy with a notebook coming and I haven't bought a ticket yet.'

'Yes, okay. But look, Ross, be careful will you? We've been delving into Leo's murky past, and we discovered that in Ireland, about six weeks before he arrived here, a racing stable lad called Lewis Roach was involved in a pub brawl and half-killed another lad with a broken bottle. The thing is that although everybody seemed to agree that Lewis was the guilty party, nobody was too keen to testify. It seems that Lewis was known to have some pretty rough friends. He disappeared soon after and they haven't seen him since. I gather they're not exactly pining for him. I faxed a picture to the racing stables and they immediately identified our Leo Jackson as their Lewis Roach. At least, they were ninety-five per cent sure. Apparently he had a beard and moustache when they had the pleasure of his company.'

'But what about his references? The Colonel said they were good.'

'Yes. It would seem that there was indeed a Leo Jackson who left just before our Leo – they're a wandering bunch, these stable lads, Lewis Roach was apparently a Londoner. And so it would seem likely that when Colonel Preston requested references for Leo Jackson, the head lad was happy to tell him that Jackson was a good worker and a fine upstanding citizen. Anyway, I just thought you should know. It's up to you what you do about him. Obviously you can't mention me, but watch yourself. This is not a man to rub up the wrong way!'

Ross laughed shortly. 'With Leo, I don't think there's a right way,' he observed grimly. 'But thanks for the warning. He's pretty much outstayed his welcome anyway.'

The Oakley Manor horses attended two shows at the weekend and performed very well. There were no disasters; Bishop won the Foxhunter class and Flo was a good second in a Grade-C class, while Simone continued to defeat all-comers in the various speed classes she entered. Even Ginger did nothing to disgrace herself or Ross.

On a more personal level the weekend was not so harmonious.

Leo exerted himself to reach new heights of insolence and awkwardness, so that even the Colonel, who kept himself comfortably distant from most of the nitty-gritty of yard business, became aware of it.

Leo was constantly rude to Ross, deliberately 'misunderstood' instructions and was found to be missing for large portions of the two days. Before the weekend was very far advanced Ross had decided enough was enough; he would give Leo his marching orders at the end of the week if things didn't improve significantly.

Fortunately, he had Danny to help him in the meantime and on the second day Lindsay as well, who had transported Gypsy to the show with them, although she spent much of the day with her parents and James, who also attended.

After Ross' Foxhunter success on Bishop, she'd brought her family across to meet him as he left the ring after the prize-giving. The moment had been a trifle awkward.

Lindsay ran forward and hugged him, eyes shining, as he dismounted. 'Ross! That was wonderful! I'm so *pleased* for you!'

Ross, blissfully unaware of her approaching family and caught up in the exhilaration of his win, swept her up off her feet and swung her round.

'We did it, Princess! Did you see him? Wasn't he great?' he demanded with uncharacteristic fervour. Then he kissed her soundly on the cheek and restored her to her feet.

'This, I take it, is Mr Wakelin,' observed Lady Cresswell coolly, appearing at Lindsay's shoulder. She extended a beautifully manicured hand to Ross with the expression of one obliged to acknowledge a shamefully poor relation. Lindsay flushed unhappily and out of the corner of his eye, as he turned to Lady Cresswell, Ross saw James come forward to put a proprietorial arm around her shoulders.

Ross removed his crash cap, ran his fingers through his flattened hair and with his most charming smile said, 'A pleasure to meet you, ma'am.'

Lindsay's mother glanced sharply at him as if suspecting mockery, but encountering only unassumed friendliness, inclined her head regally. She was an attractive woman, well into middle age but with a figure many twenty-year-olds would have killed for, and a largely unlined face that was spoiled only by the 'holier than thou' expression it wore.

'Jolly well done!' Lindsay's father spoke from behind his wife; a position which Ross suspected he habitually occupied. 'Have you qualified for something big?'

'No, not even the area finals,' Ross admitted. 'And it's too late to qualify this year, but it's a start.'

James added his congratulations and gradually the gathering broke up, but not before Lindsay's father had kindly invited the American to share the family picnic, for which he earned a brief but decidedly hostile glare from his wife.

'Don't be silly, George. Mr Wakelin hasn't got time to sit around with us, he's far too busy,' she said smoothly, with a tight smile at Ross which dared him to disagree.

He almost wished he had got time to spare, just to see Her Ladyship's expression when he accepted, but unfortunately Danny was at that very moment fetching his next ride from the lorry. He declined politely and Lindsay and her family drifted away.

As Ross loosened Bishop's girth he wondered at the instant antipathy displayed by Lindsay's mother. Did she imagine that he posed a threat to her daughter's marriage to James Roberts and his sizeable fortune? Or was it just that she looked down on everyone outside her own social circle? In which case, his being American was probably the last straw.

He smiled inwardly. Lindsay's spontaneous display of affection could hardly have been more poorly timed, but as far as he was concerned she was welcome to repeat it whenever she liked.

11

The following Monday was the hottest day of the summer so far. The heat rolled across the countryside in heavy waves soon after dawn and settled in a smothering blanket on the dehydrated land. There had been no rain for several weeks and the grass was scorched brown and dusty. Ross had risen extra early and exercised the two horses in most need of it, riding one and leading the other, before the first feeding. As the morning wore on he pottered round the semi-deserted yard doing the odd jobs that got shelved on busier days.

He thought over Franklin Richmond's problem as he worked but got no further forward. His mind was like a dog chasing its tail; no matter how hard he tried, he always ended up back at the beginning.

Who hated Richmond enough that he or she, not content with steadily bleeding money from him, wanted to see him suffering real fear at the same time? Enough to do actual harm to his twelve-year-old son.

He gave up.

After all, if Franklin himself could think of nobody who bore him any particular grudge, then how on earth could Ross hope to, when he had only known the man a few short weeks?

Shortly after noon, Leo strolled into the yard having returned from heaven knew where on his motorbike. He was dressed, like Ross, in cut-off denims and a tee-shirt. He sauntered across the gravel and helped himself to a beer from the office fridge.

For perhaps half-an-hour he followed Ross around the yard, propping himself in doorways, watching as the American worked. He was silent, which was unusual for him, and Ross felt no inclination to make conversation. Leo's presence was vaguely annoying in itself, as doubtless it was intended to be, but he was careful not to let his irritation show.

Before the midday feeding, Ross remembered he had to change the dressing on a gash Flowergirl had sustained in the horsebox the previous day. It was a superficial tread wound low on the inside of her near hind, probably caused by overbalancing on a bend. Ross tied the mare up and crouched in the straw beside her, thankful as he did so that it wasn't Bishop he had to treat. He had removed the soiled bandage and dressing, and was inspecting the wound, when a shadow fell across him.

'Get out of my light,' Ross said irritably, looking

227

up to see Leo silhouetted in the doorway, hand cupped round a cigarette he was in the act of lighting. 'And put that damned thing out!'

Leo said pleasantly, 'You put it out,' and tossed the lighted match into the dry straw directly behind Flo.

With an oath, Ross pounced on the spot where he'd seen it fall, ignoring the brown mare's indignant leap forward.

The match was nowhere to be seen.

Hoping against hope that it had gone out as it fell, Ross scrambled to his feet and stamped furiously on all the straw in the vicinity. He was rewarded by a tiny wisp of smoke curling upward to extinction.

Leo moved away, chuckling, but Ross ignored him. First things first. Taking no chances, he scooped up the affected bedding and tossed it out on to the cobbles. Grabbing a water bucket, he doused the straw thoroughly. He had once been a witness to a stable fire in the States and once was one time too many.

Flo eyed him nervously from the depths of her box, straining to turn round but restricted by her headcollar rope. Unaware of the danger that had threatened, she regarded Ross' actions with astonishment.

To be on the safe side, he tipped the remaining water into the stable before untying the mare and shutting the door. Her dressing would have to wait. He had other, more pressing business to attend to and he was good and mad.

Leo was not in the yard or the tackroom and Ross finally tracked him down to the haybarn, where he was lounging on the unopened bales, beer can in one hand and cigarette in the other.

Without a word, Ross strode forward, plucked the glowing time bomb from his fingers and ground it out beneath his heel.

Leo laughed.

'Get out!' Ross hissed. 'Get the hell out of this yard and don't ever come back!'

'Why, Yank, don't get so excited. It isn't good for you,' Leo advised, wagging a finger in Ross' face as he slid off the bales to stand in front of him.

'That's where you're wrong,' he said, accompanying the last word with a punch that had many weeks of frustration behind it. Leo staggered back and sat down abruptly. 'It's *you* it's not good for,' Ross finished with immense satisfaction. 'Now get up, get your gear and get your stinking carcass out of my sight!'

Leo climbed to his feet, wiping blood from a split lip, and with an expression that would have frightened a gargoyle, pushed past Ross and trudged out into the bright sunlight.

Ross followed him closely, intending to see him off the premises before he could do any more damage, but Leo had other ideas.

With no warning, he shot through the doorway to the covered stables, and with a muttered oath, Ross darted after him. As his eyes adjusted to the dimness he saw Leo sprint away down the corridor and slip out of sight.

Ross slowed down warily. Leo was in the toolstore. Instinct screamed at him to go back out into the yard and find help but his conscience said, just as forcefully, that to leave Leo wandering around the stables in his present frame of mind was not an option. He had already shown that he had matches on him.

His heart thumping, Ross looked round for something with which to arm himself. For the first time since coming to Oakley Manor he regretted the almost fanatical neatness of Bill Scott's regime. The corridor was clear and uncluttered from end to end. In desperation Ross lifted down the leather headcollar and rope that hung outside the nearest stable door. A muscle tightened in his jaw as he stepped cautiously forward.

The toolstore was an open-fronted recess between the central two stables in the row. Ross stopped just short of the opening, palms wet and mouth dry.

A fly buzzed and settled, walking aimlessly across the windowpane on the far side of the passageway. One of the horses began to scrape at the floor impatiently, seeing Ross and expecting its food. Ross steeled himself and hitched an eye round the corner.

The shiny double tines of a pitchfork lanced out of the opening within inches of his face and buried themselves with considerable force in the wood of the window frame.

The first thing Ross had learned about fighting from his days on his uncle's ranch in Indiana was that attack is very much the best form of defence. The second was that there is no better time than right away. He swung his handful of leather, rope and metal as hard as he could round the brickwork at head height. He was rewarded by a grunt of pain, and ducked under the quivering pitchfork handle to follow up his advantage.

Leo had staggered back to the far wall with one hand clasped to the side of his head. When he saw Ross approaching he abandoned self-pity and, glancing round, snatched up a shovel.

Ross halted abruptly, a little over six feet from Leo, painfully aware of the inadequacy of his own weapon.

'Not a man to rub up the wrong way,' McKinnon had warned. Ross guessed he could count Leo well and truly 'rubbed'. Somehow the thought failed to amuse him. Fights he had had before, and plenty, but never to his knowledge had he faced anyone so intent on doing him serious physical harm.

To try and even out his disadvantage in terms of weaponry, Ross took the initiative. Swinging wildly at Leo's head once more, he let go of the headcollar and tried to grab the shovel instead.

It was a good plan as far as it went but unfortunately it didn't work. Leo dodged the headcollar and swung the shovel at Ross' head.

Because his wild lunge had closed the gap, Ross took most of the force of the blow on his shoulder before it glanced off and grazed his cheekbone. Undeterred, he reached for the shovel.

And missed.

Leo evaded his outstretched arm and hammered the back of the implement, with sickening force, into Ross' bad knee. With no further encouragement it gave way beneath him and he found himself with a worm's-eye view of the Victorian brick floor.

A blurred white object, coming to a halt not four inches from his nose, proved to be one of Leo's trainers, and with an undimmed instinct for survival, Ross rolled away and got to his feet.

At least, that was his intention. In reality he got no further than a half-crouch before collapsing again. He grasped his leg above the injured knee as if by pressure alone he could dim the searing pain.

Leo chuckled and, exhibiting a promising talent for sadism, put his foot none too gently on the ankle of the damaged leg.

Ross swore and made a grab for him, but he skipped lightly back out of reach, still laughing.

Ross was powerless. He couldn't stand and he knew any efforts he made to crawl or scramble would be given short shrift. He watched as Leo selected another pitchfork from the tools hanging in tidy rows at the back of the store. Slowly he came round in front of Ross, away from the wall, his back to the open corridor. He laughed again, enjoying the moment.

Ross watched him come, wondering with a strange detachment if Leo actually meant to kill him. The situation seemed unreal. It was midday, for goodness' sake! *Anybody* could come.

Anybody could come too late.

Ross swallowed, his gaze steady on Leo's dark face.

Slowly the malicious grin faded.

'Aren't you scared, Yank?' Leo hissed. 'Don't you think I'd do it?' The pitchfork jabbed at the air, inches from his face.

Christ! Ross thought. I believe you, you evil bastard! I only wish I didn't.

He was lying on his side, propped up on one elbow, and he could feel the sweat running down his back under his tee-shirt. His fascinated gaze didn't waver from the lethal, shiny tines of the fork.

'This time your effing dog isn't here to save you,' Leo sneered. 'I locked him in the office. It's just you and me, Yank, and soon it'll be just me.' He peered at the American, wanting a reaction. The pitchfork was almost touching Ross' face now. 'Aren't you going to beg? Try an' talk me out of it?'

If Ross had thought it would do any good, he would gladly have tried. As it was, he didn't bother. At least that way he kept his pride intact.

'Fuck you, Yank!' Leo snarled, and suddenly the threatening tines faltered and dropped. Ross' heart jumped heavily, painfully, acceptance making way for hope. Apparently Leo wasn't beyond thought. Much as he might have liked to murder Ross, it must have been obvious to him that he couldn't hope to get away with it.

Leo turned away and as he did so, Ross caught sight of a familiar, cream-suited figure in the corridor beyond. Leo saw him and raised the fork again just as Ross opened his mouth to shout a warning.

Any warning would have been aeons too late.

From his lowly position, Ross couldn't clearly see what followed. Leo stepped forward, brandishing the pitchfork menacingly, and then appeared to trip, his legs shooting from under him, and landed unceremoniously on the brickwork just feet from Ross. His head connected with the floor with an audible crack and he took no further interest in the proceedings.

Ross looked across to where he lay, eyes peacefully closed, and thought he had never looked better. With a sigh he transferred his gaze to Roland who stood holding the pitchfork in his immaculately manicured hands, wearing a slightly comical expression of surprise on his face.

'Well, I don't know how you did that, but — thanks,' Ross said gratefully.

'This old brickwork is treacherous,' Roland observed. 'I always said someone would do themselves an injury on it one day.'

'Yeah,' Ross said dryly. 'Well, thanks anyway.'

Roland propped the fork up against the wall and regarded Ross with interest. 'I say, are you all right?'

'Oh, sure, I like it down here,' Ross said, pain and exasperation lending sharpness to his tone. Why the hell couldn't the man drop the charade once in a while?

'Well, I should get up if I were you,' Roland advised. 'You'll get frightfully dirty.'

Ross was afraid that if he got up he'd almost certainly fall straight back down again and he didn't think he could handle that. Eyebrows raised, he held up a hand.

Roland's grip was firm, and he hauled Ross to his feet virtually effortlessly. Ross caught at his cream-suited arm with his free hand while he hopped and got his balance.

Roland watched his face.

'Is it your knee?' he asked.

Ross nodded. 'The bastard went for it on purpose,' he said through gritted teeth.

Roland grunted. 'No sense of fair play, the lower classes.'

Ross let go of Roland's arm and put his left foot experimentally to the floor. Pain lanced through his knee, up to his hip and down to his ankle. He paused, biting his lip, and then tried a little weight on it.

It was pretty sore but it didn't give way, which was encouraging. It meant that probably the damage was limited. No bones broken.

He looked up, catching for an instant an unreadable expression on Roland's usually bland face. Then the mask returned.

'What are we going to do with . . . ?' Ross gestured at Leo's prostrate form.

'Oh, I expect he'll be all right,' Roland said airily. 'He'll probably have a nasty headache, though. What did you do to upset him?'

'I hit him.' Ross told him briefly what had happened in the run-up to the confrontation. 'He was intent on making trouble. I don't know whether he was drunk or something . . .'

'Shouldn't be surprised,' Roland said. 'But the thing is, what do you want to do about it? Do you want to press charges? Attempted arson? Assault? Carrying a dangerous weapon? Do you want to call the police? Take it to court?'

Ross shook his head wearily. In a way it could be said that he had started it by hitting Leo. 'I just want to see the back of him,' he said with feeling. 'As soon as possible.'

Roland nodded. 'Then I suggest we get him back on his feet and send him on his way,' he said. 'I'll see to that. If I were you I'd go and put some ice on that knee. And on your face, for that matter.'

Surprised, Ross put an exploratory hand up to his face. His cheekbone felt bruised and tender and his fingers came away sticky with blood. He sighed.

Roland grimaced. 'Nasty business, fighting. Barbaric!' he said with a theatrical shudder. 'Bruised knuckles and bloody noses. So messy!'

Ross regarded the enigmatic Englishman for a moment, finding him apparently in earnest, and then, shaking his head, limped heavily out into the corridor, pausing briefly to look back at Roland, who waved him on.

Glad to leave Leo in his deceptively competent hands, Ross carried on. Encouragingly, the further he went, the less he felt his leg was in imminent danger of collapse, though he couldn't say it became any more comfortable.

In the doorway to the yard he met both Bill Scott and the dog.

'You haven't fed the horses,' the stable manager said accusingly, then noticed Ross' face. 'What the . . .?'

'I cut myself shaving,' Ross said facetiously.

Bill looked bewildered.

'Leo,' Ross told him, 'has outstayed his welcome.'

Bill frowned at the American. '*He* did that? Well, I'm not surprised. You always were determined to pick a quarrel with him, weren't you?'

This gross unfairness hit Ross like a punch under the ribs. He looked bleakly at Bill. 'Yeah, can't think why it took me so long,' he said.

Three-quarters of an hour, two ice packs, a bandage and a handful of painkillers later, Ross emerged from the cottage to see Leo strapping his possessions on to his motorbike.

Aside from his customary thunderous scowl, his saturnine features also sported a rapidly purpling bruise, courtesy of his contact with the toolstore floor. His hair and clothing looked suspiciously damp and it required little imagination to work out how Roland had restored him to consciousness.

At that moment, Leo looked up and caught sight of Ross. He let loose a string of adjectives, which fell a long way short of being complimentary, but made no move towards the American.

Ross regarded him calmly, feeling no real animosity, rather a sort of bewilderment.

What on earth made some men so needlessly aggressive? He compared Leo's unbridled violence with Roland's controlled force. Something prodded his memory back to the night of the prowler's visit. His assailant then had dispensed physical power with the same brand of cool efficiency the Colonel's son had just displayed with Leo. It seemed unbelievable that his upper-class-twit act could conceal a decisive mind and lightning reflexes, but then, Ross had long suspected that it concealed something – Lindsay had hinted as much – and the man *had* been in the army.

Whose side was he on now? Ross wondered. If it *had* been him that night, why hadn't he come forward when Ross challenged him? He must have recognised Ross by his accent. What legitimate reason could he possibly have had for sneaking round the stables after dark?

As Leo strapped the last of his belongings into place, Roland and Bill came out of the tackroom and across the yard towards Ross. Without further ado, Leo stood astride the bike and kicked it into life.

Ross moved a little closer to the cottage wall. He had no illusions concerning Leo's apparent capitulation. It would be very much his style to try and run Ross down on his way out, and in his current state, Ross felt he would probably succeed.

Leo swung the bike round in a sweeping curve and paused beside the American just as Bill and Roland reached him. His head was bare, his helmet looped over his wrist, and if looks could kill, Ross would have been cremated on the spot.

Leo transferred his attention to Bill Scott. He had a triumphant gleam in his eye that afforded the American a sudden stab of unease. He guessed then that Leo had engineered the whole series of events – up to the point where Roland had joined the game – even if he hadn't intended the violence to escalate in quite the way it had. Nevertheless, he had expected, and wanted, to be summarily dismissed. His suspicions were confirmed with Leo's first words.

'I was going to leave anyway,' he stated, his sneer even more marked than usual. 'I don't want your stinking job any more! I've had enough of working with a cripple whose nerves are shot! Nobody can make it big when he hits the bottle like your American wonder-boy here.'

Bill was staring intently at Leo.

He's taking it all in, damn him! Ross thought. The Colonel will get it all, word for word.

Leo hadn't finished. His voice rose to a shout to combat the noise of his motorbike as he revved it up.

'Didn't you wonder why he never went out? He didn't need to. He's got his own cache of whisky in his room. Some nights he's so far gone he can't even find his way to the bathroom! I wouldn't let him ride a fucking rocking horse!'

Having delivered his parting shot, he released the clutch and with a spurt of gravel, roared out of the yard and away up the lane. As the noise of the engine died away, the three remaining men stood in uncomfortable silence.

'Well?' Bill demanded. 'Is that true?'

Ross stared bleakly at the middle button on Bill's shirt, searching desperately for a way to make the truth sound convincing; but he knew it would sound like a feeble excuse to a man who was more than halfway to condemning him already. How to say that the whisky was purely medicinal? It sounded as lame as hell.

'You're going to take his word for it?' he asked bitterly. 'You've never seen me drunk, have you?'

'Perhaps I should have looked closer,' Bill retorted.

'I get the feeling it won't make any difference what I say,' Ross suggested softly.

Bill snorted in disgust. 'I knew it! I knew this would happen! I told the Colonel as much when he first mentioned you. You can't come back from something like that. It never works.' With a final scathing look at Ross, he turned and stomped away.

Ross watched him go and sighed gustily.

Roland slapped him on his bruised shoulder.

'Never mind, old boy. Life goes on,' he observed brightly.

Ross regarded him wearily, considering this fatuous, even by Roland's idiotic standards. He began to wonder if his earlier assumptions about the man's hidden depths weren't perhaps mistaken.

Ross hobbled through the rest of the day, trying to ignore Bill's open contempt. There was little to do in the yard until the six o'clock feeding and he retired to his room after lunch to take the weight off his leg.

Bill would probably think he was taking comfort from a bottle, he thought with bitter amusement. He had no doubt that the manager would waste no time in acquainting his employer with his version of the day's events.

After the evening meal, as was his custom on a Monday, Ross made his way to the Manor to spend an hour or so with the Colonel, going over the week's events and planning campaigns to come. They had, Ross felt, been gradually building up a good working relationship founded on mutual respect and he experienced a twinge of unease at the thought of the effect Bill Scott's report might have had on the Colonel's fledgling trust. The Colonel clearly thought a lot of Bill.

He wasn't over-worried about Leo's dismissal. He knew that the groom's behaviour hadn't gone unnoticed of late, and besides, the Colonel had given him the authority to make those decisions for himself.

Ross' walk up to the house, plagued by these thoughts and considerable pain from his knee, was not a pleasant one. Masters opened the front door, stiffly correct as usual, and showed him into the Colonel's study.

'The Colonel will be with you directly, sir,' he informed Ross quietly.

Ross nodded. The door clicked shut but in spite of his knee he didn't sit. His dog lay down and watched him anxiously while he wandered aimlessly round the room, looking with unseeing eyes at sporting prints and photographs he had seen a dozen times. The room had become comfortably familiar to him over the past few weeks and he rebelled violently against the thought that his future here could be in jeopardy.

A new photograph caught his eye. It had been enlarged and framed, and someone, presumably the Colonel, had written on the mount: 'Ross on Flowergirl – Gloucester', and dated it. For some reason it touched Ross. He put all negative thoughts from his head and prepared to do battle to preserve his career, if need be.

Shortly afterwards his employer joined him accompanied by the inevitable pack of dogs, poured drinks and waved Ross into a chair.

'So you fired Leo,' he commented without preamble. He settled back, sherry in hand. 'I'm not surprised.'

Ross looked across, hopefully.

'It was past time,' the Colonel continued. 'In fact, if you hadn't done it, I would have done it myself – though not, perhaps, in quite the same way. The thing is, we don't need that kind of disruptive force in our team, and he *was* disruptive, in spite of what Bill says.'

Ross took a sip of his sherry, hardly tasting it. 'What *does* Bill say?'

The Colonel cocked an eyebrow at him. 'Oh, he says, "Wakelin never tried to get on with Leo"; he says, "Wakelin hasn't completely got over his accident yet and probably never will"; he says, "Wakelin hasn't got the temperament for the jumping game".'

Ross studied his drink, swirling it round in his glass. Bill says too damn' much! he thought with a flash of annoyance.

'And what do *you* say?' he asked finally, feeling as though he was inviting the hangman to open the trapdoor.

The Colonel regarded Ross for a long moment, his grey hair tinged copper by the evening sun.

'I still say I judge as I see, and so far I've seen nothing to give me cause for worry.' He put down his hand to fondle the ears of his favourite spaniel. 'Is that what you wanted to hear?'

Ross nodded gratefully.

The Colonel shook his head, mildly exasperated. 'You still can't trust, can you? Look, Ross, I wouldn't have taken you on if I didn't think you were up to it, Lindsay or no Lindsay. The fact is, I liked what I saw, and I still do. And I think you are a lot tougher than Bill gives you credit for. But I understand why he thinks as he does and, given time, I think he'll come round.' He paused, taking a sip from his glass. 'The thing is, we're a man short now. I'll put an advert in *Horse and Hound* next week, but do you think we'll manage in the meantime?'

'In the yard, yes,' Ross replied. 'And if we can have Danny now the schools are breaking up, at the shows too.'

'Yes, I spoke to Bill about that. He wasn't

happy, but he agreed as a temporary measure. I said I would pay the lad, of course.'

'It's a shame he's so dead set against Danny making horses his career. The boy's a natural.'

'Mmm.' The Colonel gestured at the sherry decanter. 'Another drink?'

Ross hesitated, looking at his watch. 'I was going to visit Peter this evening if I had time . . .'

'Ah, yes. I really should go myself. The thing is, I hate bloody hospitals. Spent some time in one after the war. Bloody American pilot ran me down in a jeep.' He looked sideways at Ross, who hid a smile.

'No good offering you a lift, then?'

'No,' the Colonel agreed emphatically. 'But I suppose I ought to make the effort. Tell you what, no sense in us both taking cars. I'll get Masters to run the two of us up there. We can have another sherry while we're waiting.'

'In that case, thank you.' Ross held out his glass. Much longer working for the Colonel and he might even get to like the stuff.

12

Danny turned up early the morning after Leo left, exclaimed in admiration over Ross' impressively bruised face, and did his share of the stablework with refreshing enthusiasm. Sarah too looked relaxed and happy, an indication of just how much Leo's presence in the yard had bothered her. Bill was the only one who didn't seem happier for Leo's absence. He looked bitter and barely spoke a word to Ross.

In the morning Ross worked Simone and Ginger in the school and in spite of his own physical discomfort felt good about the sessions, his spirits rising like a lark on a summer's day.

In the afternoon, Lindsay arrived to ride, accompanied, surprisingly, by Roland. This provoked a lengthy debate as to which horse he should partner. He himself, when consulted, would only say maddeningly that they all looked the same to him, which provoked exasperation in Ross and a fit of the giggles in Lindsay.

Eventually they decided that Woodsmoke was the best bet for someone who was a little out of practice. Lindsay gave up Gypsy to Sarah, who adored her, and rode the impetuous Fly instead. Ross and Danny on Bishop and Clown made up the rest of the procession that eventually wound its way out of the yard and down the lane.

Roland gave no reason for his unprecedented desire to ride with them, and on such a hot afternoon, but kept Lindsay and Sarah in fits of laughter with tall tales from his past riding experiences.

Riding behind with Danny, Ross watched the immaculately clad figure ahead of him. Despite his clowning, the Colonel's son rode with easy competence. Ross himself found that by riding with longer stirrups than usual his knee was not too uncomfortable and the ride was, in general, a great success.

When they returned to the yard, Colonel Preston was there, talking to Bill. He broke off in astonishment when he saw his son amongst the cavalcade.

'Good God, Roland! Has the heat got to you?' he remarked acidly. 'I didn't think I'd ever see you on a horse again.'

Roland dismounted a little stiffly. 'Well, I hope you had a good look, Father dear,' he responded. 'I'm not intending to make a habit of it.'

The Colonel turned from contemplation of his disappointing offspring and spoke to Ross.

'I was just telling Bill I shan't make it to the show tomorrow after all,' he said with regret. 'Those bloody hippies are camped down by the copse. I've called the police and they say they're keeping an eye on them and if they're still there tomorrow will come and move them on, but the thing is, I'd better be here. We always get this problem this time of year. They come to Stonehenge for the solstice and then hang around for weeks. It's a bloody nuisance!'

'Did you know that hippopotamus means river horse?' Roland enquired of no one in particular. '*Hippos* meaning horse and *potamos* meaning river. It's from the Greek, you know.'

'Roland, stop it!' Lindsay hissed, trying not to laugh. 'They're hippies, not hippos.'

The Colonel favoured his son with a scathing glance, which Ross felt he richly deserved, and after visiting each of his horses, left the yard, followed shortly afterwards by Roland and Lindsay.

Ross contemplated a long evening of show preparation and tried to ignore the rhythmic stabs of pain in his knee.

Ross and Danny travelled up to the Three Counties Showground at Malvern in the early hours of the next morning.

On the way, Danny remembered a childhood game that involved inventing fictitious institutions and societies using the letters on vehicle number-plates. The game started with fairly sensible suggestions such as Retired Jockeys Home for RJH, but quickly degenerated into idiocy. SSH, the Society for Schizophrenic Hamsters, rounded it off as they drove on to the showground.

The show itself was a big one and at nine o'clock, when they parked the lorry and climbed down from the cab, the area was already abuzz with the frenetic activity so familiar to Ross.

Most of the schools had broken up for the summer and flustered mothers ran hither and thither, escorting pig-tailed offspring on precocious ponies, while long-legged hunters and jumpers stalked through the throng bearing solemn-faced competitors towards white-railed rings. Grooms and helpers scurried amongst the forest of equine limbs, collecting numbers, carrying tack and mono-grammed horse blankets, brushes, and forgotten whips and gloves. Several loudspeakers vied for air space and attention, and somewhere a fairground organ added its melodic strains to the confusion. Vans selling hot dogs, candyfloss, ice creams and doughnuts kept generators humming as queues already began to form.

Ross stretched his cramped back muscles and grinned at Danny.

'Once more into the breach, dear friend?' he suggested.

'Up and at 'em,' the boy agreed.

Clown came out for his first class with springheels and wide eyes. Every fence was an exciting new adventure, to be regarded with suspicion and cleared with a wild leap. Riding him was something like sitting on a grenade with a loose pin, but somehow Ross managed to steer him unscathed through two rounds and finished with a trophy and a red rosette.

Franklin Richmond, who had watched through the viewfinder of a video camera, met Ross with a warm handshake and a demand to know just how he had pulled it off.

Tongue in cheek, Ross told him that every round was meticulously planned down to the last detail and went back to the box to collect Barfly for the next class.

The fizzy chestnut brought him back to earth with a bump. Literally. A disagreement with the fifth fence left Ross to pick himself up off the dusty ground just in time to see his erstwhile partner exit the ring, tail flying like a banner and stirrups swinging crazily against his sides.

Ross managed an apologetic grin as Franklin met him in the collecting ring.

'I'd be interested to hear the plan behind that round,' Fly's owner remarked, clapping Ross on the back and laughing heartily.

'I asked for that, didn't I?' Ross admitted, loosening the chestnut's girth.

As he walked the sweating animal back to the horsebox, he heard the familiar tones of Harry Douglas being broadcast from the public address system in the main ring and his heart sank. The man seemed to be everywhere. Ross had already received dirty looks from Stephen today.

The day wore steadily on.

Danny and Ross had to work hard to keep up with a demanding schedule but the prevailing humour was good and that made up for the lack of manpower.

Only after lunch, when Ross was warming up Bishop for his first class, did a cloud appear on the horizon. In the distance, on the edge of the practice area, he spotted Leo talking to Stephen Douglas' groom. It rocked his concentration for a moment.

What on earth was *he* doing there?

He supposed he might be asking for work, although having obviously been dismissed from Oakley Manor wouldn't be the best of references. Ross hadn't spoken of the matter with anyone outside the yard and had asked Danny not to, but it would be evident that some disagreement had occurred. Grooms didn't normally leave their jobs abruptly, mid-season. A couple of riders Ross knew fairly well had commented on his scarred face but he had passed it off with a joke and no more was said. Uneasy, he nevertheless put Leo out of his mind and concentrated on the horse once more.

Bishop performed with his customary flair but lost the class to more experienced animals. Ross could only pat him and assure him that he'd done a good job and that his day would come. The big black flicked his ears to and fro, listening, and Ross tugged his mane affectionately.

Harry Douglas had been unable to find anything more derogatory to say than to imply that it was the

American's lack of experience rather than that of the horse that had cost them the class.

Having managed a creditable third behind Mick Colby and Stephen Douglas in Bishop's second class, Ross rode him back to the box to transfer on to Woodsmoke for the final class of the day. He was so tired he hardly noticed when a rider he knew from past shows deliberately turned his back. But when he rode past a neighbouring lorry and the two grooms beside it nudged each other and all but pointed, he became decidedly thoughtful.

'Danny, is there something I should know?' he asked as he reined in beside the Oakley Manor lorry. 'The way folks here are looking, I feel like the best-dressed man at a naturist convention.'

Danny didn't laugh.

'I think Leo's been talking,' he said unhappily. 'There's . . . well, a rumour going round. Amongst the grooms, that is.'

Ross slid off Bishop, gritting his teeth as his bad knee took his weight.

'What kind of rumour?'

'They're saying . . . well, look, I didn't really hear it all.' The boy dived into the box to fetch Woody.

'Danny!'

He reappeared and stood at the top of the ramp, twisting a cloth agitatedly between his hands.

'They say, some of them do, that your nerve has gone and you drink to keep going.' He dropped his gaze and plunged on. 'They say Leo found out and you threw him out. He's been showing his bruises and, well . . .'

251

'. . . they've seen my face too.' Ross finished it for him. He laughed harshly. 'I'd be pretty stupid to fire him if I wanted to keep him quiet, wouldn't I? Surely people aren't taking his word for it?'

Danny shook his head. 'No, not all of them.' He hesitated. 'Only some of them are jealous of you, I think, and . . .'

Ross sighed. 'Yeah, I get the picture. Well, I guess it'll blow over. Some other juicy bit of gossip will turn up and nobody'll think any more of it.'

While Danny finished getting Woodsmoke ready, Ross sat on the ramp and tried to ease the throbbing pain in his leg. The knee was badly swollen and the top of his leather riding boot had become desperately tight. Though he hated to do it, Ross took his pocketknife out of the tack box and carefully slit the stitching four inches down the back.

In the collecting ring again on Woody, Ross felt eyes boring into him from all directions. He tried to convince himself it was just his imagination, but to no avail. Several of the grooms and one or two of the riders were making no secret of their curiosity. It seemed the word was spreading like wildfire.

Stephen Douglas rode alongside the American and smiled sweetly.

'Sorry to hear of your little – ah – problem,' he said, unctuously. 'If there's anything I can do?'

Ross smiled in return. 'There is one thing,' he replied. 'But there are ladies about, so I'll tell you another time.'

Douglas was young enough to let his annoyance show. Unable to think of a suitable reply, he turned China Lily abruptly away.

Ross felt little satisfaction at having won that exchange. Stephen Douglas was a comparative innocent. Other tongues would not be so easily stilled and in spite of his confident prediction to Danny, he was not so sure that the matter would blow over quickly. Although he had made many friends, Douglas had friends too and Ross knew there was a certain amount of resentment at his stepping into a job many of them would have coveted. The deliberate misquotes in Harry Douglas' article had done him no favours either.

Whether his growing ill-humour communicated itself to the usually sedate Woodsmoke or whether he was just glad to be out of the lorry and working, Ross couldn't tell, but the old horse went like a dream. The class had attracted one or two international riders and in a hard-fought jump-off against the clock, Ross was astounded when the old campaigner managed second place. He lined up for the prize-giving feeling elated, and even Harry Douglas' condescending remark about a novice having a lucky day failed to dampen his pleasure.

Franklin Richmond was full of praise and, back at the box, Danny was over the moon. His joy was touching. He could hardly have been more enthusiastic had the success been his own.

Ross relinquished Woody to the boy and exchanged his black jacket, white shirt and stock thankfully for a cool tee-shirt, and boots and breeches for jeans and training shoes. This done, he climbed into the cab and collapsed along the bench seat, glad to leave Woodsmoke to be loaded by Danny and heartily wishing the boy was old enough to drive the box as well. His leg had definitely had enough for one day.

He closed his eyes, drearily considering the latest black mark against his battered reputation. He supposed the rumour *would* gradually fade and be forgotten with no further evidence to support it, but he could very well have done without it.

'I say, old boy.' The voice came from somewhere in the vicinity of his feet.

Ross raised his head.

'The old horse did rather well, don't you think?' the voice went on.

Ross blinked into the evening sunlight, trying to focus on a coolly handsome face under a white Panama. He had had no idea Roland was even on the showground.

'Oh, hi! Where did you spring from?'

'Got a lift up with a friend,' Roland said, as though it was the most natural thing in the world for someone who professed little interest in horses to make the journey halfway across England to visit a show. 'Thing is, can't go back with him. Wondered if you'd consider giving me a lift home?'

''Fraid not, old boy,' Ross mimicked him, shaking his head regretfully. 'But you can drive, if you want.'

Roland smiled happily. 'Love to,' he said. 'If I can just remember how . . .'

'Just follow the white lines and stop at the red lights,' Ross said dryly. 'You'll soon get the hang of it.'

In due course, with horses loaded and pulling at haynets, and Ross and Danny slumped in contented exhaustion beside him, Roland proceeded to handle the heavy lorry with the offhand expertise that characterised most things he did.

After ten minutes or so of silence, Danny initiated Roland into the numberplate game and badgered Ross to join in. The game continued fitfully for most of the journey, with the suggestions becoming steadily more far-fetched and decidedly more ribald, and they arrived home in good spirits. Roland displayed a needle-sharp wit and Danny rapidly warmed to him. Even Ross, in whom memory of past behaviour advised caution, found himself unable to withstand Roland's whimsical charm.

Thursday was quiet in the yard. The sky was overcast but the heat continued unabated; a sultry, energy-sapping warmth that rendered even the smallest of tasks a chore. They gave the horses only light exercise, and Ross and Sarah devoted the afternoon to tidying and cleaning the tackroom, which was one of the coolest places in the yard with its thick, windowless brick walls.

After the evening meal, Ross reluctantly gathered hammer and nails, and armed with the necessary posts and lengths of wood, headed for the schooling arena to mend a section of fence which Fly had thoughtfully demolished a couple of days earlier.

Ten minutes later, Lindsay and James appeared. Lindsay had intended taking advantage of the relative cool of the evening to school Gypsy over a fence or two but Ross suggested she use the cross-country course instead. It would be even cooler in the wood. Lindsay agreed cheerfully and departed to saddle up.

James hesitated, watching Ross' awkward attempts to hold a post and simultaneously drive it into the hard ground with a mallet.

'Here, let me help,' he said after a moment. 'You need three hands for that job.'

They worked steadily, side by side, saying little but companionable enough for all that. After a minute or two they heard Gypsy's hooves on the cobbles as Lindsay rode out of the yard. A quarter of an hour later, they stood back and surveyed their handiwork.

'A beer, I think,' Ross said, brushing sawdust and sand from his jeans. 'What d'you say?'

They crossed the school together, carrying the tools, but in an instant the tempting prospect of ice-cold beer was forgotten as with a sharp clatter of hooves Gypsy careered into the yard, riderless and trailing a broken rein.

One look at the horse was enough. Leaf mould and twiggery adorned her head and mane, and one knee was cut. Across her lower chest a horizontal wound showed scarlet.

'My God!' James turned a stricken face towards

Ross. 'Where did she go? Where *is* the cross-country course?'

'The copse. The other side of the home field.' Ross pointed, moving to catch Gypsy's rein as she tried to dodge past. James sped off in the direction he had indicated.

Ross swore. For the first time he felt his injury as a real handicap. Instinct urged him to run after James but common sense held him back. He would be no help to anyone if his knee let him down.

Clumsily he knotted Gypsy's broken reins as she whirled round him in agitated circles and, with an inelegant flying leap, launched himself at the saddle using her momentum to swing his leg over her back. Still held tightly, she made another frantic turn, then slipped and scrabbled on the cobbles as Ross drummed his heels into her sides.

As they burst into the home field, Ross could see James disappearing through the gate on the far side. He gave the mare her head and thundered in pursuit.

At the edge of the trees he reined her in hard and slid off. In the comparative gloom of the copse he could see James' pale shirt as he moved diagonally ahead. Beyond him, on the ground, a slight figure lay motionless. Ross' heart did a slow roll and started beating with heavy, rib-thumping strokes.

After tying Gypsy to the gate, he limped after James. He saw him crouch down beside Lindsay and heard her soft cry as she sat up and buried her face in his shoulder.

Ross stopped, relief giving way to a sharp stab of

envy. He laughed sardonically at himself. What had he expected? That she would turn to *him* in her distress? She was engaged to James, for God's sake! He turned away as the two embraced, feeling like a third person in a honeymoon suite. At his feet, deep sliding hoofmarks scored the earth, evidence of Gypsy's struggle to regain her feet. Lindsay must have been thrown well clear.

'Is she all right?' he called.

'Just winded, I think.' James looked at him over her blonde head.

Lindsay raised her face and smiled tremulously at Ross through tear-filled eyes. 'Gypsy?'

'Oh, she'll be okay. What happened exactly?' He was inspecting the jump at which the mare had fallen. It was a 'bullfinch', a double post and rail fence, in-filled with brush which extended a good three feet above it and was intended to be jumped through, rather than over. Not a difficult fence for an experienced horse and Gypsy was certainly that.

Lindsay shook her head. 'I don't know. She was going beautifully and then she took off and just . . . well, tipped over. I can't explain it.'

'I think I can.' Grimly, Ross reached down into the leaves at his feet and held up the frayed end of a six-foot length of rope. It would have been a simple matter to conceal it stretched in the midst of the brush.

'Ross!' Lindsay's eyes opened wide with shock. 'Who would do such a thing?'

Well, Leo for a start, Ross thought dryly, and possibly our nameless extortionist. He shook his head, his face registering only bewilderment.

'Kids, maybe? Or the Colonel's hippies? Whoever it was, it wasn't meant for you. Nobody could have known you'd be riding here tonight. You were just unlucky.'

'Ross!' The inflection had changed. The implication of what he had just said was not lost on her.

'Never mind, Princess,' he said quickly. 'Look, if you're sure you're okay, I'll take Gypsy on back. One white knight is enough for any damsel.'

The incident left him feeling unsettled and faintly troubled. If this *had* been Leo's work then his vendetta was beginning to assume far more serious dimensions than Ross had anticipated. In spite of the violence of his leaving, Ross had not really considered the possibility that Leo would take his feud further. It certainly hadn't occurred to him that those around him would also be at risk.

He shuddered to think how badly Lindsay might have been hurt if she hadn't been thrown clear. She could easily have broken her neck or been pinned beneath the falling horse, as he himself knew only too well. The sight of her, shocked and bruised, clinging to James for comfort, haunted him all evening.

James had taken Lindsay straight to her uncle, and the Colonel had called the police who, after a perfunctory survey of the scene, said they thought it unlikely they would ever find out who had been responsible.

They showed faint stirrings of interest when Ross told them briefly of Leo's angry departure, but beyond advocating a general tightening of security could offer no further advice.

Now Ross sat in his over-warm room with the window open behind him and the dog stretched companionably at his feet, fighting an almost overwhelming temptation to make 'medicinal' use of the bottle of whisky in his suitcase. His knee ached fiercely but without the kind of intense, stabbing pain that would justify recourse to alcohol.

You're getting soft, he told himself severely.

In the end he compromised by making coffee with a shot incorporated and fell asleep on top of the bed, clad only in shorts and praying for a storm to clear the air.

Friday dawned with the same unremitting heat. Breakfast was interrupted by a call from the Colonel who said he'd had word of a dealer with a couple of useful young horses. Ross and Bill were to accompany him to look them over that afternoon.

Ross received the news with a decided upturn in spirits. New horses in the yard would help lay any rumours to rest.

At lunchtime he had a call from Franklin Richmond, inviting him out for a meal that evening, ostensibly to celebrate the success of his horses at the Three Counties. They agreed a time and place and Richmond rang off, leaving Ross to wonder if this meant there had been new developments in the war against Mr X.

Ross, Bill and the Colonel travelled to the dealer's yard in the Land-Rover rather than the Jag, to avoid appearing too obviously affluent. As they got out they were hailed from across the yard by an ageless, wiry, ginger-haired man who introduced himself as Declan O'Connell. He was as Irish as the Blarney Stone and, Ross decided, had probably been born with his lips pressed firmly against it. He greeted them all warmly and proceeded to give them a potted autobiography as an assurance of his fitness to judge good horseflesh.

According to O'Connell he had once been a steeplechase jockey of quite remarkable talent, and if it hadn't been for an equally remarkable run of bad luck he would surely have been Champion Jockey several times over in the late-seventies.

The Colonel allowed himself to be outwardly impressed by the Irishman's history but at one point, when Ross caught his eye, smiled and winked surreptitiously.

Even if one did believe all O'Connell said, Ross couldn't see that knowing a good horse was any guarantee you were selling one.

Whatever the case, the Irishman seemed good-natured and was highly amusing. One glance at Bill, however, showed that *he* didn't consider him so, at all. He was trailing behind the others, looking distinctly sour.

The yard was on the shabby side of average, with grass sprouting through cracks in the concrete underfoot. Most of the stable doors had dropped on their hinges and been chewed along the top by countless equine teeth, and the sprawling manure heap by the gate would have kept Kew Gardens in compost for the foreseeable future. Stable cats abounded, as presumably did mice, and several Jack Russell terriers followed the four of them around.

However, the occupants of these doubtful premises shone in their deep, peaty beds like diamonds in a coal cellar, radiating health and contentment.

Several of these gems were already saddled, and when the visitors had completed their tour of the yard, the horses were taken, one at a time, to a jumping ring behind the stables for Ross to try their paces.

Of these five horses two showed not more than average scope over the schooling fences, two were promising, and one did its best to scrape Ross off on the perimeter fence and declined to leave the ground at all. Of the two promising youngsters, one was regretfully discounted as not being quite up to Ross' weight, but the other, a big, deep-chested grey, was felt to be a definite possibility.

'What's the story on the brown gelding?' Ross enquired of O'Connell. Its unreasonable behaviour had aroused his interest.

'Well, you see, it's like this . . .' the Irishman began.

'The real story,' Ross cut in quickly. 'Straight up.'

Briefly, O'Connell affected hurt, then gave in.

'Straight up? All right then. To tell you the truth,

I don't know. He came to me with two others, half-brothers they were, the lot of 'em. The others jumped like stags, but him? Well, you found out for yourself. In the open, over hedges and the like, he's a grand little fella. But give him a wall alongside and you can say a fond fare-thee-well to the skin on your knees.' He shook his red head sadly. 'I almost sold him twice, but back he came like a bad penny.'

'Well, it was good of you to warn me,' Ross said with heavy sarcasm.

'I keep hoping he'll maybe take a shine to someone and behave hisself,' O'Connell explained sheepishly. 'I could see you could take care of yourself by the way you rode the others.'

Ross raised a disbelieving eyebrow at this and drew the Colonel to one side for a moment to make a suggestion. His employer nodded a time or two, then turned to O'Connell.

'We'll take the grey, subject to vetting,' he announced. 'And we'll take the brown gelding for half what you're asking and after fourteen days' trial.'

'Ah, you drive a hard bargain,' O'Connell complained, peevishly.

'Take it or leave it,' the Colonel offered. 'For my part, I think he's probably a waste of time anyway.'

'Well now, let's not be too hasty,' O'Connell suggested. 'He's a valuable horse but let nobody say I'm not a fair man. Add a hundred guineas and we've got a deal.'

The Colonel beat him down to seventy-five and they shook hands on it.

'I hope you know what you're doing,' Bill muttered from behind Ross, who ignored him. He didn't give a damn what Bill Scott thought any more.

O'Connell walked the Colonel back to the Land-Rover and then turned to say goodbye to Ross and Bill.

'Nice to be meeting you, Ross. And good luck to you.' He turned to Bill then and as they shook hands a light of recognition dawned in his face.

'Scott . . . *Bill* Scott!' he said on a note of discovery. 'Of course! I knew the name was familiar.'

He glanced at Ross. 'This fella was the brightest young talent on the steeplechasing circuit when I made my debut as an amateur. I used to copy the way he rode a finish. "The Flying Scott" we called him. Rode like there was no tomorrow. We were all convinced he'd be Champion Jockey one day and he would've been too if it hadn't been for that accident . . . How're you doing now, Bill? It's grand to see you.'

Far from looking as though the pleasure was mutual, Bill murmured something unintelligible and stared at his feet.

Declan O'Connell appeared not to notice. He managed to recall several occasions when the two of them had raced side by side, and various thrilling incidents they had shared. Bill had obviously either forgotten them or wished to be allowed to, for he edged inexorably towards the Land-Rover, and as soon as was politely possible, if not a little before, took his leave of the Irishman.

On the way back, Ross pondered Bill's obvious reluctance to talk to his fellow ex-jockey, and after they had dropped the Colonel at his front door said conversationally, 'You didn't tell me you'd ridden in the Grand National.'

'It had nothing to do with you,' Bill said in a tone that discouraged further comment.

Ross ignored the warning signals. Bill had never spared *his* feelings and he saw no reason to be charitable in return.

'Why *did* you stop racing?' he persisted. 'Was it because of the accident he spoke of?'

'Mind your own bloody business!' Bill snarled. 'And keep your nose out of mine.'

'I take it you don't want to talk,' Ross observed mildly.

Bill didn't bother to answer.

At the yard, Ross was met with the information that Franklin had rung back and rescheduled their meal for half-an-hour later. Quite frankly, he was relieved, as there was still a fair amount of preparation to be done for the following day's show.

At half-past seven, when Ross had to forsake the yard for a bath and a change of clothes, Sarah and Danny were still going strong, Sarah quietly flapping because she was expecting Darcy Richmond to arrive within the hour to take her out for a drink and she wanted time to change.

Just after eight, scrubbed and more presentably dressed, Ross climbed into the jeep and set off, written directions in hand, for a country pub called the Dovecote, a gourmet's delight apparently, hidden deep in the Wiltshire countryside.

Barely a mile up the road, he cursed and slammed on the brakes. He had forgotten the one thing Franklin had asked him to bring – Clown's trophy and rosette from the Three Counties, for Peter. He'd put them in his room ready to take, and then walked out without them.

Cursing, he backed down the road and into a field gateway to turn, then headed at top speed back to the yard.

Leaving the engine running and the dog in the back, he raced through the door and took the stairs two at a time. His door was unlocked, and making a mental note to remember to lock it on the way out, Ross pushed it open and strode in.

A noise and a half-seen movement on the periphery of his vision caused him to turn his head but the action was never completed. Something hit him hard just above his left ear and he was out cold before he hit the floor.

Ross had been knocked out several times before and it was a breeze. It was the coming round that was tiresome.

This time, hearing returned first, but for a few moments the sounds were muffled and confused. He became aware that he was lying on something soft and thought he must be in bed.

Was it morning already? he wondered muzzily. What day was it?

He heard a movement to his right and opened his eyes, turning towards it.

Shades of colour swam about, making no sense at all. He blinked. Somebody was approaching. Memory returned and alarm bells rang. He blinked again and struggled to focus, feeling desperately vulnerable. The figure, slightly clearer now, came closer. Ross felt he ought to try and move.

'I should lie still if I were you, old boy,' an unmistakable voice advised him. 'You don't look at all the thing.'

Ross closed his eyes and opened them slowly.

That was better. His vision was ninety-five per cent but with it came a crashing headache. He groaned and closed his eyes again. He was lying on the big settee in his bedsit. For some reason that he couldn't be bothered to wrestle with, Roland was there and he was holding . . .

Ross' eyes snapped open and he sat up. The room swam briefly then steadied. Roland was holding the smug-faced, mahogany Buddha which Ross had recently taken to using as a doorstop.

'Found this on the floor at the top of the stairs,' Roland said, noticing the direction of the American's gaze. 'The archetypal blunt instrument.'

Ross regarded it with disfavour. 'I never did like that thing,' he said with feeling. His head had cleared now and the worst of the pain subsided, leaving in its place a dull ache.

His first thought on seeing Roland casually holding the Buddha had been one of suspicion but common sense quickly intervened; after all, if Roland had just attacked him from behind the door, he would hardly carry him to the sofa and wait around for him to recover consciousness, would he? *Or would he?*

Ross wasn't sure. He looked at his watch and was surprised to find that only twenty minutes had passed since he had originally set out for his meeting with Franklin Richmond.

'I don't think you can have been unconscious for long,' Roland said, divining his thoughts.

'I don't suppose you saw anyone leaving?' Ross asked without much hope.

Roland shook his head. ''Fraid not, old chap. I came down to the yard – looking for you, as a matter of fact – and saw your jeep outside with the engine running. I stopped for a chat with Darcy, who'd just come to pick Sarah up, only she wasn't ready. When you didn't appear, I came on up. I seem to be making a habit of picking up the pieces, metaphorically speaking,' he added thoughtfully.

'And you didn't see anybody?'

'Not a soul. Turned the jeep engine off, though,' he added, with the air of a child expecting to be praised for its initiative.

'Thank you,' Ross said wearily.

'Not at all, old boy. Least I could do.'

'I must say you're taking this all very calmly,' Ross observed. 'Everyday occurrence in the antiques trade, is it?'

Roland's grey eyes narrowed momentarily. 'Military family. In the army myself, y'know.

Besides, you're not exactly a gibbering wreck, yourself.'

'I haven't the energy.' Ross looked round the room. 'Well, it would seem I disturbed a burglar. I can't imagine what they thought I had worth stealing.'

'A burglar?' Roland was on his way to the bathroom. He returned with a towel, dripping water. 'Here, this may help. A burglar, you say? In broad daylight?'

'What else?' Ross held the blissfully cold wad to his head, watching Roland closely all the while.

He shrugged. 'You're probably right, old boy. Thing is, are you going to call the police? Ought to really, you know.'

Ross groaned. 'No, I don't think so. I couldn't face them right now. By the way, what was it you wanted me for?'

Roland looked momentarily lost. 'Oh, nothing that can't wait. Don't you think you ought to see a doctor?'

'Probably, but I guess I'll survive. I'm already late for a dinner date.' Cautiously, he stood up. His vision fragmented then cleared.

'You'd better let me drive you,' Roland said, regarding him with a judicious eye. 'Are you going like that?'

Water had run down Ross' neck and soaked his cotton shirt.

'It'll dry.' He took a comb from his pocket and, discarding the soggy towel, gingerly tidied his hair.

His scalp was sore but the skin seemed unbroken. He thanked providence for a thick skull.

Even though he was not sure he entirely believed Roland's version of events, he accepted his offer of a lift with gratitude. His head still felt muzzy, and after all, if the Colonel's son *had* been his assailant – for whatever reason – and had wanted to do him lasting harm, he had had ample opportunity.

When they reached the yard, Sarah was just leaving with Darcy. She waved and Ross felt strangely as though time had stood still for the last half-hour or so. He put the jeep back in its parking space behind the cottage while Roland went to fetch his own car.

The Colonel's son drove his white Aston Martin at speed with casual brilliance and a fine disregard for other road users. Ross gritted his teeth and almost wished he had elected to drive himself after all. All the same, Roland deposited him safely in the car park of the Dovecote barely ten minutes later than the appointed time.

Ross thanked him and said he would call a taxi for the return journey.

He'd been undecided as to whether to mention the attack to Richmond, as he couldn't see what connection it could possibly have with Franklin's problems, but in the event, the decision was taken from him.

Franklin took in Ross' slight pallor and still damp shirt and instantly wanted to know what had happened. Ross told him the whole story, backtracking to Leo's departure and including Lindsay's fall.

'Is she all right?' Franklin asked, concerned.

Ross nodded. 'I rang earlier. She's a bit bruised but otherwise okay. She was lucky.'

'And you think it was Leo?'

He nodded again.

'And tonight?'

'I can't think who else,' Ross said, an image of Roland holding the Buddha flashing across his mind.

Franklin shook his head in disbelief. 'He must be unhinged, Ross. He could have killed you.'

Ross was already uncomfortably aware of that. Had Roland in fact saved his life by coming up to find him when he had?

It was only a relatively short drop from the window at the back of his room into the sand of the schooling area. Very easy for somebody to leave that way if they wished to remain unseen. The window had been open; it almost always was in this heat. On the other hand, Roland had said he'd found the Buddha at the top of the stairs . . .

The waiter materialised bearing their drinks and took their food orders, apparently memorising them along with those of two neighbouring tables.

'So, what are you going to do about him?' Franklin asked when they were alone once more.

Ross shrugged. 'What *can* I do? I've no proof and no idea why he should be in my room. If he was after money, he'll have been disappointed, that's for sure. I presume he didn't intend to attack me. If he saw me go out, he would've thought he was safe for a while, but then I charged back in like a stampeding rhino.'

'What if he comes back?'

Ross chuckled. 'If he tries again this evening, he'll wish he hadn't. I left old Fido on guard!'

'Seriously, though. If he's determined, he might have another try. You'd better be careful.'

'Oh, I will,' Ross promised. 'I need another dose of Leo like I need a hole in the head! He's already been busy spreading malicious rumours.' He told the businessman about Leo's efforts at the show.

Franklin was thoughtful, and later, as they tackled an excellent game pie, he sighed heavily. 'You know, I can't help feeling that it's a shame our friend Leo has such a cast-iron alibi for the time Bellboy was killed. It would be so neat if he was our man. From what you say, and what McKinnon tells me, he's ruthless enough.'

'He's nowhere near smart enough, though,' Ross pointed out. 'His idea of subtlety is a smack in the face. Your guy is devious. He's not so hot-blooded; prepared to take his time.'

'That's what makes him so frightening,' Franklin agreed. 'And so difficult to stop. And added to that, if he's as keyed in to what's going on as we think he is, he could quite possibly use Leo's mischief-making to cover his own tracks.'

Ross nodded, feeling depressed. He'd thought of that. 'I'm supposed to be helping you, not adding to your problems,' he apologised.

'It's hardly your fault,' Franklin protested.

'Look, I'm going to ask McKinnon to put a man on Leo. See if we can't catch him in the act.'

Ross stopped chewing in surprise. 'You don't have to do that,' he protested. 'You've got enough problems of your own.'

A smile hovered about Franklin's mouth.

'You *are* my problem, if you'll excuse the terminology,' he said. 'I have a vested interest in your career, remember? I need someone to ride my horses and you happen to fit the bill rather well. I don't intend to let a psychopathic ex-groom jeopardise my chances of seeing my horses jump at Olympia.'

13

The two-day show at the weekend passed off with reasonable performances from all the horses that attended, even Ginger, although none of them was quite good enough on the day to carry off a prize.

Ross was content. In all honesty, you had to expect more days like that than not.

Leo was again at the show and doing his work well. Several of Ross' friends and acquaintances came up to him, openly expressing disbelief at his ex-groom's claims. Many more, unfortunately, turned their backs on him or made disparaging remarks that he was somehow able to overhear.

'Well, it's a good way to whittle down your Christmas card list,' Ross remarked dryly to Mick Colby, who was one of those who dismissed Leo's vicious rumour-mongering for what it was.

'I must try it,' the Englishman joked. 'But honestly, you'd think people would believe the evidence of their eyes, not the word of some spiteful moron who's obviously got an axe to grind. And it's not as if he's doing himself any good by it. People may listen to him but he won't win himself any friends, and he can kiss any idea of another groom's job goodbye!'

'My heart bleeds for him,' Ross murmured.

Danielle rode alongside the pair, glancing archly through her lashes.

'And who are you kissing goodbye, Mick?' She pronounced his name 'Meek' and judging by the look in his eyes, he didn't mind a bit.

'Depends who's offering,' he responded swiftly.

'Oh, I'll ask around for you, if you like,' Danielle informed him coyly as she rode on by.

'The little minx!' Mick breathed, grinning.

Ross philosophically regarded this cementing of friendships as the silver lining to Leo's cloud.

It was hard to be philosophical, however, when on Monday morning Bill Scott passed the *Sportsman* across the breakfast table. He said nothing but the look in his eyes warned Ross that something was amiss.

The paper was open on the equestrian pages and there, amidst reports on the flat racing season and the World Dressage Championships, was Harry Douglas' column. On this occasion it bore the headline STRESS AND THE COMPETITION RIDER.

Ross read on with a deep sense of misgiving.

The article began by citing the recent, tragic case

of a flat-racing jockey who had never quite regained the winning edge after suffering a totally unexpected fall. The article went on:

It is not always the extent of injuries that determines the severity of an accident, more the level of trauma or shock suffered.

Some jockeys, three-day-event and show-jumping riders thrive on high levels of risk – others ignore it or find ways to deal with it. Most methods are harmless, such as one rider who uses yogic meditation to improve his physical and mental balance, and others who play golf or racket sports to help them wind down and relax between competitions.

Unfortunately, there will always be a few who can find no safe way to cope with the stresses of competing in these unavoidably hazardous sports. These few, and they are only a few, will either take the sensible option of retirement or, regrettably, resort to artificial stimulants such as alcohol or drugs to help them through. Neither is a lasting solution, of course. Sooner or later, each one of them will be found out and will face the censure and pity of their fellow competitors.

So are we asking too much of our horses and horsemen? No, I don't think so. In my opinion it is up to each individual and those around them to recognise their own limitations and withdraw from competition before they endanger themselves, their horses or, as in a case overseas last year, the spectators.

'Well?' Bill was obviously awaiting a reaction.

'Well, what?' Ross enquired coolly, putting the paper down. Inside, he was seething.

'Well, that's you, isn't it?' the stable manager stated baldly. 'That bit about the case overseas . . . that's you.'

'Bill!' Maggie looked unhappy.

'Well, it is. Anyone can see that.'

'I don't think it mentions my name,' Ross said, helping himself to a slice of toast.

Bill grunted. 'He doesn't need to.'

'Nobody will take any notice, Ross. You'll see.' Maggie smiled encouragingly at him. 'All the same, he shouldn't be allowed to write things like that. And to think, he used to come and drink coffee at this very table when Stephen was here.'

'Yeah, well, it's not worth worrying about,' Ross said.

All the same, it rankled. Douglas' raking over the ashes of the incident in the States was well below the belt.

There *had* been casualties amongst the onlookers when his horse had somersaulted into the crowd that day, although they hadn't told him right away. Most were minor, but one ten-year-old girl had suffered damage to her spine and was now confined to a wheelchair. He had visited the child in hospital until her mother had found out and screamed abuse at him.

Many a time when Ross rode into the ring he thought of that little girl, and her thin, brave face regularly haunted his dreams, but to suggest that he could in some way have prevented it . . .

Bitterness welled up and he pushed aside his plate, got up and made for the door. He felt, rather than saw, Bill's scornful expression as he left the room.

To avoid the sticky heat, Ross made for the cool twilight of the tackroom. Before he reached it, however, a Mercedes convertible swept into the yard bearing James and Lindsay.

'Ross!' Lindsay jumped out of the car as it stopped, looking, to the American's eyes, totally adorable in floral print trousers and a cropped, lacy top.

'Hello, Princess,' he greeted her, smiling lazily.

'Ross! Have you read it?'

Ross sighed and nodded. 'I have.'

'Well?' she demanded.

He groaned. 'Don't you start!'

'But it's not fair!' Lindsay protested, her wide, blue-grey eyes searching his face.

Ross was aware of a strong urge to take her upturned face in his hands and kiss it soundly. He stifled the impulse. He didn't think even James' tolerance would stretch that far.

'Life's *not* fair, Princess,' he said gently.

'Oh, don't be so bloody laid-back!' she said explosively. 'I know you better than that. You're hopping mad, deep down. So, what are you going to do about it? Nobody could blame you for what happened to that child.'

'Her mother did,' Ross observed. She had plagued him with vicious telephone calls and letters for weeks.

'But that was different. She was emotionally disturbed. She'd a history of it. The father didn't blame you. This article is wicked. It's libellous. You should do something!'

'It's only libel if he mentions my name,' Ross pointed out.

'Oh!' Lindsay all but stamped her foot. 'Don't you *care*?' she demanded despairingly.

'Lindsay,' James put his arm round her, 'Ross is right. The best thing to do with this kind of spite is to ignore it.'

'But it's so unfair,' she protested again in a quieter voice.

'So how are you feeling?' Ross changed the subject. 'Any ill effects from your fall?'

'I'm fine.' Her tone said it was not her that needed looking after.

'Can I get you a coffee or anything?' Ross looked from one to the other.

'Er, no, thanks all the same,' James answered for them both. 'We're just on our way out for the day. We really only called in to give you this. We've just been up to the house with the Colonel's.'

Ross looked down at the silver-edged envelope James was passing to him. His heart sank.

'It's our formal engagement party. Two weeks' time. I hope you can come.' James said earnestly, giving Lindsay's shoulder a squeeze.

Ross forced a smile. 'Congratulations! And

thank you. Though I don't know what I can wear. I don't think I packed my tux.'

'It doesn't matter. Anything will do,' James assured him cheerfully.

'Oh, I'll come as I am, then,' Ross joked, gesturing at his ragged, cut-off jeans and almost wishing he dared, just to see Lady Cresswell's face.

When they left, shortly after, he stood staring despondently at the unopened envelope in his hand and wondered what possible excuse he could find for not attending.

The wedding itself he refused to contemplate.

As the week advanced there were signs of the long-awaited break in the weather. Although it was still very warm, a fitful breeze sprang up and clouds of promising dimensions began to haunt the horizons.

The Oakley Manor horses attended the regular mid-week show at Lea Farm. Ross decided to give the bigger classes a rest and thus also Bishop and Woodsmoke. With Flowergirl and Simone he attacked the speed classes and all but swept the board. With Fly, on the other hand, he demolished practically the entire course in two novice classes and resigned himself to returning to the drawing board.

During a short breathing space between classes, Ross was sitting on the horsebox ramp trying not to mind the various cold shoulders being turned to him, when he was hailed by a familiar foghorn voice. He looked up.

'Annie!' he exclaimed with genuine pleasure. 'Good to see you!'

'Prove it to me. Buy me a drink!'

'Sure.' Ross located Danny and explained. Then, with Annie's burly figure striding beside him, he made his way to the refreshment room overlooking the indoor arena.

'Your leg's no better, I see,' she remarked as they ordered beer and made their way to an unoccupied table.

'It had a slight set-back,' he admitted.

'You ought to get it looked at again. Physiotherapy might help.'

'No, thank you! I've had a bellyful of that.'

'Coward!' she teased. 'You men are all chicken-hearted.'

'Yeah, that's me,' Ross acknowledged blandly. 'You must have been listening to the rumours. In fact, I'm surprised you want to be seen with me.'

Annie tossed her beribboned pigtails. 'Self-pity is disgusting,' she stated bluntly.

'Ain't that the truth?' he agreed with a grin.

'Anyway,' she continued, 'what does the Colonel think about it? Can't see him taking much notice of rumours.'

'The Colonel is a law unto himself. Bill, though, is another matter.'

'Well, that's not altogether surprising, is it? In the circumstances, I mean,' Annie remarked.

'Why, exactly?' Ross was bewildered.

'I should have thought that was pretty obvious,'

she said, scanning his face. 'Don't tell me nobody ever told you about Bill?'

Ross shook his head.

'Well, isn't that bloody marvellous?' she demanded. 'You of all people should have been told. You see, at your age, Bill Scott was a top-flight steeplechase jockey, much in demand. He was known for his almost ruthless determination. In fact, there were those who wouldn't have him ride their horses because they thought he'd give them too hard a race. I don't think he would have. He lived to win, but he's always had a genuine love for horses too.

'Anyway, he was bold, "The Flying Scott". Then, just as he was having the best season of his career and was well on the way to becoming Champion Jockey, it all fell apart.

'He had a fall. No different from many others he'd had by all accounts, but something in him changed and he never rode the same way again. In fact, he didn't even finish the season, as I recall. He trailed in last on several rated horses and the owners began to look elsewhere. Loyalty is short-lived where that sort of thing's concerned. Everybody was very sorry for him, but nobody wants to be associated with a failure.'

'Don't I know it?' Ross murmured. Now, Bill's vehement stand against his son's dreams of becoming a jockey made sense.

'Yes, well, Bill has never forgiven himself. Feels he let everybody down. I don't think he's been on a racetrack since he retired. He drifted in and out of jobs with Maggie patiently in tow, until eight years ago when the Colonel offered him his present position. Bill grasped the chance with both hands. He'd reached a real low point and it was like a gift from heaven. A chance to regain his self-esteem and be part of a team that was really going places. And, all credit to him, he's done his job well.' Annie paused and looked apologetically at Ross. 'And that's where you came in . . .'

He made an ironic face. 'A Yank with a shaky reputation?'

'Exactly.' She nodded. 'He was against your coming and made no secret of it. He's convinced that history is about to repeat itself. Thinks you're him all over again. He's wrong, of course.'

Ross looked up. 'You're so sure?'

Annie smiled. 'Oh yes. You're so bloody proud, you'd fight to the death before you'd give in.'

He laughed, embarrassed. 'Thanks . . . I think.' He looked at his watch and pushed back his chair. 'Look, I've got to go. Thanks for telling me about Bill.'

'It's about time you knew. Past time, if you ask me. But, Ross . . . try not to blame him. He's afraid that you're going down and will drag him down with you. We're all afraid of failing, you know. It's just we don't all define failure the same way.'

Ross paused. 'I don't blame Bill,' he said wearily. 'But fighting a war is hard enough without having partisans in the camp.'

'He'll come round,' Annie said confidently. 'He

only wants the best for the yard. He just doesn't realise yet that you *are* the best.'

Thursday morning found Ross heavy-eyed and irritable after a disturbed night. A break in the weather was long overdue. The atmosphere was almost unbearably humid again, and horses and humans alike were tetchy and ill-humoured.

Simone trod on Danny's foot, causing him to hobble for the rest of the day, and Bishop bit Ross when he was saddling up. Bill was unremittingly morose, and Ross found that understanding the reasons behind the ex-jockey's attitude was of little or no help when it came to living with it.

The Colonel sent word at lunchtime that the two horses from O'Connell's yard would be arriving the next morning, which did nothing to sweeten Bill's mood.

'Why you want to waste your time on a no-hoper like that brown horse, I really don't know,' he grumbled. 'It's not as if you've sorted out the ones we've already got.'

Ross ignored him.

'If you ask me, that animal will break somebody's leg on a wall before it's done,' Bill went on. 'It's just asking for trouble.'

'Well, you needn't worry. I won't ask you to ride it,' Ross said bluntly.

Bill stared hard at him, then coloured. 'I've got better things to do with my time,' he muttered, and got up and left the room.

Maggie watched him go, then looked at Ross unhappily.

The American sighed. 'Yeah, I know. I shouldn't have said it. I'm sorry.'

'But he asked for it!' Danny burst out. 'He's always needling you.'

'Danny!' His mother tapped him on the shoulder as she rose to fetch more coffee. 'Stay out of it.' She poured some for Ross and Sarah, and sat down again.

'That Leo Jackson seems to have fallen on his feet,' she observed, with her usual flair for dismissing uncomfortable subjects.

'Oh?' Ross was deliberately casual.

'Yes, apparently he's got a room at the Six Bells, down in the village. You wouldn't have thought he could afford it, would you? He never seemed over-blessed with money, the way he dressed and such. And having no job now . . .'

'Where did you hear this?'

'My friend from bingo works in the kitchen there,' Maggie confided, pleased to have diverted Ross' attention from Bill's behaviour. 'They're not cheap, you know. They've won awards and such. She says Leo isn't much liked but spends a lot in the bar and restaurant, so he's tolerated. She says he's not working, not regular anyway, so where does he get his money?'

Ross wondered if any of Leo's fellow guests were missing their valuables. Though, if that were his game, he couldn't hope to maintain it for long in one place. He shook his head, puzzled.

285

Later that afternoon, as Ross hosed Fly down after a long and frustrating session in the school, Franklin Richmond drove into the yard.

'Hello, Ross. How's our juvenile delinquent coming along?'

Ross rolled his eyes heavenwards. 'Don't ask.'

'What do you think the problem is?' Franklin asked, seriously. 'Lack of scope?'

'Attitude,' Ross said bluntly. 'He's got bags of ability but he just won't apply himself. He just doesn't give a damn.'

'A lost cause?' the businessman asked resignedly.

'Well, he might get better with age, but I wouldn't put money on it. I don't think you can give a horse a conscience. They either have one or they don't. This fella hasn't.'

Franklin sighed, following Ross as he led the disappointing animal inside.

'What do you suggest, then?'

'Personally, I wouldn't waste any more time and money on him,' Ross said. 'He may improve, but he'll never have the temperament to make it to the top. I'm sorry, but you did ask.'

'Oh, I know they can't all be winners,' Franklin said. 'One Bellboy in a lifetime is more than most people get.'

Mention of the unfortunate horse brought the less savoury aspect of their association back abruptly to Ross.

'Leo is staying in the village,' he told Franklin. 'At the Six Bells.'

Franklin assumed an expression of exasperation.

'There's no getting ahead of you, is there? That was *my* bit of news. How did you find out?'

'Oh, I have my spies, too.' Ross grinned and told him about Maggie's friend.

'They always say you can't keep anything secret in a village,' Richmond said, amused. 'They probably know more about him than we do. Anyway, McKinnon has a man camped practically on the doorstep, watching his every move, so Leo shouldn't bother you again. Or at least, if he does, we'll catch him at it.'

Ross still felt guilty at causing so much extra trouble and said so.

'As I said before, I see it as a way of protecting my investment. And really, as insurance premiums go, it's chicken feed. So don't give it another thought.'

Ross thanked him again and asked after Peter.

'He's much improved, thank you. The doctor thinks he'll be fit to come home in a week or so. He's been allowed out of bed but can't use crutches yet because of the torn muscles in his shoulder. He's cheerful, though, surprisingly.'

'He's a brave kid,' Ross said, admiringly. 'Tell him I'll have some more videos for him soon. Danny's been busy making a kind of documentary for him about life in the yard, too. It's not quite finished yet.'

'He'll love that.'

They had wandered out to Franklin's car and here they paused.

'I've set up the payments again, Ross,' he confessed.

'Sure, I understand.' Ross couldn't blame him.

'So we appear to have reached a stalemate with Mr X, don't we?' Franklin observed. 'Unless he makes a move, we haven't a hope of tracking him down. But he won't make one unless I provoke him by not paying, and after what happened to Peter, I can't bring myself to do that. Which is, of course, what blackmail is all about.' He sighed, looking tired. 'McKinnon agrees the decision must be mine. I think he'd like me to take the chance, but then he hasn't got so much to lose.'

Drawing on his seemingly limitless reserves of inner strength, Franklin shrugged and smiled. 'I suppose we'll win through in the end,' he said. 'We have to, really. It'll work out one way or the other. Then we'll wonder what all this soul-searching was for.

'Well, I was on my way to see John,' he continued. 'So I'd better get on. I'll have a word with him about Barfly, too, though I can't sell him at the moment, even if I decide to. That's one of the blackmailer's stipulations. Any horse I try to sell will be killed or crippled. He's a real charmer, isn't he?'

Ross watched him go, wishing he could be of more help.

The yard was quiet. Danny and Sarah had ridden out on Simone and Gypsy, and Bill had gone out in the Land-Rover without saying where. Ross headed for the tackroom. He fancied a cold beer.

In the twilight of the stable office Roland sat with

his immaculately shod feet up on the desk, a beer in one hand and the other gently pulling the dog's ears as it lay quietly beside him. He smiled pleasantly as Ross stopped short.

'Boo!' he said softly.

Ross hadn't seen the Colonel's son since the evening he'd been attacked in his room; almost a week ago now.

'Hi,' he said. 'Long time no see.'

'I was called away,' Roland said in reply to the veiled question. 'Business.'

'Oh?' Ross queried, ironically. 'A Hepplewhite in distress? A Chippendale in peril?' He helped himself to a beer and opened it. 'Do you have crises in the antiques business?'

'You'd be surprised. A rare piece comes on to the market and it's an unholy scramble to get to it first. No end of dealing and double-dealing involved.'

'You really love your work,' Ross observed with interest.

'Oh, I do,' Roland agreed with a gleam of sardonic amusement. 'It's a lot more exciting than you might imagine.'

'I can see I'm in the wrong career.'

'How's your head?' Roland enquired solicitously, choosing to ignore the sarcasm. 'Any after-effects?'

'No. No problems,' Ross said. 'Look, did you tell anyone about that business?'

'No. Did you want me to, old boy? Whom should I tell?'

289

Ross shook his head, exasperated. 'Nobody. *I* didn't bother. It didn't seem worth making a fuss.'

'Quite agree,' Roland said approvingly. 'Can't abide fuss myself.'

They were interrupted by the sound of hooves in the yard and Ross went out to meet the returning riders. Roland followed him, the dog at his heels. It occurred to Ross that the dog was very much at home with the Colonel's son and he wondered which of them it would protect if forced to make a choice. It was a sobering thought.

'I'm thinking of buying a horse myself,' Roland remarked conversationally, as they stood watching the youngsters unsaddle.

Ross turned, astounded.

'*You* are?'

'Yes, why not?' Roland enquired. 'Thought if I bought a showjumper, you could ride it for me.'

Ross raised an eyebrow. 'Are you serious?'

Roland looked hurt. 'Oh, always, my boy. Always.'

Later that evening the weather finally broke. Storm clouds gathered from late afternoon onwards, darkness fell before time, and at about ten o'clock the heavens opened. Half an hour later, as Ross and Bill finished their late rounds, the first rolls of thunder could be heard in the distance.

Back in his room, Ross lay on his bed and watched the storm through the open window, enjoying the sound of the long-awaited rain pounding the cobbles below and the wonderful drop in humidity that accompanied it.

As the storm drew closer, the dog got up and padded to the window. He cocked his head on one side, listening, and then produced a deep, rumbling growl.

Ross laughed. 'You can't chase the storm away, fella,' he teased. 'It's bigger than you.'

The dog tipped his head to the other side and whined, gazing intently into the darkness, then turned and padded across the room to the door. There, he looked back at Ross and whined once more.

'Oh, not now, you crazy mutt. You'll drown,' Ross told him.

The dog whined again, running to the window and back to the door.

Ross sighed and got to his feet. 'I guess a guy's gotta do what a guy's gotta do,' he said. 'But you needn't think you're coming back up here, soaking wet and with muddy paws.'

Oh, my God, I sound just like my aunt! he thought, groaning inwardly.

He let the dog out on to the landing.

'If you get soaked, you can sleep out here.'

The dog ran down the stairs and pawed at the door at the bottom, and when it was opened, shot out into the rain-filled darkness without hesitation.

'Desperate, huh?' Ross muttered, settling on the bottom step to await his return.

He found himself going over Roland's surprising announcement. He had a feeling it was probably a whimsical thought, spoken aloud, and that nothing would ever come of it. He couldn't really see Roland as a showjumping fan. But then, you couldn't really see Roland as anything much, except perhaps an actor. Ross wondered if he'd ever had any connections with the theatre. Now that really *would* please the Colonel!

Abruptly, he remembered where he was and why. The door was ajar but the dog hadn't come back yet. Ross opened the door wider and, squinting against the driving rain, whistled between crashes of thunder. There was no response.

He tried again.

Nothing.

He looked at his watch. It was too late for Maggie to have let him into the cottage. Ross cursed and ran back upstairs to fetch his boots. If it hadn't been raining so hard he might have left the dog out there but it was just possible he could be barking at an intruder and Ross not hearing him through the storm.

Taking his waterproof stockman's coat and wide-brimmed hat from the hook behind the door, he ran back downstairs and out into the rain.

The yard was awash. The low, security lighting revealed sheets of rain being flung earthwards from the blackness above. Lightning split the sky with jagged streaks at frequent intervals, leaving bright impressions on the retina that confused the following darkness.

Having satisfied himself that the dog was not in the yard or sheltering by the covered stables, Ross headed for the Scotts' cottage and the car parking space beyond. The lights were out in the cottage and as Ross searched the shed, the yard lights flickered off and on again as lightning struck the grid.

No sign.

Torn between annoyance and growing anxiety, Ross sprinted through the puddles to the schooling arena. The gate was shut and an accommodating flash revealed it to be empty. He trotted to the opposite corner of the yard, where the path sloped down behind the haybarn to the home field.

The haybarn door stood open. It hadn't been at half-past ten. Ross had checked it himself. The bolt was quite stiff but now the door swung heavily in the wind.

So there *had* been somebody in the yard.

Ross wished he'd had the foresight to bring something with him with which to defend himself. He hadn't even brought a torch. But then he hadn't seriously thought there would be anyone out there on such a night. Whoever it was must be mad!

Whoever it was might well be a little insane, he reflected uncomfortably.

Heart-rate rocketing, he stood to one side of the door and slid his left hand round and in to flick the light switch down.

Nobody leapt at him. Nobody rushed past him into the rain. Nobody moved at all. The barn was empty.

Relieved, Ross turned the switch off and closed the door, bolting it securely. The fact remained, though, that somebody *had* been there. Worried, he decided to check on the horses before resuming his search for the dog.

The horses were fine. All on their feet except Woodsmoke who was resting his ageing limbs, but all as relaxed as one could expect in such a storm.

Ross returned to the haybarn and began to make his way along the outside. He whistled again but the sound was pitiful in the wind-torn night. Feeling his way along the wooden wall, his foot met an obstruction and he paused, crouching to investigate. A flash illuminated the rain-sodden body at his feet just as his fingers identified the wet fur.

The sight of the apparently lifeless dog was imprinted on his mind in that one brilliant moment, and the deafening crash of thunder that immediately followed it drowned his cry of distress.

He bowed his head, shock numbing his senses so that the rain ran, unfelt, down his neck and inside his shirt. It was a moment or two before he realised that beneath his hands the dog's ribcage was moving slightly.

With urgency born of hope, Ross gathered the huge, limp form into his arms and slipped and slid his way back up the path to the yard. Somewhere on the way, the wind blew his hat off and whirled it away into the darkness. He hardly noticed, heading straight for the shed where the Land-Rover was housed. It was obvious the animal needed immediate veterinary attention and a journey in his own open-topped jeep was plainly out of the question.

Wishing there was a light in the shed, Ross laid

the dog in the back of the Land-Rover, removing his coat to cover him with. He retrieved the ignition key from the ledge over the doorway and climbed into the front. Before he could fit the key into the ignition, however, a beam of light caught him directly in the face.

'What the hell?' he gasped, throwing up his hand to shield his eyes.

'What's going on?' a voice demanded. 'Ross?'

'Roland!' Ross was equally astounded.

The beam of light dropped and a flash of lightning through the doorway illuminated the unmistakable features of the Colonel's son. He too was hatless and, unsurprisingly, drenched.

'Out of the way!' Ross shouted above the drumming of the rain on the tin roof. He gunned the engine.

'What's wrong?' Roland flashed his torch round the interior of the vehicle. 'Oh, hell! What happened? No. Forget it. You get going. I'll ring Roger and let him know you're coming. Go!'

Ross switched the lights on and accelerated out into the downpour. The headlights stabbed out bravely through the shining rods of rain as he drove up the lane but it was like looking through frosted glass. The windscreen wipers scraped frantically at the screen but could make little impression.

Ross drove craned forward in an effort to see more clearly, his knuckles white on the wheel. Twenty-five miles an hour seemed suicidal. He did forty.

Water was cascading along the sides of the road

and flooding across it in places. Trees tossed and swayed in the gusty wind and small branches littered the tarmac. The twelve or so miles to Roger West's house took an eternity, and Ross prayed he hadn't missed his way in the chaotic darkness. He'd only been there once before.

The vet, alerted by Roland's call, had switched on an outside light and when Ross drove up was waiting in the doorway of the small animal surgery that his partner normally occupied during working hours. A flash and simultaneous crack of thunder as Ross opened the door of the Land-Rover proved that the storm was at its peak, directly overhead.

'Go on through!' Roger shouted as he stood back to let the American and his sorry burden go by. 'Lord, what a night!'

It seemed a lifetime that Ross stood making pools of rainwater on the grey linoleum while Roger examined the battered and bedraggled animal on his operating table, occasionally darting questions at Ross. The dog had regained consciousness at some point during the wild drive but he had neither the inclination, nor perhaps the ability, to move. Blood mingled with the water running out of his fur.

Now that the need for urgent action on Ross' part had passed, so had the sustaining adrenalin. Into its place crept a miserable resignation.

From somewhere in his past, a line from Kipling repeated on his consciousness: *Brothers and sisters, I bid you beware, of giving your heart to a dog to tear.*

How true, he reflected, but a lesson never

learned. He'd been stung before and still he had come back for more.

Well, never again.

Roger was looking up, his expression sympathetic. Words were not needed.

'If it's that bad, end it.' Ross was surprised at the steadiness of his voice.

The vet pursed his lips. 'There is a chance. Just a slim one but I'm willing to try . . .'

The dog raised its black muzzle and gazed through pain-filled brown eyes at the two men. Blood oozed in the wet fur and his legs lay limp on the tabletop.

'What d'you think's wrong with him?' Ross asked.

'It's hard to tell, exactly,' Roger said. 'I would've said he'd been hit by a car but you say he was nowhere near the road. However, his injuries suggest he's been hit by something and probably more than once. There's one gash here, on his head, but he's also got several broken ribs and there are massive contusions. There may be internal damage and his spine may be affected.'

'Are you saying he'll be paralysed?'

Roger shrugged. 'It's a strong possibility. It may be only temporary, I can't tell. He could possibly make a full recovery, though at this point I'd have to say that that was doubtful.'

Ross nodded, digesting the information. His throat ached with grief.

'What do you want me to do?' Roger asked gently.

Ross watched his dog for a moment longer, then turned away, unable to bear the unshaken trust in those beautiful eyes. 'You decide,' he said. 'Make a clinical decision. I can't think straight. You decide and send me the bill.'

'*Ross*, I can't do that!' Roger protested. 'It's your dog. I need your permission, your *written* permission, strictly speaking.'

'You have my permission to do what you think is best,' he said, making for the door. He knew he was shirking the responsibility and wasn't proud of himself. But equally, he trusted the vet to do the right thing by the dog.

'Don't you want to stay, in case . . .?' Roger delicately left the question unfinished.

'I have to get back, to check on the horses. Let me know what happens. Send me the bill.'

Ross stepped forward and gently fondled the dog's ears. He bent and kissed the top of the sodden head, then left the surgery and went out into the storm. Within seconds he was back in the Land-Rover.

For a moment he sat and stared through the rain-lashed windscreen with unseeing eyes. He hadn't realised how fond he'd become of the dog. Stupid to let himself get so attached.

To Ross it felt as though his life was predestined to go round in circles and he never seemed to learn from his past mistakes. He got bitten and he just went back for more. What did that say for his character? he wondered, as he started the engine. He supposed it denoted either a lack of intelligence

298

or monumental stubbornness. He wasn't sure he liked either analysis.

The image of the helpless dog haunted him and he pressed his eyes with the palms of his hands, running his fingers up through his dripping hair. Deliberately, he smothered the grief with anger. Putting the vehicle in gear, he drove out of the yard on to the treacherous roads again.

Who could do such a thing?

Had someone been in the yard waiting for the dog, or had it surprised someone bent on other unlawful business?

Leo was being watched, wasn't he?

Was it Franklin's Mr X who'd clobbered the dog?

And what of Roland? What could *he* possibly have been doing in the yard at nearly midnight in such weather?

Ross remembered Roland sitting fondling the dog while they talked, earlier that day. The dog had trusted him. Could someone befriend an innocent creature and then viciously attack it just hours later? Wearily, he had to admit that he didn't know any more but if he ever found out who *was* responsible . . .

He hit the steering wheel with a clenched fist as he drove.

By the time Ross returned the Land-Rover to the shed by the Scotts' cottage, the worst of the storm was over. Thunder still rolled in the distance but it grew fainter all the time and the rain had settled to a steady downpour. Wonderful healing rain to

299

wash away the dust and soften the ground. Wonderful relief for showjumpers' legs.

He put the ignition key back on its ledge and sloshed across the yard to the tackroom. The door was secure. One by one, Ross checked all the horses again, reflecting that if Roland had been up to no good, he had certainly left the way clear for him.

All appeared to be peaceful and in order. The Scotts' cottage was still in darkness. Ross was grateful that they were heavy sleepers. He felt he could do without either Bill's acrimony or his wife's sympathy at that moment.

He climbed the stairs to his room feeling lifeless and drained of emotion. Even the anger had abated a little, drifting away with the receding storm.

The light was still on in his bedsit. Roland lay sprawled on the sofa, a towel draped round his neck and his hair spiky from rubbing. It was the first time Ross had seen him in a less than polished state. It made him seem far younger and somehow much more likeable.

'How is he?' he asked, with what appeared to be genuine concern.

Ross felt he was past knowing who was genuine or not. He shook his head. 'Not good,' he said. 'I left him with Roger but I don't think there's much he can do. He'd probably be paralysed anyway.'

'Oh, I'm sorry. How did it happen? Did something fall on him in the storm?'

'I think somebody clubbed him,' Ross said bluntly, watching Roland closely for a reaction.

It was minimal. His eyes narrowed slightly and a muscle tightened in his jaw. 'Oh, hell,' he said, quietly but forcefully. 'Why? Why would somebody do that?'

Ross shook his head. 'You tell me,' he said, wondering if Roland could, if he chose to.

'Not Leo again, surely?'

Ross shrugged, unable to say why it couldn't have been. How had life ever got so damned complicated? he wondered wearily, shivering a little with delayed shock and the cold sogginess of his clothing. The stockman's coat he had dropped in the shower cubicle in the bathroom, saturated as it was with rain and the dog's blood. He'd see to it in the morning.

Roland was quick to notice. 'Get dry. I'll make you some coffee,' he said briskly. 'Move on. Put it behind you.'

Ross turned obediently, then stopped. There was one thing he had to know.

'What were you doing in the yard?'

Roland spooned coffee into mugs. 'I was watching the storm from the house. I saw torchlight and came to investigate. I found you.'

Ross changed into dry clothes and accepted coffee, which he found to be liberally laced with his own whisky. Hazily, he wondered where Roland had found it. He would have to be more careful, with *his* reputation; though hiding the bottle was even more likely to be seen as an admission of guilt.

He couldn't win.

The liquid restored him halfway to life, and halfway was all he cared to experience for the time being.

After a period of brooding silence, Roland drained his mug. Patting Ross sympathetically on the shoulder as he passed, he announced his intention of returning to the main house and his bed. 'Have to get my beauty sleep, don't you know?'

Ross thanked him, but he was out of the door before it occurred to the American that that was the first time in the past hour or two that Roland had affected his upper-class-twit persona.

So, it *was* just a front. Lindsay was right. And one that had to be consciously maintained, too.

Hot on the heels of this discovery came the realisation that he hadn't been carrying a flashlight when he'd searched the yard. Therefore, either Roland had seen the light carried by whoever had attacked the dog – in which case he had certainly taken his time coming to investigate – or he was lying.

On the whole, Ross hoped it was the former. He had, admittedly, borne the appearance of someone who had rushed out in a hurry, hatless and wearing only shoes rather than boots in the torrential rain. But why so long? Ross must have been in the yard for a good ten minutes before he'd found the injured animal and *he* had seen no light.

Too depressed to think straight, he finished his coffee and fell into bed.

14

Midway through the next morning the O'Connell horses arrived.

The six-year-old grey with the deep chest and long, plain head went by the name of Saxon Blue. He stood at the top of the horsebox ramp with head upflung, gazing at his new surroundings, then strode steadily down into the yard. His companion, the brown gelding with the fence fetish, was known as Trooper Joe.

Ross watched them as they were safely installed in their new quarters; neighbouring boxes for reassurance as they had come together. After a certain amount of whinnying from them and the resident horses they seemed to settle.

With all the excitement generated by the arrival of the new horses, nobody appeared to notice the absence of the dog, which habitually kept to shady corners out of everybody's way. Ross was relieved.

He didn't particularly want to talk about it just yet. In his experience, well-meaning sympathy was a bitch for re-opening wounds.

When the inevitable questions came, he had decided to let it be known that the dog had been hit by the haybarn door swinging in the wind. In fact, if it hadn't been for the fact that *he personally* had shut and bolted the door the previous evening when the storm was just starting, he might have considered that a plausible explanation himself. That fact and the telephone call he had received at breakfast time.

He missed the dog more than he would have expected. Theirs had not been a demonstrative relationship, indeed the animal had rarely even wagged its bushy tail, but it had always been around and Ross realised that he had made a habit of talking to it as he passed by.

Later in the day, Ross took some tack to the saddler's to be repaired and phoned Franklin from the car park.

Franklin greeted his call with pleasure swiftly followed by wariness.

'Hello, Ross. Is anything wrong?'

He briefly related the events of the night before. 'They didn't go after the horses,' he finished. 'This was either payback for me, or getting rid of the dog before Mr X makes his next move.'

'God, Ross. I'm sorry!' the businessman exclaimed, genuinely upset. 'If I could only get my hands on this bastard! I'm not normally a violent man, but just this once! You didn't see anything, of course . . .'

'No, nothing.' Ross thought fleetingly of Roland but stayed quiet. He had no real evidence against his boss's son, and besides that, he even liked the guy, in spite of his oddball affectations.

'I suppose it's not possible Leo could have given McKinnon's men the slip?' he said after a moment. 'I mean, this is just his style, isn't it? He never liked the dog and we all know what he thinks of me.'

Franklin sounded doubtful. 'It would certainly have been the night for it,' he allowed. 'But that's assuming Leo knew he was being watched, and unless McKinnon's men have been very careless, there's no way he could have. Those men are professionals, Ross. I can't see an amateur like Leo catching them out.'

'It does sound unlikely,' he agreed. 'The thing is, I had a phone call this morning. Somebody wanted me to know that what happened to the dog was no accident.'

'They called *you*?' Franklin was surprised and not a little alarmed. 'Oh, God, Ross! I'm sorry! I feel responsible for all this. After all, I got you into it.'

'No way!' he protested. 'It's as much my fight as yours now. This guy has made it personal.'

'No use asking if the voice rang any bells with you, I suppose?'

''Fraid not. And he wasn't so helpful as to give me his name. I wouldn't have described it as an Irish accent, though. It was kinda muffled. Hard to hear what the guy said at all.'

'And the dog?' Franklin asked. 'Have you heard from Roger yet?'

'I called him this morning but he still couldn't say one way or the other. He made it through the night but it's still touch and go. Roger didn't sound too hopeful.'

Cutting through Franklin's sympathy with the excuse that the mobile phone's battery was low, Ross said goodbye and switched off, sitting for a moment in thought.

'Be careful,' Franklin had said as he disconnected. Ross *would* be careful. Had to be, if he wanted to get through this with his career intact.

Oakley Manor and the horses had become his life now; became more so with every day that passed. The trouble was that if his mystery caller was to be believed, his life might be the price he had to pay.

Somehow, somebody had found out that he was trying to help Franklin. 'Your dog is dead, Yank,' the harsh, indistinct voice had told him that morning. 'And if you don't learn to mind your own business, you could be next!'

The big show of the weekend was on the Sunday and when Darcy Richmond arrived late Saturday morning with the intention of taking Sarah out to lunch, Ross gave her the afternoon off. Delighted, she hurried off to change.

'She's a good kid,' Ross told Franklin's nephew as he took him to see the two new horses. 'She works her socks off here.'

'She loves her job, I know that,' Darcy told the American. 'She never stops talking about it.' He smiled, showing that he didn't mind. 'Well, sometimes she does,' he amended, with a cheeky wink.

Ross smiled in return, thinking again what a strange pair Darcy and Sarah made.

Having duly admired the new arrivals, they made their way out into the sunshine once more.

'Jeez! What've you been up to?' Ross asked, seeing Darcy's face properly for the first time. His left eye bore signs of a fading bruise of quite impressive proportions.

'I could ask the same of you,' Darcy laughed, looking at Ross' grazed cheekbone, legacy of his encounter with Leo. 'Although Uncle Frank told me about that.' He put his fingers up to touch his own marked face. 'You ought to have seen it a couple of days ago. I'd like to say I got it fighting for a lady's honour but the sad truth is that I ran into a friend's racket, playing squash.'

'Ouch!' Ross said as Sarah emerged from the cottage, washed and changed. 'Now, don't forget. Back by six to help get the lorry ready.'

Barely had Darcy's silver Nissan swept out of the yard than something much heavier was heard approaching. There was the sound of rapid braking as the two vehicles passed in the long driveway, and then shortly after, a massive, gleaming new horsebox nosed into the yard, dwarfing the older one in the way a touring coach would dwarf a minibus.

Danny and Bill appeared from the tackroom and came to stand by Ross as he stared in awe.

'Wicked!' Danny breathed, slipping into schoolboy lingo. His father favoured him with a withering glance, but secretly Ross couldn't agree more.

Hot on the heels of this shining monster came Franklin's Merc, which disgorged not only Franklin himself but Colonel Preston and his son also.

'I had to see your faces!' Franklin said as the horsebox engine shuddered to silence. 'Isn't she a beauty?'

A man in logoed overalls jumped down from the cab. 'Mornin', Gov'nor,' he said to Franklin, adding somewhat unnecessarily, 'Here she is, then.'

He watched the reception committee move closer to study the vehicle and cleared his throat. 'I don't norm'ly work on Saturdays as a rule,' he informed them meaningfully. 'But the Gov'nor 'ere, 'e said as how 'e wanted it this weekend and there weren't no one else, so 'ere I am.'

Franklin good-naturedly took the hint and fished out a note which he passed to the driver, advising him to buy himself a beer.

The driver blinked at the note before coming to his senses and slipping it into a trouser pocket. Forget the beer, his expression had said for a moment, I'll put in an offer for the brewery! He murmured his appreciation and, having collected Franklin's signature on the delivery documents, departed in a company van, driven by a colleague.

A good half-hour of delighted discovery followed, as the assembled group embarked on a tour of inspection. The lorry held five horses in comfort, six at a push, with storage space for equipment and fodder, and had both rear and side ramps.

Another advantage it held over its predecessor

was the living quarters. A kitchen, complete with hob, microwave, washing machine and dryer, tucked neatly into a corner of the sitting-cum-dining area which also boasted a stereo and television, and whose soft chairs converted to narrow beds if need be. It even had a toilet, washbasin and shower cubicle.

Ross found himself grinning from ear to ear at the prospect of such luxury.

'I'll be moving out of my room upstairs,' he joked. 'This is unbelievable! I had no idea you were thinking of something like this. It must have cost . . .'

'Enough to buy a small house,' Franklin admitted. 'But worth every penny. It was a joint investment, you know. John put a substantial amount forward and even our Scottish friend was persuaded to part with a penny or two. We're moving into the big league now, my lad.'

'Talking of Robbie Fergusson,' the Colonel said to Ross, 'he's hoping to come and watch his horses again tomorrow, so you'd better put on a good show.'

'I'll do my best,' Ross promised, wondering if the Scotsman's presence at the show owed anything to the adverse publicity he had recently been receiving. Ross was sure that it wouldn't have gone unnoticed.

Before Franklin departed for lunch with the Colonel, he managed to draw Ross aside for a moment on the pretext of having a look at one of the horses.

'McKinnon's men have nothing to report on Leo,' he said quietly. 'He certainly neither left by the front door nor took his motorbike. They say it's possible he could have left by the back door and made his way across the fields under cover of the storm, but that would mean that he knows he's being watched and McKinnon can't see how that's possible. I'm afraid we're no further forward.'

Sunday dawned dry and bright but with a much fresher feel than in the recent past. Gone was the awful dragging heat of the last few weeks. The sky was a clear blue, the sun warm and a light breeze began to evaporate the worst of the surface water, leaving the turf soft and springy.

As the Oakley Manor team parked their new acquisition proudly amongst the first arrivals at the showground, Ross experienced the buzz the start of a show always gave him.

This was probably the biggest show, in terms of prestige, he had so far attended in England. In the shining new lorry, Bishop, Woodsmoke, Ginger, Flowergirl and Simone waited with barely controlled impatience for the action to start.

Everyone except Sarah was attending the show. She preferred to remain in the yard where she felt under less pressure. Sally, the farmer's daughter, usually came in to help when she was on her own.

On this occasion, Danny and Bill had accompanied Ross in the horsebox, Bill sharing the driving at the Colonel's suggestion, to leave Ross fresh for riding.

He accepted this arrangement gladly, although he was a little concerned that Colonel Preston was having doubts about his fitness, and made a mental note to try and minimise his limp when his employer was around.

The Colonel himself was to arrive later in the morning in the Jaguar, and there had been talk of Franklin obtaining permission to bring Peter out of hospital for the afternoon. It seemed Ross would have quite a crowd of interested onlookers, with Robbie Fergusson also promising to be there.

As a matter of fact, it was Ginger who produced the best result of the morning, winning her Grade-C class with a neat and obedient double clear round. Ross should have been elated but somehow could feel no enthusiasm for her performance. She seemed to lack any spark of enjoyment. Unfortunately, Fergusson had not arrived by that time and so missed his mare's finest hour.

Simone and Flo worked eagerly to provide their usual sprinkling of placings in the speed and agility classes, including a thrilling battle in the Top Score competition where they took second and third places behind Danielle Moreaux on her experienced little horse.

The show was well organised and well attended, with many of the top British names and a scattering of international riders competing. Stephen Douglas was there and so, unfortunately, was his father. Mick Colby had travelled King and several novices up, and Ross saw many other familiar faces, some of whom greeted him amiably, while some cut him dead.

Lindsay and James had travelled independently of the Oakley Manor team, bringing Gypsy to the show in a trailer. They seemed in high spirits and Gypsy obliged by winning a speed class for her delighted owner.

The big chestnut, Telamon, appeared in the collecting ring for the first class of the afternoon, ridden by a rather heavy-handed young man who was one of those who had earlier turned his back on Ross. His relationship with the stallion appeared to be one of perpetual opposition. The horse looked full of fight and Ross was entirely on the animal's side. He wondered idly if he himself could ride the giant chestnut, and half-wished he could try.

Telamon and his passenger, Jim Pullen, were drawn fairly early in the class and, as expected, the round was an unmitigated disaster, the chestnut taking three fences at hurdling pace before determinedly bucking his jockey off at the far end of the ring.

Lindsay rode alongside Ross.

'You really should try to disguise such unholy glee,' she admonished severely, with a twinkle in her eye.

'The guy's a moron,' Ross said. 'But I didn't realise I was quite so easy to read. I guess I'll have to be more careful!'

'Well, it was obvious to me, but then perhaps I know you better than most.'

'Do you often read my mind?' he asked jokingly.

'Oh, all the time,' Lindsay declared, laughing. 'You'd be surprised the things I know about you!'

And you'd be surprised the things you don't, he thought, ruefully.

Aloud, he said, 'I shall *definitely* have to be more careful!'

'So, can you come on Saturday?' she asked, unaware of the track on which she had set his thoughts.

'Saturday?'

'Our party. James' and mine,' Lindsay reminded him.

Ross noticed she avoided calling it an engagement party. Was it possible that she was starting to get cold feet?

'*This* Saturday?' he said, in the tone of one who had thought it at least a month away. 'Oh, hell! I'm sorry, Princess, I can't. I'm – that is, I've arranged to go out with Danielle.'

'Bring her along,' Lindsay said brightly. 'The more the merrier.'

'Well, I'll ask her, thank you,' Ross said, unable to think of a further excuse and making a mental note to advise Danielle of the plans he had inadvertently made on her behalf.

Bishop was in fine form, winning his first class and only missing a place in the next after slipping on a difficult turn in the jump-off. Ross put it down to his inexperience and was well satisfied.

As the afternoon wore on and the prize money became more and more enticing, the bigger names began to emerge.

The Colonel had appeared just before lunch,

apparently having been chauffeured by Roland, and was soon joined in the grandstand by Robbie Fergusson. The Scotsman made no effort to come down and see his horses or their rider at close hand. Instead he sat in the members' stand with an auburn-haired beauty at his side and drank champagne while his horses performed for his pleasure below.

Ross had no particular desire to talk to the man but the situation made him feel a little like a gladiator doing battle to amuse his noble patron. He knew he was being over-sensitive, but then the man *was* only a chess player himself, albeit a stinking rich one.

Franklin had arrived in a brand-new Range Rover which he had parked at the ringside to give Peter the best view possible without having to leave the vehicle, and Ross made a point of taking each of the horses round for the boy to see between classes.

Both Ginger and Flo were entered for the penultimate class of the day and as Ross trudged round the ring beforehand, pacing out the combinations and rehearsing the turns in his mind's eye, he tried to keep his mind off the increasing discomfort in his knee.

Pain, in moderate proportions, he felt he could deal with but he prayed that pain would not give way to weakness. Time off now for more operations wasn't an option. The horses were just coming good. Woodsmoke, Bishop and Simone were well on their way to qualifying for the top international shows and if he lost the rides now, he would lose them for ever.

The fences in this class were as big as anything Flo had ever tackled at a show but she launched herself at them with enthusiasm and gave a very creditable performance. In fact, she only came to grief at the very last obstacle, a formidable wall which was jumped diagonally across the arena, heading for the corner where a group of disabled children brandished candyfloss and helium-filled balloons.

Whether it was these silver balloons which caught the mare's eye Ross didn't know, but she badly misjudged the wall and crashed through the top of it, scattering wooden blocks and pecking badly on landing. Somehow she found the mysterious 'fifth leg' which some horses seem to keep for such emergencies, and stayed upright.

Disappointed, for the Colonel's sake as much as anything, Ross patted her shoulder and they left the ring to sympathetic applause.

Harry Douglas, who had so far that afternoon been quite restrained in his comments, could apparently find no fault of Ross' to account for her mistake and contented himself with observing that they would not take part in the jump-off. Ross wondered if perhaps the vendetta had run its course.

'Bad luck, Ross.' Danielle smiled as she rode past him into the ring and Ross remembered guiltily that he hadn't told her of their supposed date the following Saturday He made a mental note to do so when he returned to the collecting ring on Ginger.

Danny appeared out of the milling crowd leading the chestnut mare and Ross passed Flo's reins to him in exchange. He accepted a leg-up from the boy, wincing as his knee took the strain. Settling into the saddle, he tightened the girth and gathered up the reins. Danny made no move to leave.

'Is anything the matter?' Ross asked, his mind on Ginger, who felt mulish. She had already worked up a sweat, just on her way from the horsebox.

'She's acting a bit weird, Ross,' he said, frowning. 'Back there, when I led her past the beer tent, some idiot opened a can of lager practically under her nose. She nearly blew her top! I thought I wouldn't hold her for a moment. I've never seen her like that before.'

I have, Ross thought grimly.

'She's got a thing about bangs and popping noises. Something must have frightened her pretty badly at some time. I expect she'll be all right now,' he said

Danny's face reflected the doubt that Ross himself felt but he nodded and turned away with Flowergirl.

Ross rode the chestnut mare towards the main ring, wishing that the general public was not so trusting. Sun-bronzed women in skimpy skirts trundled toddlers in pushchairs within inches of Ginger's back legs and children reached out to pat her as she passed, unaware that the sudden, unseen contact made her flinch and jump.

She was being very good, really, and Ross thought, not for the first time, that whatever it was that made her react so unreasonably at times, it was not a basic fault of her nature. For the most part she was a fairly placid animal, until something sparked off one of her illogical panics.

He wondered if horses could suffer from schizophrenia.

They reached the collecting ring without mishap and joined the whirling mass of horses and riders warming up for the class. The practice area was far too small, a common fault at non-permanent showgrounds, and as other competitors rode past in all directions, occasionally brushing the mare with whips or swishing tails, Ross could feel the tension building within her again. He fought to stay relaxed himself, knowing that any anxiety he felt would be transmitted to the horse and could only make matters worse.

Mick Colby rode alongside on a novice Ross didn't recognise.

'Hi, fella. How's it going?' He looked harder at the American. 'Are you okay?'

Somebody had just cut in front of Ginger, their whip flicking her face, and Ross felt the sudden, jerky signs of panic shudder through the mare. In spite of himself, he froze inside. Her ears began to flick back and forth agitatedly and through the reins her mouth felt hard and unresponsive. She was on the verge of breaking but there was nowhere to go.

'Ross?'

He had a sudden mental picture of those excited

children with their silver balloons. In his mind's eye he saw them screaming, falling over each other in their efforts to flee.

Dear God, half of them were in wheelchairs. They couldn't get away! Ginger would run them down. She wouldn't turn; not in one of her hysterical flights.

'Look, I've got to get her out of here,' he said urgently to Colby. 'Could you tell the stewards? I can't jump her like this. Please?'

Colby was plainly bewildered. 'But, what . . .?'

'Will you do it?'

'Yes, of course. But what's the matter? Are you okay?'

'Thanks.' Afraid to touch her with his heels, Ross jumped off Ginger. Gripping her nostrils tightly with his left hand so that her breath whistled, he led her tentatively forward. She went in a series of short, jerky steps, alternately towing Ross along and pulling back. In this fashion he left the collecting ring and headed for the lorry park.

Halfway there, she stopped shaking and started to walk more sensibly. Ross heaved a sigh of relief. He supposed if he took her back to the ring now she might be all right, but then again she might not and he could hardly scratch her a second time without some form of explanation. He dismissed the idea without much hesitation.

'You're one crazy horse, aren't you, girl?' He looked at her wide, worried eyes and felt pity for her.

The upset caused by his unexpected withdrawal

from the class caught up with him even sooner than he'd thought it would. Bill said little as he took the chestnut from him, apparently accepting Ross' terse excuse that she was a little off-colour. He called to Danny to have Woodsmoke ready for him in three-quarters of an hour or so, and wandered slowly back to the ringside to see Franklin and Peter.

'The Colonel's looking for you,' the businessman said. 'Or at least, he sent Roland to find you. I gather you've scratched Ginger. Is anything wrong?'

'She's had enough,' Ross said, economically.

'So how does Woody look for the last class?' Franklin enquired, thankfully accepting this at face value.

'He's fine. Jumping out of his skin,' Ross assured him, wistfully wishing that Fergusson would be as easily satisfied. 'Hiya, Peter. How's it going?'

'Hi, Ross. This is great!' the boy declared, eyes shining. 'Much better than hospital. I wish I didn't have to go back there.' He stopped, looking a little shamefaced. 'The nurses are really nice but . . . Well, you know what I mean.' He looked at Ross almost pleadingly.

'Sure I do,' he told the boy. 'I spent nearly two months in one, myself. It's the pits.'

Peter looked cheered by this whole-hearted endorsement of his views and even Franklin had to smile. 'Will Woodsmoke win, Ross?' Peter asked eagerly 'Will he beat Sandy Peterson?'

Peterson was one of the leading money-winners in England so far that year and Ross grinned. 'Well, he might but I can't promise anything,' he told the excited boy. 'Keep your fingers crossed for me.'

'Ah, Ross, my boy.' As Ross left the Richmonds' ringside position, Roland approached unseen and laid a heavy hand on his shoulder. 'My esteemed papa sent me to find out if everything is all right. Our mutual friend Mr Fergusson is, to put it mildly, hopping mad. It seems he expected to be consulted before you . . . er . . . scratched his horse.'

'Consulted? There wasn't time for that! What was I supposed to do – use semaphore?' Ross exclaimed indignantly. 'Besides, what's the point? He doesn't know the first thing about the animal. He probably wouldn't even recognise her if she wasn't announced by name!'

Roland put his hands in the air, dramatically. 'Don't shoot me, old boy, I'm only the messenger! I take it you had a good reason for not riding the beast?'

'I did.'

'But you're not going to burden me with it,' Roland observed mildly. 'Okay, that's fine by me. I'll tell him the animal got its fetlocks in a tangle or something.'

Ross smiled in spite of himself. 'Tell him the mare had done enough. That was a very big course, you know.'

They were passing within feet of one of the fences in the ring: huge parallel bars some four foot six in height with a similar spread.

Roland stood and looked at the jump, as on the

other side of the rails a horse swung towards it and with a thudding, snorting, leather-creaking effort, cleared it and thundered on.

He shuddered. 'You can see why some people lose their nerve,' he commented. 'Nothing would induce me to approach one of those on the back of a horse.'

Ross looked at him sharply but it seemed his remark had been perfectly innocent.

'The jumps,' he muttered, 'are the least of my problems.'

Roland seemed disinclined to return to his father and Fergusson, and when the current class ended, with a victory for Mick Colby and his new ride, he waited while Ross walked the course for the last class, then accompanied him back to the horsebox to collect Woodsmoke.

On the way they narrowly escaped being mown down by Telamon, who was proceeding crabwise through the crowd in spite of, or perhaps because of, Jim Pullen's best efforts to restrain him.

Roland seemed impressed by the giant chestnut.

'Now that's a spirited creature!' he exclaimed. 'A real old-fashioned charger. Carry one into battle, don't you think?'

Ross looked sideways at his companion.

'I suppose so. If one had a battle to go to,' he agreed, sardonically.

'Exactly so,' Roland said, typically appearing to miss the intended sarcasm. 'Well, well. There's old Perry. Nice to see you again, Perry old chap.'

Perry Wilson, who, Ross remembered, had been

the Colonel's rider for a good many years, was not in fact as old as Ross had imagined he would be. Slight, with a thin face and wire-rimmed spectacles, he looked to be around forty, maybe younger.

'Hi. Ross Wakelin.' Ross held out his hand in greeting.

'Hello. Well done, too.' Perry had a ready smile. 'You're doing a great job with those horses.'

'Perry was plagued with back trouble, poor chap. Had to give up,' Roland explained for Ross' benefit. 'Cruel shame. Wicked. Cut off in his prime, you know the sort of thing . . .'

'I'm sorry,' Ross said with genuine sympathy. There but for the grace of God. Who could say? It might be him before long. *Plagued with an old injury, you know. Such a shame.*

'Oh, it wasn't quite that tragic,' Perry said, laughing. 'I wasn't ever going to be another David Broome.'

'Well, you won the Hickstead Derby!' Ross pointed out. 'That's no mean feat!'

'My moment of triumph,' Perry agreed. 'That was the horse of a lifetime, though. The trick is being able to get the best out of any mount.'

On impulse, Ross asked, 'What did you think of Ginger when you used to ride her?'

Perry frowned. 'She seemed a nice mare. Very novice then, of course, but plenty of promise. Why? Are you having trouble?'

Ross was uncomfortably aware of Roland by his side and began to wish he hadn't spoken but it was too late now.

'I wondered if she'd ever been badly frightened in any way? She gets very uptight sometimes.'

'Not that I know of,' Perry said, shaking his head. 'She always seemed fairly placid. I started her as a youngster but then she became unsound and was put in foal. She came back into training last summer, not long before I gave up. She'd miscarried, I believe. There was some sort of upset . . . I can't remember the details, sorry. You could ask Annie Hayward, though. The mare was with her at the time. Anyway, I really didn't ride her a lot.'

'Thanks. I don't suppose there's anything in it but it never hurts to ask.'

'Too right,' Perry agreed. 'Well, I must get on. I'm course-building these days, you know. Nice to meet you, Ross. Roland.'

The last class of the day in the main ring had attracted a high-profile field and Ross found himself queuing for the practice jump with partnerships the likes of which he had only previously seen on television.

Woodsmoke was not daunted, however, and they swept out of the ring with a clear round, marred only by a momentary lack of concentration on Ross' part which almost resulted in Woody taking the wrong fence.

Ross was furious with himself. Just because he had caught sight of a face in the crowd that reminded him of someone – someone who was most unlikely to be there – he had almost thrown the competition away before he started.

The public address system crackled. 'I should take more water with it, Ross,' Harry Douglas advised. 'But seriously, that was a nice round. At least the horse had his mind on the job! A clear for Ross Wakelin and Woodsmoke.'

The crowd laughed, unaware of the barbs hidden under the smooth tones.

Ross could see from a few of the sideways glances in the collecting ring that the implication hadn't gone unnoticed there. He ignored them, his face set in a mask of indifference. Changing on to Black Bishop, he concentrated on settling and suppling him.

For some reason, the horse didn't give him the usual, well-oiled, confident feel. Afraid that he was letting his own tensions communicate themselves to the animal, he consciously tried to empty his mind and relax.

'Don't let 'em get to you, Ross m'boy.' Mick Colby circled past on King's Defender.

Ross raised his eyebrows theatrically. 'Who?' he asked.

Mick grinned. 'Atta boy!'

Stephen Douglas rode by, wearing what could only be described as an unpleasant smirk. 'Found a drinking partner?' he enquired of Ross.

'Yes, you're too late!' Mick responded swiftly and the smirk faded.

'Thanks, but don't bother,' Ross said wearily as Douglas rode on. 'Besides, there's no point in joining me in the stocks.'

'Oh, I don't mind the odd rotten tomato,' Mick

said, grinning. 'And anyway, we Brits always support the underdog. It's in our nature.'

Ross grimaced. 'You're doing wonders for my self-esteem.'

'I never thought Stephen would let himself be poisoned like that, though,' Mick went on thoughtfully. 'He used to be a nice lad.'

Mick was directly before Ross in the jumping order and so the American didn't see his round. Instead, he concentrated on gaining Bishop's full attention and obedience.

For once, the horse seemed reluctant to respond, feeling awkward and unwilling, and Ross had to work really hard. He heard the hooter go for the start of King's round and voices hush around the arena as the horse went to work. Bishop still didn't seem himself. Ross slowed him up and let him walk. It would only be a minute or two before he was called and nothing more could be done.

Suddenly, from the arena came an appalling crash and splintering of timber, and the grunting thud of horseflesh hitting the ground. A gasp, magnified by many throats, sounded around the ringside and died into silence.

Ross stood in his stirrups to see.

Midway across the ring and partly obscured by another fence, King was struggling to regain his feet amongst a tangle of red and white poles. Six feet or so away, lying ominously still, was his rider.

A stab of apprehension twisted through Ross. He sat back in the saddle and began to walk Bishop round once more. All the riders knew it could happen but it was nevertheless a shock when it did, and it was all the worse for being a personal friend too.

St John's Ambulance workers bustled by, ducking under the ropes and running across the ring. Ross hoped Mick was just winded. Nine times out of ten, that was all it was.

A speculative buzz of conversation began to build up once more and a moment or two later an ambulance could be heard, its siren sounding intermittently, threading its way through the crowds towards them.

The riders in the collecting ring drew to one side as it passed. Scores of tired day-trippers, who had been heading for the exits, now turned with re-newed interest to flock, vulture-like, to the ringside.

Ross remembered that day almost a year ago and wanted to shout at them to go away; to mind their own business. Tragedy is a personal thing and should be kept that way.

He knew it wouldn't do any good. Accidents exercise a compulsive attraction for the average human being and human nature will rarely be denied.

At least for Mick it was a long-distance affair. Nobody could see if his face was sweating and drawn with pain. Nobody could hear if a groan was forced from him when they moved him. And nobody else was involved.

Ross shook the memories away. That way lay madness.

He concentrated on Bishop's ears. The big black

flicked them to and fro, sensitive like all his kind to atmosphere. It seemed an age that they circled the collecting ring, weaving between the other waiting competitors, but eventually the ambulance reappeared, moving slowly across the uneven ground, and made its way back through the collecting ring and across the showground.

Shortly after this, King was led past by his girl groom. The horse seemed unhurt although his saddle didn't look to have much of a future. The girl seemed upset. Several people besieged her, asking for news of Colby, but she merely shook her head and shrugged, apparently knowing nothing.

The loudspeakers crackled, apologised for the delay and said that they hoped, as they were sure everybody else did, that Mr Colby would be all right. Next to jump, they said, would be Ross Wakelin on Mr Robert Fergusson's Black Bishop.

Ross was waved in by the stewards and while he trotted Bishop in steady circles, waiting for the team of army cadets to finish rebuilding the shattered fence, he could hear the ambulance siren blare out to clear a way through the traffic on the main road.

The cadets retreated, the hooter sounded and Ross turned Bishop towards the first fence. It was a low, rustic pole and brush fence that would ordinarily have caused the black no problem at all, but on this occasion he approached it at a choppy, unbalanced canter so unlike his usual fluent self that Ross was seriously worried that he might be lame. They cleared the obstacle, though not by much, and Ross swung him towards the second, a formidable spread fence.

Bishop still wasn't happy. His ears were back and his head held high. As he saw what was expected of him he faltered, and when Ross tried to drive him forward he dug in his toes and refused.

For Ross this was more than enough to tell him that all was not right. The horse had never before refused. Normally, the problem, if anything, was to hold him back. With a young horse, nothing could be gained by forcing him on, even if it could be achieved, and everything stood to be lost.

Glancing towards the judges' caravan, Ross touched the brim of his crash hat and nodded, the accepted signal for retiring from the competition. With a sigh of disappointment he let the black walk from the arena on a long rein. The next competitor rode past him without so much as a glance and the crowd clapped unenthusiastically. In the commentary box, Harry Douglas cleared his throat.

Wait for it, Ross thought. This should be good.

'I don't think we can blame Ross if nerves got the better of him there,' Douglas said sympathetically. 'It isn't easy to tackle a big course like this one at the best of times, and especially not when you have just witnessed a nasty fall.

'Still, I'm sure our next competitor won't be put off, for next we have Derek Campbell on Summerlane. Derek is one of our most promising young internationals, who has just returned from competing in Europe . . .' He went on to give a brief résumé of the redoubtable Derek's recent triumphs.

Ross reached the collecting ring and dismounted, wearily wondering if Douglas Senior would ever tire of his sport.

'Ross!' Danielle was beside him, leading her grey mare. 'He has no right to say such things! He goes too far. Anyone with half a brain could see that Bishop was not right. It was no fault of yours.'

'Good thing I'm not sensitive,' he said with the ghost of a smile.

'Ah, but he smudges your reputation, no?'

'Smears,' Ross corrected helpfully.

Danielle tossed her head, her dark eyes sparkling. 'Smears, smudges – what's the difference? He should now be stopped.'

Ross was busy running his stirrup irons up and loosening Bishop's girth. 'What do you suggest I do?' he enquired mildly. 'Pull him out of the commentary box and punch him out?'

'It would do him good!' Danielle declared.

'Maybe,' Ross agreed. 'But I'm afraid, much as I'd enjoy it, it's not a good idea. The thing that bothers me is that people are beginning to believe him.'

'Ah, pooh! They do not know you. Me, I have seen you ride horses they would not believe! I know you are not afraid.'

Ross watched her dark, animated face with its engagingly expressive features and felt a sudden rush of affection. He leant forward and kissed her cheek. 'Thank you, Danielle,' he said earnestly.

'But I have not helped!' she cried in exasperation.

'Sure you have. More than you know,' he told

her warmly. 'Now you'd better get on board, they'll be calling you in a moment. I'll give you a leg up.'

She obediently bent her knee and he boosted her into the saddle. She was as light as thistledown and he was smiling as he turned back to Bishop – and came face to face with the Colonel and Robbie Fergusson.

The Colonel was obviously concerned and looked at Ross with a question in his eyes. Fergusson was coldly furious.

'Is there a problem, Ross?' the Colonel began, but Fergusson cut in abruptly.

'Yes, there's a problem! *He's* the problem! He flunked it! He's a spineless has-been who should never have been allowed back on a horse – anyone's horse – let alone mine!'

Ross flinched inwardly and a muscle tightened in his jaw but he held his temper.

The Colonel was visibly upset.

'Look, steady, Robbie. We agreed we'd listen to what Ross has to say. It's only fair.'

'Oh, yes. By all means,' Fergusson sneered. 'This should be good. Let's hear why a promising young horse with a brilliant career ahead of him was retired from his first major class after only one jump!'

Ross had never felt less inclined to explain anything to anyone in his life. Only his desperate need to retain the ride on Bishop kept him from speaking his mind.

'Ross?' The Colonel spoke softly but there was

no mistaking the underlying steel. *Don't let me down*, he was warning. Quietly, Roland came up to stand behind him.

'The horse wasn't comfortable,' Ross stated with a studied calm. 'And I'm not about to ruin a potential Grand Prix horse for the sake of a single class. If that's what you would have me do, then you'd better get someone else to ride your horses.'

'Bravo!' Roland murmured almost inaudibly. No one took any notice.

'Is the horse lame?' Fergusson snapped.

'No, I don't think so.'

'Then what?'

'I can't say, exactly. I just know he wasn't happy.' Ross didn't even begin to try to explain to Fergusson, who could know nothing of the special bond between horse and rider, just how a horse could communicate its discomfort to its jockey.

'More likely *you* didn't feel happy,' Fergusson suggested. 'I think that Douglas man was close. You lost your bottle after seeing that other bloke being stretchered off.'

'That's not so,' Ross asserted quietly.

'No? Are you trying to tell me that it didn't affect you at all?'

'No, of course not. I'm not stupid. I don't like seeing anyone get hurt, least of all a friend, but it had nothing whatever to do with the way Bishop behaved.'

'Robbie . . .' The Colonel decided it was time to intercede. 'Ross has another horse to jump. Couldn't this wait until we've all calmed down?'

'One minute.' Fergusson shrugged the Colonel's hand off his arm. 'What about Red Queen?' he demanded of the American. 'Why was she scratched? Another bad feeling?'

Ross' heart sank. He could smell defeat. Damn Ginger! Why today, of all days? He stared at Fergusson steadily, aware that anything he could say would only plunge him deeper into the mire.

'Well?' Fergusson barked the question like an irate schoolmaster.

'Ginger's different . . .' he began, and it sounded feeble even to his own ears.

'She won a class this morning!' Fergusson almost shouted. 'And this afternoon, for no reason at all, you pull her out of a class for which *I* – I'll have you remember – paid the entry fees.' He leaned closer. 'If you're not up to the job, Mr Wakelin, why can't you at least find the guts to say so?'

A number of possible replies occurred to Ross, none of which would tactfully defuse the situation. He remained silent. The Colonel, he could see, was bristling indignantly but it was Roland who spoke.

'I think,' he said diffidently, into the awkward silence, 'that this gentleman would rather like us to move. I believe we are somewhat in the way.' He indicated a hovering steward who thanked him and looked apologetic.

'Of course.' The Colonel seized on this diversion as an exhausted Channel swimmer might seize on a lifebelt. 'I think enough has been said for now. Let's get the horse back to his box.'

Fergusson glared at him and then glared at Ross

again for good measure. 'I'll be leaving now anyway,' he said. 'No sense in staying. I'll ring you in the morning to make arrangements about the horses,' he added significantly to the Colonel as he turned away.

The steward, who was still hovering, looked relieved as the remaining three men and the horse began to move towards the lorry park. Several other people in the vicinity watched the group curiously as they left the collecting ring.

It wasn't surprising, Ross thought dispiritedly, Fergusson had hardly been discreet. The gossips and backbiters would have fuel for weeks to come. He supposed that within minutes everybody would know he had all but been given his marching orders. He wondered miserably who would get the ride on Bishop.

Not Stephen Douglas. That would be *too* much. It wasn't likely either, he reflected more sensibly, as he had reportedly fallen foul of Fergusson too.

'Awfully upset, wasn't he?' Roland said thoughtfully to no one in particular. No one in particular answered him.

Out of the thinning crowds Danny appeared riding Woody. He looked worried. 'I heard,' he said, 'over the loudspeakers. Is Bishop all right?'

Ross sighed. 'Something wasn't right, Danny. Maybe he hurt himself when he slipped earlier on.'

The Colonel looked sharply at him.

'Do you think that was it, Ross?' he asked. 'Why didn't you tell Fergusson?'

'I'd forgotten it,' he said truthfully. 'Not that it would have made any difference. He wasn't looking for answers.'

When Ross entered the ring on Woodsmoke some thirty minutes later for the jump-off against the clock, he was in no mood for taking prisoners. Thirty minutes of other people's carefully averted eyes, thoughts of his own crumbling career and bitterness at the way events seemed to conspire against him had combined to harden his resolve to granite. Woodsmoke would jump round that course if Ross personally had to pick him up and carry him.

Old campaigner though he was, Woody was not immune to the messages being transmitted to him. He jumped as he had never jumped before. Ross was fairly early in the jumping order and the time to beat was not yet desperately tight, but Woody smashed it.

Riding with more verve than sense, Ross cut corners impossibly close, pushed on where he should have steadied and took two whole strides out on the gallop to the last fence. The crowd gasped, as with an indignant grunt, Woodsmoke flung himself at the final wall, his front legs reaching forward to clear it, and landed way out on the other side.

When Ross pulled him up, the old horse was snorting with excitement and his ears flicked to and fro in agitation. He danced from the ring, dripping with sweat, unable to settle. Ross patted his brave old neck.

'That's our new leader, Ross Wakelin on Mr Franklin Richmond's Woodsmoke, with a time of thirty-five-point-oh-four seconds. That's the time to beat, ladies and gentlemen.' Harry Douglas obviously felt he had made enough mischief for one day. Ross felt like giving the commentary box the finger but didn't feel it would advance his cause.

He was touched by a twinge of guilt as he dismounted and saw the trembling, heaving flanks of his mount, but the round had done more for Ross' flagging spirits than any amount of reassuring words could have. It had done the trick where the competition was concerned, too, although that had become of secondary importance to him. Nobody came near to beating him. He won the jump-off by two clear seconds from the redoubtable Derek, with Danielle in third place.

Ross limped back to the horsebox with Peter Richmond's excited congratulations ringing in his ears, along with the rather more reserved praise of his father. Ross' mood was not lost on the businessman, nor had his eyes missed the hyped-up condition of his horse.

At the lorry, the Colonel greeted him with a certain coolness. 'I daresay you feel better for that,' he observed. 'And I hope you've got it out of your system – because if you ever ride any of the horses in my yard in that way again, it will be the last time you ride for me.' He spoke quietly, stating a fact. 'That was beyond competitive. That was stupid!'

Ross knew the reproof was justified.

'I'm sorry,' he said. 'It won't happen again.'

15

The night following the Berkshire show was one of the longest of Ross' life.

Though both mentally and physically fatigued, neither his mind nor his body would relax. He kept going over the row with Fergusson in his head, wondering if there had been anything else he could have said, or anything he *had* said that he shouldn't have. The Colonel had not exactly taken his side, but then again he hadn't backed the Scotsman either.

Ross supposed Colonel Preston had to keep on the right side of the other owners as far as he could, as he relied on the money coming in from them to help balance his own outlay.

Damn Ginger! he thought for the thousandth time. *Should* he have taken her into the ring?

In his mind's eye he saw again the children in wheelchairs with their happy, trusting faces, and knew that he couldn't have.

Ross tossed and turned, tension keeping him wide-eyed and staring into the gloom. His left knee ached with a grinding intensity which gradually developed into a throb. It hadn't been this bad since he'd left hospital.

The pain nagged, adding to his worry. The surgeons had hinted that it was possible there could be a chip of bone they had missed, which, should it prove troublesome, might have to be removed at a later date. Ross was becoming more and more convinced that this was the case. On some occasions it would catch him with a stab of pain sharp enough to take his breath away.

Right now, though, it was just pounding monotonously. The three-quarters-full bottle of whisky on the shelf across the room began to exercise a powerful attraction.

He ignored it successfully for four long hours, trying to force his restless mind to relax, to release the tension in his tired muscles.

It was hopeless.

In the still, dark hours of the early morning, despair began to creep in. His career was on the rocks again and it mattered even more this time than last. This time he had had a taste of the success he had been working for. He had been given good horses, wealthy backers, a second chance – and somehow he had blown it. People had been prepared to believe in him and he had let them down.

No matter that he couldn't see how he could have played it any differently. He had failed when he had been given every chance to succeed.

He frowned in the darkness.

Was it possible he *had* lost his nerve? Could somebody imagine confidence to conceal a lack of courage even from themself?

Surely his final round on Woodsmoke was not that of a nervous rider? But then he had been stung into recklessness by frustration and disappointment. Maybe anybody could ride like that if the provocation was great enough – even a nerveshattered has-been. Fergusson's comments came back to haunt him in the darkness.

Had he lost his job – or just the ride on Black Bishop? Ross didn't know, or particularly care if it came to that. Bishop was the horse of a lifetime and without him, prospects for the yard, in Ross' present black mood, seemed bleak and unexciting.

As he heard the clock in the village strike three o'clock, Ross decided enough was enough. Rolling off the bed, he limped across to the bookshelf and reached for the bottle. Without giving himself time to think, he removed the cap and tossed back three long pulls, coughing slightly as its fire burned his throat.

A comforting warmth began to spread through his body. He wiped his watering eyes and regarded the remaining liquid with a longing that dismayed him.

Oblivion, albeit only temporary, was a temptation but it provided no answers. With a groan, he replaced the cap. He was within a whisker of proving Leo right. It was perhaps only his pride that saved him.

He remembered what Annie had said and laughed softly in the darkness. If she could see him now . . . Pride was no help at all at three o'clock in the morning when you couldn't sleep.

At six o'clock he gave up the struggle, got out of bed and had a cold shower. His head and his knee were in fierce competition for his attention and he catered for both with painkillers and a scalding cup of black coffee.

Sitting in the open window with the chill morning air blowing through his thin shirt, he looked down at the yard below him. Beyond the Scotts' cottage, the new horsebox gleamed in the sunlight. Ross regarded it wistfully, wondering what the future held.

In the yard, the horses in the outside boxes leaned over their doors, enjoying the cool air and beginning to think of breakfast. Ross scanned the familiar faces with affection, seeing not only their physical features but also, as with old friends, their characters. Idly, he wondered where Bishop was. Usually the big black was one of the first to demand his feed.

Ross watched for several minutes longer, a sense of unease growing, then shoved his feet into his boots and hurried down to the yard.

A chorus of whinnying greeted him as he headed for Bishop's box. Just as he reached it, the horse swung his head over the half-door and glowered at him. This was normal behaviour for the young prodigy and it was with some relief that Ross took the headcollar from the hook beside the door and deftly slipped it on, avoiding the snapping white teeth.

Once inside the stable, however, Ross' fears returned. The big black was standing resting one hind leg, his back slightly hunched in discomfort, and when Ross asked him to move he did so with bad grace. With a sinking heart he gave the animal a cursory examination before turning him loose and going in search of Bill.

He found the stable manager in the cottage, drinking coffee, and imparted the bad news.

Bill favoured him with a look that wasn't long on welcome and grunted.

'His back, you say?'

'Or hip.'

'Better call Annie, I suppose, if you're sure.'

'Of course I'm sure,' Ross said evenly. 'I know an uncomfortable horse when I see one.'

The little man grunted again.

'I suppose you're happy now,' he said, getting up from his chair.

'Happy?' Ross was astounded.

'Lets you off the hook, doesn't it?'

Ross blinked. The way Bill said it, you would think Ross had engineered the back problem himself, if that were possible. No matter that the horse could possibly be out of action for some while.

He shook his head in disbelief and turned away. That Bishop's injury more or less exonerated him from blame for their non-performance the day before, had not in fact occurred to Ross until Bill had pointed it out. His only concern had been for the horse.

He had his hand on the doorknob when Bill spoke again.

'I'll ring Annie, then. And I'll let the Colonel know. Fergusson may ring this morning.'

It was something, Ross supposed. He nodded. 'Thanks. I'll start the feeds.'

Annie arrived mid-morning, driving as usual as though she were midway through a stage of the World Rally Championships.

'Ross! Bill!' she boomed in greeting. 'Where's the lad?'

Bishop was already wearing his headcollar, and without hesitation Annie marched up, clipped the lead rope on and opened the stable door.

The black made no attempt to bite her, Ross noted wryly. He obviously knew when he'd met his match.

'Did it at the show yesterday, did he?' she asked. 'Seems to have been a day for accidents. Heard anything about the lad who rides King? Chap in the pub said it was a nasty fall.'

'I rang the hospital this morning,' Ross said. 'He'll be out later today. Broken collarbone, concussion, that sort of thing. He'll be sore for a week or two but he'll be okay.'

Ross held Bishop while Annie began her inspection. After a few moments she looked up.

'Found the problem,' she announced 'One of

you like to come back here and hold his near hind up for me?'

Ross obediently relinquished the lead rope to Bill and moved to the black's quarters.

With no further ado Annie set to work. With Ross in position, she placed one hand on the horse's back to re-locate the problem and then, with the heel of her palm and most of her not inconsiderable strength, she hit the animal.

Bishop staggered, nearly sending Ross flying, and flashed a warning look at his attacker.

Annie ignored him, feeling along his spine once again. 'Once more, I think, just to be sure,' she declared.

This time, Ross *was* sent flying. Bishop regained his footing and his dancing hooves came uncomfortably close, but Bill pulled him forward, away from Ross.

'That seems to have done it,' Annie observed with satisfaction. 'Just a slight misalignment, pressing on a nerve. Luckily not too serious, though it could have done a lot more damage if left. Are you all right?'

Ross grinned, accepting a hefty tug up.

'Probably the result of a slip,' she judged, looking at the horse again. 'Wouldn't have thought it would have caused him that much pain but perhaps he's a bit of a baby. Men tend to be,' she added, with a sideways look. 'Rest him for a couple of days. Some heat treatment wouldn't hurt, then plenty of lungeing to build the muscles up. Barring accidents, I see no reason why it should happen again.'

Bishop did indeed look happier already.

'Beer?' Ross suggested, as they left the stable. Then, with a gleam in his eye, 'Or is it too early for you?'

'It's never too early, Ross, you know that.'

While they were quenching their thirst, the Colonel called into the yard on his way out for the day. He came to enquire after Bishop and as he left, told Ross he would see him as usual that evening. He was naturally pleased that Bishop's setback appeared to be only temporary but gave no hint of his disposition towards Ross.

Annie left soon after. She leaned out of the Land-Rover window as Ross stood by to see her off.

'Trouble?' she asked, meaning the Colonel.

Ross shrugged. He wasn't sure.

'You look after yourself, kid. You look awful.'

'Thanks,' he said ironically. 'You're a great morale booster.' He paused, looking behind him.

Bill was nowhere to be seen.

'Are you going to make me an improper suggestion?' Annie asked, intrigued.

'Would it do me any good?' Ross quizzed her, smiling.

'Not in the least. Handsome men are always bastards in love. And besides,' she added, eyes twinkling, 'I make it a rule never to get involved with men who are smaller than me!'

Ross eyed her six-foot-tall, beefy frame and laughed with her. 'Actually, it's Ginger I wanted to ask you about. I believe you had her for a while?'

'Yes, two winters ago. Fergusson put her in foal when she was throwing up a couple of splints.'

Ross raised his eyebrows.

'Well, no, not Fergusson himself – it was a thoroughbred stallion as I recall. Though I wouldn't put it past him, bloody man!' she added as an afterthought.

'And she lost it?'

'Yes. Look, I don't know why I'm telling you this if you already know . . .'

'What exactly happened?'

'Some hooligans with a box of firecrackers,' Annie said, remembering with disgust. 'Got a kick out of seeing the horses run, I suppose. They'd have got more than a kick out of me if I'd caught them at it, I can tell you! I had two mares in foal out together. Sherry dropped hers early but it survived. Ginger wasn't so far on and she miscarried. Poor old girl, she was in a terrible state. She wasn't lame by that time, so we abandoned the idea of breeding from her and Fergusson put her back in training. Bloody shame! She's a sweet mare. Would have made a super brood mare. Anything else I can tell you?'

'No. Thanks, I think you've told me exactly what I wanted to know.'

'Problems?' she asked, eyebrows raised.

'I'm not sure. She does seem to have a rather extreme reaction to loud noises, and I wondered why. And she's a little moody.'

Annie laughed. 'Mare's privilege,' she asserted. 'But I'm not surprised about the noises. That was

344

quite a trauma she suffered. She'll probably get over it, given time.'

'Sure. Well, thanks anyway.'

'Glad to be of service.'

Annie put out a hand to touch his arm briefly. 'Roger told me about your dog, Ross – I'm so sorry. It's a damned shame. I hope he pulls through for you.'

Ross nodded. 'Thanks. He's in good hands.'

Annie withdrew her hand briskly, the fleeting softness smothered, and started the Land-Rover engine.

She winked at Ross. ''Bye then, lover boy. And, hey, take care of yourself, okay?'

He laughed and waved a dismissive hand.

Being a Monday, the yard was deserted in the afternoon. Even Bill had gone off somewhere in the Land-Rover and Ross decided it was a good time to tackle his two difficult pupils.

He began with the new horse, Trooper Joe. The brown horse had settled in quickly and was proving to be quite a character. He was a likeable rogue though and, Ross suspected, highly intelligent.

He worked quite happily in the schooling area until Ross started to apply stronger leg aids to ask him to bend. As soon as Joey felt his rider's leg move back he scuttled crabwise for the nearest fence and it was only Ross' quick reactions that saved his knee from being ground against the woodwork. He tried once more, with a similar result. Joey didn't get uptight about it; it was just a technique he had developed for getting his own way. Ross decided that at some time, somebody had probably used spurs roughly on the horse and he had never forgotten.

Sorting out problem animals had been Ross' business in the States and he enjoyed the challenge. From the tackroom he fetched an old driving bridle and fitted it over Joey's existing bridle, adjusted it so the blinkers were in the right position and stepped back into the saddle.

The horse seemed untroubled by these new attachments. Ross applied his leg hard, just behind the girth. Joey took one step sideways and then paused, unsure. His vision restricted to the front, he could no longer tell where the fence was exactly.

Seizing the moment, Ross urged the horse forward. He repeated the exercise several times and when Joey tried to turn his head to locate the fence, Ross kept him straight. He popped him over the only jump that was standing in the arena at that time, parallel bars at about three foot six, which he jumped with no hesitation and some style.

After half an hour, Ross judged he had had enough and dismounted with a feeling of achievement. It would probably be many weeks before he could dispense with the blinkers but from the feel of the horse over a jump, the wait would be worth it.

A few spots of rain were falling as Ross led Ginger from her box, and the sky promised more. He rode into the school with little optimism. The only way he could see of reducing the mare's fear

346

of loud noises was by letting her grow used to them gradually. The thing was, it would take weeks, possibly months, and he couldn't see Fergusson allowing him the time. The thought that it might already be too late he pushed resolutely away. He *had* to keep the ride on Bishop.

He warmed the mare up as for a normal schooling session and took her over one or two jumps. She behaved well, apparently in one of her better moods. Ross' spirits rose a notch or two. The rain increased to a steady drizzle.

From his pocket, he took two small flat pieces of wood that he had dug out of the toolshed earlier. Letting the mare walk round the school on a loose rein, he gently tapped the pieces together. The mare flicked her ears back enquiringly. He patted her, talking all the while, and then tapped them again.

Gradually he increased the volume of the taps. Ginger became a lot more edgy, but didn't panic. Ross made much of her. He was so absorbed that he didn't see a mackintoshed figure come and lean on the gate. After another ten minutes or so, Ross began to allow himself a glimmer of hope. The mare was trying hard.

In the field beside the school, one of the Colonel's spaniels, on a rabbiting expedition, put up a brace of pheasant with a flurry of clucking and flapping wings.

Ginger's nerves, already stretched, snapped. She bolted blindly.

Ross was ready for her. With his legs clamped

hard on her sides, he put both hands on one rein and pulled her head round. With her muzzle touching his boot and her white-rimmed eye almost at his knee she could do no more than stagger sideways for a few yards.

For a moment, Ross thought she would fall but she managed to retain her balance and halted, splay-legged and shuddering violently. He could feel her extreme tension still and knew that if he released her head she would probably bolt again. Keeping the rein tight over her neck, he slid off the opposite side and stood talking quietly to her.

Slowly, she relaxed. Ross found he was shaking with reaction as he released the rein. She stood beside him, the picture of dejection, and he felt sorry for her.

He considered getting back on but couldn't raise much enthusiasm for the idea. The rain was now a steady downpour; he had just lost half-an-hour's progress in a split second and he hadn't the heart to start again.

He shied away from the thought that he just plain hadn't the heart.

Patting the mare's rain-sodden and steaming neck, Ross unsaddled her and turned her loose. He took off his crash hat and let the rain run through his hair and down his face. Tired and dispirited, he limped back towards the yard with the saddle over his arm. He was almost at the gate before he lifted his head enough to see that someone was there and he'd been watched. His spirits fell another notch.

When he saw the blonde hair under the waxed

cotton hood, Ross didn't know whether to be relieved or sorry. On the one hand, Lindsay was the person to whom he had always found it easiest to talk; on the other, he was slightly ashamed that she had witnessed his weakness in not remounting.

He scanned her face for scorn but found none.

'Hi, Princess,' he said wearily.

'Hello.' Her tone was absent-minded and she was gazing at the horse.

Ross balanced the saddle on the top rail of the gate and leaned on it, too down to care that the rain wasn't doing the leather any good. He would oil it later.

Lindsay looked sideways at him.

'Is it because she's a chestnut?' she asked abruptly.

Ross didn't pretend to misunderstand her. It was a question he had asked himself a thousand times. Ginger . . . the horse in America . . . the one in his nightmares . . . they were all the same colour. Was it possible that his trouble with Ginger stemmed from a subconscious connection he'd made between them? Was he tense, and communicating his tension to the mare?

Maybe a little, he admitted, but surely the basic problem was with her. Why couldn't anyone else see that she was crazy? *Could* it be his imagination?

'Simone is a chestnut,' he reminded her defensively.

'*What* then, Ross? What's happened to you? You used to ride all the roughest, baddest horses. People said you had no nerves at all.'

349

Ross sensed that Lindsay longed for him to reassure her. After all, it was she who was responsible, in the main, for his being in England and riding the Oakley Manor horses. He noted her use of the past tense.

'Perhaps I should have quit while I was ahead,' he said, taking refuge in flippancy.

Lindsay wasn't amused. 'But she bothers you, doesn't she? You surely can't deny there's a problem?' she demanded. 'Especially after what happened just now.'

'And what do you think happened just now?' Ross asked in brittle tones.

'I saw one of the toughest riders on the circuit let a novice horse get away with blatant disobedience. I saw him break the first rule of training – any training – that you should always end on a good note.' She was watching his face closely as she spoke. 'Oh, come on, Ross! Don't you know what they're saying about you?'

'People always talk,' he observed mildly. 'You don't have to listen.'

'Damn you!' Lindsay cried vehemently. 'Don't give me that "I don't care" routine. I know you better than that.'

He turned his back to the gate and stared into the middle distance, eyes bleak, face shuttered.

There was silence for a moment, then she put a tentative hand on his shoulder. 'Don't shut me out, Ross,' she pleaded. 'We used to be friends. I just want to help.'

Ross didn't respond. Rain dripped off his hair

and ran down his neck inside his denim shirt, which was in any case plastered to his back. He wished she would go and he needed her to stay, but each word she uttered twisted the knife a little more. How would it help to admit to her that he was beginning to doubt himself?

'Ross!' Losing patience, she gripped his arm and pulled him to face her. 'Talk to me, damn you!'

She caught him off guard. For a moment he gazed down at her upturned, impatient face, glistening with rain, and then his control slipped. With one finger he tilted her chin and when she made no move to resist, bent to kiss her in a fashion far removed from the brotherly embraces of the past.

Lindsay froze for an instant, then her hand stole up into his wet hair and pulled him closer.

For a moment nothing else mattered until, abruptly, Ross pulled away.

'That was bloody stupid!' he said roughly. 'I'm sorry. Better forget it.'

Lindsay recoiled, hurt. 'Consider it forgotten,' she retorted roundly, and turned to open the gate.

Ross put out a hand to stop her. It seemed more important than ever that she should understand about Ginger.

'I'm not afraid for myself,' he said, trying to find the words to explain. 'At least, I don't think so. It's just – the nightmares – the children – that child, screaming. I can't let it happen again.'

Lindsay heard the desperation in his voice and turned back, her eyes full of compassion. 'But it won't, Ross. It was a once-in-a-lifetime fluke. You have to put it behind you. Vixen had a tumour. Ginger's a completely different horse.'

'Ginger is insane,' he stated bluntly.

'She doesn't *look* it,' Lindsay said doubtfully, surveying the chestnut mare who stood quietly, tail turned to the driving rain. 'Are you sure?'

'Last year at Annie's she was frightened by some idiots with a firecracker and lost her foal. I don't know whether it turned her mind or what, but now any sudden loud noise makes her freak out. She stops thinking and just runs. Won't stop for anything. If anyone got in her way . . .'

'Is that what happened just now?'

Ross nodded. 'It would have, if I hadn't caught her in time.'

'Can't she be accustomed to loud noises? You know, desensitised or something?'

'I don't know. That's what I was trying but I can't see Fergusson giving me the time. He's just as likely to whisk the horses off to some other yard if I say I don't want to compete on the mare for a bit, and I can't risk that. I'm already in danger of losing the ride on his horses, if not my job.'

Lindsay watched him steadily, rain running off the tip of her nose.

'It won't come to that, Ross, surely? Won't Uncle John speak to him?'

'I saw your uncle this morning and he said he'd talk to me tonight. He didn't look like a man about to increase my paycheque,' Ross told her dryly. 'He wasn't happy yesterday. He stands to lose a lot if Fergusson pulls out.'

Lindsay bit her lip. 'I don't suppose it'd do any good for me to have a word with him?'

'Thanks, but no, I think it's beyond that now. If your uncle is going to stick with me, it has to be his decision.'

She glanced at Ginger again, frowning. 'Are you sure about her, Ross? Is she really dangerous?'

He studied her thoughtful face for a moment, realising that she still wasn't convinced.

He sighed. 'I don't know, Princess. Perhaps you're right and I *am* biased against chestnut mares. I suppose time will tell. I just have a bad feeling about her and I don't want anyone else to be hurt. Least of all me,' he added with a self-deprecating grin.

Lindsay still looked troubled and Ross felt enough had been said. He smiled brightly at her. 'Come on. Let's go in and have some coffee. Maggie's been baking. If we stay out here we'll get wet.'

Lindsay surveyed his sodden clothing and laughed. 'That would be a shame,' she said. 'Honestly, I shouldn't think you could get much wetter if you went and jumped in the river. Why on earth didn't you put a coat on?'

'I don't know.' Ross whistled to Ginger, who came willingly towards him. 'I guess I need someone to mother me.'

'Like hell!' Lindsay spluttered. 'Look, I really came to see Gypsy. She cut herself yesterday and I wanted to make sure it hadn't swollen up.'

'It's a clean wound,' Ross said, leading Ginger to the gate. 'Couple of days and she'll be fine.'

They wandered down into the yard where Ross took the mare back to her box and rubbed her down.

'So, where's your dog?' Lindsay asked, following him back to the tackroom. 'He's not usually far away.'

It still hurt, to think of the dog. Ross gave her the potted version that he had already given the others, about the storm and the swinging door.

'Oh, I'm sorry, Ross! Oh, the poor lad!' Sympathetic tears shone in her eyes and he longed to take her in his arms again.

'So how is he now?' Lindsay scanned his face. 'You haven't rung, have you? Oh, Ross, you must! You can't just leave it like that.'

'I know. I'll ring later.' Impossible to tell her that even if the dog should recover, he couldn't take the chance of having him back.

Lindsay checked on Gypsy and together they headed for the cottage and Maggie's fresh bread and cakes.

They were back on an even keel, their easy relationship apparently restored, but Ross could not help but feel that it would never be quite the same again.

'I want you to be straight with me,' the Colonel said by way of opening the inquest. They had both settled into leather armchairs with glasses of sherry to hand.

'Sure.' Ross nodded.

'I don't mean to imply that you haven't been in the past,' the Colonel added. 'It's just that

354

sometimes I find you – shall we say, inscrutable? I find I have no idea what's going on in your head.'

You and me both, Ross thought, ironically. He surveyed his sherry glass, smiled faintly and said nothing.

'By the way,' the Colonel said, glancing round, 'where's your dog tonight?'

'He's at the vet's. Had an accident Friday night,' Ross said shortly.

'Poor old chap. What happened?' The Colonel, who was very fond of his own small pack of dogs, seemed genuinely concerned.

'He was hit by something. It happened in the storm.'

'What? On the road? A car?'

Ross shrugged. 'I don't know. I found him in the yard. The barn door was swinging – I thought it was probably that.' It was a good start for the policy of *glasnost*, he thought wryly. But how else to explain without a long, involved account that would undoubtedly stray into forbidden territory? Interesting that Roland had apparently said nothing of the matter to his father.

'Is he going to be all right?'

Ross had spoken to Roger West's partner earlier in the evening and learned that the dog was holding his own but no more than that.

'He may be paralysed. It's touch and go.'

'That's a damned shame,' the Colonel said. 'He's a nice dog.'

'Mmm.' Ross had no wish to talk about it.

They sat in silence for a moment, the Colonel

355

thoughtfully swilling the sherry round his glass. Ross, for his part, felt strangely detached now that the crunch had come.

'Robbie Fergusson called this morning,' his boss said finally, holding his glass up to view the contents and then watching Ross over the top.

Ross waited, poker-faced.

The Colonel half-smiled to himself. 'I told him about Bishop and explained that he was obviously uncomfortable yesterday. Robbie conceded the point but doesn't accept that you were right to withdraw the mare.'

'Surprise, surprise,' Ross murmured. 'So what now? Have I lost the ride?'

'I think that's up to you,' the Colonel said. 'Fergusson may be a pompous, overbearing bastard but he's not stupid. He's a tactician by profession and even *he* realises that you get a sweet tune out of Bishop. The thing is, we obviously have a problem. He's not happy about the rumours he's been hearing concerning you.'

'Which one in particular?' Ross asked, flippantly. 'The one that says I'm practically an alcoholic or the one that says I've lost my nerve? Or do you subscribe to the popular view that I drink to conquer my fear?'

'I take no notice of hearsay, myself. You should know that by now.' The Colonel wasn't amused. 'But, quite apart from that, you must admit there's some kind of problem with Ginger?'

'I do.' Ross had a strong sense of *déjà vu*.

'And?'

'And I don't care if I never sit on her again,' he said bluntly.

'Are you going to tell me why?'

'I don't believe she's safe. She's mentally unstable.'

'I see.' The Colonel raised his eyebrows but sounded neither surprised nor incredulous. On the other hand he gave no sign of being precisely convinced, either. 'Given that, what do you intend to do about her?'

Ross sighed. 'If it's a choice between riding Ginger and losing them both, I'll ride the mare. But I'd like it to go on record that in my opinion she'd be far better retired to stud. If her instability arises from a trauma, as I believe it does, it wouldn't be hereditary.'

The Colonel shook his head.

'Fergusson wouldn't hear of it,' he stated with conviction. 'He doesn't believe the mare's at fault.'

'And you?'

The Colonel considered his reply. 'I believe that some horses and riders are incompatible, just as some people find it impossible to get along with one another. But having said that, I respect your judgement.'

'Thank you.'

'Well, I've seen nothing so far to persuade me otherwise.'

Ross sipped his drink, wishing it was a beer, and wondered how far the Colonel's trust would stretch. God knows, there were enough people determined to put it to the test.

'Look, Ross,' he said suddenly. 'As far as I'm concerned, you don't have to prove a bloody thing. If you don't want to ride the mare – for whatever reason – it's not the end of the world. I'm sure we can withstand the loss of Fergusson's horses. No one here would blame you.'

Ross looked up, surprised and grateful for this gesture of support. 'It wouldn't do my reputation much good,' he observed. 'Besides, Bishop is by far the best horse I've ever ridden, maybe the best I'll ever ride, and I've no intention of watching somebody else ride him into the ring if I can possibly prevent it.'

'Fergusson wants to see the mare jump at the New Forest Show next week,' the Colonel warned softly. 'She's entered in the Open and he says he'll be there to watch.'

'Fergusson's a pain,' Ross said, with feeling. Danny had told him just the day before, how much of a tourist event the Brockenhurst show was. Hardly ideal conditions for a nervy horse.

'Privately, I agree,' the Colonel said. 'But in this instance I'm afraid he holds the reins.'

'I'd be happy to let him,' Ross responded dryly.

'Another sherry?' The Colonel rose and poured two without waiting for an answer. He held one out to Ross.

'What about my reputation?' Ross asked, lifting one eyebrow ironically as he accepted the glass.

The Colonel collapsed back into his chair, narrowly missing a spaniel which had taken up residence in his absence. 'Should I be worried?' he asked, his shrewd grey eyes on Ross' face.

'No.' Ross returned his gaze steadily.

The Colonel pursed his lips and nodded, apparently satisfied.

Not for the first time, Ross felt he was very fortunate in his boss.

'Were you aware that my son was intending to buy a horse?' the Colonel enquired.

Ross blinked. 'No. Well, not exactly. I mean, he did say something once but, no offence meant – you know how it is – I didn't pay much heed.'

'I know exactly how it is,' the Colonel said heavily. 'But apparently, this time Roland was quite serious. The horse is to arrive on Wednesday but beyond that he will tell me nothing. God knows what sort of animal he'll have turned up.'

Wednesday was progressing in the manner of many Wednesdays past when the sleek blue horsebox pulled into the yard.

It was mid-afternoon and Ross had just finished a satisfying schooling session on Trooper Joe when the new horse arrived. Roland swung his immaculately shod feet off the office table where he'd been lounging, drink in hand, since lunchtime and wandered out into the yard. Sarah and Danny emerged from stable doorways and Bill turned from his discussion with Ross to regard the vehicle with reluctant curiosity.

Ross knew the stable manager considered Roland's unexpected venture into ownership as a frivolous and very likely short-lived affair, dreamt up on a whim. Ross was not so sure. He'd begun to suspect that Roland put a lot more thought into his actions than he would have anyone believe. What those thoughts were, though, was often anyone's guess.

The box driver, a young chap with a piece of straw between his teeth, called a cheerful 'Afternoon' and strode round to the rear of the lorry.

'Glad to get shot of this one, we are,' he said with debatable tact, undoing the bolts and clips which secured the ramp. 'Beats me why you'd want him. Still, I wish you luck!'

Sarah and Danny looked intensely curious, Bill glowered and Roland smiled with unruffled calm.

As the ramp was lowered and the partitions swung to one side, those waiting in the yard were treated to a dim view of a massive chestnut rump at the same time as their ears were assailed by a piercing shriek. The horse was untied and led to the top of the ramp, where he stood with upflung head and eager eyes, surveying his new surroundings.

Bill Scott swore under his breath and for once Ross was inclined to agree with him.

Completely dwarfing the man who held him, Telamon the failed racehorse marched purposefully down the ramp and shrieked a challenge to the world.

From the stables, half a dozen excited voices answered him.

Bill swore again. 'Shit! That's all we need. A bloody stallion!'

Ross glanced at Roland and was amused to see a

look of almost comical dismay cross his face. Could it be that for once the Colonel's son had failed fully to appreciate all the aspects of a situation? As swiftly as the expression had touched his face it had gone. The upper-class idiot returned.

'Well, can't it be muzzled or something?' he enquired with wonderful innocence.

Ross smothered a laugh.

'It's not a bloody dog,' Bill observed witheringly, including the American in his disapproval.

Roland looked hurt. 'Of course not. He's Ross' battle charger.'

'Most likely break his neck!' Bill grunted, ever the pessimist.

'Ross'll manage him, won't you, Ross?' Danny stated with easy confidence.

'Oh, sure,' he said lightly. 'No problem.'

Roland beamed happily.

His charge duly handed over, the box driver lost no time in getting on his way. Probably, Ross thought, afraid that they would change their minds and decide to send the horse back.

After discussion, Telamon was installed in one of two empty boxes on the opposite side of the yard to Bishop and Flo.

Roland seemed anxious to see the horse ridden and reluctantly Ross agreed to try him that evening. Reluctantly because he guessed that the event, having been announced in advance, would inevitably attract all the Oakley Manor crew and he would far rather have had a chance to become acquainted with the horse in private.

As he had feared, when Ross accepted a leg-up from Bill at half-past seven that evening, the rails of the school positively bristled with interested onlookers.

Not only had Roland reappeared with his father, but Lindsay and James had also come with them. Sarah had returned to the yard after going home for her tea and was accompanied by Darcy Richmond, with whom she was apparently spending the evening. Even Maggie had come out, a fluffy pink cardigan buttoned over her apron, and to cap it all Danny was there with his video camera to record the event for posterity.

'Shoulda sold tickets,' Ross observed to Bill as he settled into the soft leather of Butterworth's temporarily redundant saddle.

The stallion, which had proved surprisingly quiet to handle in the stable, sidled restlessly beneath him, back hunched and tense. He proceeded across the yard to the school on legs which punched the ground like steel pistons. With jaw set, he tossed his head, anticipating resistance from Ross.

Ross sat quietly, trying not to interfere with the big chestnut more than was necessary. Only in Bishop had he ever felt anything approaching this power, but whereas in the German horse it was controlled and smooth, in this animal it was raw and rebellious. Ross felt his own adrenalin begin to pump as a thrill of excitement rose in him.

As soon as he heard the gate click shut behind him he sent the chestnut on, sensing the frustration and bottled energy that would have to be released before he could even hope to communicate with the horse.

Telamon hesitated fractionally as his head was set free. A succession of riders who had strapped him down ever harder in an attempt to control his wildness had left him unprepared for this abrupt change of tactics.

Then, with a squeal of pure pleasure, he erupted into the centre of the school and proceeded to buck himself almost inside out. Ross stayed with him, gripping hard with his long legs and letting his body follow through. The stallion reached the end of the school and turned, still bucking, to make his way back.

Unsure how much longer he could cling to the wildly lurching horse, Ross sat down hard, pulled its head up and drove it forward. Gradually the leaps levelled out and the chestnut began to run.

Ross let him go. From Telamon he received no feeling of hysteria. This horse, though unruly, was not about to do itself any harm. Sure in this knowledge, Ross relaxed and began to enjoy himself.

The area was too small for the stallion to reach any great pace and after four or five circuits he started to steady. Ross steered him towards one of the low schooling fences and he skipped over it, barely bothering to break his stride. Encouraged, he inclined him towards the big parallel bars in the centre of the school. The jump was five foot square and had been erected when Ross was schooling

Woodsmoke earlier in the day. It was not something Ross would normally have asked of a comparative novice but he wanted to see how the big chestnut would react.

Telamon flicked his ears forward, snatched at the bit and forged fearlessly ahead. Ross let him go, and as the massive hindquarters bunched and lowered, threw his weight forward. The red and white poles flashed by a good twelve inches below the stallion's hooves and the landing was smooth and effortless.

A cheer broke from the lips of those watching and Telamon shied violently and bucked again, almost catching Ross out. One more circuit of the school and the horse allowed Ross to slow him to a trot and finally to a halt by the fence.

The American's little crowd of supporters looked as excited as he felt. He patted the arching chestnut neck and slid off the horse. Telamon turned to eye him, froth cascading from his chomping jaws, but the expression held no malice. Ross had the distinct impression that the horse was very satisfied.

'I've never seen anything quite like it!' The Colonel was the first to find his voice. 'What do you use, Superglue?'

Ross grinned. 'I did a lot of horse-breaking in the States,' he said. 'They weren't all like that, of course – these days we try to do it gently – but occasionally you come across a bad one. It's just practice and a measure of luck.'

'Play it down if you like,' the Colonel said, 'but

I don't know of many riders who could have stayed on that or who would have cared to try.'

'Well, *I* knew he could do it,' Lindsay said smugly. Her protégé had proved himself.

'He's far from gentled,' Ross cautioned them, mildly embarrassed. 'It'll be a whole different ball game when we get him to a show.'

'Nonsense! I shall expect you to win at Brockenhurst,' Roland stated confidently. 'He's entered in the Open, you know.'

'Oh, boy!' Ross said with feeling, thinking of Ginger. 'That should be quite a class!'

'Wicked!' Danny agreed.

Ross decided it was time the stallion was put back in his box. It would be best to wait until the horse had settled in before he tried turning him loose to roll in the sand. As he ran the stirrups up and loosened the girth, Darcy and Sarah took their leave. Darcy clapped the American on the back.

'Uncle Frank will be sorry to have missed that,' he said. 'Quite a performance.'

'I've got it on video,' Danny reminded him. 'Peter will enjoy it too. He's some horse!'

'He is that,' Ross agreed.

Lindsay and James drifted off with the Colonel, and as Ross led the horse back to the yard, Roland fell in beside him.

'My dear papa was convinced I was trying to murder you when he found out about Telamon,' he told Ross, who reflected that the thought had crossed his own mind. 'But I told him it was just what you needed to revive your tattered reputation.'

'My battle charger?' Ross remembered, amused.

'Exactly,' Roland said.

As Ross settled the stallion he pondered Roland's real reason for buying the horse. It would be easiest to take him at face value and believe that the huge, powerful chestnut had appealed to him and that he had bought it on a whim with no thought for the possible consequences, but this Ross couldn't do. Surely a man with Roland's past experience of horses couldn't fail to see what a potential minefield of problems having the stallion might entail, not least the difficulty of riding him?

'You made a good job of that.' Bill had come up, unseen. 'D'you think you can cope with him in public?'

Ross finished rubbing Telamon down.

'Well, we'll have to see, won't we?'

He shut the door and stood looking at the stallion for a moment. He was a magnificent beast. Not beautiful, his frame was perhaps a little too angular for that, but his chest was broad and deep, his legs strong and clean, and his hindquarters immensely muscled. He turned, munching hay, to glance curiously at the two men. His long head wide between the eyes; plenty of room for brain.

'I wasn't sure you'd ride him,' Bill said after a moment, and Ross knew he meant that he'd doubted Ross' nerve, not his ability.

He didn't say anything.

'I suppose you had to, with everybody watching like that.'

That's right, don't make the mistake of paying

me a compliment, Ross thought with wry amusement.

'I suppose I could have said I had a headache,' he said aloud. 'Damn! Why didn't I think of that?'

The stable manager regarded him thoughtfully. 'Is the mare really unsafe?' he asked, in the manner of one reluctantly relinquishing a long-held belief.

Ross looked at him, surprised. '*I* believe she is,' he said quietly. 'But I guess I can't prove it to you.'

He switched off Telamon's light.

'See you later, big fella,' he murmured, and started back across the yard with the saddle and bridle.

'He'll never be up to much,' Bill said mulishly. 'He's too full of himself. He's a waste of money.'

'It's Roland's money,' Ross observed mildly.

Bill grunted and moved away.

Ross shook his head, smiling in the half-light. He supposed it had been an olive branch of sorts. Not much of one, admittedly, but then Noah's dove had only managed a twig.

16

'Ross Wakelin!' a voice said forcefully, just behind him.

It was Saturday. He was near Guildford at a novice show with Clown, Barfly and the new horse, Saxon Blue. So far, things had been going well.

He turned with interest but no premonition of disaster, to find himself looking at a face he'd hoped very much was firmly in his past.

'Mrs Faulkner,' he acknowledged without much enthusiasm.

The woman looked older, thinner, and if possible, even more bitter than the last time they had met. Once an attractive woman, the accident that had maimed her only daughter had twisted both her features and her mind.

She hated Ross with an unflagging vigour, blaming him completely and utterly for the child's paralysis. She had written him dozens of poisonous letters and called him countless times with ugly threats, even once trying to run him down in her car. Then, by chance, Ross' father had found out and used his legal connections to force her to stop, threatening her with a charge of harassment.

Hers was the face that had swum in and out of his nightmares, relentlessly accusing. Hers, too, the face he thought he'd seen at the ringside the previous weekend.

His heart sank.

He needed Diane Faulkner like he needed a contract placed on him by the Mafia. She could mean nothing but trouble.

He was on his feet temporarily, taking a rest between rides, and now searched the crowds hopefully for a sight of Danny with his next mount.

'I didn't believe it when I heard,' Mrs Faulkner said, shaking her head to support her statement.

Ross regarded her warily. 'I'm sorry?'

She didn't leave him long in the dark.

'How can you live with yourself? My poor baby is in a wheelchair, crippled, her life ruined, and you're back playing your games as if nothing had happened!'

If only you knew, lady! he thought bitterly. He edged away, still looking for Danny.

'I thought you'd quit. I thought you'd finally done the decent thing. I suppose you thought I wouldn't find you if you ran away to England? But I did find you and now I'll tell everybody! People should know. You shouldn't be allowed to carry on. You're a murderer!'

Nobody had died, logic protested, but Ross didn't think it would help his cause to point that out.

He stopped edging away. The only obvious effect it was having was that of encouraging her to speak louder, and that he could do without. He knew from bitter experience that reasoning with her was useless. Diversion was his only hope.

'Who told you where I was?'

She was not noticeably put off.

'Someone who recognised you for the louse you are!' she said, stepping closer. 'Someone who knew –'

'How is Naomi? Is she with you?' Ross cut in, trying again. Diane Faulkner's voice had a distressingly carrying quality, accentuated by its being broadly American in a very English crowd, and many of those in the vicinity were beginning to take a more than covert interest.

This time it worked. She stopped in mid-sentence and stared at him.

'You bastard!' she hissed, and dealt him a stinging slap across the face.

She was not a big woman but hatred lent her strength and the unexpected attack rocked Ross back on his heels. He gasped and caught her wrist firmly as she swung at him a second time.

She tugged back ineffectually.

'Take your filthy hands off me!'

Suddenly a camera flashbulb went off somewhere close to Ross' left shoulder and he turned, astounded. With a grin of triumph, the photographer pressed the shutter again.

'Gotcha!' he said.

Ross cleaned tack with absentminded thoroughness in the yellow light of the tackroom that evening. The yard was quiet. Only muffled sounds of munching and snorting disturbed the warm stillness. Occasionally, from the other side of the yard, he could hear bursts of canned laughter and clapping from the open window of the Scotts' cottage. He supposed the Colonel and Roland would be getting ready to go to Lindsay and James' party. The thought did nothing to improve his mood.

He soaped and buffed the leather to a rich, gleaming suppleness, lost in gloomy contemplation of the latest vigorous stirring his own particular nest of hornets had received.

Danny had arrived with Fly in time to provide Ross with a respectable means of escape, and one he'd had no hesitation in making use of.

Diane Faulkner had screamed more abuse, most of which was mercifully unintelligible, and was finally shepherded away by the collecting ring steward and a nurse from St John's Ambulance. Barfly surprisingly did not take advantage of his jockey's preoccupation and jumped what was for him a reasonably sensible round.

It didn't take long for word to get round, and for three more long hours, Ross had endured a host of curious and censorious stares. He seemed to be making his mark on the English circuit all right but for all the wrong reasons. Whoever said 'There's no such thing as bad publicity' should have his head seen to, he decided bitterly.

He was immensely grateful for Danny's unquestioning loyalty and his spirits were further lifted by two competent performances from Saxon Blue.

The fact remained, though, that someone had deliberately searched out Diane Faulkner in order to set her on to Ross. Someone who hated him enough to make sure there was a press photographer handy with camera poised to witness the confrontation.

Although Ross had to admit that there seemed to be no shortage of people who wished him less than well, he felt that given his connections the person in this case was almost certainly Harry Douglas. It was criminal that someone in his position should be allowed to get away with so deliberate a campaign of ruin. However obviously unfair, this latest publicity would go down a storm with the American's growing band of detractors.

'Hello, Ross.'

Lindsay stood in the doorway. God only knew how long she had been standing there. She wore ski-pants and a long, loose shirt, her hair hidden under a cotton headscarf.

Ross smiled. 'Hi, Princess. I hope you're not going to make a habit of sneaking up on me. It's not good for my blood pressure, you know.'

'I'm sorry. Actually, I wasn't sure you'd still be here. I thought you were going out.'

'Out?'

'With Danielle,' Lindsay reminded him.

Ross could have kicked himself. 'And I thought *you* were having a party,' he countered. 'Shouldn't you be getting ready?'

'I came to check on Gypsy. She's re-opened that cut on her leg.'

'*This* time of night?' he asked, incredulously. 'You should have called. The cut's fine. I changed the dressing an hour ago.'

'Actually, I had to get out of the house,' she admitted, carefully tracing the line of a scratch on the doorpost with her fingernail. 'Mother's getting on my nerves. She's so overpowering. She has to try and organise everybody and they don't need it. They're all professionals – the caterers, the musicians, even the florists. It's *so* embarrassing. You can see they're all wishing her at the devil.' She sighed. 'I suppose she means well, but . . .'

'Sure she does. She just wants everything to be right for you.'

'Not for *me!*' Lindsay burst out, looking all of a sudden younger and very unhappy. 'She wants it for herself. Everything has to be how *she* wants it, so her toffee-nosed friends will be impressed. I'm even marrying the man *she* chose for me. The most eligible of eligible bachelors.' She stopped short, biting her lip. 'No, I didn't mean that. James is a great guy. I'm very fond of him.'

Ross supposed it was natural to get cold feet at the last minute, and for Lindsay it must almost feel like the final commitment with the scale of the

373

celebrations, but he fervently wished she hadn't chosen to unburden herself on him. *Fond* was a strange choice of word, though.

'You'll be fine. You make a great pair,' he assured her. 'Look, can I get you something? A coffee? Beer?'

Lindsay shook her head. 'No. Thanks all the same. I'd better get back. I've got to change and finish getting ready. I'll probably get a rollicking as it is.'

She made no move to leave, however, concentrating on the scratch on the doorpost once more, a little crease between her brows.

Ross finished soaping the last bridle and started reassembling it. The silence was loud between them and he wished she would just go. He wasn't by any means the best person to advise her on affairs of the heart, and after last week he would have thought she'd have known that.

'Why don't you want to come tonight, Ross?' she asked abruptly, turning to face him.

He blinked. Whatever he'd expected, it hadn't been a direct challenge.

'I . . . er . . . I don't have anything to wear,' he said lamely. 'I wasn't expecting to have to dress up when I packed to come over.'

'It doesn't matter. There'll probably be all sorts there.'

Ross raised an eyebrow. 'Not jeans and cowboy boots,' he said. 'Your mother would crucify me!'

'Stuff Mother!' Lindsay countered forcefully. 'But it's not just that, is it, Ross? You could have borrowed. Why don't you want to come? Is it Danielle?'

Ross felt cornered. 'No, it's not Danielle. I never did ask her to go out tonight. Sorry, Princess. It's just . . . I don't know. I guess I'm just not in the mood for partying.'

'Me neither,' Lindsay confided with a smile. 'Look, please say you'll come? Even just for a little while. Roland will lend you something to wear. He's about your height and he's got tons.'

Ross was taken aback. 'He might not want to . . .'

'He doesn't mind. I asked him yesterday, just in case. Please say you will? It won't seem right otherwise. Do it just to annoy Mother, if nothing else!'

Ross gave in. He'd had it in the back of his mind that he really ought to put in an appearance, anyway.

'You say *your mother* organises everybody,' he said pointedly. 'Okay, I'll come but it won't be until later. Now you'd better be on your way, hadn't you?'

Lindsay nodded. She turned away and then stopped and said over her shoulder, 'I knew you weren't going out with Danielle tonight. She's coming to the party with Roland.'

'You devious little . . .!' Ross threw his cleaning sponge at her and she ducked and ran out of the door.

Ross travelled to the first day of the New Forest Show on the Tuesday with his mind all over the place. Behind him in the lorry, four excited horses shifted and stamped on the straw-covered matting but for once he had little thought for them.

He'd spent less than an hour at Lindsay's party. Roland and Danielle were the only people he'd known apart from the Colonel and the engaged couple themselves, and he was not in the mood for making small talk to strangers.

He nibbled a couple of canapés, drank a glass of champagne and slipped away when the dancing began, feeling he'd done his duty and unable to bear the sight of Lindsay, gorgeous in emerald silk, smiling up at James as they circled the floor.

He slowed the box as they approached the bottleneck of Lyndhurst High Street, tapping his fingers on the wheel.

Monday's article in the *Sportsman* had not spared him. The photograph of Diane Faulkner and himself was a masterpiece, surpassed only by the wording of the headline, which ran AMERICAN RIDER IN CRIPPLED CHILD TRAGEDY.

The accompanying report rated Ross as little better than a child molester. He was labelled a 'controversial rider', his accident in America was termed an 'incident' and Mrs Faulkner was described as 'understandably bitter'.

She was quoted as saying that Ross had tried to buy her silence with a wheelchair for Naomi, and made it sound as though his reckless or incompetent riding was to blame for the tragedy. No mention was made of Vixen's brain tumour.

The article was careful to draw no conclusions and make no direct accusations on its own behalf. It really didn't have to.

Ross' Monday night session with the Colonel had not – for the second week running – been a bundle of laughs.

'Life certainly hasn't been dull since you came to ride for us, has it, Ross?' his boss said by way of an opener as they sat down together.

'No, sir.' Ross returned a steady gaze.

'Accidents, prowlers, break-ins, fights amongst the staff, and now this . . .' He indicated a copy of the *Sportsman* which lay open on his desk.

Ross said nothing. There didn't seem to be anything he could say.

'A reporter from the local rag woke me at half-past seven this morning, wanting to know my feelings on the matter,' the Colonel told him. 'I think he got rather more of them than he bargained for! I detest such intrusions, especially by the press, and especially before breakfast. I threatened him with trespass!'

Ross smiled, picturing the scene.

The Colonel picked up the paper. 'It doesn't read well, though, does it? We can do without this sort of thing if we're going to try to attract sponsors next year.'

It was the first Ross had heard of looking for a sponsor, although it was something that became a necessity for most riders when they started competing at a higher level.

'I'm sorry,' he said, helplessly. 'It wasn't the way

they make it sound. They twist everything round to suit themselves.'

The Colonel nodded, seeming calm enough. 'It hasn't gone unnoticed the way Harry Douglas has singled you out, you know. Several people have remarked on it. Franklin is of the opinion we should put some pressure on the editor to make Mr Douglas toe the line. Would you like to make a statement in your own defence?'

Ross considered this. 'No, I don't think so,' he said after a moment. 'You can't convince those that don't want to be convinced, and the others won't believe this rubbish anyway. I think if I ignore it and Douglas can be persuaded to give it a rest, the whole business will die a natural death.'

The Colonel raised an eyebrow. 'Well, yes. I suppose that's one way of looking at it.' He tapped the photograph with one finger. 'I assume there is a reasonable explanation for this?'

Ross shrugged. 'She'd hit me once and was going to do it again. I had to stop her somehow.'

The Colonel regarded him long and thoughtfully. 'For a quiet, unassuming chap, you certainly seem to have a genius for upsetting people,' he said finally.

Ross smiled. 'Don't I just?'

He explained to the Colonel about the wheelchair; how it was offered as a gift. 'I wanted to try and help somehow and I couldn't think of anything else. God knows it was little enough but it was something. She threw the offer back in my

378

face,' he remembered regretfully. 'I guess it was a dumb idea.'

Telling the Colonel had helped, in a way. It was a long time since he'd talked of it to anybody, even Lindsay, and it helped to get it out into the open. To stop it festering away inside.

Nevertheless, the matter preyed on his mind as they travelled the short distance to Brockenhurst.

Several people had gone to the trouble of ringing the yard to spout verbal abuse at him, linking the article – as Douglas had no doubt intended – with the earlier one about drinking. Two callers Ross had spoken to himself; the others – he didn't know how many – had been fielded and dealt with by Bill. Knowing the censure was unjustified didn't stop it leaving a nasty taste in his mouth.

He began to think about issuing a statement in his defence, after all. It seemed he had underestimated the depth of feeling the article would arouse.

At the show, waiting just inside the collecting ring on Simone and trying not to notice the nudging and whispering, he was hailed by Mick Colby who was attending the show as a spectator.

'Does everybody read that bloody paper?' Ross asked, as Mick came over.

'What paper?' his friend enquired innocently. 'No, don't you dare touch my shoulder.' He moved his bandaged arm back out of Ross' reach. 'But honestly, I shouldn't worry. They'll get over it. It'll be somebody else another day. You're just flavour of the month at the moment.'

'Some flavour,' Ross remarked dryly.

By midday he discovered he had become more or less immune to the stares and pointing fingers, and when during the afternoon Clown unseated him in the practice area and he heard several smothered giggles, it troubled him not at all.

In fact, when he had remounted the flighty skewbald, he rode past the offending group, said with a creditable imitation of Roland, 'Hilarious, wasn't it?' and had the satisfaction of seeing their faces redden in discomfort.

At least it seemed the horses were on his side. They all jumped competently and behaved well, and the lorry cab was decorated with a smattering of rosettes as they joined the queue of slow-moving traffic leaving the showground that evening.

By the time the horses were unloaded and settled for the night, all their gear sorted and cleaned, and the horsebox made ready for the next day, there was only time for a few hours' sleep before the whole performance began again.

Four horses made the journey to the show on Wednesday. The two mares, Ginger and Flo, occupied the two foremost stalls in the lorry, with the stallion, Telamon, at the very rear. In between was one empty section and the solid figure of Woodsmoke, who effectively quelled any romantic notions the big chestnut might otherwise have nurtured.

Ross had another busy day. Ginger behaved herself, although she could not, by any stretch of the imagination, have been described as eager.

Robbie Fergusson was at the show, Ross knew, but he kept himself to himself which suited Ross just fine. Flo excelled herself, placing in both her morning classes – one an important qualifier. The Oakley Manor team ate lunch on the hoof, and the first of Ross' rides for the afternoon was Telamon.

The horse had behaved impeccably throughout an uneventful morning and when Danny boosted Ross into the saddle did no more than sidle, respecting the boy's hand on his rein. When Danny stepped back, however, the chestnut launched himself skywards.

Ross had been ready for something of the sort. They were on a patch of exercise ground behind the horseboxes and he let the animal have his head as much as possible, hoping that he would ease the kinks out of his system and settle down before he had to head for the ring.

When, half an hour later, they made their appearance at the practice ring for Ring Two, they caused quite a stir. Telamon had settled into a high-stepping trot, his dark copper neck arched and tail streaming like a banner. Although, mercifully, he took no notice whatsoever of the mares while he was being ridden, a few of them noticed him and neighed excitedly.

From the goggle-eyed expressions his appearance provoked, Ross concluded that news of Telamon's purchase had not yet filtered through the grapevine.

'You sneaky sod!' was Mick Colby's comment.

'If you can pull this off, my friend, the scoffers will have to eat their words.'

'If,' Ross agreed. 'But he's just as likely to pile me in the middle of the ring for all the world to laugh at!'

Somebody had erected a good-sized practice pole and Ross put Telamon at it. He pinged it just for fun, jumping high and wide, putting in a spirited buck on the landing side for good measure. Ross cursed at him, caught between annoyance and amusement. He let the stallion walk round quietly then until his number was called.

That Telamon was wildly excited as he entered the ring was immediately obvious even to the most uninformed spectator. He crossed the turf in an extravagant trot, tail held high and nostrils cracking. To Ross he felt like a tightly coiled spring with a hair-trigger release. His champing jaws periodically tossed back streams of white foam to decorate Ross' black jacket. The crowd began to buzz with anticipation.

He concentrated on staying relaxed, hands gently playing on the reins to keep the horse's attention, and after stopping to acknowledge the judges, gave the stallion a fraction more rein, letting him spring forward into a canter. As the hooter sounded, he swung the horse between the timing beacons and approached the first fence, an inviting, rustic affair that Telamon negotiated with the kind of mini-explosion that with him passed for a jump. A stride after landing, he was airborne once more. Ross sat the buck quietly then pushed him forward.

Telamon took the next two fences without appearing to notice them and then allowed himself to be guided round the first turn and towards the fourth.

A double of gates, a wall, parallel bars and a tricky upright were all traversed with almost scornful ease and Ross began to enjoy himself. He was leaving the horse to find his own stride as much as possible, knowing that interference only served to provoke conflict.

Coming to the second last, however – parallel bars that you could comfortably have driven a small car between – he couldn't resist squeezing slightly with his calves to ask for extra effort.

Extra effort was unquestionably what he got.

Telamon shot into the air with an indignant grunt, giving the black-and-yellow poles at least eighteen inches' clearance, and landed running. Ross attempted valiantly to make the turn to the last fence but by now Telamon was convinced that running was the order of the day. They missed the jump by a good yard, still accelerating, and began to circumnavigate the ring.

It was at this point that Ross' memory chose to dredge up a snippet from a few weeks before, and he heard Bill Scott saying disparagingly: *He's a failed racehorse, you know . . . Used to run away going down to the start.*

Rejecting the sensible course of action, Ross concentrated on steering, and with forward planning and a fair degree of luck managed to thread the horse between the jumps to arrive on line with the last fence a second time. Obligingly, Telamon picked his feet up at the appropriate moment and they skimmed between the timing beacons to finish the course.

The stallion plainly thought it a huge joke, for as Ross sat back to try and ride him to a halt, he put in a buck of gargantuan proportions that sent the American over his head without a hope in hell of saving himself.

The crowd gasped collectively, then clapped and laughed as Ross picked himself up with a self-conscious grin and dusted himself down, waving away the stewards who were running to his aid.

He saw with amusement that no one had yet attempted to catch the stallion, who was standing by the exit watching the other horses in the collecting ring. He patted the horse's sweaty neck with no resentment and led him out.

'Well, don't say we don't give you entertainment value,' the voice behind the loudspeaker said as they departed from the arena. 'That was, amazingly, just four faults for circling. Four faults for Ross Wakelin on Mr Roland Preston's Telamon.'

Ross was heartily grateful that Harry Douglas wasn't commentating at the show. His reception in the collecting ring was mixed but mostly good-natured. It seemed that his supposed indiscretions were momentarily sidelined in the face of this new interest.

Outside, where Danny waited with a cotton sheet to throw over the chestnut's loins, Ross was greeted by Lindsay, James and Roland.

'I see what my revered father sees in the sport now,' Roland said in the tone of one finally understanding an enigma. 'It really is quite exciting, isn't it?'

Lindsay gave her cousin a playful push. 'Roland! Stop acting the fool.'

'You should have seen it from where I was sitting,' Ross suggested.

James laughed. 'I don't think many of us envied you. I know I didn't! But he did look rather good when he behaved, didn't he? Even to my untrained eye.'

Lindsay agreed wholeheartedly.

'Well, I'm looking forward to his next class,' Roland said with the enthusiasm of the newly converted. 'Now Ross has got used to the horse, we should have a good chance in that one.'

'Oh, sure,' he said ironically. 'I shouldn't be surprised if we win it!'

The afternoon continued apace. Ross rode Flowergirl once more and Ginger twice, before bringing Woody out for the bigger classes.

He was constantly changing horses and numbers and rings. Bill and Danny worked like termites, scurrying to and fro to make sure the right horse, wearing the right tack, reached the right collecting ring at the right time.

Woodsmoke managed a very creditable second place in his first class and a sixth in his second, but he seemed to be feeling the hard ground with his ageing limbs and, knowing Franklin would agree were he there, Ross consulted with the Colonel and withdrew him from the last class.

By this time he was bone weary and his knee felt as though someone had it in a vice and was trying to reshape it with a mallet.

He would have been quite happy to have gone home had Telamon not been down to jump in the last class, and if the hope of salvaging the final shreds of his reputation had not, very probably, rested upon his partnering the horse a second time.

If Telamon was any less excited on this, his second outing, it would have taken a keen observer to have spotted it. He entered the ring with the same high-stepping trot and screamed his excitement to the world in general, in the way that only a stallion can. Several hopeful mares answered him, which seemed to do his ego good for he shook his head and tried to break into a canter.

Ross restrained him and nodded to the judges, hoping that they would sound the starting hooter without too much delay.

His wish was granted. He eased the stallion forward and inclined him towards the start of the course. These jumps were considerably bigger than those in the earlier class but Telamon accorded them the same glorious lack of respect. Ross once again chose a policy of non-interference, restricting his part in the proceedings to steering towards the appropriate fences and tentative suggestions about moderating their heady speed.

It was only when the last combination had been cleared and they were passing the finishing markers that he realised they had, incredibly, jumped a clear round. The appreciative crowd cheered, enjoying the stallion's highly individual style, and Ross felt the chestnut gather himself for another huge buck. He hauled his head up and the buck became a fairly harmless leap instead.

Despite his weariness, Ross could not prevent an idiotic grin from spreading over his face as he returned to the collecting ring.

This horse was one big, crazy son of a bitch but, hell, he could jump! And he, Ross, had the ride!

The Oakley Manor team and followers couldn't have been more delighted if he had just won an International Grand Prix. It was a feather in their collective cap that the horse was jumping well for their yard when others had failed to produce the goods. Their obvious pride in his achievement lifted Ross as nothing else had done for a long time.

Half-an-hour later, he and Telamon were back in the collecting ring, waiting to be called for the jump-off.

There had been only five clear rounds. One of these was accomplished by Stephen Douglas on China Lily and Ross would have been less than human if he hadn't felt a great deal of satisfaction when he saw the tight-lipped discomfort of Telamon's former jockey.

The jump-off course was tight and twisty, and didn't suit Telamon's wide, galloping turns, but the chestnut jumped clear again, and when two others faulted, Ross found himself lining up for a third-place rosette. The stallion was greatly diverted by the notion of a lap of honour, doing his best to overtake the first- and second-placed horses as they circled the ring, and bucking when his attempts were foiled.

As they filed out, one of Ross' fellow competitors turned in the saddle and said, 'Rather you than me, mate!'

Ross grinned widely.

As he slid off the horse and loosened his girth, Ross heard a plummy, upper-class voice declare: 'They say he drinks, you know.'

'Well, if that's Dutch courage,' a second voice replied, 'I'm going to try some!'

The American caught Danny's eye and laughed.

While Ross was having supper with the Scotts that evening, the Colonel rang to say that Robbie Fergusson had requested that as Bishop would not be fit to jump in the two classes for which he was entered on the final day of the show, Ginger might take his place. Ross agreed, reluctantly, although he was fairly sure that the request was more in the nature of a command.

Putting the handset down, he sighed. He'd been relieved to have got the mare safely through her classes and had been looking forward to a Ginger-free day. In some instances she would not have been eligible for Bishop's classes, as she was graded below him, but as luck would have it, the two classes tomorrow were qualifiers and open to all.

As he climbed the stairs to his room, he found he

was really too tired to worry about it. Tomorrow would have to take care of itself.

Ross was greeted first thing the next morning by a note pushed under the door at the foot of the stairs. It read: *King Rat has bolted. The cat is in pursuit.*

It wasn't signed and Ross smiled to himself. McKinnon was obviously exercising his individual brand of humour at Leo Jackson's expense.

At the show he found another note awaiting him in the secretary's tent when he went to declare the change of horses.

The rat has grown wings at Bournemouth and is going across the water. Cat now enjoying a saucer of milk. Good luck today.

Ross experienced mild relief at the thought that Leo was out of the picture. Now at least Mr X wouldn't be able to use the ex-groom's spite as a cover for his own activities. A faint sense of unease persisted, however.

Why *had* Leo suddenly decided to leave? Had he realised he was being watched and was therefore unlikely to get away with any more mischief-making? Ross had done a lot of thinking before he got to sleep the previous night, and the half-conclusions he had come to didn't fit at all with Leo's abrupt departure this morning.

Back to the drawing board, he thought resignedly. At this particular moment, though, five fit and eager horses awaited him in the horsebox and he had a very busy day ahead. It was neither the time nor the place to try to sort out Franklin's problems.

By lunchtime, Ross and his crew had expended a great deal of effort and energy, and had in return collected a sprinkling of rosettes and one silver trophy. This last was won by the ever-consistent Simone in a hotly contested Top-Score competition.

Ross' success with Telamon the previous day seemed to have earned him a reprieve with some of his critics, and several of his fellow competitors came up to congratulate him on Simone's win.

The afternoon got underway with another speed class, in which Ross and Flowergirl had to be content with second and which Lindsay and Gypsy won. She was delighted and teased him about his second place as they lined up to receive their prizes. They circled the ring in a lap of honour and as Ross watched her slim, black-jacketed figure cantering ahead of him he ached with the intensity of his feelings for her.

When she slid off Gypsy outside the collecting ring, however, it was to James that she turned, accepting his congratulatory kiss and demanding of him: 'Wasn't Gypsy wonderful?'

James agreed dutifully but his eyes were on Lindsay and his love for her shone like a beacon on a clear night.

Ross rode on by.

By mid-afternoon he had ridden in four more classes, including the Foxhunter Qualifier on Ginger. A vague hope that there might be a problem with substituting the mare for the absent

Bishop had been dashed by a helpful official and Robbie Fergusson had appeared uncharacteristically in the vicinity of the collecting ring, as if to physically compel Ross into the ring.

He had watched, unsmiling, as Ross had coaxed the mare round the course to collect a total of eight faults for two fences down and didn't speak to him when he came out, except to say that he hoped the American would wake her up a bit for the next class.

Ross refrained from saying what was on his mind, for the sake of their future relationship. Instead, he promised to do his best, then sent Danny off with Ginger with instructions to take her somewhere quiet and settle her down.

If the mare had looked as though she needed waking up, Ross knew it was entirely due to his own efforts to keep her calm. As soon as he'd sat on her that afternoon, he'd sensed she was in one of her irrational moods.

There was no time to worry about her, though. Ross still had Telamon and Simone to ride in the Foxhunter before he rode Ginger and Woodsmoke in the last class.

He warmed up the stallion himself and the route he took from warm-up area to collecting ring was tortuous, due to the discovery that the effect of bringing Telamon face to face with a fairground organ, of which there were several dotted around the showground, was similar to directing a blow torch on to a box of fireworks.

The journey was accomplished without undue

drama and as Ross entered the collecting ring he was amused to find himself the focus of many expectant gazes. People had learned quickly that the stallion was likely to provide a spectacle worth viewing.

He didn't disappoint them. A band striking up nearby caused him to explode into the ring in a leaping, snorting flurry of hooves. Once there, he resisted Ross' efforts to steady him, completing one circuit of the arena before settling a little and turning his attention to the job in hand.

The course was a fair one, straightforward and not too big, and Telamon played with it. He treated the fences with contempt, skimming over them and bucking in between.

He flew the second last, a triple bar, picking up speed, and in spite of Ross' advice to the contrary, galloped flat out to the last wall, uncharacteristically missed his stride and uprooted it in a cascade of red-and-white wooden blocks. Madly excited, he then proceeded to put on a rodeo display that tested Ross' powers of adhesion to the limits.

The onlookers clapped and cheered delightedly, which helped not at all, but somehow Ross regained control of sorts and persuaded Telamon to leave the ring in a reasonably dignified fashion.

The indefatigable Simone, whom he jumped ten minutes later, redeemed the Oakley Manor reputation by achieving a faultless clear round and following it with a fast clear in the jump-off, to snatch first place from Danielle Moreaux. The Colonel was quietly delighted.

392

'Another step on the ladder to Birmingham, Yank,' he said, clapping Ross on the back. 'You made a bloody good job of that!'

The last class was the biggest of the day, in the size of both the jumps and the prize money, and was sponsored by a car company whose advertising banners fluttered on every available railing around the arena. An impressive line-up of competitors was entered and the crowd stood five or six deep. The Colonel and Robbie Fergusson had seats among the privileged, in the grandstand.

In the crowded collecting ring, Ross rode Woodsmoke round quietly alongside, amongst others, Jim Pullen, Derek Campbell, Danielle Moreaux and Stephen Douglas. Presently Lindsay joined him and they wove through the masses together, chatting amiably.

From their elevated viewpoint they watched the first few competitors to see how the course was jumping. Judging by the performances it was a course for a bold, experienced horse but there were no particular black spots.

Satisfied, Ross went back to warming Woodsmoke up. He had not jumped the old horse so far that day, saving him for the big class, and Woody didn't disappoint him. He jumped a beautiful, polished clear, leading Ross to wish wistfully that the horse was six years younger.

Lindsay did not fare so well. The course was a little on the big side for Gypsy at the end of a busy day and she collected twelve faults. She didn't really mind. She rode back with Ross to the horsebox, voicing her intention of putting her mare in the trailer and returning to watch Ross win the class.

'James won't mind waiting a little longer,' she said. 'He'd like to see you win too.'

Ross laughed. 'There's just one little flaw in this plan of yours,' he informed her. 'Has it occurred to you that Woody might *not* win?'

'Absolutely not!' she declared. 'Think positive. Nobody can touch you. You can't lose!'

'Oh, good, no pressure then,' he observed, sardonically.

James, when questioned, said he wouldn't dream of leaving before seeing Woody jump again.

Ross could have wished them and everybody else a mile away ten minutes later when he mounted Ginger and found her to be, if anything, several degrees more strung up than she had been earlier.

All the danger signs were there: agitated ear movements, the whites of her eyes showing, and her stride short and jerky. She gazed worriedly around her on the way to the ring, but most of all it was the telepathy she conveyed to Ross that made his palms suddenly sticky and his mouth dry.

She seemed totally spaced-out. He flirted with the idea of taking her back to the lorry and be damned to Fergusson, but the thought of someone else riding Bishop at Olympia kept him on board and circling the collecting ring.

'She looks a bit wound up,' Lindsay commented from the rails as Ross paused for a moment. 'Is she okay?'

'No,' he said, matter-of-factly. 'She's crazy as a snake but only I seem able to see it.'

'She *does* look a little distressed,' James said judiciously. 'Perhaps it's nerves.'

'Let's hope so, buddy,' Ross said heavily. 'Let's hope so!'

It seemed an eternity before his number was called; a lifetime in which Ross' mind ran unbidden through every possible scenario that might result from Ginger having one of her attacks of hysteria in the ring. He wondered how much would have to happen before Fergusson would consider him justified in retiring from the competition.

When the moment arrived, however, Ginger seemed to have shifted from spaced-out to faintly mulish, in one of her typical mood swings. In this mode, Ross felt they were less likely to storm the grandstand than have two refusals and be disqualified at the first fence. Either way, his chances of keeping the ride on Bishop didn't look very bright.

Fortunately the first two fences were jumped coming back towards the collecting ring and the lure of the other horses, and Ginger jumped them, albeit begrudgingly. Ross sat down hard and used all the strength he could muster to bully and coax her round the turn and towards the third fence, an imposing green-and-white parallel.

All the way to the fence he knew he was fighting a losing battle. Nothing in the world can make a horse jump if it has its mind set against it, and

Ginger had her mind firmly set against it. She dug in her toes a full stride away from the take-off point and would go no further.

Ross swore under his breath.

With little expectation of success, he swung the mare round, bullied a few more strides of canter out of her and turned her back towards the jump.

Suddenly, in the crowd, not six feet from the mare's heels, a balloon burst with a sharp crack.

Nothing could have been calculated to upset her more. With a sound that was somewhere between a grunt and a squeal, she ripped the reins through Ross' fingers and bolted.

The abrupt change from recalcitrant to hysterical caught him out and the mare was away and running before he could stop her. She was heading away from the exit and the other horses, proof – if it was needed – that her mind had ceased to function rationally. This was swiftly borne out by her flattening the mound of floral decorations which stood as a centrepiece to the arena.

Fighting a sense of unreality, Ross tried to force his mind to think. Urgently he calculated angles and distances but could see no hope of avoiding either a collision with the boundary railings and the fragile bodies beyond, or the double of white gates which formed fence ten and stood close to the side of the ring. Grimly, he chose the gates.

As the distance between Ginger and the side of the ring dwindled, Ross abandoned any faint hope he might have harboured that she would come to her senses in time to swerve.

History was repeating itself and he had lived it so many times in his dreams that now it was happening it was almost a relief.

He felt calm and detached. His vision was filled with the stupid, staring faces of the crowd. They knew they were safe. The horses always stayed on the inside of the rails. Tragedy was never expected, it was something that happened to other people.

They would never understand, Ross thought savagely as he suddenly threw all his weight on to Ginger's left rein and stirrup in an attempt to throw her off balance and off-line.

It worked.

She stayed in the ring, hitting the first gate without making any effort to leave the ground and carrying it forward for a stride before it tangled in her front legs and her momentum sent her sprawling into the second one.

Ross gripped instinctively, staying with her as she fell, his mind refusing to abandon the hope that she might yet make it back to her feet.

The shiny white paintwork tilted crazily as Ginger ploughed into the base of it. Ross kicked his feet free of the stirrups a fraction too late and threw up his right arm to protect his head as the whole eight-foot length of the gate collapsed on top of them.

For a moment Ginger seemed winded. She lay with heaving sides for the space of perhaps five heartbeats and then erupted into frantic action. Her body pinning his left leg to the turf, Ross could do no more than twist on to his face as the mare struggled to her feet, trying in vain to protect himself from her scrabbling hooves. Her weight lifted from his leg twice, and twice fell back, before she finally made it to her feet.

Ross bit the sleeve of his jacket as a passing hoof thudded into his shoulder and another clouted the back of his crash cap. The gate dragged sideways a foot or so and then dropped, and Ross heard Ginger move away.

He was finding it difficult to breathe. Each lungful was agony. Lack of oxygen made his head spin and noise receded, replaced by a buzzing sensation. Vision was hazy, swimming. He closed his eyes against the chaos and felt a soft darkness overtake him.

Voices filled his head. Many voices.

Voices asking if he could hear them. A voice suggesting he be rolled over. Another, sharper, saying to leave him be, the ambulance was coming.

Ross blessed that last voice silently. He lay still, with his eyes closed, feeling mostly numb. Wishing everybody would go away and let him sink back into the darkness; knowing at the same time that they wouldn't, that they would want to move him; knowing that with movement would come pain.

'Stay back, miss!' a voice commanded. 'Please leave the ring.'

'I have to see him!'

That sounded like Lindsay. Ross opened his eyes. Grass filled his vision. Grass and a length of shiny, white-painted wood.

'We're family,' another voice announced. Ross considered this hazily. *Family?* It had sounded like James.

'Well, all right. But stay back.'

'Is he badly hurt?' Lindsay again.

The voices didn't know.

Ross felt it was time he took a more active part in the proceedings. With an effort he used the arm he wasn't lying on to push himself over on to his back. Pain clamped his stomach and upper body in a vice-like grip but he'd been winded often enough to know that it would pass.

The voices exclaimed and hands reached out towards him.

'Just let me be,' Ross said as forcefully as he could manage.

The hands drew back sharply. He heard an ambulance enter the arena.

'How do you feel?' a voice enquired solicitously. 'Any broken bones, do you think? Can you move?'

Breathing was becoming easier now. Ross opened his eyes again and rolled his head to look about him. Lindsay came into view, looking pale and distressed.

He smiled.

'Hi, Princess,' he said and was rewarded by a watery smile in return. Encouraged, he sat up just as the ambulance came alongside.

The voices protested. They really thought he should lie still. He shouldn't try to get up too soon.

Ross' vision swam and steadied. On the whole, he thought, they were probably right, but once the medical fraternity got their hands on you they were loath to let go, and he knew his medical notes would make interesting reading. There would be X-rays, tests; he would have to stay overnight. His leg would be examined. Questions would be asked and his fitness to ride would come under scrutiny . . .

'I'm okay, really,' he assured the new array of faces that had gathered round him. 'Has someone caught my horse?'

The horse was being taken care of, he was told. How about himself? Could he stand? Could he walk as far as the ambulance?

'I'm fine,' Ross assured them brightly. 'Just winded for a moment. I've got another horse to ride yet.'

'Oh, yes?' the doctor in charge said, eyebrows raised. 'We'll see about that.'

With the doctor's help, Ross climbed to his feet. A hot stab of pain burned through his ribs on the left side and he caught his breath. He could have cheered though. His bad leg, put cautiously to the ground, didn't buckle. It created its own kind of hell, which made him grit his teeth, but it held.

Ross looked up and grinned broadly in relief.

The doctor, far from being reassured by this, seemed to regard it as further evidence of the need for treatment but contented himself with persuading Ross to accept a lift out of the ring in the ambulance.

Applause rippled round the arena as the vehicle made its way out. Ross reflected that he had probably made their day.

Outside the collecting ring, he climbed stiffly down from the ambulance, thanked and reassured the medical crew for the umpteenth time, and was nearly bowled over by an enthusiastic embrace from Lindsay.

'Ross!' she cried. 'For a moment I thought . . . I mean, it was just like last time. I was *so* scared! And you *were* right about Ginger, weren't you?'

He unwound her arms from about his neck, partly in deference to James, who was watching with an expression that was unreadable, and partly because her hug was making contact with a lot of sore places in a way that made his vision swim a little.

'I expect it looked worse than it was,' he said steadyingly. 'I was winded, that's all.'

He turned to where Danny was leading Ginger up for the vet to see. Her panic spent, she looked dejected, her chestnut coat dark with sweat and ears drooping unhappily. It didn't take an expert to see that she was heavily lame. She could hardly put her near fore to the ground.

Ross wondered what Fergusson would have to say about the afternoon's events and felt suddenly tired and depressed, himself. He accompanied Danny and Ginger back to the horsebox, limping almost as heavily as the mare.

The Colonel joined them en route, concerned for Ross' well being and anxious for the horse. He firmly vetoed the American's declared intention to stick to his schedule and ride Telamon but eventually gave way on the question of Woodsmoke.

'All right. But if you do yourself any further injury, I won't be answerable to Franklin,' he warned. 'What did the vet have to say about Ginger?'

'He wasn't happy,' Ross reported. 'He thinks she may have cracked a bone in her pastern. She'll have to be X-rayed. There could well be a problem with her back, too.' He looked round significantly. 'Where's the worried owner?'

The Colonel sighed. 'He said to forward the vet's report. He's gone home. Bloody man!'

Ross grunted an amen to that.

By the time Ross had jumped Woodsmoke to second place in the jump-off and all the horses were loaded and ready to travel, almost two hours had passed and he was feeling pretty much like a football must feel after a particularly gruelling Super Bowl.

Dismounting from the big bay, the ground had threatened to jump up and hit him, and he'd sat down rather rapidly on the horsebox ramp.

Riding had been a less than joyful affair but not quite as bad as he had feared it might be. Even so, had it been any horse but Woodsmoke, he would probably have been forced to admit defeat. With Woody though – steady dependable Woody – it was mostly a case of pointing him in the right direction and staying on. The horse did the rest.

In the end, there were only two clear rounds in the jump-off, other riders trying too hard for speed and sacrificing fences. Ross was easily beaten on the clock by Stephen Douglas, who jumped a fast clear on China Lily but for once seemed to have no inclination to gloat.

Ross travelled back to the yard sprawled on the sofa bed in the living-quarters of the lorry. Danny had offered his company but Bill had said with surprising insight that he thought Ross would prefer to be alone.

Ross did prefer it. On his own he didn't have to maintain a stoic façade. He reflected that probably Bill spoke from experience. After all, who should know better than a steeplechase jockey what it felt like to be trampled by half a ton of struggling horse?

By the feel of it, now the adrenalin had ebbed and subsided, he would soon be sporting several hoof-sized bruises. His head ached heavily, as did his ribs, and if he twisted or tried to bend too far, a sharp pain discouraged him in no uncertain manner.

None of these discomforts worried him unduly. He would be stiff, he knew, but it wouldn't be the first time and he felt very sure it wouldn't be the last. Time would heal.

What did worry him was the added damage that had undoubtedly been done to his knee. The mare had to pick *that* leg to roll on. Still, he supposed being very lame on one leg was better than being lame on two.

His thoughts turned unhappily to Ginger. If anything, she had looked to be in a worse state than he was. Her best hope lay in being unfit to finish the season, then maybe Fergusson would sell her on to someone who had time to tackle her problems.

At some point in this unsatisfactory train of thought, and despite the fierce competition between head, ribs and knee for his attention, Ross drifted off to sleep.

17

Consciousness returned quite suddenly.

One moment wild and muddled dreams, the next a hazy light and the heavy ticking of a clock. Ross lay and watched the light from behind his lashes. He wondered what time it was, hoping he didn't have to get up too soon.

It seemed like any other morning until he shifted position and a thousand damaged nerve-endings screamed in protest. It was a bad moment, and as he lay still, waiting for the sensation to pass, he realised he couldn't actually recall going to bed.

The stairs creaked and the door swung open. Not used to receiving company early in the morning, Ross rolled his head to view his visitor, hoping fervently that whoever it was wasn't bent on doing him harm. In his present state, he'd be a pushover.

Maggie Scott appeared round the dividing

curtain. 'Oh, you're awake then,' she observed, somewhat unnecessarily. 'How do you feel?'

'I've been better,' he admitted. 'What time is it?'

'Gone midday,' she said, walking round the bed and drawing the curtains at the window. The sun streamed in, making Ross wince. 'You had us worried last night, you know. Fainting like that. The Colonel was proper cut up. Said he never should have let you ride Woody in that last class.'

'I've never fainted in my life,' Ross protested.

'Well, you did last night, or something like it. We had a job to wake you at all when the lorry got back. You were very groggy. Anyway, halfway across the yard you collapsed again; nearly pulled Bill over. James had to half-carry you upstairs. Proper to-do it was.'

Ross frowned. 'James carried me?'

'It was touch and go whether we called the doctor or the ambulance,' Maggie went on, relishing the memory of the drama. 'The Colonel was afraid you had delayed concussion, but I said I was sure they would have checked you for concussion in the ambulance at the show.'

'They did,' Ross agreed.

'I said they would have,' Maggie said knowingly. 'I said all you probably needed was a good sleep, and the doctor agreed. He knows I've done some nursing and was quite happy to leave you in my care.'

'Thank you.' Ross was genuinely grateful. 'I'm sorry I caused such a fuss. Uh . . . did the doctor say anything else?'

Somewhere along the line he had changed, or been changed, from his riding gear into the shorts he wore in bed, and it was too much to hope that his heavily strapped knee would have gone unnoticed.

'He said he thought you had some sore ribs and there would be a lot of bruising. Oh, and he asked about your knee but the Colonel said that was an old injury.'

'The Colonel was in here?'

'No, of course not. Just Dr Brougham and me,' Maggie said, full of self-importance. 'The Colonel waited in the cottage with Bill and the others. Anyway, the doctor said you were lucky to have got off so lightly, by the sound of it.'

'And Ginger?'

Maggie hesitated, uncharacteristically. 'She's not too good, poor old girl. But there'll be time enough to worry about that when you're on your feet again.'

Ross eased himself gingerly into a sitting position. 'Well, if you'll excuse me, that won't take too long,' he said.

Maggie protested, her maternal instincts aroused. The doctor had said two or three days, she argued.

'I'll get bedsores!' Ross exclaimed in mock alarm. 'No, honestly. The sooner I'm up and about, the sooner the stiffness will wear off. I'll be okay.'

Though unconvinced, Maggie eventually conceded defeat and when all her offers of help were politely refused, left the room. She would have something to eat ready for him in the cottage, she said.

When Ross finally made it to the yard, after taking a ridiculously long time to shower, shave and dress, he found it a hive of activity. Lindsay, Sarah and Danny were hosing down Joey, Blue and Fly; Roger West's Range Rover was parked by the stable office, dusty as ever, and its owner stood talking to Bill and the Colonel outside the tack-room.

Ross eased away from the doorpost he had been leaning against and limped across to them.

'Ross!' The Colonel was the first to see him. 'Should you be out of bed?'

'I figured I'd had a long enough lie-in,' he said, embarrassed as always by the concern focussed on him. 'How's the mare?'

He could tell instantly, by their faces, that all was far from well.

'I'm afraid there's not much we can do for her, Ross,' Roger said unhappily. 'I took a couple of X-rays of that near-fore earlier and I'm afraid it confirmed what we feared.' He held up one grey picture, pointing with the corner of the other. 'See, there. She's chipped her short pastern, just behind the coronet. And here.' He indicated the other X-ray. 'What do you see?'

Ross looked, gloomily. 'She's cracked her pedal bone,' he said, recognising the crescent-shaped bone within the hoof. 'Poor old girl. She must be in a lot of pain.'

The vet nodded. 'She must have clouted it pretty

hard. There's evidence of damage to the ligaments and tendons, too. The Colonel thinks she may have got her leg through that gate yesterday and wrenched it trying to pull herself free. In addition to that, she's not at all comfortable in her back and seems mentally distressed too. She'll not jump again; may not even be fit enough to ride, and from what I've been hearing, it would be a bit of a risk to breed from her. Basically, we're just waiting to hear from Mr Fergusson.'

'I see.' Ross had expected it, deep down, but it didn't make the thought any the more palatable. The mare had run out of time. 'I'll go see her.'

'I've given her a sedative,' Roger said, 'and a pain-killer but she's still not happy. I hope Fergusson isn't too long getting back to us.'

Ross nodded and made his painful way over to the covered stables. Out of the corner of his eye, he saw Lindsay start towards him, then pause as she read his expression. Silently, he blessed her for understanding his need to be alone.

He spent quite a while with the mare. Talking to her, trying to calm her. Apologising for not understanding soon enough and finally telling her that she had nothing to fear; soon everything would be all right.

As ever, he couldn't reach her. She seemed to be in her own private hell. A world not only full of fear and mistrust, but now filled with pain, as well. He couldn't reach her but he experienced empathy with her. In some ways, he felt, they had had a lot in common.

Ross was with the mare also, three hours later, when two men came from the local hunt kennels and she was destroyed humanely in the home field, out of sight of the other horses, with her head in a bucket of oats and carrots.

It was not the first time he had stood with a horse in its final moments but it never got any easier. One moment a thinking, feeling being, a personality you knew and with whom you had shared moments of joy and sadness; the next an awkward, undignified corpse, dull-eyed and insentient.

Ross turned away as soon as it was over, leaving the two men to finish their unpleasant but necessary task alone. Behind him he heard the drone of the winch motor as the heavy body was hauled into the van.

Bill was waiting at the field gate. He had offered to take Ross' place but even though circumstances had dictated that they never became close, Ross had felt he owed the mare his company in that last act. What always got to him was the sense of betrayal he felt. Horses stood so quietly. Infinitely trusting. He supposed it was better that way. No apprehension. No fear. Just suddenly – nothing.

'Bloody business,' Bill growled as Ross reached him. 'You never get used to it, do you?'

Ross shook his head. 'You always wonder if there was anything else you could have done.'

'You do the best you can at the time,' Bill said. 'No use torturing yourself. And if it's any comfort, I should have listened to you about that mare. I'm sorry.'

Ross was surprised. 'It helps,' he said. 'Thanks. But it's too late.'

They wouldn't let him work or ride, so Ross had a hot bath to try and ease his bruises and stiffening muscles, and then spent an hour or two stretched out on his bed, prey to self-pity and depression.

The only thing about the day that held any promise was the news from Roger West that, contrary to expectation, the dog had begun to rally. There were signs of movement in his back legs although it was still too early to say whether he would regain full mobility.

The vet suggested that in a day or two, if he continued to make progress, the dog should go to Annie Hayward's to convalesce. She had a way with sick animals of all kinds, he said, and had immediately offered to help when she heard about the dog.

Ross was deeply grateful.

The evening found him making his way up to the main house in response to a request from the Colonel. Although the walk was irksome, on the whole it was preferable to an evening spent in his own company or the doubtful entertainment of British TV.

The Colonel was not alone in his study when Masters showed Ross in. Roland lounged nonchalantly in one of the worn leather armchairs, sipping sherry.

'Hail the all-conquering hero, bloody but unbowed!' he declared.

Ross glanced disdainfully at him, which bothered him not at all, and moved to one of the empty chairs, trying to minimise his limp as much as possible. The Colonel handed him a glass of sherry. Ross took it, wondering what effect it would have when mixed with the various pain-killers he had taken during the day.

'How do you feel, really?' his employer asked, regarding him keenly as he sat down. 'You had us worried last night, you know.'

'Yes, so I hear. Sorry about that. I guess I was pretty tired, but I'm fine now.'

The Colonel raised an eyebrow.

'Well, a bit rough, maybe,' Ross admitted. 'But it'll wear off.'

'You look exhausted,' the Colonel stated bluntly. 'I was working it out: you must have ridden thirty-five or forty rounds over the past three days. And that was a nasty fall. If I'd known how badly bruised you were, I'd never have let you ride Woodsmoke.'

Ross made a dismissive movement with his hands, wishing the Colonel would leave the subject alone.

'All's well that ends well,' Roland remarked, from the depths of his armchair.

Colonel Preston regarded his son with open contempt. 'Haven't you anything better to do?' he asked sharply.

Roland considered this. 'No. Don't think so.'

412

Ross didn't know whether it was a result of yesterday's kick to the head, but he was beginning to join Lindsay in finding Roland amusing.

'Damned shame about that mare,' the Colonel said, ignoring his disappointing offspring. 'You were right about her all along. I couldn't blame you for saying "I told you so".'

Ross felt no inclination to do so. 'I would rather have been wrong.'

'I must say, I've never seen anything like it, and I've had horses all my life. She appeared to go completely berserk.'

'I have,' Ross said grimly.

'Of course. I was forgetting. You must feel the fates are against you. I mean, the chances of its happening twice to the same person must be millions to one.'

'That would depend,' Roland mused.

'On *what* precisely?' The Colonel showed a marked lack of patience.

'On what triggered it.'

'And what the devil do you mean by that?' his father demanded.

'Keep your hair on, Father dear,' Roland advised, in his infuriatingly calm way. 'I was just thinking aloud.'

'Well, I appreciate you have to practise but try to do it quietly and in your own time.'

Gotcha, Ross thought delightedly. You could see who Roland took after.

A respectful tap on the door put an end to the sparring. Masters took half a step inside at the

Colonel's invitation, keeping his eyes lowered so as not to intrude.

'Phone call, sir. Lady Cresswell.'

'Thank you. I'll take it in the hall,' Colonel Preston said, rising from his chair.

As the door closed behind him, Ross leaned forward, ignoring a twinge from a protesting rib. 'What *did* you mean by it?' he asked Roland softly.

Roland shrugged. 'Oh, just that Leo was at the show yesterday.'

Ross stared. 'But, that's imposs—' Too late, he realised he was treading on dangerous ground.

'Impossible?' Roland hoisted a lazy eyebrow. 'Why should you say that, I wonder? Nevertheless, he *was* there.'

'How do you know? I didn't see you there.'

'Oh, but I was,' Roland replied smoothly.

'You kept yourself to yourself, then,' Ross observed.

'I went to see Danielle. No reason I should tell you,' he pointed out.

'So, where did you see Leo?'

'Um. . . in the beer tent as I recall. Don't remember him having a balloon, though.'

Ross' eyes narrowed.

Roland wore his habitually bland expression, as if they were just exchanging platitudes. What he was implying, however, put an entirely new complexion on the previous day's events.

It hadn't occurred to Ross that the bursting balloon had been anything other than an unfortunate accident. Though *why* it hadn't in

414

hindsight he had no idea. After all, he had had enough experience lately of malice aforethought to make even the rosiest of spectacles mist up a little. Enough to make him suspicious of anything, one would have thought.

So much for Leo being out of the country. The fact that he had gone to such elaborate lengths to make them think so, made it obvious that he knew he was being watched. What *wasn't* clear was for how long he had known.

How many times in the past had he pulled the wool over their eyes?

Professional McKinnon's men might be, but they'd been operating in the belief that Leo could not possibly know he was being staked out. They were too practised, according to McKinnon, to have given the game away themselves. Therefore someone must have tipped Leo off.

But who? Who could have known? Who would have cared? And where was Leo now?

Ross all but groaned aloud. Fit and healthy, he'd win no prizes for detection. In his present state . . .

'A penny for 'em,' Roland remarked lightly, getting up to replace his empty glass on the drinks tray. 'Well, it's been nice talking to you, old boy, but I must be going. A date with the delicious Danielle. Glad to see you on your feet again. Tell my revered papa not to wait up.'

In the event, father and son met in the doorway. Roland bowed ironically. 'I bid you farewell,' he said grandly. 'You may now bemoan my lamentable lack of character to your heart's content.'

The Colonel grunted. 'We've got far more interesting things to discuss,' he said dampeningly.

'Oh, unkind, unkind!'

When he had gone, the Colonel topped up Ross' glass and his own, collapsed into his chair and proceeded to do just what Roland had suggested.

'Where did I go wrong?' he asked with a sigh. 'He used to be such a nice boy. So . . . well, so normal!'

'Was that him?' Ross indicated a framed photograph which stood on a nearby trophy case. It showed two teenage boys holding aloft a large trophy between them.

'The one on the right.' The Colonel nodded. 'The other boy is Darcy Richmond.'

'Is it?' Ross looked more closely. 'I didn't realise they were friends.'

'They weren't, really. They went to the same school. The cup was for rowing or some such thing.'

'That would have been after Darcy's father was killed, I presume?'

'Yes, a couple of years. Though he wasn't exactly killed, you know. He committed suicide.' The Colonel shook his head sadly. 'A bad business. Took an overdose and drowned himself in his bath.'

'Thorough,' Ross commented. And somewhat different from the story Darcy had told, he thought.

The Colonel grunted. 'It was about the only thing he *did* do properly. He just couldn't see that

Franklin had got where he was by plain hard work. Always trying to take short cuts, Elliot Richmond was. It's hard to believe two brothers could be so different.'

'But Darcy fell on his feet.'

'Oh, yes. Although Franklin had always paid for his schooling and suchlike, anyway. He hadn't a child of his own at that time and was a very good uncle to the boy. God knows what would have become of Darcy if he hadn't been. He bailed his brother out a time or two as well, until it became obvious that Elliot was never going to learn to be responsible. Then he stopped and concentrated on the boy.'

'And Darcy's mother?'

'Long gone,' the Colonel said. 'An empty-headed bimbo who ran out when the money did. It seems the two brothers were alike in their choice of women, if nothing else. Marsha was just the same. More classy perhaps but essentially the same. Franklin freely admits the only good thing to come out of the marriage was Peter.'

'Darcy told me his father was killed in a car accident,' Ross said, gently probing.

Colonel Preston nodded. 'It was extremely hard for him to come to terms with at his age. First his mother running out on him – as he saw it – then his father killing himself. I imagine he suffered from feelings of guilt, like many children in divorce proceedings. You know, thinking that it's somehow their fault. Franklin managed to keep the whole affair very quiet but I think the lad invented the accident story to comfort himself. I didn't realise he was still using it.'

He sipped his sherry thoughtfully.

'He's a nice enough boy really, though I think perhaps Frank indulged him a little too much. And there were times when he showed tolerance when quite frankly a sound hiding would have answered better. The business with . . . er . . . women,' he said, apparently changing his mind mid-sentence. 'Still, it's always easy to criticise and he's turned out well enough. Darcy's been good to young Peter in his turn, you know. No true brother could have treated him better, and the kid worships him.'

'I've seen that,' Ross agreed. 'He seems to have a way with the boy. Doesn't share Peter's passion for horses, though.'

'No. He had every opportunity but never took to it. A lot of boys don't, I find. They prefer toys with push-button controls. Darcy took up sailing, something his father was fond of, too. He's quite good, I believe.' The Colonel turned his attention back to Ross. 'But what about you? When do you think you'll be back in the saddle again?'

'Tomorrow.' He didn't hesitate. 'We've got the Frinkley Show on Sunday and the stallion will need to be exercised.'

The Colonel reached for the decanter and raised his eyebrows at Ross, who shook his head. His boss poured himself a drink with great deliberation.

'Frinkley is out,' he said finally, in a voice that brooked no argument. 'And the stallion can be lunged or turned out for a day or two.'

418

He held up his hand to silence Ross' protest. 'The doctor was quite concerned, you know. Said you should go in for X-rays. There was a lot of bruising and he couldn't tell exactly what damage might have been done. Your knee, for example, and a bloody great hoofprint in the middle of your back.'

'Steeplechase jockeys get them every other week,' Ross protested. 'Ask Bill. And my knee is an old story. It's getting better all the time.' And my nose is getting longer, he thought wryly.

The Colonel didn't look convinced. 'All right, but you take at least two clear days off or I'll march you off to the hospital myself!'

Ross rose early the next morning after an uncomfortable night and spent some time nursing a cup of coffee and going over his conversations with the Prestons, Senior and Junior, in his mind.

At half-past seven the yard began to come to life as usual. Horses whinnied, doors banged, and water rushed as buckets were filled at the taps.

Ross managed to shower and dress in a marginally quicker time than he had the day before but his agility wasn't going to win him any medals for a day or two to come. The bruises were developing colourfully and the swelling beginning to subside. He told himself determinedly that he was on the mend.

In the yard and ready to work, he was greeted with firmly shaken heads. Bill and Danny told him to go to the cottage or back to bed, and Lindsay, whom he met coming out of Flo's box with a mucksack, exclaimed, 'Oh, no, you don't! Uncle John's orders. You're not to lift a finger for at least two days. Go and sit down, we've got it all under control.'

Ross was astounded. 'He called you?'

'No,' she said. 'I just came.'

'I thought you'd come back to England to be sophisticated and get horses out of your system.'

'That was Mother's idea, not mine. Anyway, it'll only be for a day or two. Now do as you're told and go and put your feet up or something.'

He pottered aimlessly about the tackroom for three-quarters of an hour while the mucking out was taken care of, remembering his very first morning at Oakley Manor when he had done just the same. So much had happened since then, it was hard to believe it could be only eight weeks or so ago.

As the Colonel had pointed out, life had not exactly been dull since his arrival. What Ross didn't know was how much of his troubles could be ascribed to Franklin's extortionist, and how much to Leo.

It was quite possible that if he was as clued-up as he seemed to be, the extortionist could be using Leo's activities as a smokescreen. There was no way of knowing.

Ross felt like a blind man in a cactus forest: whichever way he turned he seemed to be stung, but he couldn't see who was doing the stinging.

It had occurred to him that morning that

Roland's tip about Leo's supposed presence at the show on Thursday might have been no more than a smokescreen to hide his own involvement.

But where was the motive? Surely *he* was not the blackmailer, the infamous Mr X? Ross could not imagine Roland had ever lacked for money. Besides, he had a good job. A senior position in a London company, trading in antiques.

Or did he? He was very vague about it and certainly didn't spend much time there.

Ross made a mental note to ask McKinnon if Roland's finances had been scrutinised. He sighed, catching his breath sharply as his ribs complained. The more he tried to reason it out, the more confused he became.

After breakfast, a roster was drawn up to allow all the horses exercise of some sort, and finding the prospect of a completely inactive day a drag, Ross decided to give Danny a jumping lesson in the school on Flo.

He waved aside Lindsay and Maggie's protests that this didn't come under the heading of rest, but as a concession accepted the offer of a shooting stick and was privately very glad of it by the time the session was over.

Danny was delighted with the whole idea and Ross smiled, remembering the boy's determination to become a steeplechase jockey. At this rate he would be after the job of second rider in the Oakley Manor yard.

And why not? he thought, watching how easily the fifteen-year-old managed the bouncy, excitable mare. The lad had a way with horses and they responded well to him. All he needed was experience.

After the session, as Danny was hosing down the mare to cool her, Ross was sitting on the edge of the water trough, daydreaming and feeling a hundred and one, when Franklin's new Range Rover swept into the yard, bearing not only him but Darcy and Peter as well.

Ross limped across to meet them and was greeted with warmth and concern by Franklin.

'It's good to see you up and about, but are you sure you should be walking on that leg? It looks pretty painful.'

'Sure. It's okay, just a bit stiff,' he lied.

'I should never have let you ride Woody after that fall,' Franklin said, shaking his head regretfully. 'Why on earth didn't you say something?'

'I honestly didn't feel that bad,' Ross assured him, then, feeling that a change of subject was probably called for, 'Look, Danny and I were just going in for a cup of coffee. Why don't you join us? Maggie's been baking.'

'Those are the magic words,' Franklin said. 'There is nothing we Richmonds like better than Maggie's home-made scones and gingerbread. Isn't that right, Peter?'

The boy smiled a little wanly from the back seat of the Range Rover where Darcy was preparing to lift him out.

'He's feeling a bit under the weather. Just been for a physio session,' Franklin explained.

'Oh, bad luck, kid,' Ross said with real sympathy. 'It's pretty much like hell, isn't it?'

Peter nodded. 'Did you cry?' he asked. 'When you had it?'

'Oh, buckets!' Ross assured him.

Peter surveyed him doubtfully, then grinned. 'I bet you didn't.'

'Well, only when no one was looking.'

'Come on, young 'un,' Darcy said, scooping Peter up. 'Let's go see what Maggie can find for you, shall we?'

They all made to follow but hearing the clatter of hooves in the lane, Ross and Franklin turned back, and presently Lindsay, Bill and Sarah rode in. With Danny's help the horses were soon settled and the whole crowd made their way to the cottage for coffee.

Maggie was in her element with eight people in her kitchen. She produced quantities of fruitcake and scones, and poured coffee in varying colours and degrees of sweetness. Shortly after everybody had found a place to perch, the door opened and Roland looked in.

'Is this a private party or can anyone join in?' he asked, and without waiting for an answer, came in. Everybody shifted up good-naturedly to make room.

'Don't squash the invalids!' Franklin warned. 'Now tell me, Ross, how is it, really?'

Before he could form a reply, Lindsay broke in. 'He won't tell you, Frank. You're wasting your time. It's this macho American hang-up he has. He could be at death's door and all he'd say would be, "Oh, I'm doin' fine." '

She mimicked Ross' accent perfectly and he joined in the general laughter, glad of the diversion. He wasn't used to being molly-coddled and had ridden for several weeks in the States with a broken collarbone without anybody even knowing.

But Franklin wouldn't have it. 'No, *really,* Ross?'

His mouth twitched. 'Oh, I'm doin' fine,' he drawled and laughter broke out anew.

Only Darcy seemed unamused. Strangely, he was scowling at Peter, who had cheered up no end and was laughing louder than anyone. After a moment, Darcy seemed to sense Ross' scrutiny, smiled at him and relaxed.

The telephone rang and Maggie went to answer it. Lindsay started to make more coffee, and halfway through the making of it, James arrived and was called in. Lindsay kissed him affectionately as she passed by handing round mugs, and Ross felt a prickle of jealousy.

'I didn't know you were here,' James said, settling next to her on the arm of her chair. 'I called at your parents' house. I thought we were going to Winchester for that exhibition.'

Lindsay put a hand to her mouth. 'Oh, James, I'm sorry! I totally forgot. Forgive me? The thing is, with Ross out of action they need some help here.'

'Yeah, well, you could have let me know.'

It was the first time Ross had seen James even

slightly impatient with her but he couldn't really blame him. For someone who didn't ride, Lindsay's preoccupation with the yard and its business must have been sorely trying at times.

She looked downcast. 'How can you ever forgive me?' she asked him with a lost-puppy look.

James was human. He relented.

Moments later, Maggie reappeared. 'That was Doreen at the pub,' she announced to the room in general. 'A terrible thing happened in the village last night. You know little Alice Ripley from the Post Office?'

Most of them nodded.

'Well, she was stood at the bus stop opposite and some maniac drove straight into her. They say he was doing sixty miles an hour! Poor kid didn't stand a chance. Sixteen she was. Just had her birthday last week, poor little mite.'

There were general expressions of shock and sympathy. Franklin glanced uneasily at Peter to see how he was taking the news. He didn't appear unduly distressed.

'What's more,' Maggie went on with a certain morbid relish, 'they caught the blighter. He'd been drinking. Three times over the limit, he was!'

There was a sharp crack as Roland slammed his mug down on the wooden table and stood up. As he released it, the mug handle clinked on to the scrubbed pine to lie beside the bowl. He looked down at the broken pottery with slight surprise, as if unaware of having been the cause.

'They don't make things like they used to, do

they?' he joked, the mask slipping back into place. 'Sorry, Maggie. Look, I must go. Thanks for the coffee.'

As the door closed behind him, those remaining exchanged glances.

Maggie was stricken with remorse.

'Oh, I'm sorry, love!' she exclaimed, turning to Lindsay. 'I didn't think . . .'

'It's not your fault,' Lindsay reassured her kindly. 'I know it was eight years ago but Roland still finds it hard to accept what happened to Aunt Caroline and Harriet. They were a really close family and it's just such a waste when it happens like that.'

'The worst of it is that people don't ever seem to learn,' James agreed. 'You hear about it happening again and again . . .'

Franklin evidently decided that this conversation was not ideal for his convalescing son and stood up, announcing that he had things to do before lunch. His move signalled the break-up of the gathering.

Lindsay and James left, presumably to get ready to go to their exhibition, with Lindsay voicing her intention of returning in the morning.

Franklin departed for the main house and some business with the Colonel, and Peter asked if he could watch the horses being fed. Bill offered to wheel him round the yard, so Darcy fetched his wheelchair from the Range Rover.

When feeding was complete and Clown plied with extra carrots from his young owner, Peter was

426

wheeled back into the yard, where Darcy was found to be engaged in what appeared to be a very heated discussion with Danny. They broke off immediately they saw the others and Danny marched off towards the cottage, scowling.

Coming back from the house, Franklin passed Danny and looked curiously at Darcy. 'What was that all about?' he asked, as he bent to lift Peter out of the chair.

Darcy shrugged, looking quite upset.

'Danny says he gave me a videotape to show to you and Peter. The one he's been filming of the horses. But I haven't seen it. He says he left it on the passenger seat of my car the other day, but he didn't. Or at least I never found it if he did.'

Peter, peering over his father's shoulder, looked disappointed.

'Was that the one where Ross rode Telamon and he was like a bucking bronco?'

'I don't know. It could have been,' Darcy said dismissively, then smiled at his young nephew. 'Never mind. I'll buy him another tape if he doesn't find that one and we'll make you up another film.'

'But it won't have Telamon's bucking bronco act on it, will it?' Peter was unusually persistent.

'No, but we'll find something just as good,' Darcy said, adding, 'I could murder Danny.'

'I expect it'll turn up,' his uncle said soothingly. 'Come on, it's high time we were on our way.'

As Bill and Ross waved goodbye to the Richmonds and made their way back to the cottage, the stable manager wasn't happy.

427

'Danny's such a cloth-head, he's probably still got the tape somewhere himself,' he said. 'But whatever the case, he should know better than to argue with owners like that. I'll have to speak to him about it.'

Ross wasn't sure. It was true Danny could be absent-minded at times but he wasn't stupid and was invariably truthful. If he was adamant that he'd left the videotape in Darcy's car, then he had. It was probably Darcy who had misplaced it and didn't want to be the one to disappoint Peter.

After lunch, Maggie dragged Bill off under sufferance to visit friends in Dorset and Ross spent the first hour or so of the afternoon sitting on the school fence watching Sarah and Danny exercise Woody and Fly.

When he judged that they had done enough, he announced his intention of driving to the saddler's to pick up a saddle that was in for repair. He asked them to have Telamon ready for him to lunge when he returned.

It was a yard rule that no one except Bill or Ross should go in with the stallion on their own because, however well behaved, a stallion is always a stallion and by nature unpredictable. If Danny or Sarah needed to attend to him, they had to do so together or with another person present.

Driving the jeep was not the height of luxury at the best of times, but with ribs that protested at every bump in the road and a knee that was daily less co-operative about bending, it was getting to be a decided grind. Ross began to think seriously about an automatic.

Sitting in the car park at the saddler's, he called McKinnon on his mobile.

McKinnon's answerphone said he was out and could it take a message?

Ross explained briefly about Roland's theory with regard to his fall at the show and his own vague suspicions with regard to Roland. As he switched off he saw a familiar figure filling the tank of a racy black hatchback at a petrol station on the far side of the road.

At the same moment, Roland looked up and saw Ross. He waved and the American waved back.

Ross started the jeep, thinking that wherever he was these days, Roland never seemed to be far away, and wondered idly about coincidence and intent. He wondered also why Roland had forsaken his Aston Martin. Too conspicuous, perhaps?

Such was his state of mind that he checked his rear-view mirror several times as he drove on, but the black hatchback didn't appear.

You're getting paranoid, he told himself severely. Snap out of it.

Because of roadworks and the inappropriately named rush hour, Ross was twenty minutes later than he had estimated. When he turned back into the yard Telamon's door stood open and neither the horse nor its minders were anywhere to be seen.

He cut the jeep's engine and left it where it was,

almost immediately hearing a flurry of powerful hoofbeats in the school. Ross hurried towards the sound, an uneasy premonition settling on him.

At the gate he was met by a highly excited stallion with reins and stirrups flying. He deftly caught a rein as the horse made to swing away again and peering past the animal, could see Danny climbing to his feet, a rueful expression on his face.

'What in hell's name do you think you are playing at?' Ross demanded thunderously.

Danny flushed red and came over. 'I was just – that is, I thought I could ride him. I was going to surprise you . . .' His voice tailed off unhappily as he saw the look on Ross' face.

'And whose horse is this?'

'I never meant any harm. I wouldn't have let anything happen to him.'

'Whose?' Ross repeated sharply.

'Roland's,' Danny said miserably.

'Did *he* say you could ride him?'

Danny shook his head.

'Then what on earth possessed you?'

'I'm sorry.' The boy was looking at his feet, fiddling with the strap on his crash hat. 'I wanted to see if I could ride him. Looks like I can't,' he said then with the ghost of a self-conscious grin. His jeans and shirt were plastered with wet sand.

Ross opened the gate and let himself into the school. In spite of his fury, he had to admire the lad's courage. And after all, it was something he had done a time or two when he was younger, stealing a ride on a forbidden horse. He'd got caught once, too, and thrashed for his disobedience.

'Are you hurt?'

Danny shook his head.

'Well, the worst thing you can do is let him win,' Ross said after a moment. 'You'd better get back up. Then sit quietly and do exactly what I say. Don't touch his mouth. Think positive and picture him walking slowly. Horses are highly telepathic, as you know.'

Danny came round to the near side and bent his left leg at the knee, looking hopefully at Ross. With one hand on the reins Ross tossed him aboard the huge chestnut, where he sat looking puny and wholly impotent.

Ross laughed. 'You've got guts, I'll give you that! Now just walk him quietly. Don't ask for anything more. He's being very good at the moment and that's what we want him to remember when we finish.'

Danny followed his instructions and Telamon behaved, but it was a close-run thing. Ross could sense that another explosion was never very far away.

'Okay, that'll do,' he called, and Danny walked the horse back to the gate with a huge grin on his face.

'He thought about it, didn't he, Ross?'

'Yup. He sure did,' Ross agreed, glad to get his hand back on the reins. 'And that's the last time you'll sit on that horse until I say different. Do you understand?'

'Danny! Get off that horse and go inside!' A low, furious voice spoke from behind Ross. Bill had returned, unnoticed by the pair.

Danny's face fell and he obediently slid to the ground. He made to run the stirrups up.

'Leave the horse and go!'

Danny left, giving Ross an anxious look and pausing fractionally by his father as if to speak, but what he saw in Bill's face discouraged him.

'Bill, it's no big deal –' Ross began.

'No big deal?'

'The horse is okay. The boy's okay.'

Bill stepped closer and over his shoulder Ross could see Maggie standing, looking on awkwardly.

'Danny could have been killed, or crippled like you!' Bill asserted bitterly.

Ross' eyes narrowed.

'How can you stand there and say it's no big deal? That horse is dangerous! He's no fit ride for a boy. He's no fit ride for anybody, come to that. What the bloody hell were you thinking of? Are you mad?'

Bill wasn't in the mood to accept excuses, and besides, Danny was in enough trouble already. Ross waded in.

'I know it was wrong, but the kid has to learn. You can't shield him from all the knocks, you know. He's got a healthy appetite for a challenge. Do you want him to be a sissy? I'd been bucked off dozens of horses by the time I was his age. That's how I learnt. It's the *only* way to learn.'

If Ross had thought Scott angry before, now he was apoplectic.

'*Don't* you tell me how to raise my son!' he thundered. 'You're hardly a fit example to follow!'

Ross' eyes flashed but he held his temper with an effort. In the background he heard Maggie say reproachfully, 'Oh, Bill!'

'Maybe not,' Ross said steadily. 'But it's wrong to limit the boy with your own fears. He's got to make his own life, his own mistakes. What happened to you was your bad luck, not his!'

He led the stallion out of the school and down into the yard, pushing past the ex-jockey where he stood.

Bill watched him pass, his face full of anger and bitterness.

It seemed their uneasy truce was over.

Sunday was a drag.

Bill wouldn't speak to Ross beyond what was strictly necessary and Danny crept around looking miserable and guilty. Lindsay had rung to say could they manage without her for a day or two because she was rather busy, which Ross had interpreted as meaning she was in hot water for spending so much time at the yard.

In the evening, when he had given up trying to find anything worth watching on TV and had decided to settle for an early night, he heard a knock at the door.

He hesitated. Events had made him cautious. But deciding that, in general, bad guys were probably not in the habit of announcing their arrival, he crossed to the door, unlocked and opened it, to reveal a rather sheepish Danny on the landing outside.

'Hi!' he said, opening the door wider. 'Come on in.'

'Do you always lock your door?' Danny asked curiously as he passed Ross.

'Oh, always. I'm the nervous type.'

The boy glanced suspiciously at him.

'Park your butt,' Ross suggested. 'Coffee?'

'Aren't you mad at me?' Danny asked, sitting on the sagging sofa.

'Should I be?' Ross enquired over his shoulder as he put the kettle on.

'I got you into trouble,' the boy said, not shirking the issue. 'And I can see Dad's not speaking to you.'

'He'll get over it,' Ross said lightly, spooning coffee into mugs. 'Sugar?'

'One, please.' He sat silently for a few moments, apparently deep in thought.

Ross brought the coffee and sat at the other end of the sofa, angled to face Danny.

'Why didn't you tell him it was my fault?' the boy blurted out suddenly. 'He's blaming you and that's not fair!'

'Life's not fair,' Ross observed placidly. He seemed to be saying that a lot lately.

'Don't patronise me,' Danny said irritably. 'I tried to explain but Dad wouldn't listen. It's like he'd rather blame you. I don't understand him.'

'He's just worried about you, that's all. Feels I should be more responsible. He's probably right,' Ross added.

'But *you* didn't know I was going to try and ride Telamon. If you had, you'd have stopped me.'

'That's right, I would,' Ross agreed. 'Which is precisely why you didn't ask me.'

Danny looked uncomfortable. 'I know it was wrong, I wasn't thinking straight, but it's not as if anything happened.'

'It quite easily could have, you know,' Ross said soberly. 'A stallion is one of the most dangerous and unpredictable creatures on earth. You have to treat them with respect. You know the old saying?'

Danny shook his head.

'They say, when dealing with horses, "You tell a gelding; you ask a mare; and you consult a stallion." It's worth remembering.'

Danny laughed. 'He didn't consult me,' he said. 'He just dumped me like so much rubbish!'

'Let's hope it taught you a lesson.'

'I said I was sorry.'

'So you did.' Ross nodded. 'Now let's forget it, shall we? We're in the local paper again, did you see?'

He leant forward to reach for it and caught his breath sharply as the movement shifted a rib.

'It still hurts then? Dad doesn't reckon you'll be fit to ride for another week.'

'He told you that?' Ross passed him the paper, opened on the relevant page.

'Well, actually, no. He told Mum. I was

listening,' Danny admitted, unashamed. 'He also said –'

'Okay, okay! Didn't anyone ever tell you it's wrong to eavesdrop?'

'I wasn't eavesdropping,' Danny protested. 'I was in the same room. Dad thought I was watching telly.'

'That's just as bad!' Ross exclaimed, amused. 'I don't want to hear any more.'

Danny fell obediently silent, reading the article in the paper. It was a general account of the show with several pictures, one of them being a murky shot of Ginger falling, obviously taken from across the ring. The text, uncorrupted by Harry Douglas' poison pen, was sympathetic and detailed several of the yard's recent successes to balance the unflattering picture.

'It's not a very clear photograph,' the boy said, peering closely. 'I can't even see you.'

'Bloodthirsty little sucker, aren't you?' Ross said, laughing. 'By the way, have you come across that videotape yet?'

Danny scowled. 'No, and I don't expect to. I left it on the front seat of Darcy's car, like I said I did. Why doesn't anyone believe me? You all think because I'm young I'm automatically stupid!'

'Hey!' Ross raised his hands. 'Not guilty! I never said it and I never thought it. I think it's far more likely that Darcy's lost it. Try to take it easy. You'll have ulcers by the time you're twenty-one!'

Danny grinned reluctantly. 'But it's just *so* annoying when nobody believes you.'

'Tell me about it! But the best thing you can do is stick at it and prove them wrong.'

'Is that what you do? With Harry Douglas and the others? I thought you just didn't care. You never seem to.'

'Hide like a rhino, that's me,' Ross agreed wryly. 'More coffee?'

'Yes, please.' Danny looked sideways at Ross as he walked by. 'I never know whether you're kidding or being serious.'

'Oh, quite serious. I've got plenty of coffee.'

'You see what I mean?'

When Ross came back with the drinks, Danny was wandering around the room restlessly, looking at the Stubbs prints on the walls and the half-a-dozen books that Ross had.

There wasn't much to see. He hadn't made any effort to impose his personality on the spartan room. It was probably a legacy of his unsettled past.

He set the coffee down, watching the boy pick up a volume of English history, and his heart missed a beat as he remembered what stood next to it, partly concealed. He saw Danny freeze momentarily then reach slowly for the bottle.

Ross said lightly, 'Now that really *would* get me into trouble, if you were to go back smelling of whisky.'

Danny jumped as if he'd been shot. Snatching his hand back as though the bottle was burning hot, he whirled to face Ross, holding the book, his cheeks flaming.

437

'That's not a bad book, actually,' Ross said pleasantly. 'Read it if you like – but I expect you already know most of it.'

Danny replaced the volume but remained standing, glaring a mixture of disappointment, accusation and defiance at Ross.

In spite of himself, he burst out laughing.

'Don't look so tragic! It's not life and death.'

'Is it true then, what they said about you?' Danny demanded. 'Don't laugh at me! I want to know.'

' "One swallow doth not a summer make",' Ross quoted. Then, more seriously, 'No. I promise you, it's not true, Danny. I've had that one bottle since I got here. I can't sleep sometimes when my knee's playing up. It seems to help. Hell, I don't even like the stuff much!'

Danny looked torn. 'You promise?'

'I promise.' Ross hoped to hell that the boy did believe him. He could imagine Bill's reaction if he learnt of this.

Danny came forward slowly and sat down.

'Why did you hide the bottle, then?'

Ross sighed. 'It wasn't exactly hidden, more – discreet. And because I didn't want anyone jumping to the same conclusions you just have.'

Danny picked up his coffee. 'Life's a bummer, isn't it?'

Ross relaxed, making a mental note to put the whisky back in his suitcase.

'Ain't it just?'

18

The next morning brought another note from
McKinnon. Ross found it pushed under his door,
as the first one had been. He smiled as he read it.
McKinnon was clearly enjoying their little game.

*Confirmed. The rat has doubled back, bolt-hole as
yet unknown. The antique has provenance. Hope you
are recovering.*

Amused, Ross wondered how Roland would feel
about being called an antique. He was glad that the
Colonel's son seemed to be in the clear but much
about him was still puzzling, not least, on
occasions, his behaviour.

Ross sighed. The idea that he himself could
discover anything that the professionals had failed
to seemed as unlikely as ever.

His return to the saddle the following day could
not have been described as an unqualified success,
but neither was it a total failure. From past

experience, he knew he'd just have to grin and bear it. It was nothing new and it was nothing like as bad as it had been after the original accident. He knew Bill was watching him for any signs of weakness to report to the Colonel and, if nothing else, that spurred him on.

At the end of the day he felt as though he had had an argument with a steamroller, but although his knee had protested vigorously, it hadn't let him down. He felt a kind of weary elation as the last horse was settled for the evening and he limped up the stairs to his room, to rest and freshen up before the evening meal.

He spent a couple of hours with the Colonel, as usual, and was cheered by the news that Robbie Fergusson had agreed to leave Bishop at Oakley Manor for the time being.

'He wouldn't go so far as to admit that he was wrong about you,' the Colonel told Ross. 'So I should tread carefully around him for a bit.'

'I'll tug my forelock to him if it means I can keep the ride on Bishop,' Ross assured him. 'That horse is sensational. It's tough that he has to be owned by an awkward bastard like Fergusson!'

The Colonel nodded his agreement. 'And, according to Franklin, Fergusson's not the only one you're not flavour of the month with.'

'What d'you mean?'

'Well, apparently it's young Peter's birthday on Saturday and Darcy had planned a big day out for him, but it seems Peter would rather go to the Somerset and Avon Show to see you jump Clown.'

'Oh, dear. I guess that wouldn't go down too well. Darcy doesn't really see the attraction, does he?'

'No. And to be honest, I think he's a little bit jealous of you. You must know Peter thinks you're the bee's knees?'

'Well, yes,' Ross acknowledged. 'But that's just the age he's at and because I ride Clown. Surely Darcy doesn't take it seriously?'

The Colonel got to his feet to replenish their glasses.

'Oh, no,' he said, shaking his head dismissively. 'It just put his nose out of joint, that's all. He's taking Peter out on Sunday instead, so everybody's happy.'

He passed a second sherry to Ross.

'Tell me, what's happened between you and Bill? I thought you were beginning to get on better but now he's going round with a face like a bulldog chewing on a wasp.'

Ross gave him the gist of the Telamon affair and the Colonel responded with a chuckle.

'Yes, I can see how that would have upset him,' he said. 'Have you ever heard of diplomacy?'

'He was determined to blame it on me anyway,' Ross pointed out. 'There didn't seem any point in getting Danny into any more trouble. I'd already bawled him out.'

'Oh, well. Bill will come around again,' the Colonel observed with the comfortable complacency of one who didn't have to work with him.

★

Ross didn't see any outsiders at all the next day, for which he was profoundly grateful. He had spent a long night tossing and turning, kept awake by a disturbing train of thought as much as by his knee.

He worked hard that day, trying to shut out the unwelcome suspicions that were nagging at him, but by the time evening stables were finished, he knew he was fighting a losing battle. He waited until Sarah cycled away down the lane and Danny and Bill headed for the cottage, and then let himself into the stable office and telephoned Franklin Richmond.

Franklin himself answered.

Aware that there was a risk, ringing him at home, Ross said hurriedly, 'I can't talk now, but could we meet up later?'

'I have some business calls to make but I could be free by half-past eight or nine. Is it important?'

'It might be,' Ross said guardedly. 'Same place as last time?'

'Okay. Make it nine then, to be on the safe side, and if I'm not there, wait for me. I *will* come.'

Ross replaced the handset and sat looking at it, blindly. He hoped, beyond all hope, that he was not making a mistake. He felt, more than anything, like someone who has just completed the arrangements for a duel, although pistols at dawn might be preferable. He was not looking forward to the evening at all.

A sound from the tackroom sent Ross swiftly to the door. Roland stood there in the gloom, his pale-suited figure easily recognisable.

'Looking for me?' Ross asked pleasantly.

'As a matter of fact, yes,' Roland replied. 'Thing is, I've been stood up and wondered if you'd care to come out for a drink this evening?'

Ross was greatly impressed with this barefaced lie, as he was ninety-nine per cent certain that Roland had been eavesdropping and ninety-eight per cent certain Roland knew that he knew.

'I'm afraid I can't,' he said, in tones of deep regret. 'I already have a date.'

'And who is the lucky lady?'

Ross shook his head, grinning. 'Oh, no, you don't. I've already lost one of my girlfriends to you. I think I'll keep this one to myself.'

Two hours later, under a sky that threatened rain, Ross set out for the Dovecote with an open map on the seat beside him in case he missed his way. Roland had driven him last time.

He supposed, looking doubtfully at the clouds, that he would soon have to think about trading-in the jeep for something more suited to the vagaries of the English climate. Something with a roof. Before he'd covered half a mile, however, all such mundane considerations had been driven from his mind by a discovery altogether more urgent.

He was being followed.

He might never have noticed the car if it hadn't been for the fact that in his preoccupation with wondering how Franklin was going to react to what he had to say, he'd missed his turning and had to double back.

As he back-tracked, a black hatchback passed him going in the other direction and a minute or two later, when he was held up by a tractor, the self-same car appeared behind him. Sure, it was two or three cars back but it was there.

Scanning his memory, Ross placed it. At the garage three days ago. A black hatchback and Roland. Just how often *had* he been followed? he wondered. And *why*?

His old suspicions came flooding back. With a surge of annoyance, Ross determined to lose Roland. The job would have to be done sooner rather than later, too, because the Dovecote was located in a quiet backwater with very little around it but farmland. Once in the vicinity, it would not take a genius to guess where he was going.

His opportunity came sooner than he'd expected. Coming to his missed turning, he swung into it only to be brought up short by a queue of traffic at a red light. Twenty yards or so of deserted roadworks blocked the road on the left-hand side and a steady stream of vehicles was coming through from the opposite direction.

When the lights changed and Ross' queue moved forward, he dawdled in the right lane, level with the green light, revving his engine and making out that he had trouble until the signal changed to red once again.

Then, leaving behind half a dozen hooting and honking motorists, no doubt calling him all the names under the sun, he accelerated down the single carriageway, swerving round a large oncoming lorry at the far end, and sped away down the road.

In his mirror he could see the lorry still moving forward and beyond it two cars – one of them the black hatchback – who had tried to follow him and had now met it head on.

Ross allowed himself a moment of smugness. With any luck Roland would be held up for quite a while, as it was unlikely that the lorry driver would be willing to reverse. It had been *his* green light, after all.

All the same, Ross took a couple of diversionary turnings before resuming his journey. The way Roland drove, it was quite possible he could still have overtaken the slower jeep.

Back en route, Ross checked his watch. *Damn Roland!* What with his initial mistake and his subsequent detours, he was going to be late meeting Franklin. He put his foot down.

About two miles from the pub, as he turned into the lane that would lead past it, he was held up again by a Land-Rover that pulled out of a gateway directly into his path, causing him to brake hard. He leaned on the horn, his patience already stretched. The driver waved a careless hand in apology.

'Okay, but shift your butt!' Ross muttered under his breath. He looked at his watch again. Five past nine. The Land-Rover was in no hurry.

DRH. Damn Roland's Hide, Ross thought, reading the numberplate out of habit.

Suddenly, as if remembering an urgent appointment, the Land-Rover picked up speed substantially and disappeared round a bend in the road.

Ross shook his head in disbelief. They were all out tonight! Following, he found himself brought up short by a diversion sign flanked by two orange and white traffic cones. He pulled up.

The suggested route was a left fork that looked to be little more than a glorified farm track. In the distance he could see the roof of the Land-Rover just as it disappeared behind a stand of trees.

According to the map it was just a roundabout way of getting to the same place, taking in a small wood and a handful of farm buildings on the way. He was going to be very late indeed. Ross shifted gear and started down the lane.

It was very rough. Dried mud and stones littered it, and through the cracks in its tarmac, grass had begun to grow. Over the sound of the jeep's engine, Ross could hear the drone of a motorbike behind him. The lane was probably seeing more traffic in this one night than it had in the past ten years.

Turning into the gloom of the stretch that was flanked by the copse, Ross swore. Skewed across the road, with its nose buried in the hedge on the right-hand side, was the Land-Rover he had been following. Just to Ross' side of it was an open gateway leading into the wood. It almost looked as though the vehicle had tried to make the turn and missed.

From his viewpoint, Ross couldn't see whether anyone was still inside the Land-Rover but as there was a complete absence of anyone outside the vehicle, looking at the results of their handiwork, he had to assume that the driver was still inside and possibly hurt.

He switched the jeep's engine off, slid out and went to investigate.

The Land-Rover's engine was still running but from his angle of approach he couldn't see anyone at the wheel. Thinking it was possible the driver had fallen sideways on to the passenger seat, he approached the window and looked in.

Not a soul.

There was the slightest whisper of sound behind him and then a stunning blow to the base of his neck sent Ross sprawling against the side of the Land-Rover. His hands were grasped and pulled roughly behind his back, and he was pushed sideways until he was face-down on the bonnet with his nose pressed to the engine-warmed metal. What little he could see from that position was whirling crazily and he closed his eyes, feeling nauseous.

His captor reached into the vehicle and switched off the ignition. The absence of vibration was an improvement. Through the fog in his brain, he heard another engine approaching. The motorbike.

Any hopes of assistance that might have been forming in Ross' woolly consciousness were dashed as the man behind him spoke.

'Get that bike out of sight. Move the jeep, then give me a hand before somebody comes,' the voice commanded in broad Irish tones.

Ross felt he should try and see what was going on but his attempt to raise his head was rewarded by a sturdy push back towards the bonnet. His face connected painfully with the metal and his damaged ribs complained sharply as they were forced against the angle of the wing. Cravenly, he abandoned the idea.

He heard the jeep being moved, and after a moment or two the motorbike man came over and Ross' hands were tied, none too gently, behind his back. Then he was pulled upright, turned round and propelled through the open gateway into the wood. Behind him he heard the Land-Rover start up again, move – presumably out of the hedge and back to the side of the road – and stop.

After a few strides Ross stumbled, still muzzy, and his shirt collar was grasped by whoever was behind. An arm came over his shoulder and a shiny, six-inch blade flashed in front of his face.

'Would you be knowing what this is, mister?' a soft voice enquired.

Ross did know, only too well. He nodded.

'Well, if you do as you're told then maybe I won't stick it in you,' the voice informed him generously. 'Now walk, and don't even think of trying anything.'

The copse, which consisted of thickets of overgrown hazel coppice interspersed with larger beech trees, was at that time of the evening growing rapidly more gloomy, and conditions didn't improve the further they went. Ross found it increasingly difficult to avoid stumbling over brambles and looping roots. He just hoped that his captor wouldn't mistake such mishaps for 'trying anything'.

As his head cleared, the significance of that Irish accent had become all too depressingly clear.

When they had gone perhaps a hundred yards, Irish grasped Ross' collar again, swung him round, and with a foot hooked deftly behind his knee, dumped him unceremoniously at the foot of a youngish beech tree.

Ross eased himself sideways so that he was no longer lying on a root and looked up for the first time at the mysterious Mr X.

The man who stood before him, the deadly blade held so casually in his hand, was of medium height and build, and wore jeans, a tee-shirt and a black balaclava.

Ross blinked and looked again. The balaclava was still there. For a moment, in spite of the gravity of the situation, he found it amusing. It seemed so melodramatic. This was a Wiltshire wood, for Chrissakes, not exactly a terrorist blackspot!

'What's so funny?' The other man had caught up. Unmistakably familiar tones.

Ross looked beyond Irish. Lean, wiry form and again a balaclava. He needn't have bothered.

'Hi, Leo,' Ross said conversationally.

'You fool!' the first balaclava said contemptuously. 'I told you to keep your bloody mouth shut!'

'I don't care. I want the Yank to know who's doing this to him.' Leo pulled his balaclava off and stepped closer. 'I've got a score to settle with this bastard. I want him to know, and I want him to shit himself with fear!'

Ross looked back at Irish. 'You certainly mix with the low-life,' he observed.

There was a flurry of movement as Irish was shoved to one side, and Ross' heart missed a beat as he found himself looking down the barrel of a gun.

Suddenly the melodrama didn't seem so amusing. Everything inside him seemed to freeze. He stopped breathing. For the sake of his pride he hoped the terror he felt wasn't reflected on his face.

Long years of concealing his emotions from the telepathy of horses came to his rescue. Ross made himself relax, forced his fascinated gaze away from the deadly black hole, and looked up at Irish.

'Is this part of your plan?' he asked, in a voice that sounded a thousand times steadier than he felt. 'Who's in charge here anyway?'

Irish put out a hand and tipped the gun barrel down.

'Put that damned thing away, for God's sake. If you want him to beg you're wasting your time, you should know that by now. And you're wasting *my* time, so get a grip on yourself and let's get it over with.'

Leo glared at Ross for one more long moment and then glared at Irish for good measure.

'One day . . .' he promised, before turning away. Neither Ross nor Irish felt any need to ask him to enlarge on it.

Ross closed his eyes, and clenched his fists and jaw to stop them from trembling. He should have learned by now not to antagonise Leo. You don't tease a mad dog.

Irish had also turned away now but any thoughts Ross might have had of rushing him were effectively quelled by the thought of Leo's gun. That and the obvious drawbacks entailed in trying to rush anyone from a sitting position with his hands tied behind his back.

One consideration alone cheered him, although *cheered* was probably pitching it a little too strong – Irish evidently craved anonymity, which suggested he had no intention at present of permanently removing Ross from circulation. Just what he *did* intend Ross preferred not to contemplate. It possibly also suggested that without the balaclava he was somebody Ross would recognise. On the other hand, it could just be insurance against future recognition.

Suddenly, both Irish and Leo were back. They stood one on each side of Ross and hauled him to his feet. Leo then moved behind him and with a swift tug the rope tying his hands together came undone, remaining attached to his right wrist only.

Ross swore silently. The rope had obviously been secured with a quick-release knot such as were used, for safety's sake, to tie horses' headcollar ropes. If he had known that, there was a strong possibility he might have managed to release it himself.

Leo pulled on the rope, bringing Ross' right hand round in front of him, and reached across to seize the left also. Ross made no move to resist.

Irish stood not three feet away, hefting his knife casually in his hand, and he had no doubt Leo still had his gun stowed somewhere about his person. With a deftness that would have brought tears to the eyes of a Boy Scout, Leo tied Ross' wrists firmly together in front of him.

No quick-release knots this time.

A further rope was tied around the one that bound his hands and thrown over a sturdy branch about three feet above his head so that his wrists were pulled upward. Leo tugged on it until Ross was on tiptoe and then tied it off. As the knot slipped tight, Ross found he could stand flat-footed again, for which he was grateful. The strain on his arms and bruised body was quite painful enough as it was and his broken rib made its presence felt with every breath.

Leo stood back with an unpleasant smirk to survey his handiwork.

'Not such a wise-guy now, are you, Yank?' he observed with satisfaction.

Ross didn't feel at all wise. He watched with a kind of fatalistic calm while Irish rummaged in a haversack Leo had presumably brought with him, and drew out a full bottle of what looked ominously like whisky.

'This shouldn't be too much of a hardship,' he said, standing up and coming towards Ross. 'I hear you have a liking for the stuff.'

'That's right.' Leo grinned unpleasantly. 'He's got quite a reputation.'

With a jolt, Ross guessed something of what they

intended and depression settled on him like a dark blanket.

'I did warn you to keep your nose out of what didn't concern you,' Irish said reasonably. 'You really should've listened.'

Leo leaned close. 'Got any smart remarks now, Yank?'

Offhand, Ross couldn't think of any.

Irish removed the screwtop and stepped to Ross' side. He watched, trying to see something, any little thing that could give a clue to his identity, but the light was fading fast now and somehow all he could see was that bottle.

From the other side, Leo grasped the front of Ross' shirt and shoved him roughly back against the tree, then put a hand under his chin and forced his head back.

Ross tightened his jaw muscles, instinctively preparing to resist. He needn't have bothered. With admirable teamwork, Irish slugged him in the stomach with his fist, and as Ross' mouth opened and the breath left his body in a painful rush, Leo's hand clamped round his jaw. Something cold and metallic forced its way between his teeth, bruising his lips, and any intended resistance was effectively quelled.

'You know what this is, don't you?' Leo was enjoying himself hugely.

Ross did but he was hardly in a position to answer. He could feel sweat running down his face and body and tried not to think about the horrendous consequences of any slip on Leo's part.

453

'Let's get on with it.' Irish seemed as weary of Leo's gloating as Ross himself was.

The neck of the bottle slid between Ross' teeth next to the gun barrel and he closed his eyes helplessly. The strong, smoky-tasting liquid burned over his tongue and down his throat, filling his mouth. He tried not to swallow, breathing through his nose, and a quantity of the spirit ran down his chin and soaked into his shirt. His eyes began to water.

With a muffled exclamation, Irish used his free hand to pinch Ross' nostrils. It became either swallow or drown.

Ross swallowed.

His mouth filled up again instantly. Twice more he swallowed huge gulps of the fiery liquid, then his throat and lungs constricted in panic. He tried to twist away.

Irish seemed to recognise his predicament, for the pressure on his nose released and he drew in a blessed lungful of air. The relief was short-lived, however. Moments later the hand was back and the process was repeated.

Some time later the gun barrel was removed and the hold on his nose ceased. He was beyond resistance. The whisky flowed. Gagging and coughing, he swallowed, though a certain amount dribbled out and soaked his shirtfront.

'How much will it take?'

The words sounded echoing and distant, like someone calling through a tunnel.

'A little more. We don't want him getting out and wandering off.'

That was a different voice, he felt. Not Irish or Leo but familiar all the same. How many more people had come to watch?

Ross opened his eyes but his head was still tipped back and all he could see was a pattern of light and dark blotches moving about hypnotically.

They didn't make sense. Nothing seemed to make sense.

Later still, he realised that the bottle had gone and he was sitting down. He tried to open his eyes again but someone had attached lead weights to his eyelids. He thought hazily that he'd better get going, that he'd be late, but he couldn't remember where he was supposed to be going or why.

Moments later, or it could have been minutes, he found himself lying face down in the leaf mould. It seemed fairly comfortable so he stayed there.

Ross couldn't precisely say when consciousness left him or when it returned. The sensation was more that of drifting on the borders – sometimes one side, sometimes the other. The first vaguely tangible thing that made it through to the reasoning part of his brain was a dazzling light, which was shining uncomfortably, straight into his eyes.

He blinked owlishly.

'This one's well gone,' a voice remarked from behind the light.

The light hurt and Ross closed his eyes again. Perhaps it would go away.

It didn't.

'Come on, son. Sit up.' A hand caught hold of his shoulder and tipped him back. Pressure that he hadn't been aware of on his chest now eased and something softer supported his back.

'No sign of injury. Smells like a distillery,' the voice said.

'Shall I get the breath box?' Another voice.

Ross opened his eyes once more but couldn't see a thing.

'Waste of time. He couldn't blow a candle out. We'll have to take him in.'

'Do you think he drove here like that?'

'Yeah. Bloody marvellous, isn't it? I suppose we should be glad he wasn't on the motorway.'

'You can say that again!'

The light swung away. Ross could now see the windscreen of the jeep, but beyond it, pressed against the glass, was a tangle of leaves and stems.

He couldn't remember why it should be like that. He stared, puzzled.

Somebody leaned in front of him, switched the jeep's lights off and removed the ignition key.

Careless of him to leave them on. Not like him. He tried to look up at the man but his head was too heavy.

'Come on then. We'll take a little ride, shall we?' Strong arms reached under his armpits and lifted.

Memory stabbed back.

'No, please . . . No more,' Ross said thickly. 'For God's sake . . .' He turned his head away.

'I should say you've had enough already,'

somebody said with grim amusement.

'Bastards!' Ross said suddenly, vehemently, surprising even himself.

'Yeah, yeah, and life's a bitch,' the nearest voice said patiently. 'Come on, mate. Bring that bottle, Steve.'

Ross half-walked and was half-carried towards a blue flashing light which made his head hurt. The ground seemed to roll away under his feet. He closed his eyes and was hazily aware of being laid on something soft before oblivion closed in.

More lights. A rough blanket beneath him. Voices echoing off cream-painted walls. A king-sized headache.

'Is this the RTA? What have you brought him here for?'

'No other vehicles involved. Just drove quietly into the hedge. No injuries I could see.'

Somebody grunted. 'Better get the doc to check him over. Need a blood test anyway.'

'Why bother? Just light a match and stand well back.'

Someone obviously thought that funny. Ross didn't. He tried to say so but it didn't come out right.

'He's coming round again.'

'Has somebody gone for the doc?'

'He's on his way.'

Ross opened his eyes a fraction more. Vision was a kaleidoscope of colours and lights. He blinked and the colours grouped themselves into vague shapes. It was like looking through the glasses of an acute myopic.

He tried to concentrate. Four dark blobs resolved themselves into two police uniforms. The effort made his head pound and he groaned, feeling abysmal.

One of the uniforms bent over him.

'I think he's beginning to see the error of his ways,' he remarked. 'Can you hear me, sonny? Can you tell me who you are?'

Ross knew perfectly well who he was. He wasn't stupid. Telling them proved to be a different matter. With the best intentions, all he could manage was an unintelligible mumble.

'Where . . .?' He frowned with the effort.

'Nought out of ten for originality,' the nearest uniform said. 'Harnham Police Station. Cell three.'

Still Ross couldn't grasp it. 'What for?'

'I'll give you three guesses,' the uniform said sarcastically.

Ross blinked stupidly at him.

'Give it a rest, Steve. He's in no fit state.'

Another voice said, 'This the new arrival?'

Ross rolled his head to look. A mistake. When the room steadied again he saw a weary-looking, grey-haired man regarding him with scant pity.

'Has he said anything?'

'Nothing that makes much sense.'

Grey-hair put a bag down and opened it. 'Any injuries?'

'None apparent.'

He sighed. 'Better check.' He unbuttoned Ross' shirt and pressed a cold disc to his chest. 'There's some old bruising here. Where did you find him?'

'Got a tip-off and found him draped over the wheel of his car. Had an empty bottle on the seat beside him. Whisky.'

'I can smell it,' the doctor confirmed. After a moment he put the stethoscope away and produced a slim torch, which he proceeded to shine into each of Ross' eyes in turn.

'That looks okay. No concussion.'

His strong, practised fingers moved over Ross' scalp and touched the bruise on his neck.

Ross winced.

The fingers paused, pressed again.

He winced again.

'That hurt,' the doctor commented. 'He's got a bit of bruising there too but he'll survive. Better take some blood.'

Ross couldn't see the logic in this. His sleeve was pushed up and he felt the prick of a needle.

'Smells as though he's bathed in it,' the doctor said, wrinkling his nose. 'It's early too. I wonder what his story is. Well, I think he's fit to be detained but keep an eye and call me if you're worried. I'll look in on him in the morning.'

The sounds receded and a door banged. Ross groaned and rolled over.

The next time he surfaced, his head was clearer. Unfortunately, sensation had returned to the rest of his body with a vengeance too.

He looked around him. Four walls, the bed and a john. It was hardly the Hilton.

With an effort, he slid his legs over the side of the bed and sat up. At once, his head set up a hammering that would have done a pile-driver proud. He groaned. The back of his neck was stiff and tender, as were his shoulders and arms, and his ribs told of new damage. The way his stomach felt, he couldn't contemplate ever facing food again.

He sighed and tried to recall the events of the previous evening but it was all a muddle of confused images. He remembered Roland following him and he remembered somebody in a balaclava, but couldn't see the connection between that and his being where he was now. His mind skittered over the period in between as if afraid to face it.

The door rattled and opened.

A fresh-faced young PC looked in. 'Cup of tea?'

'No, thanks,' Ross said with feeling.

The door opened wider and the grey-haired police surgeon of the night before came in. He took the cup from the youngster and held it out to Ross. 'Better drink it, you know. It'll help.'

He doubted whether anything short of a hefty dose of chloroform would help but he took the cup obligingly and sipped. His mouth was cut and bruised, and felt as though it had been scrubbed out with wire wool, but if the hot tea sat a little heavily on his stomach, at least nothing cataclysmic happened.

'So. How are we this morning?'

'Well, I can't speak for you,' Ross said flippantly, 'but I've had better mornings.'

'I'm not surprised,' Grey-hair said. 'You'd polished off the best part of a bottle of Scotch, apparently.'

Ross frowned as a memory flickered on the edges of his consciousness. He shook his head. 'I didn't. I mean, I . . . I don't even like the stuff.'

'Well, you certainly gave it a fair trial, I'll say that for you,' the doctor observed sardonically. 'Now, do you have a name?'

Ross bit back another facetious reply and sighed. There was nothing to be gained by antagonising them.

'Ross Wakelin,' he said. 'But I assume you've got my wallet and driver's licence, so you already know that.'

'True, but you managed to bash the back of your head somewhere along the way and we can't be too careful.' He looked at Ross thoughtfully. 'So what's the story? Why the binge? Were you celebrating or trying to drown your sorrows?'

'Neither. I don't drink. What I mean is – not like that.' An image almost settled in his mind's eye. 'There was somebody else . . .'

'Well, if there was, they should be shot for letting you drive like that,' the doctor remarked. 'Let's just have another little look.'

He took the slim torch out of his bag again and, asking Ross to look straight ahead, shone it into his eyes.

'Yes, that's okay,' he said after a moment.

'You'll be right as rain just as soon as you get rid of that massive hangover you must have. I just hope it was worth it.' He put the torch away. 'You're moving very stiffly. Let's take that shirt off and have a proper look.'

'How did they find me?' Ross asked, obediently undoing buttons. 'I remember being in a wood.'

'Not when they found you,' the doctor said. 'Member of the public reported a car in a ditch. We sent out and there you were.'

Ross shook his head. It didn't make sense. He stood up and let the shirt slip from his shoulders, catching it as it reached his hands.

The doctor frowned as his eyes flickered over Ross' colourful torso. Sucking his teeth, he moved round behind Ross and came back to face him. 'You've been in the wars already, it would appear. How did that happen?'

'Riding accident,' he said briefly.

Grey-hair looked sympathetic. 'You're not having much luck,' he observed. Then the penny dropped. 'Ah, yes. Now I've placed you. You're that American showjumper. I saw it in the paper. Nasty fall. Were you drinking to dull the pain?'

'No. I told you. I didn't drink by choice,' Ross persisted. 'There was someone else there. I was forced to drink.'

'Ah, yes. So you said,' the doctor remembered. He finished his examination. 'We get dozens of cases like yours in here every week and most of them have some story to tell. Accept it, lad. I'm afraid they have all the evidence they need. Blood-

462

alcohol levels probably three or four times the legal limit. Found at the wheel of a vehicle on a public highway.' He shook his head. 'Your driving days are over for a while, I'm afraid. In England that is,' he added as an afterthought, putting his instruments back in his bag. 'You can put your shirt back on.'

'What happened to the bottle? Fingerprint it, then you'll see,' Ross said desperately. 'I never touched it.'

The doctor shook his head again, sadly. 'Give it up, lad. I don't know what they've done with the bottle. They may have thrown it away by now, for all I know. You are all the evidence they need.'

'Well, can you ask? Please?'

'You're serious, aren't you?' The doctor regarded him thoughtfully. 'Okay. I'll see what I can do, but don't get your hopes too high.'

'Thanks,' Ross said gratefully. He didn't know if it was the hot tea, his groggy state or a combination of the two, but suddenly he had begun to feel shaky and a sweat broke out on his body. He sat down weakly on the bed and was starting to roll up his sleeves when the doctor put out a hand and caught his wrist.

'What's this?'

Ross looked down. Both his wrists were red raw and slightly puffy. He frowned. 'I can't remember. I don't know what happened.'

The doctor fished in his bag once more.

'I think we should have a record of those,' he suggested, producing a camera. 'In case your memory returns. They look like rope burns to me.'

Ross held his arms out to be photographed, trying to force his mind back past the blackout. It stubbornly refused to go.

'When can I go home?' he asked, when the doctor had taken a number of shots from all angles.

'That depends. The amount you had, you'll still be way over the limit, but you're rational, so as long as you don't intend to drive, I expect you'll be able to leave as soon as you've been charged. But it's really not up to me, I just advise.'

'So when will that be? And what *is* the time, anyway?'

Ross' new watch had vanished, along with his wallet, belt and boots. To prevent him from doing himself an injury, he supposed. Like he had the energy.

The doctor lifted a wrist. 'Just gone eight. The custody officer will be with you in ten minutes or so. You'll have to take a breath test, then he'll formally charge you and you'll be bailed to appear in court at a later date. We won't have the results of your blood test for a week or two. Oh, and you'll have to sign a form giving permission for that. If you refuse, that's an offence in itself.'

Ross nodded and sighed deeply, both of which he immediately regretted.

As the door closed behind the doctor, Ross lay back on the bed and pieced together what little he could remember with what he'd been told. Most of the previous evening remained a blank but one thing began to be depressingly clear.

He'd been neatly set up.

19

In due time the custody officer appeared and Ross, his boots returned to him, followed the officer and the young PC to the charge room. He was led across to what looked like a piece of office equipment, where he stood swaying dizzily until the constable fetched him a chair. He sank on to it gratefully and presently the room began to behave as a room should; that is, the floor stopped heaving and the walls looked more or less vertical.

'Take a deep breath and then blow into this tube until I tell you to stop,' one of the policemen instructed him.

Ross complied, the effort making him light-headed once more.

Presently, the custody officer's voice penetrated the mists. He seemed to have started without Ross. '. . . are charged that at twenty-three-hundred hours on the evening of Tuesday the second of August . . .'

They'll be finishing morning stables by now, Ross thought. What would they be saying? If he hadn't been missed the night before, they would certainly have discovered his absence by now. What would they be thinking? What had Franklin thought when he hadn't shown up last night?

The officer's voice drifted back, reciting the charge automatically from long experience: '. . . on a road called,' he consulted his paperwork, 'Sandy Lane, while the proportion of alcohol in your blood thereof exceeded the prescribed limit.'

A drunk driver, Ross thought, crushed. Oh, God! What would the Colonel say? And Lindsay? Would she believe him guilty?

'Do you understand the charge?' the officer asked in the tone of one who has been obliged to repeat himself.

'Yes,' Ross said dully. 'But I wasn't driving. The jeep was parked.'

'With its lights and ignition on,' the policeman said, glancing at the report. 'Do you normally park in the hedge?'

'If you'd just fingerprint the bottle,' Ross said desperately. He scanned the officer's face and gave up. He reached for the proffered pen. 'Okay. Where do I sign?'

A few minutes later, the rest of his belongings restored to him, Ross found himself in the reception area trying to gather his rambling thoughts. In his pocket a printout from the station breathalyser recorded a reading more than twice the legal limit of thirty-five microgrammes of alcohol to one hundred millilitres of breath. It seemed the deciding factor in the matter of his early release was the lack of any previous record.

His jeep had apparently been left where the police had picked him up, which was, he was informed, current policy. The custody officer had offered to ring Oakley Manor and arrange for him to be collected but Ross declined. He decided a taxi would be infinitely preferable to Bill Scott's company, just at the moment.

His mobile phone hadn't been among his belongings and while he wavered between finding the payphone, and the altogether more tempting option of collapsing on to the nearest seat, an immaculately suited figure unfolded itself from behind a newspaper and stood up.

'Well, I must say it's about time,' Roland said peevishly, coming forward. 'I've been sitting here for absolutely ages and the coffee is diabolical.' He indicated a vending machine on the wall. 'Bloody instant stuff! I say, do you feel quite well? You don't look at all the thing.'

Ross found Roland's idiotic chatter more than usually irritating.

'Oh, I feel just tickety-boo,' he replied waspishly.

'That's all right then,' Roland said, happily. 'The car's outside, if you're ready to go.'

He put a supporting hand under the American's elbow, much as one would to assist an elderly relative, and steered him towards the door.

Ross would dearly have liked to have pulled his arm free and made his own way out but felt that falling flat on his face would rather rob the gesture of its effect.

Outside the door and squinting uncomfortably in the unsympathetic sunlight, Ross was assailed by four or five aggressive reporters bristling with microphones, tape-recorders and cameras. For a moment, he didn't associate their presence with his own but then the flashbulbs went off and the questions started.

Beside him, Roland tensed and swore.

'Someone's been busy,' he muttered. 'Don't say anything. Not a word!'

Taking him firmly by the arm, he guided Ross purposefully across the road to his parked car, jostled all the way by the predatory news-gatherers. Opening the passenger door, he propelled the American inside and then slid across the black bonnet with surprising agility and opened his own door.

Still standing, he held up a hand to silence the persistent voices.

'I don't know what you've heard, but there's obviously been a mistake,' he announced, clearly and with authority. 'There is no story. Go and report a church fête or something.'

He slid smoothly into the car, started the engine and drove away while the reporters were still looking at one another in disgust.

Glancing in his mirror, Roland laughed. 'It wouldn't have worked on Fleet Street,' he said. 'But with the local press . . .'

'You've done that before,' Ross said thoughtfully. He was watching the Colonel's son closely and almost saw the upper-class-twit mask slip back into place.

'Oh, all the time,' he agreed airily. 'I used to manage a rock band, you know.'

Ross' eyes narrowed.

'I don't believe you,' he said after a moment.

'Quite right. I'm an inveterate liar,' Roland said cheerfully. 'I shouldn't believe half of what I say, if I were you.'

Ross subsided into silence. He was in no fit state for verbal sparring. Besides, he remembered abruptly, he was sitting in the very same car he had worked so hard to lose the evening before.

'Why were you following me last night?' he asked, with bluntness that a clearer head might have tempered.

Roland was not noticeably disconcerted. 'I wanted to see where you were going,' he said reasonably, throwing the car into a right-angled bend with no perceptible slackening of speed.

'I should have thought you already knew that,' Ross said, instinctively leaning into the bend.

'That office door is thicker than you might think,' Roland observed unashamedly as the hatchback settled comfortingly back on to all four wheels.

Ross was speechless. He thought Roland might at least have had the decency to look a little embarrassed.

He glanced sideways and smiled disarmingly. 'Ah, I see I've shocked you. Call it incurable nosiness, if you will. I've always suffered from it. Lamentable, I know, but we all have our faults. Don't we?' he added, almost as an afterthought.

Ross let that pass. A mile or two slid by and he closed his eyes, feeling lousy.

'Just where did you abandon your jeep, exactly?' Roland asked after a few blissfully silent minutes.

Ross stirred and gave approximate directions. 'The police said it was called Sandy Lane.'

'Uncommonly helpful fellows, the police,' Roland said approvingly.

'How did you know where I was? And how the hell did the press know?'

'I don't know how the local press knew, unless some public-spirited individual saw you being brought in and told them,' Roland said, skilfully passing two cars and a crawling tractor in the teeth of an oncoming juggernaut.

Ross winced.

'As for me,' Roland continued, 'I'm here on Father's orders. He was woken at half-past seven this morning by an enthusiastic correspondent from the *Sportsman*, demanding to know if he was aware that his star employee was at that moment languishing in the local nick, faced with a drink-driving charge.'

Ross' heart sank. No chance then to break the news gently and plead his own, edited side of the story. Though quite what he could have said was debatable. There was no need to ask how the Colonel had received the news. His anger and disgust were all too easy to imagine.

'You're very quiet,' Roland observed, seemingly unaware of the bombshell he had just dropped. 'Probably just not a morning person, I expect.'

Ross couldn't be bothered to summon another withering look.

The jeep, when they came up with it, was exactly where it had been left the night before. It had no wheels, headlights or windscreen, and what was left was completely burnt out, but it *was* still there.

Ross stared at the blackened wreck and made the discovery that he was beyond feeling. With the news about the Colonel, he had touched rock bottom and there was nowhere lower to go.

'Drunks, I expect,' Roland said judiciously. 'There are a lot of them about.'

Ross had had enough. 'Why don't you just shut the hell up?' he demanded, rounding on him savagely.

Roland put his hands up in surrender. 'Okay, okay. But really, you can't deny it's an odd place to choose for a booze-up.'

'Oh, I don't know. It's a nice quiet spot,' Ross retorted. 'Or used to be,' he added with a glance over his shoulder as two cars drew up behind them and disgorged a bevy of determined reporters.

Roland wasted no time in getting underway once more, and in the door mirror Ross could see the press cameramen busily snapping the burnt-out jeep.

'So, which particular sorrows were you trying to drown?' the Colonel's son asked casually as they turned homewards.

471

Ross groaned from a combination of physical discomfort and mental frustration.

'For Chrissakes, I wasn't trying to drown anything! I didn't drink by choice. Why the hell would I? And *if*, for argument's sake, I *had* intended to, I would hardly have driven ten miles out into the country and run the risk of being picked up by the police, when I could have stayed in my room and done it, would I?'

'So what are you saying? That somebody forced you? That you were set up?' Roland sounded curious, but not incredulous. 'By whom exactly?'

One of the few things Ross clearly remembered was Leo's gloating face but he couldn't expect anyone to believe that the ex-groom had done it on his own, and until he knew more he felt it would be wisest to pretend ignorance.

'I don't know,' he said, shaking his head. 'They kept their faces covered.'

'Well, did you tell the police?'

'I tried,' Ross said tiredly. 'You can imagine what they said. I tried to get them to fingerprint the bottle too but they weren't interested. They've heard it all before.'

Roland looked sharply at him. 'Fingerprints, you say? Because you didn't touch the bottle. That's an idea.' He looked thoughtful. 'But why should anybody want to set you up?'

'I don't know. You tell me,' Ross replied guardedly. 'Someone with a grudge, perhaps, trying to ruin my reputation. There seem to be plenty of people who'd like to see me go down big time.

I'm not exactly Mr Popularity, in case you haven't noticed.'

'You've put one or two backs up, I know. But there's a big difference between spreading rumours and doing something like this. I mean, it can't be easy to subdue someone and force a bottle of whisky down their throat,' he said. 'Not that I've ever tried it, of course. But I would've thought one man would've had his hands full.'

Unless he had a six-inch blade and no compunction about using it, Ross thought, another chunk of memory slotting into place.

With no warning, Roland suddenly swung the car into a lay-by and stopped. Leaving the engine running, he opened his door and got out.

'Won't be a moment,' he said airily. 'Got a call to make. Personal.'

He brandished a mobile phone, which he had produced from somewhere about his person, shut the door and walked away from the car.

Ross couldn't imagine what could be so urgent that it couldn't wait the two or three miles back to the yard but he supposed it was no business of his. He wondered what had happened to his own mobile phone. Presumably it had either suffered the same fate as the jeep or Leo had pocketed it. The latter seemed likely.

He leaned back, closed his eyes and found himself wondering, uncharitably, if Roland owned a knife. For no particular reason he remembered the ease with which Roland had handled Leo that day at the yard and it occurred to him that for a man who appeared to spend most of his life masquerading behind a false personality, an Irish accent would hardly be a problem. He hadn't ever seemed over-keen to involve the police, either.

But then, last night the time-scale hadn't been right. Surely Roland couldn't have reached Sandy Lane before him when Ross had left him in that muddle at the traffic lights.

Or could he?

Ross had wasted more time after leaving him behind, trying to cover his tracks, and he knew that Roland drove everywhere like a rally driver. That would of course presuppose that he had known where the American was going in the first place, in which case – why bother to follow him?

Of course, if he had known Ross was intending to meet Franklin he could make an educated guess at the meeting place, having driven Ross there the evening he was knocked out. But it was difficult to imagine Roland and Leo as partners in crime, unless all that had gone before had been a smoke-screen. And if that was the case, then who had driven the Land-Rover?

Nothing seemed to make much sense, but all the same Ross decided to tread carefully.

Grimacing, he circled his shoulders while he waited, trying to ease a growing stiffness. The muscles almost creaked in protest.

Roland reappeared, sliding back into his seat.

'So, how many were there?' he asked, as if the conversation hadn't lapsed. 'How many ruffians

474

does it take to subdue our All American Action-boy and persuade him to take a drink?'

'Only one, if the knife is big enough,' Ross said dryly. 'But there were two. As to who they were, though, your guess is as good as mine. I'm afraid most of it is still a blank.'

'Post-traumatic amnesia,' Roland said matter-of-factly.

Ross slid him a sideways look. 'Meaning?'

'Meaning,' Roland said, calmly negotiating another bend on two wheels, 'that the mind recalls what it wants to recall and tends to blank out events too recently painful to remember. A kind of safety-net for your sanity.'

'And the antiques trade teaches you all this, does it?'

'No, but active service in the army and a tour in Northern Ireland does,' Roland replied placidly.

Of course. Ross subsided once more, feeling stupid. So easy to forget Roland's original career. He *made it* so easy to forget.

Roland swung between the limes into the long drive to the stableyard, giving the nearside gatepost a fright.

'My revered papa said he wished to see you the instant you got back, but I convinced him he would do better to wait until this evening.'

He drew to a smooth halt in the yard and held out a packet of Alka-Seltzers to Ross. 'Take a couple of these, stay off the coffee – the caffeine won't help – and try and get some sleep.'

'Yes, Doc.' Ross climbed stiffly out of the car.

There didn't seem to be a soul about. 'And, uh, thanks.'

'Don't thank me. Father's orders, old boy. Just doing my filial duty.'

Ross waved a hand and turned away.

By the time Ross presented himself at the door of the main house, ten long and miserable hours had crawled by.

He'd followed Roland's advice with difficulty and found himself recalling the old joke about not liking Alka-Seltzers because they were too noisy. It hadn't seemed so funny this morning. Swallowing wasn't a bundle of laughs either; it was almost as though the whisky had burned his throat, but at least after a while the nausea began to subside a little. Sleep, however, had never been further from him.

From the yard below, the noise of business as usual floated up to taunt him. He wondered how they would exercise Telamon. Nobody came up to see him and he wasn't sure whether to be sorry or relieved at that. On the whole he thought it was probably a good thing. With a shadow of stubble, a waxy complexion, swollen, cut lip and bloodshot eyes, he looked almost as bad as he felt.

He wondered if Lindsay was helping in the yard but couldn't hear her voice. He remembered her declaring vehemently, on that bright sunny ride to the river, that drink-drivers should be publicly flogged. It did nothing to improve his state of mind.

Apart from the nausea and the shivers, he

476

supposed he was in no worse shape than when he'd last spent the day on his bed, after the New Forest Show. The difference was that then he'd been wounded in action, so to speak. Now, from everybody else's point of view at least, he had only himself to blame.

During those ten sleepless hours, Ross had plenty of time to think. Too much time. But his thoughts were largely unprofitable.

If, as seemed probable, he had been waylaid to prevent him from passing on information to Franklin, then the strategy had succeeded They'd made sure he never reached the Dovecote, and not only was the larger part of the evening an incomprehensible blur but whatever thoughts had prompted him to approach Franklin in the first place were also staying stubbornly in the darkest recesses of his mind.

He remembered his careful call to the business-man and Franklin's query: 'Is it important?' He'd replied that it might be, and with those few words, quite possibly sealed his own fate.

What had been so important that he had rung the man at home?

Frustration at his own inability to remember added to his general malaise.

On the other hand, whoever had waylaid him could not have banked on Ross' memory loss, so he assumed their aim had been either to scare him into minding his own business or to discredit him to such an extent that no one would be inclined to take him seriously anyway.

Maybe they figured that in the circumstances the charge would be enough to lose him his job; and maybe, he thought mordantly, they were right.

Masters bowed him into the hall and through to the study in tight-lipped silence. He was the first person Ross had seen since returning in disgrace that morning and if his demeanour was anything to go by, he was in for a rough ride.

The Colonel didn't rise when Ross was shown in and his usual welcoming smile was noticeably absent. He was sitting not in an armchair but at his desk and waved the American into the leather-seated carver's chair opposite. Ross felt like a disgraced pupil called before the principal and the comparison was no comfort.

Colonel Preston regarded him solemnly for a moment and then his gaze dropped to the desktop. The silence was brooding. The Colonel was apparently undecided as to how to begin and Ross wanted to see how the land lay before he said anything at all. The ticking of the mantelpiece clock was deafening.

In his present fragile state, the tension made Ross feel slightly dizzy. He began to count the seconds in his head, to concentrate his wandering senses. When he reached thirty-five the Colonel spoke, quietly.

'Some weeks ago I asked you if I should be worried about the rumours of your drinking and you said no. Like a fool I believed you.'

It wasn't the best possible opener.

Ross looked his employer straight in the eyes.

478

'It was the truth,' he asserted earnestly. 'It still is.'

'Then how do you explain this?' The Colonel reached into a desk drawer and produced a bottle of Scotch, two-thirds empty.

Ross didn't have to ask where it had come from. It was the one from his room. He felt a momentary flash of anger at the intrusion but stifled it. After all, it was quite possible Maggie might have found it when she was cleaning and mentioned it to Bill. Roland, too, had known he had it. He found himself hoping Danny hadn't betrayed him, though he couldn't really blame the boy if he had.

'Well?'

Ross realised he was staring at the bottle. Reluctantly, he raised his eyes to the Colonel's face once more.

'I can't sleep sometimes. My knee gives me a bit of trouble. The whisky helps. Just a mouthful or two, never more.'

The Colonel raised his eyebrows.

Ross tried again. 'I've had that one bottle for weeks. I bought it at the airport. I might even have the receipt somewhere . . .'

The Colonel shrugged. 'That proves nothing. You could have bought any number since you've been here. Probably have,' he added, as if to provoke Ross.

'I can't prove I haven't. You can't prove I have,' he countered bitterly. 'Did you find any more while you were looking?'

The Colonel didn't reply. He seemed lost in

thought, his face set in hard, uncompromising lines. His very silence was damning.

Ross could see it all slipping away from him. His career, the respect of his new-found friends and this wonderful chance of a lifetime he'd been given.

He was at a loss. Even if he mentioned Leo he had no proof, and his silence over the previous attacks would be seen as highly suspicious. Without the background information, which he had promised not to divulge, his story would test the gullibility of the average six-year-old, and the Colonel was neither six nor gullible.

'I spent the day hating you for the sake of my dear, sweet wife and daughter,' Colonel Preston said then, lifting his head to regard Ross with an intensity that was deeply unsettling. 'I couldn't understand how you could have done anything so stupid. You've always seemed so straight, so strong. But then I thought that perhaps all those people were right. Perhaps you *were* losing your nerve and drinking to keep going. The sporting pages are full of your unlucky past; hinting at irregularities, at an unreliable reputation. I've never known so much attention focussed on an unknown before. I began to think that perhaps they *were* right after all and I'd been wrong . . .'

Ross was silent. Sick at heart and unable to defend himself, he could only await his sentence. The mantelpiece clock continued to count out the seconds towards the inevitable. He wondered miserably what his father would say.

'Franklin rang this morning,' the Colonel went on after a while. 'He asked if you were all right. Said you were supposed to meet him last night but you didn't show up. He hadn't heard about – this, and flatly refused to believe it when I told him.'

'Then this evening Robbie Fergusson rang. He's threatening to take Bishop away again.' The Colonel's voice was flat and unemotional. He picked up the bottle once more and began to regard it closely.

'Somebody had phoned him with the news. He said he'd always known you were a windy bastard and now you'd gone too far. I argued with him,' he said, sounding surprised at himself. 'I tried to change his mind. I said he'd never find a better rider. I said he'd regret his decision and told him I was sure there would be some explanation. He wouldn't listen but I found I was halfway to convincing myself.'

Ross' heart began to beat in slow, painfully heavy thumps.

The Colonel looked up, directly into his eyes. 'Now I don't know what to do,' he said. 'I feel that to keep you on would be to betray the memory of my family, and yet somehow . . .'

Ross returned the Colonel's gaze with an effort, uncomfortably aware of the unprepossessing spectacle he must present. He still hadn't shaved, unable to trust the steadiness of his hand with a blade and too ashamed to ask for the loan of Bill's electric shaver. Although he'd combed his hair, the image in the mirror had resembled a person in the latter stages of galloping consumption.

'*Why*, Ross?' the Colonel beseeched suddenly. 'Tell me why. Give me a reason. Damn it, I liked you! I didn't want to believe you'd do it. At first I couldn't, and that's the only reason I'm speaking to you now. Was it the pressure? You seemed to be handling it so well . . . *Why* did you do it?'

'I *didn't* do it,' the American said, stung into self-defence by the disillusionment in the older man's face and aware, as he spoke the words, that it was probably the one thing he could say that wouldn't help him at all. Why try to deny the obvious?

He tried again.

'I was set up. Framed. It wasn't my doing.'

'Who then? Who did it?'

'I don't know. They wore balaclavas . . .' He tailed off, knowing it sounded ridiculous.

The Colonel had looked away and was shaking his head slowly.

'I trusted you,' he said sadly. 'This whole business has turned sour on me. I haven't the heart for it any more. I think you'd better go now.'

Waved away, Ross left the Colonel sitting in his chair looking at a photograph of his dead wife. He limped wearily out and when Masters closed the front door disapprovingly behind him, sat down heavily on the step, his aching head in his hands.

The Colonel's quiet disillusionment had been far worse than the anger he had steeled himself to meet. Fergusson's ultimatum was just another bee-sting in a swarm. What would it signify if the yard broke up anyway?

He groaned and thought fleetingly of the bottle

on the Colonel's desk. *Hair of the dog.* It hadn't seemed a good idea to ask if he could take it with him, all things considered.

He thought of the Colonel as he'd left him, his dreams sliding away from him, of Franklin's worry and Peter's pain, of Clown's bloodstained terror, the dog's agony and the loss of Bellboy and Ginger.

He thought of his own persecution and somewhere, deep down, a slow-burning anger was kindled.

What right had any man, or men, to ruin so many lives and cause so much distress?

Anger got him up on his feet and all the way back to his room. There he made strong black coffee, in defiance of Roland's advice, and fell asleep, fully clothed, before he could drink it.

20

Ross awoke feeling stiff from his night on the sofa and the ongoing effect of his bruises, but otherwise a lot better. He still hadn't reached the full fried breakfast stage but felt he might be able to face coffee and toast. Although the heavy, throbbing pain had largely retreated, his head felt tender, as though it was bruised inside.

Much as he dreaded having to face the Scotts, he knew the moment had to come, so he showered and dressed and made his way over to the cottage. Maggie was alone in the kitchen and responded to his tentative greeting with tight-lipped civility.

The atmosphere in the yard was, if anything, worse. Sarah and Danny looked at him with awkward embarrassment, as though unsure of how to approach him, whereas Bill could barely bring himself to look at him at all. Hardly a word was spoken. Ross himself tried to behave as though nothing was amiss, although it wasn't easy. The horses, at least, treated him the same as always.

After breakfast, eaten in strained silence, the roster for the day had to be set. Ross asserted that he was fit and ready for business as usual, whereupon Bill favoured him with a doubtful look, heavy with scorn, and said he supposed they would have to take his word for that. Ross was heartily glad when he was back outside with the horses.

Mid-afternoon, Roland appeared in the yard and, after kicking his heels aimlessly for a while, followed Ross into the tackroom.

'So how's the fallen hero?' he enquired, resting his spotless cream corduroys against the sink unit.

Ross was almost pleased to see him.

'Beneath contempt,' he said, ruefully. 'But otherwise much better, thanks. How's the Colonel?'

Roland waved a dismissive hand. 'Oh, he'll get over it. Franklin rang again this morning and pleaded your case. Seems he said you were stone cold sober at half-past six and he couldn't see why you would drink yourself silly when you'd just made arrangements to meet him. He suggested that perhaps somebody else might have had a hand in it, so to speak. I believe he mentioned Leo . . .' He paused, watching Ross beneath his lashes. 'Well, anyway, gave Father something to chew on.'

Ross was mildly surprised. 'The Colonel told you all that?'

'Well, no. Not exactly,' Roland said apologetically. 'I sort of happened to overhear it. You know how it is.'

Ross knew precisely how it was. He shook his head in wonderment. With his talent for eavesdropping, Roland was wasted on the antiques trade; MI5 would welcome him with open arms.

'Have you seen the papers?' Roland said, following Ross into the stable office and back out again. 'They've had a field day. Terrific pictures.'

'It's an ill wind . . .' Ross observed dryly.

He wasn't sure if Roland was trying to provoke him or just chattering in his usual, careless way. Quite frankly, he didn't much care. The news that Franklin was pleading his case with the Colonel had cheered him considerably.

Remembering Roland's very real distress over the accident in the village, though, Ross wondered at his easy attitude now. Presumably *he* also believed Ross to be innocent. Ross couldn't be sure whether that was because Roland trusted his word or because he knew it to be true. One thing was for sure: no one would know better than he just how damning such a conviction would be in the Colonel's eyes. *Could* he have been involved?

Ross looked at the bland, pleasant face with its sweep of immaculately styled, sandy hair, and had absolutely no idea.

The two of them were just emerging into the sunlight when Lindsay's red MG turned into the yard. She sprang out, dressed for riding, and came over immediately to where they stood.

Ignoring Roland, she took in Ross' decidedly below-par appearance at a glance and gave him the benefit of a blazing stare.

'So it's true,' she observed flatly. 'I was in London yesterday and when I got back the whole village was buzzing with it. They say you were drunk and crashed the jeep. I didn't believe it at first. I couldn't believe you'd be so stupid! Then I saw the papers and they were full of it. Photographs, the lot.'

'It must be true, then,' he said whimsically. 'If it's in the papers.'

'I told you the pictures were good,' Roland said, pleased.

Lindsay stopped glaring at Ross to glare at her cousin for a moment.

'Are you denying it?' she said, then, turning the full wattage of her anger back on to Ross, 'Looking like that?'

He was stung by her doubt. 'What do you want? A full confession?' he asked. 'You seem to have made up your mind pretty much on your own!'

'You forget, I've seen you hit the bottle before,' she stated accusingly.

'Once!' he countered angrily. 'What do you want? Perfection? You'd better go back to James for that.'

Lindsay stared at him, clearly hurt.

'Ouch!' Roland murmured from behind Ross. The American swung round to glower at him and he quickly looked down at his toes.

'You're right,' Lindsay said shakily. 'I always expect too much. It's just – I thought I knew you. I guess I don't.'

487

'I guess not,' Ross agreed, his anger still running high.

Lindsay took a step back, running a hand through her thick, blonde fringe. 'James was right. He said I shouldn't come. I should have listened.'

' "To honour and obey . . ." ' Ross suggested.

She blinked at him, eyes bright with unshed tears, and he felt a stab of conscience.

'I don't know why I'm wasting my time. You obviously don't give a damn, so why should I? I just feel so sorry for Uncle John! And I wish I'd never told him about you.' With this parting shot, she turned on her heel and walked back to her car.

Ross watched her go, his temper gradually ebbing and leaving him feeling tired and depressed.

Why had he flown at her like that? Was it because she was a soft target? He shook off that unpalatable thought. He'd lost his temper because of *all* people it hurt most that Lindsay had condemned him out of hand.

All the same, he wasn't proud of himself. She hadn't even stopped to ride Gypsy, which had obviously been her original intention.

'You've done it now,' Roland remarked.

'Oh, shut up!' Ross said wearily.

'Hell hath no fury like a woman disappointed,' Roland misquoted, shaking his head knowingly. 'So, have you remembered anything else about Tuesday night?'

Fragments of memory were returning but in view of his suspicions he didn't particularly want to share them with Roland.

Ross shook his head. 'Not yet. I guess I must still be traumatised, huh?'

'It'll pass,' Roland said easily. 'Trust Uncle Roly.'

Just after evening stables Franklin dropped in. He greeted Bill, then waited until the two Scotts and Sarah had left the yard and walked round the horses with Ross.

'I gather from the dirty looks that it's not the done thing to talk to you?' Franklin said as the cottage door closed behind Bill and Danny.

'No, I'm not exactly in favour,' Ross agreed lightly.

'Tried and convicted, eh?' Franklin stopped and turned to face him. 'That don't-give-a-damn front is all very well, Ross, but it won't do for me. You look awful. How are things, honestly?'

He looked away. 'Oh, pretty much like hell,' he said conversationally. 'It's really hit the fan this time. Our Mr X has done himself proud. He certainly knows how and where to hit.'

'So it *was* a set-up! I *knew* it had to be,' Franklin exclaimed triumphantly.

'Sure it was. But it was a damn' good one,' Ross said with feeling. 'The Colonel is gutted – to use one of Danny's favourite words.'

'He would be,' Franklin said soberly. 'John has never really got over the deaths of Caroline and Harriet. I don't think he ever will. It was a criminal waste of two precious lives, and the imbecile who did it walked free after a couple of years. I don't think anything could discredit you more in the Colonel's eyes than to find you guilty of being drunk at the wheel of a car.'

'Thanks,' Ross said ironically. 'I feel a whole lot better now.'

'I'm sorry.' Franklin was contrite. 'Have you spoken to John yet?'

Ross nodded. 'I hope I never have to live through another twenty minutes like that again,' he said. 'But thanks for the back-up. I think it was the only thing between me and the breadline last night.'

'I didn't know what to say, so this morning I told John I wondered whether Leo might have had a hand in it, just to give him something to think about. What *did* happen?'

'I set out to meet you as planned but they knew I was coming and laid on a little diversion – just for me. As a matter of fact, Leo *was* there,' Ross confirmed. 'And I'm pretty sure our extortionist friend was too, but no,' he said, seeing hope in Franklin's eyes, 'I still don't know who he is. He wore a balaclava throughout.'

'I wonder how long Leo's been involved,' Franklin mused. 'You're sure it was our Mr X and not just some thug Leo had found to help him get his own back on you?'

'If it was, he was Irish,' Ross remarked sceptically.

'Ah, I see what you mean. I wonder how long Leo *has* been involved, then. Did he seem to know what was going on? Did he say anything significant?'

490

Ross thought back, rubbing Telamon's nose absentmindedly. 'I remember Irish saying he'd warned me to mind my own business so I'd only got myself to blame, or words to that effect. I don't think Leo said anything important. He was enjoying himself too much.'

'Do you think Leo knew who the other man was?'

'Must have done. I mean, you don't go out and commit a crime with a complete stranger, do you? Besides, in that case, how would Irish have approached him in the first place? He can't wear that balaclava all the time.'

'He could have used the phone,' Franklin observed.

Ross looked heavenwards. 'I didn't think of that. Brain dead, I guess. But seriously, try this for size. While I've been frozen out, so to speak, I've been thinking and I thought: what if Leo worked out who Mr X is and some of what he's up to? After all, he must know who he stole that business card from and wouldn't have to be Einstein to make the connection with the Clown affair, even if he didn't go the step further and pick up on Bellboy. What if he faced Mr X with it and wanted to be cut in? We wondered how he managed to afford to stay at the Six Bells for so long, and it was certainly no accident he got thrown out of here when he did. He was actively asking for it.'

Franklin was looking very interested. 'You might have something there,' he said. 'But do you think it's Mr X's style to allow himself to be blackmailed?'

'Maybe not,' Ross admitted. 'But he might also think that Leo could be a useful tool, for a while at least. I mean, it really fogged things up, didn't it? Not knowing who was responsible for what.'

'But now we know they're working together, what's to stop us, or rather McKinnon, picking Leo up and persuading him to tell all?'

'Nothing. Except I think Mr X will make sure Leo keeps his head down from here on in. He certainly didn't intend me to know who either of them were, but Leo just couldn't keep his mouth shut. Our friend could've cheerfully slaughtered him.'

'And might still do,' Franklin observed darkly, 'with the stakes this high. He could already be charged with attempted murder for running Peter down.'

'Yes, I hadn't thought of that.'

They wandered on in silence for a moment, both thinking hard.

'Can you tell me more about Tuesday evening?' Franklin asked after a moment. 'I waited for about an hour but when you didn't show up I called the cottage and Bill said you'd gone out and weren't back yet. I rang your mobile but it was switched off and I didn't know what to think, except that your jeep might have broken down. I even drove the route I thought you'd have used but there was no sign of you or the jeep. I didn't know what to make of it until the next day when I rang John. So tell me, what did happen?'

Ross frowned. 'The whisky really messed me up

and I still can't remember everything, just snatches. For instance, I remember I was late because I thought I was being followed and I was trying to lose them.' He didn't think he'd mention Roland at this point. 'There was a Land-Rover, a diversion sign and some traffic cones – I'd guess they were probably just for my benefit – but I can't remember what happened next. When they forced the whisky down me I think I was in a wood. I remember branches overhead and being tied to a tree. My arms still ache . . .'

He paused by Clown's box, turning half away from Franklin. It was intensely painful to remember. So humiliating; so *frightening* to be that helpless. His mind still flitted around the edges of it.

'I . . . um . . . remember that Leo had a gun,' he said, and a cold sweat broke out on his body at the memory. 'And I remember Irish saying I should have minded my own business, but the rest . . .'

His voice cracked and he shook his head, staring hard at nothing in particular. 'I can't even remember what I wanted to talk to you about.'

Franklin perceived his distress and put a hand on his shoulder.

'Never mind now,' he said gently. 'A gun, though? My God! Did you tell the police?'

Ross laughed harshly. 'Oh, sure, they'd have loved that! "A gun?" they'd have said. "What, no hand grenades?" No, I figure they've heard just about every story there is concerned with drinking, and then some. They weren't exactly receptive.

Apparently I was found in the jeep, three times over the limit and with the whisky bottle beside me. They just weren't interested in excuses.'

Franklin shook his head. 'I'm *so* sorry, Ross. How much have you told the Colonel?'

'Nothing.'

'Why not?'

'Well, how could I? How much could I say before he started to guess there was a lot more to it than he was being told? If I didn't tell him the whole, he would just think it was a tall story. And who could blame him?'

Franklin studied Ross' taut profile as they stood watching Clown pulling at his haynet.

'I'm sorry,' he said again. 'I had no right to get you involved in all this. It just didn't occur to me there'd be any danger to you, personally.'

Ross disagreed. 'It wasn't your fault. You and McKinnon only asked me to keep my eyes and ears open. It was my idea to start stirring the hornet's nest. The way I see it, it's my fault if I got stung.'

Franklin pursed his lips. 'Well, whatever the case, it's gone far enough. I'm not having your career ruined for my sake. The Colonel must be told, whether McKinnon likes it or not. Personally, I would've told him in the first place but McKinnon wouldn't have it, and since I employed him to advise . . .' He shrugged.

'Look, let's wait a bit,' Ross urged. 'The Colonel hasn't sent me packing yet – though God alone knows why! His attitude towards me would be bound to change if he knew the truth. Other people

494

would notice and wonder, maybe even Mr X himself. This thing could snowball and we don't want anyone else getting hurt. Let's just let it ride for the moment.'

'But Bill and the others – they're treating you like dirt,' Franklin protested. 'It's not fair to let you carry the can for something you didn't do.'

'Bill and I have never seen eye to eye,' Ross pointed out. 'And now I know that *you* believe me, I think I can cope with the others.'

Franklin was still doubtful. 'If you're sure, but I don't like it, Ross. It's getting out of hand.'

'Well, we've obviously got him worried,' Ross observed. 'Maybe he'll make a mistake. Or maybe I'll remember something useful.'

Franklin wasn't convinced. 'He's made one push to get you out of the way. If he sees it hasn't worked he may make another. What then? Have you thought of that?'

Ross had and he didn't like it any more than Franklin appeared to.

'I just wish I knew what it was he thought I was close to discovering. It's so frustrating.'

'Perhaps he doesn't know either. On the phone you told me you thought you might have something important to discuss,' Franklin said. 'What if he listened in somehow and decided to nobble you before you could share it with me, whatever it was?'

'I thought of that. But he couldn't have bargained on me not remembering,' Ross said. 'So he can't have thought I knew anything very important. The whole thing must just have been a precaution. I was nosing around and he wanted me out of the picture.'

Franklin ran his fingers through his hair and sighed. 'Sometimes I feel perhaps I should have the horses destroyed and finish this business once and for all, but then there's Clown. I could never do that to Peter. He's had a rough enough time of it already.'

'I don't know that it would help, either. It might even make things worse. I mean, he's already shown he's not unwilling to use other targets. If it's a grudge, it's not just going to go away because the horses do.'

'You're probably right,' Franklin said wearily. They had completed their circumnavigation of the yard and stopped beside his Range Rover.

'Listen, Ross, I don't know how to thank you . . .'

'What for?' he enquired. 'Getting myself in a hole? I've blundered around making trouble for myself and upsetting a whole lot of other people and for what? I just seem to have muddied the waters a bit more, if anything.'

'The professionals have done no better,' Franklin observed. 'But I meant, thank you for caring enough to try. And I can assure you that when you go to court you'll have the best legal defence in your corner that money can buy.

'Anyway,' he glanced at his watch, 'I must be going. I called in on my way to the Chinese take-away. It's Cook's night off and we normally go out but Peter has got it into his head he wants a Chinese.' He grimaced. 'Not my cup of tea, I'm afraid. I prefer good, traditional English cooking myself. You can't beat roast beef and Yorkshire pudding. Strange thing that – it's the only thing I really miss about Peter's mother. When she could be bothered, Marsha was a dab hand in the kitchen, though to look at her you wouldn't think she could make toast without a recipe.' He smiled at the memory.

Ross hesitated only fractionally, then gave voice to a suspicion he had long harboured. 'When did you find out about Marsha and Darcy?'

Franklin raised an eyebrow. 'You don't miss much, do you?'

Ross relaxed. It appeared he hadn't offended and, furthermore, had guessed right.

'I suspected,' Franklin said. 'But Darcy himself told me in the end. I couldn't blame him, exactly, though I was disappointed. She was an attractive woman and almost always got what she wanted, sooner or later. Usually sooner. If she had her eye on him, he wouldn't have stood a chance – he wasn't much more than a boy, after all.'

'So you didn't fall out over it?' Ross thought his forbearance remarkable.

Franklin smiled and shook his head. 'No, not really. The marriage was over by then, in all but name, and I couldn't see what good it would do to alienate the boy just when we needed to stick together as a family. He'd owned up and apologised, said it only happened once and the affair was over. As far as I was concerned, that was an end to it.' He opened the door of the Range Rover and paused. 'What made you think of that?'

Ross shrugged. 'Oh, I don't know, something he said once. More the way he said it, I suppose. I can't really remember.'

'He's always had an eye for the girls,' Franklin confessed. 'Takes after his father, I suppose.' He started the engine. 'Look, Ross, take care of yourself, okay? Leave the detecting to the detectives for a bit. Your first concern should be getting fit and winning classes.'

Ross grinned. 'Okay, boss.'

'And if you change your mind about telling the Colonel . . .'

'Sure. I'll let you know.'

The next day, Friday, started promisingly with a note from the Colonel to say that if Ross felt up to it, the horses would compete as planned that weekend and he should prepare them accordingly. The note was brief and businesslike and gave no hint as to the Colonel's disposition, but Ross considered it a hopeful sign.

Although it was clear that his workmates still regarded him with disgust, the prospect of action lifted everybody's spirits a notch or two and gave the team a common aim. The atmosphere in the yard improved noticeably.

Ross worked hard all day, riding all the horses that were entered for the show at the weekend, assessing their performance and demeanour after the enforced break in their routine. His own condition improved hourly, although the state of his cracked ribs hadn't been improved by the attentions of Leo and Irish and would clearly be tender for some days to come.

As he finished his last session of the day and leaned on the gate watching Clown roll luxuriously in the soft sand of the school, Danny came to stand beside him.

'Hi, kid,' Ross said, without turning his head.

Danny was silent.

Ross sighed. 'Come to add your two cents' worth?' he enquired.

Danny shuffled his feet. 'No,' he said finally. 'I've been thinking about what you said that night. You know, about the whisky and jumping to conclusions?'

'Uh-huh.' Ross waited.

'Well, the thing is . . . I wanted you to know I don't believe you did it. Drink and drive, I mean. You wouldn't. It's just not the sort of thing you'd do. I know what they're saying but I don't believe it. I just wanted you to know.' His somewhat wandering avowal of faith having reached its end, he rather spoilt it by adding, 'You didn't, did you?'

Ross supposed it was a measure of his low physical and mental state that a simple show of confidence could bring a lump to his throat, but his mouth twitched in response to this postscript.

'No, Danny. I didn't,' he said gravely, still not looking round. 'And thanks.'

'I just wanted you to know,' Danny repeated.

499

Saturday morning dawned fair but with a blustery wind, which had sprung up overnight. The preparations for the show ran smoothly, every member of the team carrying out their own particular tasks like parts of a well-oiled machine. Nobody spoke much, although that was not unusual. Time was at a premium and they were all working hard.

Maggie came out with a well-stocked lunchbox just as they were loading the horses and handed it to Danny. Normally she wished Ross good luck. Today she hardly glanced at him.

When all the four-footed passengers were safely aboard and the last bolts fastened, Ross made his way round to the driver's side of the cab and opened the door.

'I think not,' Bill said firmly, coming up behind him. 'The Colonel would rather I drive.' He stared defiantly up at Ross like a bull terrier taking a stand.

Ross felt quick anger rise in him but clenched his jaw against the retort. After all, he really couldn't blame them. He shrugged and turned away. 'Suit yourself,' he said. 'I'll travel in the back.'

The show was a big one, which suited Ross. The less the concentration of people who knew him, the better. As it was, he was sure it hadn't gone unnoticed that Bill had driven the lorry. He kept his head down and concentrated on the job in hand.

The competition was fierce but the horses were

jumping well and more than held their own, and in spite of his antipathy Bill couldn't hide his pleasure as first Simone then Bishop qualified for classes at the bigger shows later that year. Ross was pleased too but he couldn't help wondering gloomily who would be partnering the horses by then.

The Richmond clan turned up to see Clown jump in two classes but, try as he might, Ross wasn't able to win a rosette for the birthday boy.

Peter accepted the disappointment with his customary good manners but he was very quiet, and once or twice Ross found he was being regarded with a particularly solemn stare. He wondered what the boy had been told.

Before they left, Franklin drew Ross to one side and told him that in place of the written-off jeep, he had an old Land-Rover that Ross was welcome to use for as long as he liked.

Or until they take my licence, Ross thought, thanking him.

'Well, actually, it was Darcy's idea,' Franklin admitted. 'It only sits around doing nothing. It's a bit rough, I'm afraid, but roadworthy.'

'You want to watch the clutch,' Darcy said, coming over. 'It's a bit of a sod. And one of the front wheels needs balancing, as I remember, but basically it's okay.'

Ross thanked him as well and he shrugged and waved a dismissive hand. 'Hey, forget it. It's no big deal and it'll do it good to be used. We'll drop it by later.'

'That's great. I need to go over to Amesbury on

Monday and I'm not quite sure whether I'm allowed to use ours at the moment.'

If Darcy had indeed been jealous of Ross' popularity with Peter, as the Colonel had suggested, then he appeared to have got over it now, Ross reflected as he trudged wearily back to the horsebox with Clown after they left. He couldn't have been more amiable. Perhaps he found it easier to contend with a tarnished idol. Peter had certainly seemed subdued. No doubt it was uncharitable, but Ross couldn't help wondering just what Darcy might have said to the youngster.

'A penny for 'em,' a voice said at his elbow

'Mick!' Ross turned, delightedly. 'Nice to see you. How's tricks?'

'Collarbone's good as mended and I'll have the plaster off my foot next week, all being well,' Mick Colby declared cheerfully. 'All in all, better than you, from what I've been hearing. How're you doing?'

'I'm workin' on it,' Ross said. 'I suppose you read the papers?'

Colby nodded, grinning. 'You just can't bear to be out of the news, can you? So, who got you into that little mess?'

Ross looked at him sharply. 'Why do you say that?'

Colby shrugged. 'Oh, I don't know. I've seen enough of you, one way or another, to know that it's not your style. Crazy you might be but you're not stupid.'

'Thanks. I appreciate that,' Ross said sincerely.

'So, how's that red tornado you've been riding lately? Is he here today?'

'Not today,' Ross said, pleased to let the uncomfortable subject drop. 'He's got two classes tomorrow, though, and he's fighting fit.'

Mick seemed disposed to stick around and with his cheerful company the rest of the day passed very pleasantly. He got on well with Danny and when Roland turned up shortly before lunch, good spirits turned to hilarity. Bill regarded their determined light-heartedness with open disapproval but said little.

Ross' success with Telamon appeared to have dampened the rumourmongers' efforts a little and for the first part of the day he encountered if not friendly smiles, then at least no open hostility. As the day wore on, however, it became apparent that someone had been busy spreading the details of his latest misdeeds and his reception in many quarters turned a little frosty.

He found he'd grown used to the cold.

By the time the last round had been jumped and the horses loaded, the Oakley Manor team had collected two trophies, several rosettes and a respectable amount of prize money. Ross was dog-tired and never happier to leave the driving to Bill.

'You should take it easy, Yank. You look like death only slightly warmed up.' Mick seemed genuinely concerned.

'Thanks! The original Job's Comforter. Couldn't you think of anything really depressing to say?'

Mick laughed. 'I just thought you could do with a little advice from a friend. See you tomorrow, maybe.'

'Sure, Limey,' Ross responded. 'If I make it through the night!'

In fact, Ross slept through most of the return journey, shifting restlessly to ease the discomfort of his cracked ribs and throbbing knee. Despite his light-hearted banter with Mick, in his waking moments he seriously wondered how much longer he could keep going with his troublesome knee, even if he was given the chance.

The second day of the show was almost as successful as the first, although the proceedings were complicated somewhat by the wind, which had strengthened still further overnight and blew the ring decorations and some of the flimsier fences over with what became a monotonous regularity.

The horses reacted variously to this when it happened, ranging from Woody's bombproof reliability to Telamon's professed terror, which Ross suspected was a total sham. Nevertheless, counterfeit or no, it didn't stop the stallion bucking him off in the middle of the main ring when nearly five foot of planks collapsed dramatically a few yards away.

Ross picked himself resignedly up off the turf and followed the chestnut from the ring to the accompaniment of sympathetic applause.

In the collecting ring he found Stephen Douglas had caught the horse, and walked over, expecting to be on the receiving end of a snide remark or two.

504

His rival, however, seemed disinclined to gloat. 'He's a bugger, isn't he?' Douglas remarked with what looked suspiciously like the beginnings of a friendly smile.

'You can say that again,' Ross agreed, slightly bemused by this completely unheralded behavioural swing. Thanking Stephen, he took back the reins.

When Telamon more than redeemed himself later by winning one of the biggest classes of the afternoon, ahead of Stephen Douglas and Danielle Moreaux, Ross was over the moon. He felt a certain affinity with the rogue horse. After all, they were both badly in need of proving themselves.

'You did it, you crazy son-of-a-gun!' he said, slapping the arching red neck as he remounted for the prize-giving. Telamon tossed his head, sensing as some horses do that he'd done well and feeling pleased with himself.

As they lined up to receive their rosettes, Stephen Douglas glanced across at Ross with an uncertain smile.

'Well done. You gave him a great ride,' he said, reddening a little.

Ross blinked. 'Thanks,' he said.

It appeared to be a day for surprises and not all of them pleasant.

After having collected an unlucky four faults on Woodsmoke in his final class, Ross rode Bishop into the ring feeling heartily glad that it was his last ride of the day. The black had fully recovered from his injury and jumped with smooth precision, giving each obstacle a good clearance and never looking like making a mistake. In spite of his own fatigue, Ross was lifted by admiration for the horse.

As he gave him a loose rein and walked him towards the exit, the loudspeaker announced, 'A lovely clear round there for Ross Wakelin and Black Bishop. Maybe one of the last times we shall see this partnership, as I believe the horse has been sold. A shame, that. Next to jump we have number two-two-five, Sally Patterson on her own Magpie.'

Ross was stunned.

Where the hell had they got their information? How could it be that the show commentator knew before he did? His face stony, he rode through the collecting ring and on to the public thoroughfare before he dismounted.

'Ross! Is it true?' Danny was instantly beside him. 'Who told them that?'

'How do you feel about losing the ride, Mr Wakelin?' a voice enquired unctuously at Ross' shoulder, and he turned to find Harry Douglas smiling at him from behind a hand-held tape-recorder. 'Oh, I'm sorry. Can it be that you didn't know? Mr Fergusson phoned me this morning.'

'And you didn't waste any time spreading the glad tidings. I should've guessed it was you,' Ross added through clenched teeth. 'Don't you ever give up? What have I ever done to you to make you hound me like this? Surely it's not still about Stephen? Can't you see he's better off where he is now?'

'Hound you? You're imagining things, Ross. I'm a reporter. I merely report what I see. People have a right to know.'

'And you have a right to stir things up when they get a bit quiet, I suppose?' Ross was aware that they were attracting a fair amount of attention, both inside the collecting ring and out, but he was too incensed to care. 'Well, I hope you're happy now you've dragged my reputation through the mud, because there's one advantage to being in my position – I've got absolutely nothing to lose!'

There and then, heedless of the fascinated gaze of the gathering crowd, he hit Harry Douglas with all the weight of weeks of frustration powering his fist.

The *Sportsman*'s star reporter reeled back into the arms of the startled onlookers and slid down to sit on the trampled grass with an almost comical expression of amazement on his face.

'Put that in your bloody paper!' Ross said with tremendous satisfaction and turned away without a second glance. The crowd parted to let him through, and a ragged cheer and amused applause followed his departure. It seemed he wasn't entirely without friends after all.

Stephen Douglas materialised at his side as he plodded across the showground in the wake of Danny and Bishop.

'I've been wanting to do that for years,' Douglas Junior said, casting a satisfied glance back to where his father was being helped up and dusted down. 'He's been interfering in my life ever since I can

507

remember. He tried to make me hate you because you took over my rides, but I lost that job before you ever came to England. I can see that now. He's sick! He told me you were going around telling people I couldn't ride to save my life. Said you were always bad-mouthing me, but nobody I spoke to could ever remember you having said anything against me at all. And then I was talking to Annie the other day – you know, Annie Hayward who does backs – and she put me straight on a few things. And well,' he paused, awkwardly, 'I just wanted you to know I'm sorry. I hope you'll believe I had nothing to do with the things he wrote.'

Ross waved a hand wearily. 'Forget it,' he advised. Then, mindful of the courage needed for such a speech, 'But thanks. And don't worry about it. You can't choose your relations.'

With evident relief, Stephen drifted away to his next ride and Ross was joined first by Roland, then Lindsay and James.

'Is it true about Bishop?' Lindsay demanded immediately.

Ross hadn't seen her since she'd confronted him in the yard and didn't know where he stood with her exactly. He hesitated.

'Well?' she prompted, impatiently.

'Who knows? Probably,' he said, depressed now that the euphoria of delivering Douglas' come-uppance was ebbing away. 'Harry Douglas said so.'

'By the way, lovely right hook, old chap!' Roland declared. 'Couldn't have done it better myself.'

'But how could Harry Douglas have found out first?' Lindsay persisted. 'Surely if it's true Uncle John would have been told? So why didn't he say anything?'

'Perhaps it was Fergusson's way of getting back at me,' Ross suggested. 'There's no love lost, you know.'

'But that's too much! It's so unfair!'

'Oh, Princess. When will you ever learn?' he said despairingly. 'Not everyone has your sense of fair play, you know. You just have to roll with the punches.'

'There speaks a man of the world,' Roland observed dramatically, adding gently to his cousin, 'He's right, m'dear.'

Lindsay stopped in her tracks, glaring first at Roland, then at Ross. 'All right, make fun of me! But if you had a little more backbone, perhaps you wouldn't be in this mess!'

She turned away abruptly and, with a patient shrug, James peeled off and followed her.

'Oh, dear!' Roland murmured as they departed. 'Well, can't you think of any way to insult *me*? I warn you, I'm frightfully thick-skinned but I am particularly touchy about my ears . . .'

In spite of himself, Ross smiled. 'I can see why,' he said with a sly grin.

Bishop managed a very creditable sixth place in the jump-off, against stiff opposition, but Ross could find little pleasure in it now. He travelled home lying on the sofa-bed while Bill drove slowly in the ever-strengthening winds.

Soon after they reached the yard the Colonel phoned Bill at the cottage to confirm that Fergusson had received, and was likely to accept, a substantial offer for Bishop from a wealthy farmer with a string of horses in Yorkshire.

As Bill imparted this news to the team, his eyes rested on Ross with bitter accusation, and the unloading and settling of the horses was carried out for the most part in depressed silence.

To Ross, the news seemed to signal the beginning of the end and even the memory of Telamon's wonderful performance failed to keep his spirits afloat. He wondered gloomily what Roland would do with the horse if the yard did break up.

The other horses would doubtless find places in other yards but he couldn't see Roland bothering to find another rider for the stallion that he'd bought on a passing whim. Judging by the horse's past record, he wouldn't find it easy to place him either. Ross wondered if Roland would consider selling Telamon to him.

Alone in his room, after a late meal eaten half-heartedly, Ross sprawled on the sofa listening to the wind howling round the stables. Bill had said that Ross needn't bother to come down for the late rounds, the implication being that he would rather do them alone. Having climbed painfully up the stairs once, Ross was quite content to let him.

The pain in his knee was many times worse than it had been when he first came to England and he knew he couldn't put off consulting a specialist for much longer. They would say he ought not to have left it so long. He was supposed to have had a check-up at the end of June but had known they would probably want to operate and surgery would put him out of action for several weeks.

So what? It probably wouldn't matter now.

Three weeks ago he'd been measured for a new pair of leather riding boots with an elastic insert in the left one to ease the pressure. He was due to pick them up in the morning. It hardly seemed worth the bother.

He gave himself a mental shaking. Self-pity would get him nowhere. After all, England was just one country. If he was determined he could go to another part of Europe where he wasn't known and start over. Or even Asia. Horse sports were booming in places like Japan.

No, the future could take care of itself, he decided. What caused such deep, aching misery was the prospect of leaving Oakley Manor under a cloud. Of leaving behind any chance of regaining the respect of the people he had come to know and like.

Franklin would speak up for him, he had no doubt, but if after all that had happened the extortionist was still at large, what had he achieved? If only he could remember what he'd been going to tell Franklin that night . . . But then, if he had a dollar for all the 'if onlys' in his life, he'd be a rich man indeed.

Sighing, Ross levered himself off the sofa and limped towards the kettle to make himself a cup of instant caffeine. Halfway there, a knock at the door halted him in his tracks. Warily, he made his way over.

'Who is it?' he asked through the panel.

'Lindsay.'

Mystified, Ross opened the door. Lindsay it was, clad in a soft, jade-green jersey dress that clung invitingly to her slim curves.

Ross transferred his gaze reluctantly to her face. Her blue-grey eyes met his for a moment and then fell to a point somewhere in the region of his shirtfront. She looked vulnerable and very unsure of herself.

'What's wrong?' he asked, concerned. He looked past her, out of the door. She appeared to have come alone. 'Has something happened?'

'I – er –' Lindsay hesitated, biting her bottom lip.

Ross reached forward to touch her arm. 'What's wrong, Princess?' he repeated, softly.

'I'm surprised you'd still want to talk to me,' she said with a rush. 'After some of the things I said to you.'

'I guess I can force myself,' he said nobly, mouth twitching with amusement. 'But, as I remember it, there was a fair bit of mud-slinging on both sides!'

'Well, I came to apologise,' Lindsay said, with the air of one determined to discharge their duty whatever the case. 'I shouldn't have said what I did but it just makes me mad when I see people I care for being treated like that!'

'Well, thank you,' Ross said, caught between

frowning and laughing. 'But what brought this on? What made it so urgent that it couldn't wait till morning?'

Lindsay looked up at him, her eyes huge and suspiciously bright.

'I *had* to come. I've been so miserable. I mean, you must have been feeling pretty awful anyway. You didn't need me making it worse. I mean, about Bishop and Ginger, and Tuesday night – I never really thought you did that but you wouldn't defend yourself and it hurts Uncle John so. I wanted you to tell me that you hadn't. You see, it's just that it *matters*! Can I come in?'

Having tried with limited success to follow this emotional cloudburst, Ross was somewhat taken aback by this final plea. His heart started to thump heavily. It was nearly eleven. It might not be such a good idea . . .

'Sure,' he said. 'But . . . um . . . what about James? Does he know you're here?'

'James told me to come,' Lindsay said in a small voice. 'He said he knew when he was beaten, and . . .' She studied her feet, face reddening.

'And?' Ross prompted. He had to be sure he was getting the right message.

'He said any fool could see that you loved me.' Her voice rose on the last words, turning them into a question.

'Oh, Princess!' Ross groaned, gathering her into his arms. She clung to him, half-sobbing, the top of her fair head barely reaching his shoulder. 'What do you want with a crippled saddle tramp like me?

James has everything: looks, wealth, charm. He's a great guy.'

Lindsay pulled away for a moment. 'Well, *you* marry him then,' she suggested. 'Oh, don't be so bloody noble! I'm very fond of James but I've never loved him, I know that now.'

Ross put his arms round her and drew her into the room.

'What *will* your mother say?' he enquired, teasing.

'Sod Mother!' Lindsay said indistinctly, her head against his chest.

With a delighted chuckle, Ross kissed the top of her head. 'I'd carry you across the threshold, Princess, but my ribs are still a bit sore.'

'Not *too* sore, I hope?' she enquired.

He shook his head. 'Nowhere near that bad.'

21

Lindsay left at first light the next morning, before anyone was up and about.

'I want to tell Mother myself,' she said when Ross urged her to stay. 'I think I owe her that much. She doesn't know the engagement is off yet. I was dining at James' parents' last night and I expect she thinks I stayed there. Besides, I couldn't face going down to the yard when Bill and the others are there.'

Ross raised an eyebrow. 'Ashamed of me?'

'Don't be silly,' she said. Then, with a carefully straight face, 'I don't think I'd want to be seen with you in public, that's all.'

'You little minx!' Ross breathed, lunging to get between her and the door.

Lindsay dodged easily, giggling.

'See you later,' she called as she skipped down the stairs and out into the windblown morning.

From the window, Ross watched her cross the yard, a slim figure incongruous in a jade evening dress, and smiled as she turned and waved before rounding the corner. Her subterfuge was almost certainly wasted as the Scotts would hear the engine of her MG as she left and draw their own conclusions.

In due time, having showered and dressed, Ross made his way down to the yard. It was something of a shock to encounter the depressed faces of his workmates as they fed and mucked out the horses.

Ross' whole world had taken on a different complexion overnight and the atmosphere in the yard was totally at odds with the warm glow he felt within. True, his problems hadn't miraculously disappeared, but neither did they seem so desperately overwhelming. Wherever he found himself in the future, he wouldn't be alone.

In the cottage, he ignored the usual copy of the *Sportsman*. If Douglas had written anything about him at all, it wouldn't be complimentary and he didn't want anything to spoil the way he felt this morning.

After breakfast, which was eaten for the most part in a deafening silence, Ross announced his intention of going to pick up his new boots. He wondered aloud if Danny would like to accompany him.

'Danny's got things to do here,' Bill said shortly.

'Young Peter is coming over for the day, Ross,' Maggie explained, taking pity on him. 'Danny offered to keep him company and they're going out this afternoon.'

516

'Masters is taking us to Beaulieu, to the motor museum,' Danny put in. 'They've got some wicked cars there! I haven't been for ages.'

Bill scowled at his son. 'Don't have time to cart you all over the bloody countryside,' he muttered. 'Got far too much to do here.'

So Ross set off alone in the borrowed Land-Rover, eyeing the windblown trees a little apprehensively. Last night's gale had not died down. If anything, it had strengthened and the roads were strewn with leaves and broken branches. In the yard that morning, empty buckets, haynets and discarded rugs had taken on a life of their own, flopping and rolling across the ground in a way that startled the horses and would have been quite amusing had anyone felt like laughing.

Cutting across the hills to the northwest of Salisbury via the back roads, Ross' thoughts dwelt with pleasure on the previous night.

When a car came at him in the middle of the road on a blind corner, he swerved violently to avoid it, cursing the other driver as the nearside wheels of the Land-Rover bumped heavily into a pothole. It would follow his recent run of luck, he reflected ironically, if after Lindsay's declaration of devotion he had to spend the next few weeks in hospital recovering from a road accident.

He shifted down a gear or two and pulled back on to the road. The steering wheel juddered a little under his hands. Darcy was right, the wheels *did* need balancing.

His thoughts drifting again, he reached the brow

of the hill and saw with pleasure the Wiltshire countryside spread out like a patchwork quilt below him. The road followed the ridge for a few hundred yards, curving round the head of a steep-sided valley, and here the rising wind buffeted the Land-Rover so heavily that Ross had to steer into it to stay on course.

Avoiding another traveller on the not over-wide road, he again had to bump on to the side and as he pulled back on to the tarmac had the uneasy feeling that the vehicle wasn't responding as it should.

It seemed now to be pulling hard *into* the wind. As the incongruity of this dawned on him, the road banked a little as it rounded the valley head and the Land-Rover, without any warning, lurched violently to the right.

Resisting his instinctive attempts to correct its course, it swerved wildly across the opposite carriageway, hit the grass verge and launched into the air.

The brakes, applied moments too late, had no effect at all on the temporarily airborne vehicle, and the view that had so delighted Ross just moments before now looked likely to be the last he ever saw.

The valley was deep and incredibly steep-sided, its slopes stepped by the feet of countless generations of grazing sheep. The Land-Rover tipped crazily towards it, held up only by three disturbingly rusty strands of barbed wire and a series of ancient, lichen-greyed fence posts. The wire screeched and twanged like a violin in the hands of a toddler and one weary strand gave way under the strain.

It seemed an age that the Land-Rover hung there, tilted suicidally over the precipice, but it could only have been a matter of moments before the fence, having stretched to its limits, swung back with surprising elasticity, tipping the vehicle back on to three of its wheels.

Hardly daring to breathe, Ross lost no time in unfastening his seat belt and opening the door. His heart missed a beat as he saw the yawning emptiness beneath his offside front wheel, and although the Land-Rover appeared to have settled fairly firmly, he decided that in this case discretion was definitely the better part of valour, and slid across the front seat and out of the passenger door.

With his feet back on terra firma, he took three quick steps to distance himself from the vehicle, as though fearing it might yet drag him over the edge, and then turned with morbid fascination to look over the fence.

It didn't take a genius to see just how close to oblivion he had come. He was standing on a rough, grassy verge barely a yard wide upon which rested two of the Land Rover's four wheels. Immediately to the other side of the fence the turf dropped away, and some two hundred and fifty feet below, at the bottom of a slope that must have been one in three, a flock of startled sheep gazed anxiously up at him.

The wind whipped through his hair and rocked

him on his feet. Feeling suddenly light-headed, Ross turned away from the valley and sat down heavily on the tough, brownish grass of the verge.

Now that the danger was past, his body reacted to the surge of adrenalin it had produced with a hefty dose of the shakes. He closed his eyes, rested his head on his knees and took slow, deep breaths to steady himself.

The low drone of an approaching car swelled and stopped as the driver pulled up alongside. A window lowered, unheard above the gale, and a man's voice enquired, 'You all right, mate?'

Ross looked up.

'Yeah. Fine now, thanks.'

'Anything I can do?'

'I don't suppose you know where I could find a garage with a tow truck, do you?' Ross asked hopefully. Even if he'd still had his mobile phone, he would have had no idea who to ring.

The car driver nodded. He could do better than that. There was a repair garage down in the valley. He knew the mechanic and would call in on his way by. With a final glance at the balanced Land-Rover he offered his opinion that Ross had been incredibly lucky and went cheerfully on his way, no doubt to describe the accident, with relish, to everybody he encountered during the day.

Where are the press with their cameras snapping? Ross thought sardonically. They've missed this one. They're slipping!

In the next ten minutes or so, several more cars and two lorries came by, all either stopping or slowing to view the spectacle of the precariously perched vehicle.

'It's all under control,' Ross told those that stopped. 'Yes, I'm fine, thank you. Somebody's on the way.'

During a lull in the traffic, he climbed to his feet and wandered round to the back of the Land-Rover, wondering if it was carrying any rope with which a passing lorry might be persuaded to tow it back on to the road, if the recovery vehicle failed to materialise.

The wind was howling across the ridge with unrelenting vigour and the Land-Rover rocked under its assault. Ross found a rope, although it had seen better days, and a number of other tools including a spade, presumably for digging oneself out of snowdrifts.

'I'd say you were pretty lucky there,' a voice remarked close behind him with a marked lack of originality.

Ross jumped. He hadn't heard a car approach. 'There's a tow truck on the way,' he said, turning, hoping as he said it that it was true. 'It's all under control . . .' His voice tailed off as he saw before him the navy uniform of one of Her Majesty's finest.

'Oh, Jeez!' he groaned, recognising one of the officers from the week before.

'Well, well,' the policeman said with dawning recognition. 'If it isn't our American friend. For a moment there I didn't recognise you, standing up.'

'Very funny,' Ross said, not laughing.

'I must say, your parking hasn't improved,' his

tormentor remarked, standing back to survey the vehicle. 'Just what exactly happened? Did the wind blow you off course or were you trying to get the cork out of a bottle?' He was clearly enjoying himself.

'The wind,' Ross pointed out, 'is blowing the other way.'

'Well, I think in view of your previous form we ought to just make sure you aren't under the influence,' the policeman said, and called over his shoulder, 'Jim! When you've finished putting those cones out, bring the breath box, will you?'

By the time the tow truck arrived, some five minutes later, Ross had had about enough of Police Sergeant Steve Deacon and his sidekick.

After the negative breath test, the two had amused themselves by asking Ross numerous questions and requesting vehicle documents. These last he was able to produce. Franklin with his usual thoroughness had left them in the glove compartment and they were all, to the almost visible disappointment of the sergeant, up to date.

'I'll give the name and address of your insurer to the farmer who owns this particular fence,' he said helpfully, as the Land-Rover was dragged back on to the road by the cheerful, round-faced mechanic in the tow truck. 'And if I were you and I wanted to travel in the next couple of weeks, I'd take a bus. You'll have to get used to it sooner or later anyway. See you in court.'

With this parting shot he beckoned to his partner and headed for his car.

'Bloody charming!' the mechanic said, getting out of the truck and looking at the departing police car. 'Know him, do you?'

'We've met,' Ross said dryly. 'But I sure wish we hadn't.'

'Know what you bleeding mean!' the mechanic agreed. Then, turning his attention to the Land-Rover, 'Not hard to see what's happened here.'

Ross followed his gaze. If one discounted the four-foot length of barbed wire which decorated the front bumper, the vehicle looked little the worse for its adventure, except for the fact that while its nearside front wheel pointed slightly left, its offside companion was pointing determinedly in the opposite direction.

'Looks like the track rod's come off the joint, at a guess,' the mechanic said placidly, rubbing his bristly chin with a grimy paw.

Ross was thoughtful. 'Does that happen often?'

'Nah, not very. You'd spot it was loose on the MOT most likely.'

Ross continued to gaze at the offending wheel. He had seen from the documents that the Land-Rover had been tested within the last month.

'Would it be possible for someone to arrange for it to happen?' he asked after a moment.

'Bloody hell! That's a bleeding question, that is!' the mechanic said, looking curiously at Ross. 'Who do you work for? The sodding Mafia? Yeah, I suppose it would. Very easy. All you'd have to do would be slacken off the nut on the steering rack joint – or take it right off. You could even drive round with it like that. No telling when it would finally come apart. Could be one mile, could be ten.'

'Unless you hit a pothole . . .' Ross said absent-mindedly.

'That would probably shake it loose,' he agreed. 'Bloody nasty if it happened in traffic.'

'Or on a bloody hill,' Ross suggested with amusement.

'But you don't seriously think somebody did it on purpose?' the mechanic persisted, appearing not to notice the mickey-taking. 'What did you do to him? Shag his soddin' wife?'

Ross shook his head. 'Pay no attention to me, I'm paranoid,' he said with a slight smile. 'Can you fix it for me?'

Seated in the tow truck, heading for the workshop, Ross' mind was busy with several unpleasant but increasingly convincing suspicions. The police sergeant had unwittingly given his memory a prod when he'd checked the numberplate with the registration papers.

The first three letters were DRH. 'Damn Roland's Hide' Ross' subconscious had immediately quoted, and in an instant, memories of the previous Tuesday evening came flooding back.

DRH had been the registration of the Land-Rover that he'd followed through the diversion, and therefore was almost certainly the one that had stopped across the road, setting up the ambush. It would be stretching coincidence too far to believe that his near-calamitous accident in the same vehicle was just that: an accident.

'It was Darcy's idea,' Franklin had said when he had offered the Land-Rover to Ross at the show. When it arrived Ross hadn't looked twice at it. There were so many four-wheel-drive vehicles on Wiltshire's roads, it just hadn't occurred to him to look closely at this one.

Was Darcy the Mr X they were looking for, or had somebody, possibly Leo, 'borrowed' the vehicle that Tuesday evening? And *who* then had loosened the nut on the steering rack?

'I reckon you're lucky old George Collins is bloody skint.'

This somewhat cryptic utterance cut across Ross' thoughts.

'If that had been a new fence it would prob'ly have snapped when you hit it,' the mechanic supplied obligingly. 'Stretch 'em like bloody pianer wire they do these days. That old wire's looser and got some give left in it. Bloody lucky.'

At the garage, he showed Ross the tapered joint on which the steering track rod end sat.

'When that comes apart, your chances of controlling the car are sod-all. One wheel goes one way and one the other. I tell yer, you were lucky you didn't roll the bugger!' He pointed with one blackened finger. 'See here. It's been greased to help it slide. The other one hasn't been touched for donkey's years. Looks like you were right, mate. Bloody stupid sort of joke to play!'

'Bloody stupid,' Ross agreed. 'I'm sure he didn't realise what he was doing.'

'I should bloody hope not,' the man said, shaking his tousled head as he went to work on the Land-Rover. 'Well, I suppose it's your sodding funeral, but if it was me, I'd half bloody kill him!'

'Mmm. I might just do that,' Ross agreed. 'I bloody might.'

Finally catching on, the mechanic looked up and grinned good-naturedly.

Having been assured that the Land-Rover was once more roadworthy, Ross settled his account, adding a generous percentage in true gratitude. He then resumed his journey, driving slowly in deference to the wind and the state of his nerves. Besides which, he had a lot on his mind.

Working on the premise that Darcy Richmond was indeed the extortionist and conveniently leaving aside the matter of motive for the moment, he tried to fit together the pieces of the puzzle. He had no doubt that Franklin's nephew had the brains to pull off the blackmail and he was in a position to do it, having access to the stableyard and the financial know-how needed to bank the proceeds without trace. But where then did Leo come in?

He, in Ross' opinion, was strictly minor league, criminal by inclination rather than by design. Perhaps, as he himself had suggested to Franklin, Leo had stumbled on to Darcy's trail by stealing his wallet and finding the business card. This would have led him to the connection with Clown, if no further, and given him at least enough leverage to threaten to expose Darcy if he wasn't cut in. In effect, blackmailing the blackmailer. It was quite possible he still didn't know the whole of it.

Ross remembered the day Darcy had turned up at the yard with a black eye. Perhaps the two men had come to blows when Leo faced him with what he had guessed. Ross had had proof enough himself of Leo's propensity for violence.

If Darcy was indeed their Mr X, it would explain how he had managed to stay one step ahead of McKinnon's men all the time. It had been a clever move to bug the telephone outside Franklin's house, thereby directing suspicion towards an outside listener, when all he would need to do would be pick up an extension, casually question his uncle or glance through his papers when he was not at home.

Although Darcy had his own pad, Ross knew he still had a room at his uncle's home. It was not to be supposed that Franklin would leave details of his business with McKinnon lying around for casual eyes to see, but neither would he have expected Darcy actively to seek it. Besides, McKinnon had worked for Richmond Finance before. It would be a natural progression for Darcy to suppose that his uncle would use the company in this other matter.

Why had McKinnon eliminated Darcy from his enquiries? Ross wondered. He supposed it was because of a lack of perceptible motive and the existence of an apparently watertight alibi for the night of the Bellboy incident.

Darcy himself had told Ross he was away sailing that weekend. He was sure McKinnon would have checked that Darcy had indeed taken his boat out, but what if he had moored again elsewhere and slipped back to Oakley Manor to slaughter the horse? Almost impossible to trace. And if Darcy *were* their man, it would account for Leo's knowing that McKinnon's men were watching him.

Ross sighed. He hoped, for Franklin's sake, that he was wrong but the more he thought about it, the more probable it all seemed.

Ross had his own ideas as to the reason behind Darcy's campaign against his uncle but one fact stubbornly refused to fit the overall picture. Darcy had apparently been prepared to risk Peter's life to gain his ends.

However consummate an actor Darcy might be, Ross felt sure he had never faked his devotion to the boy. It was there for all to see, whenever they were together. It was, even for cousins, an unusually strong bond and he clearly resented anyone who threatened to replace him in the boy's affections.

Maybe that was why he had 'lost' Danny's videotape that had contained footage of Ross riding the bucking stallion. Too young to fully understand the bad feeling surrounding Ross, Peter already regarded the American with a certain amount of juvenile hero worship, as the Colonel had pointed out, and seeing him ride the rogue horse could have done nothing but enhance that image.

So, taking this possessive devotion into account, how could Darcy possibly contemplate harming the boy?

For a few moments, Ross was fully occupied manoeuvring the Land-Rover through the traffic to the bootmaker's shop. The boots tried for fit, approved and paid for, he began the homeward journey.

Now that he had the skeleton of a solution to build on, Ross found that many of the remaining pieces slotted quite easily into place.

He remembered the evening they had gone out for a drink, ostensibly on a whim. It now seemed more likely that Darcy had engineered the whole thing. It had been about a week after Ross had confronted the prowler in the yard. Perhaps, even then, Darcy had been sizing him up as possible trouble. Or perhaps Ross had merely been his alibi for the time of Peter's accident.

That innocuous evening at the pub had thrown up several significant facts in hindsight. The undisguised warmth and admiration in Darcy's eyes when he had spoken of Franklin's ex-wife had set Ross thinking, and remembering how easily he had mimicked Fergusson's Scottish accent, it was plain that assuming an Irish one would be no problem to him.

It wasn't possible to be sure exactly who had done what, and at whose instigation, but Ross was beginning to see that Darcy had been extremely adept at harnessing the hostility of others for his own ends.

This said, he was willing to bet that Leo had engineered most of the physical 'accidents'. Things like the rope between the trees and the attack on the dog bore the ex-groom's hallmark of spite. Leo it had been, too, who had worked on Ginger's neurosis while he was at the yard, bringing her to breaking point and finally beyond, with tragic, not to mention painful, consequences.

It was easier to accept Leo's part in it than Darcy's. Leo had never pretended friendship but Ross had liked Darcy and now experienced a sense of betrayal. They would never have been bosom-buddies but he had seemed easy-going and good-natured and Ross had considered him a friend.

If he was right, then it seemed likely that Sarah had been taken in too. Ross had always thought them an ill-matched pair but what better cover for Darcy making visits to the yard than to see her? He imagined that she would have needed very little encouragement to keep him up to date with the business of the yard, either. The horses were her passion.

Using Leo as a willing tool, Darcy had tried again and again to weaken Ross' position in the yard. It was quite possible he had manipulated Harry Douglas in some way too. When, in spite of everything, the Colonel and Franklin had stood by Ross, it was no wonder Darcy should have decided that the time had come to get rid of him once and for all.

It was no wonder, but it was no excuse.

Ross felt bitterly angry. He felt anger for himself;

for Franklin, who had shown his nephew nothing but kindness; for Peter, Ginger and the dog, all of whom were totally innocent victims; and for the Colonel and Lindsay and all the other members of the Oakley Manor team who had suffered because of Ross' disgrace.

Driving back to the yard, with only the howling wind for company, Ross began to plot Darcy Richmond's downfall.

Back at the stables, the wind showed no sign of abating. It was a nerve-shredding, relentless shriek. Leaves and branches littered the gravel and somewhere a door was banging. Anything that wasn't tied down was rolling around or pinned against the first upright it had fetched up against. The horses were shifting uneasily in their stables, upset by the noise and transmitting their tension to one another.

Ross put the Richmond Land-Rover in the shed in place of the other, which he parked in the yard. Bill appeared, grumbling about the weather, and together they did the midday rounds; feeding, filling water buckets and tidying stables. All the while, Ross was engrossed with the problem of what had to be done and how to do it.

He ate a light meal, for which he had little appetite, with Bill, Maggie and the two boys. During lunch, the wind seemed to drop a little and shortly afterwards Masters collected the eager youngsters to take them on their promised visit to the motor museum. If the loving care lavished on the Preston Jaguar was anything to go by, the excursion would be no great hardship for Masters either.

As the big car swept sleekly out of sight, Ross made his way over to the tackroom. For an hour or more he cleaned tack dirtied at the show, his mind busy with the conclusions it had reached that morning, going over and over the evidence, wanting to be quite sure he was right. Finally, reluctantly, he turned his steps towards the house. He needed to use a telephone and he dared not use the one in the stable office. To be overheard at this stage would foul everything up.

The oak trees behind the house tossed and strained in the fitful wind, their towering bulk looking slightly menacing, and the broad sweep of gravel opposite the imposing front door was strewn with twigs and greenery. The wind was rising again, from a different direction now, the brief lull apparently over.

Ross wished he could postpone his plans for the afternoon but the circumstances would never again be so ripe for exploitation. It *had* to be today. If, that was, McKinnon and Franklin agreed.

In the absence of Masters, the Colonel opened the door himself. His enquiring expression faded to one of resignation as he saw Ross. He stood back and waved the American past and into the study where a pack of assorted dogs greeted him with varying degrees of enthusiasm.

'What a day,' the Colonel observed moodily, following him in. 'Bloody wind! I hate it! Can't relax with that noise going on.'

Ross turned to face him and the Colonel's eyes narrowed.

'Has something happened?'

'I . . . um . . . have something to tell you,' Ross said, feeling that as statements went, it was a fair candidate for understatement of the year. 'But first, I need to use your phone.'

The Colonel waved a hand towards his desk. 'Help yourself,' he offered, interest sharp in his face.

'Thanks,' Ross said, and went to work.

22

Two hours, a glass of sherry and a cup of coffee later, Ross sat back in one of the Colonel's armchairs and watched his employer's face as he mentally digested what he'd heard.

He had been a good listener, interrupting only occasionally and then with intelligent questions. Once past the initial astonishment, he had assimilated the information remarkably quickly, considering that it was presumably all new to him. Ross supposed that was all part of his military training and probably what had helped to raise him to the rank he had attained.

It had begun to rain about half an hour ago and now it was lashing down, or more accurately along, periodically thrown against the window like sea spray. Ross watched it absentmindedly and pitied anyone caught at sea on a day like this. He hoped the motor museum was a mainly indoor affair and that the boys' visit would not be spoiled. They had planned to go to the cinema after Beaulieu, so they wouldn't be back for several hours yet.

Finally the Colonel lifted his thoughtful gaze from the desktop and looked directly at Ross.

'I suppose I should say that I've been guilty of misjudging you,' he said then. 'But, quite frankly, I haven't. All along I've struggled to reconcile what I was hearing of you with the impression I was forming of your character. The two just wouldn't mesh. It's a relief, in many ways, to know the truth. I'm not usually guilty of poor judgement.' He sighed. 'If only the whole thing wasn't such an infernal tangle. I mean, *Darcy*! I can hardly believe it. Poor Franklin! The thing is, I can't see an easy way out of it. Whatever we do, people are going to be badly hurt. It's a bloody mess!'

Ross nodded his agreement.

'I wish you'd told me before,' the Colonel said, not for the first time.

'I wish I could have, believe me,' Ross said. 'But it wasn't my decision to make. I'm sorry.'

In spite of the unhappy situation, it was good to be back on the level with this man for whom he felt a good deal of liking and respect.

'I understand,' the Colonel said. 'But is there no other way to resolve it all? This plan of yours seems sound enough but I don't like your involvement. If Darcy falls for it, he'll be like a cornered bear, lashing out at whoever's closest, and that will be you. Heaven knows, you're hardly his favourite person as it is!'

Ross shook his head. 'I wish there was but it's important to catch him red-handed. It's the only way to be certain. I'm not out to play the hero, I can assure you. McKinnon's men will be there to take over as soon as we've hooked our fish. I don't think there'll be any danger.'

It was one of those statements, blithely made, that he was to remember later.

The telephone on the desk rang, forestalling any further comment.

The Colonel answered it, listened and handed it wordlessly to Ross. It was McKinnon calling back, rather faint and crackly due to the effects of the high wind on the line, but what he had to say was clear enough.

'Okay, it's on. You'll have all the back-up you need. One of my men will be with you about seven o'clock to fit the wire. And, Ross – be careful, will you?'

As he replaced the receiver his heart was thudding heavily.

'It's set,' he told the Colonel, calmly. 'All we have to do now is bait the trap.'

'Are you going to ring from here?'

Ross shook his head. 'Better not. I'd normally use the one in the stable office. I don't know how closely Darcy's monitoring the yard now but he's pretty smart and I don't want to run any risk of giving the game away at this late stage. Just remember, when your phone rings don't answer it.'

The Colonel stood up with Ross and accompanied him to the door.

'You'd better borrow a coat,' he said, following Ross out into the hall. 'Otherwise you'll be soaked to the skin by the time you get back to the yard.'

In the comparative gloom of the hall Roland was standing, apparently absorbed in study of the telephone directory.

'I thought you'd gone out,' his father grunted, without ceremony.

'I came back,' he stated somewhat unnecessarily. He put the directory down on the highly polished table beside the phone. 'Awfully breezy out there. Not the day for golf.'

The idea of anyone setting out at any time that day with a view to playing golf was so preposterous that Ross had to smile. Roland touched an imaginary cap and disappeared through the open door into the kitchen.

The Colonel wasn't amused. 'I sometimes wonder if my son isn't one or two beagles short of a pack,' he said, shaking his head.

Ross laughed, then looked thoughtfully from the kitchen doorway to the telephone on the hall table, and thought that Roland might just be the cleverest one of them all.

An hour and a half later, just before eight o'clock, Ross was in Woodsmoke's stable, directly beneath his own room, awaiting Darcy Richmond's arrival. The rain had stopped but the wind, if anything, had increased. He had been there perhaps ten minutes but didn't think he'd have to wait much longer. Ross didn't doubt that Darcy would come, for a quarter of an hour earlier Franklin's nephew had been on the receiving end of a very disturbing phone call.

Knowing that Franklin would not be at home, because he was at that moment with McKinnon, Ross had telephoned and asked to speak to him.

'Ross!' There was a pause while he imagined Darcy frantically speculating as to what might have gone wrong with his plan. 'Er, Uncle Frank's not here at the moment,' he went on, recovering his poise. 'Can I take a message?'

'Sure, thanks. Just tell him he needn't pick Peter up this evening because I've got to go out and can drop him off on the way, if you like. I've just got a couple more phone calls to make, then I'll run him home in the Land-Rover.'

He had put the receiver down smartly, pretending not to notice Darcy's urgent protests, and then lifted it again and left it lying on the table.

The Scotts had been evacuated, at Franklin's request, to the main house, and the Colonel would let his telephone ring unanswered. Unless he had miscalculated badly, Ross felt sure that Darcy would by now be well on his way to the yard in a state of near panic. He could almost find it in himself to feel sorry for the guy.

Almost.

Woody munched steadily on his hay, showing the unconcern of a veteran towards both the gale and Ross' unusual behaviour. Suddenly, though, he pricked his ears and swung his head towards the door. In the same instant, Ross heard the roar of a rapidly decelerating engine above the howl of the wind.

Instinctively, he pressed himself flat to the stable wall as Darcy leapt from his car and immediately began shouting alternately for Peter and Ross. He sounded panicky and, receiving no answer, ran to the door that led up to Ross' room. He took the stairs two at a time, judging by the speed of his ascent, and banged briefly around before charging down again and out into the yard.

Peering through the stable window, Ross saw him check the tackroom and the stable office and, on the way out, pause to read the numberplate of the yard's Land-Rover. What he saw obviously didn't reassure him and he began yelling again with renewed vigour.

'Ross! Peter! Where the hell is everybody? Ross! Damn you!'

He ran over to the cottage but found to his frustration that the door was locked. It said something for his state of mind that he didn't apparently find it strange that both of the Scotts should be out, when the Land-Rover was parked in clear view in the yard and their family car was beside the cottage. Instead, he made a sound that was something between a howl and a groan, and kicked the door hard in desperation.

'Where are you?' he yelled at the top of his voice. 'Peter! Ross! For God's sake, somebody! Maggie! Oh, God, they can't have gone. Please don't say they've gone! Ross, damn you . . .' He rattled the door frantically, then stood back from the cottage looking up at the windows.

Ross judged it was time to make his presence known. He stepped quietly out of the stable, pushing aside Woody who had finally succumbed to curiosity and was standing with his head over the door, steadily winding a length of hay into his chomping jaws. Darcy had now given up at the cottage and was running towards his car.

'Looking for someone?' Ross called.

Darcy stopped mid-stride and whipped round. His eyes narrowed as he saw Ross and he looked quickly past him for a sight of Peter.

'Where is he? Where's Peter?' he hissed. 'And where did you come from?'

'I was hiding,' Ross said, as if it were the most natural thing in the world. 'I wanted to see what you'd do when you couldn't find us. Your reaction was pretty interesting. Why, for instance, should we not go? What could possibly be wrong?'

For a moment Darcy appeared to consider caution, but his hatred was stronger. With a very ugly expression he stepped a pace or two closer. 'You sneaky bastard! You set this up, didn't you? How did you find out?'

'About what?' Ross would have liked to take a step or two back but in this wind he wasn't sure what the effective range of the wire strapped to his chest would be.

'Don't act stupid! About the Land-Rover. Why didn't you go out this morning? You said you were going out.'

'I did,' Ross said, coldly furious now that Darcy had confirmed his guilt beyond doubt. Something in him had clung to the hope that he was wrong, in spite of all the evidence to the contrary. 'You damn' near killed me, you evil son-of-a-bitch!'

'I meant to!' Darcy had thrown caution to the winds now, his easy-going, Mr Nice Guy image gone as if it had never existed. 'I wish I had, you bastard! You've ruined everything with your interfering nosiness. I should have hit you harder that night in your room. You sucked up to Franklin. You tried to turn Peter against me. I warned you twice and I thought, after the other night, you'd be finished! I thought the Colonel would throw you out. And Uncle Frank . . . he thinks the sun shines out of your arse. I thought it would show him you're no better than the rest of them . . . But he stuck by you. Why?'

The last word sounded agonised and Ross got the impression that Darcy's hatred of him had now become even more prominent in his mind than the extortion plot. He felt the hairs prickle on the back of his neck. Being the target of such undisguised venom was not a comfortable experience. He wondered how much McKinnon would need to hear before he considered moving in.

'He stuck by you too, fella,' he said steadily. 'Even when you didn't deserve it.'

'He had a guilty conscience!' Darcy declared scornfully. 'He cheated my father and felt he had to make it up to me. So he played the Good Samaritan – helping his penniless nephew; sending

541

him to expensive schools; giving him a job and shares in the company; forgiving all his sins. I screwed his wife, did you know?'

Ross nodded. He felt a pang of sympathy for Franklin, who was no doubt listening with McKinnon.

'And he forgave me!' Darcy gave a great shout of laughter. 'What a bloody saint! I told him it was just once but it was right from the start and he never guessed! God knows how he ever made any money, he's a pushover. It should have been half mine, you know, the company,' he added bitterly. 'My father owned half of it.'

'But he sold it to Franklin for gambling money,' Ross observed mildly.

'That's a lie!' Darcy cried, his face suffused with hatred. 'Franklin tricked him and I'm going to make damned sure he doesn't do the same to Peter and me.'

'Is that why you tried to blackmail him?'

'I *did* blackmail him!' Darcy asserted proudly. 'I was going to bleed him dry. I'd have done it, too. I would have bled him dry and then taken Peter from him. He was running scared until you came along and fouled it all up!'

Gotcha! Ross thought, triumphantly. That should be all that McKinnon needed to hear. The wind gusted mightily and a shower of slates slithered off the roof. Somewhere in the distance a tree groaned and toppled with an impressive crash.

Darcy ignored the slates, stepping nearer to the

542

American. 'What have you done with Peter?' he asked then, remembering why he had come.

'Nothing. He's at the cinema, as far as I know.' Ross stood his ground, caution battling with pride. 'He's quite safe. He still has to rely on that wheelchair, though, doesn't he? Tell me, how do you live with yourself, knowing you did that to your own son?' He had no proof, but everything pointed to it: their physical similarity, Darcy's affair with Marsha and his jealousy over Peter's admiration for Ross.

Darcy's reaction removed any lingering doubt.

'No!' He almost screamed the word and Ross took a step back in spite of himself. 'I never meant that to happen, I swear it! The driver was incompetent. He wasn't meant to hit any of the children, just scare them – to scare Franklin. It was just another threat. He was an incompetent fool!'

'You're the fool, fella!' Ross said contemptuously. 'You had everything going for you but you just couldn't get rid of that chip on your shoulder. Well, you've had it now.'

'Says who?' Darcy sneered, stepping ever closer, menace in every line of him. 'There's no one else here. Who's going to believe a drunken, nerve-shattered cripple with a grudge?'

Without taking his eyes off the American, he reached into an inner pocket and produced a flick knife with which Ross was uncomfortably familiar. The blade clicked open smoothly.

Where the hell was McKinnon?

'Especially,' Darcy went on, 'when they find

you've tried to commit suicide by cutting your wrists. Or maybe they won't find you until it's too late. "Poor Ross," they'll say. "He just couldn't take it any more." And I'll be as shocked and upset as the rest of them.'

He appeared to find the prospect immensely satisfying and Ross felt his temper rising. It was no part of the plan to tell Darcy he was wired, but the cavalry should be arriving any moment now and he doubted that revealing it would put him in any more danger than he was in already. It might, if anything, give Darcy pause for thought.

Ross patted his torso. 'Maybe nobody *would* believe me,' he admitted. 'But I'd say you've been pretty convincing yourself.'

Darcy's rapidly changing expressions were almost comical. He ran quickly through surprise, disbelief and dismay, and settled once more for vicious loathing.

'You sneaky bastard!' he hissed a second time. 'You're wired!'

Ross thought that rich, coming from someone who had unashamedly listened in on countless occasions, but his amusement was short-lived. Only a few feet separated them now and Darcy was advancing with a disturbing light in his eyes.

'Who's listening?' he demanded. 'Who, damn you? Is it McKinnon?'

Ross stood his ground, keeping a wary eye on the knife. Because his temper was high, he smiled maliciously, gaining a perverse enjoyment from the moment.

'McKinnon. Your uncle. The Colonel. Do you want me to go on? I'd say they've heard enough, wouldn't you? They'll be here any minute.'

It was too late to back down now. Ross could only hope he could fend Darcy off for as long as it took them to get there.

Where the hell were they? How long could it take to drive up the lane from the road, for heaven's sake? With a sudden, sickening sense of foreboding, he remembered hearing a falling tree. If it had been one of the limes at the end of the drive . . .

With an inarticulate cry, Darcy launched himself at Ross, his knife hand swinging for the American's belly. Ross blocked the thrust instinctively, stepping aside as he did so, and Darcy's foot lashed out, smashing sickeningly into his knee.

Ross' desperate defence crumbled. He fell back in agony, to land sitting against the stable wall. Inside the box, Woody snorted in alarm.

Darcy stepped forward to follow up his advantage and Ross could only watch him come. There was nothing within reach that could conceivably be used as a weapon and he would be damned if he was going to give Darcy the satisfaction of seeing him try to crawl away.

Darcy leant forward, his lip curling unpleasantly as he held the knife up for Ross to see, and Ross was calculating the merits of pulling him on to a head butt when two things happened almost simultaneously. Another tremendous gust of wind blew a second shower of tiles on to Darcy's head and shoulders and three burly men sprinted, shouting, into the yard.

Darcy was not beyond thought. He decided to cut his losses. As two of the men ran forward, leaving one at the entrance to the Manor drive, he raced for the nearest vehicle, which happened to be the yard Land-Rover. Ross groaned inwardly. The keys were in it, as they almost always were. It was yard policy in case of emergency and had become a habit.

Darcy wrenched the nearside door open, slid in and along the seat and gunned the engine. For one short moment Ross thought it wasn't going to start. It was known for being temperamental.

Not today.

It gave a polite cough and started obligingly. Within moments Darcy had it in gear and, ignoring his pursuers' commands to stop, had swung it round and was accelerating across the yard.

At this point, Ross wouldn't have given much for the chances of the single man guarding the drive but, much to his surprise, Darcy turned the vehicle the other way and drove hard at the five-bar gate into the home field.

The gate was a heavy wooden one, built to last, but it hadn't been fashioned with the idea of withstanding an assault from an accelerating Land-Rover, and it didn't.

By this time, Ross had dragged himself up to a standing position by hanging on to the stable door. His left leg, when put gingerly to the ground, felt as though it had been forcibly filleted and set up a protest that brought him out in a sweat.

The three burly individuals looked at the departing Land-Rover, then at each other, and raced in unspoken agreement for Darcy's abandoned car.

'We'll take it from here,' one of them called to Ross as the powerful engine burst into life.

Not in that, you won't, he thought sardonically, watching the silver beauty skid as it hit the wet grass of the field.

He briefly considered the other Land-Rover, hidden away in the shed, but doubted if his knee would co-operate enough even to get it in gear.

With an ungainly action somewhere between hopping and skipping, he crossed the yard to get a better view of the pursuit and found himself outside Telamon's box, hanging on to the door to stay upright. In front of his nose hung the stallion's bridle, swinging in the wind. It was left there in case of emergencies. This, he decided with a flash of inspiration, definitely qualified as an emergency.

Without giving himself time to think better of it, he grabbed the bridle and within moments had caught the big chestnut, who seemed surprised but not displeased to be going out at such short notice.

Ross had neither the time nor the energy to spend fetching a saddle. He led the eager stallion outside and with a flying leap that owed more to desperation than athleticism, reached the sleek back and clung to it instinctively as the horse surged powerfully forward. The leading rein, which he had hastily knotted back to the bit to give him more control, was almost ripped through his fingers.

He heard shouts and four more men burst into the yard; two from the drive to the Manor and two, who could have been Franklin and McKinnon, from the lane. Ross shouted about the other Land-Rover as he passed and, with more luck than judgement, managed to guide his excited mount through the shattered remains of the gate to thunder in pursuit of the two vehicles.

Halfway across the field he passed the abandoned sports car. Superb on the road, its performance on the wet and rutted surface of a grassy meadow had obviously left a lot to be desired.

A few strides further on, Ross passed McKinnon's men running gamely in the wake of the Land-Rover, which had by now disappeared into the wood on the far side of the field.

Giving the stallion his head, Ross tried to guess where Darcy would make for. He decided that if, as seemed to be the case, he was familiar with the lie of the land, he would bear right inside the wood, heading for the track which led into a field beside Home Farm Lane.

If Ross cut the corner, he estimated he could catch up with the Land-Rover before it reached the lane. It would mean jumping two sizeable hedges but such was Ross' confidence in the stallion's ability and courage that he didn't hesitate. He twisted his fingers in the flowing red mane and swung the horse right-handed across the field.

As it turned out, it was not the horse's ability that was put to the test but that of his jockey.

Telamon leapt with such power that Ross was hard put to keep his seat on the satiny-smooth chestnut coat. He prayed that they would encounter no farm machinery on the landing side of the hedges.

The gamble paid off, however. Landing – halfway up the stallion's neck – in the field that flanked the lane, Ross somehow managed to retain his seat and the vestiges of control and steady the horse, and after a moment he caught sight of a figure hurrying through the half-light towards the road.

The Land-Rover had presumably come up against an insurmountable obstacle, probably a fallen tree, Ross thought, as he sent the horse once more in pursuit. He'd not properly considered quite how he had intended to tackle the moving Land-Rover from the back of a horse but thankfully the problem had resolved itself. A running man certainly presented less of a dilemma.

Because of the howling wind, Darcy didn't become aware of the approaching horse until it was nearly upon him. Then he sent a desperate glance over his shoulder before veering sharply away.

Telamon entered into the spirit of the chase, altering course obediently to follow, and as they drew level once more, Ross stuck out his foot and pushed. Darcy stumbled sideways and pitched headlong into the grass.

Attempting to stop and turn in one movement proved to be Ross' undoing. The stallion lost traction with his hind feet on the wet grass and almost fell. Sliding hopelessly, Ross abandoned all hope of staying with him and half-fell, half-leapt to the ground, feeling pain shoot through his knee as he did so.

Darcy was clambering to his feet not two yards from where Ross had landed, an action the American discouraged by throwing himself at him in a flying tackle that would have gladdened the heart of a major-league football coach. Darcy subsided into the grass again and stayed down, moaning weakly, even when Ross cautiously raised his weight from him. He appeared to be winded but Ross was taking no chances.

A quick search revealed the flick knife in an inside pocket and an all-purpose scout's knife attached to his belt by a clip. These Ross transferred to his own pockets.

Well aware that Darcy's incapacitation was likely to be only temporary, and having little inclination for further fisticuffs, Ross removed the belt from his jeans and used it to secure his captive's hands firmly behind his back. Then, as his own breathing was far from easy, he sat on him.

'Now you know what it feels like!' he told his winded adversary with satisfaction.

Darcy declined to comment.

Ross looked round hopefully for Telamon but the horse had prudently taken himself off. He sighed, resigning himself to the fact that from here on in he would have to walk; a prospect that gave him little pleasure. Still, if the stunt had done no good at all to his knee or ribs, it had done immeasurable good to his soul.

As his own breathing steadied, Ross looked back at the dark mass of the wood from which Darcy had run. The trees dipped and swayed in the wind and, though he strained to see in the low light, Ross couldn't see any sign of McKinnon's men.

Although it could be no later than half-past eight, the sky was incredibly heavy with the threat of more rain and the effect was a sort of eerie twilight. McKinnon's men were probably still floundering about in the depths of the wood. Ross would have shouted if he'd thought it would do any good but the noise of the wind was far too great.

Darcy had begun to move beneath him now, and reluctant to tramp back through the muddy woodland paths with timber raining about his ears, Ross decided to head for the lane in the hope that someone would have thought to try and head the fugitive off there.

Nothing could be gained by waiting any longer, so he rose painfully to his feet and hauled his protesting prisoner up after him.

'I've got your knife, so shut up and walk,' he said unsympathetically, giving him a push in the appropriate direction.

Darcy walked, out of necessity, but he didn't shut up. He started by calling Ross all the uncomplimentary names he could think of, which was quite an impressive number, and gradually worked round to offering him a princely sum for his freedom. Ross' opinion of Franklin's nephew reached an all-time low.

'What makes you think Peter is your son?' he asked finally, as they reached the gate into the lane.

Darcy half-turned. 'What? Of course he is! I've always known. You only have to look at him . . .'

'Oh, I don't think so,' Ross said in his ear. 'That kid is twice the man you are, already. I'd say the most you've got in common is your name.' He grinned to himself as Darcy renewed his vitriolic attack on his character and ancestry.

The gate was padlocked and, for an instant, Ross' heart sank. The thought of trying to clamber over, with his knee refusing to bend properly or take his full weight, was bad enough. Couple that with the problem of keeping Darcy under control at the same time and he was in big trouble.

Then a thought occurred. He had, in his pocket, the keys to two of the gates on the far side of the copse. Sometimes they rode that way and the Colonel liked to keep all the gates on the perimeters of his land locked to keep out undesirables. He hardly dared to hope, as he fished for them, that one of the keys would fit this padlock.

One of them did. He could have cheered.

Once through the gate and standing with his captive on the grass verge of the lane, Ross felt less like cheering.

To his right, about twenty yards away, a sizeable tree lay squarely across the tarmac, effectively blocking any form of passage, be it on foot or in a vehicle. To his left the way looked, for the moment, to be clear but to go that way would involve a walk of at least a mile and a half before he reached a road where there was any likelihood of flagging down a car. It might as well be half a continent away for all the hope Ross had of walking to it.

Where is McKinnon? he thought, for what seemed like the hundredth time that day. He was forced to concede the probability that this time, as last, his way was blocked by fallen timber. Never had he needed his mobile phone more.

'What now, smart arse?' Darcy enquired annoyingly.

Annoying, because Ross wasn't sure. If he walked as far as the tree on their right, who was to say that McKinnon would be able to get even that far? On the other hand, if he went left, would he be going away from possible help, and might he not find the road similarly blocked around the next corner?

'We wait,' he told Darcy, trying to sound confident. 'I'm still wired, don't forget. So I just have to say, "I've got Darcy. We're in Home Farm Lane", and someone will come.'

'You hope! What range does that transmitter have?'

Ross ignored him. He had no idea about range but neither did he have any choice. Leaning against the gate to take some of the weight off his bad knee, he waited, trying not to mind that it was beginning to rain.

In the event, he was right. Someone did come. Above the gusting wind he heard the sound of an approaching vehicle and, pushing Darcy ahead of him into the lane, was almost immediately blinded by a set of powerful headlights sweeping round the bend towards them.

Ross' relief was immense. He waved a weary arm to make sure the driver saw them, and waited for the situation to be taken out of his hands.

It was.

The lights, still blinding, came to a halt barely ten feet away, shining through the rods of rain and making the surrounding gloom seem darker than ever. A figure sprang from the vehicle and strode towards Ross and Darcy, silhouetted by the glare.

'Jeez, am I glad to see you!' Ross declared, giving Darcy another push.

The figure in the lights halted some four or five feet away.

'Why, Yank, I'm touched!' an all-too-familiar voice sneered.

Leo! Ross froze in disbelief, his hand tightening instinctively on Darcy's arm. How the bloody hell did he come to be here?

Darcy seemed to find the situation amusing. 'What now, *Yank*?' he asked over his shoulder, with heavy emphasis.

Ross didn't answer, for the simple reason that he didn't know. He wondered briefly, if he pushed Darcy hard at Leo to unbalance him, whether he could use the advantage gained to overpower the man. He was never to know. Just as he was steeling himself to try, Leo spoke again.

'I want you to meet an old friend, Yank. A great friend of mine. Do you recognise him?' He held one arm out sideways against the light and Ross was forced to reconsider. Leo was carrying his gun.

Without a moment's hesitation, Ross pulled Darcy close in front of him, using him as a shield.

Leo laughed out loud. 'A good idea, Yank! Very good. Always supposing I gave a shit about him. But I don't. He was just a means to an end. A bit of easy money. If I have to shoot him to get to you, well,' he shrugged, 'that's okay.'

He lifted the gun in front of him to shoulder-height, using both hands.

Ross' pulse rate accelerated into the hundreds. Surprisingly, though, what he felt was more excitement than fear. The situation seemed so unreal. The wind, the rain, the deadly silhouette in the blinding light – it was almost as though he were watching from a distance. As though it were some fantastic dream from which he would awaken, by and by. That was a dangerous way to think and he gave himself a sharp mental kick in the pants.

Deeply disappointed to have failed at this late stage, his inclination was to goad Leo, to shake him out of that irritating self-satisfaction and hope that anger made him careless. It also occurred to him that it mightn't be a bad idea to try and redirect that anger towards Darcy.

'Yeah, I guess you must be pretty mad, if you've found out how much Darcy's really been making from his little racket,' he said, sympathetically. 'So much for honour among thieves, eh?'

'What do you mean?' The gun dropped six inches or so. He had Leo's interest. He'd gained some time.

In front of him, Darcy was perceptibly shaking. 'He's just talking,' he said urgently. 'He doesn't know anything. Don't listen to him.'

'Shut up!' Leo said sharply. 'Go on, Yank.'

'I bet he never told you the half of it,' Ross said, warming to his task. 'We're talking hundreds of thousands here. What he offered you was mere chicken feed. If I were you, I'd want fifty per cent, maybe sixty. After all, you've done a lot of the hard work lately. Taken most of the risks.' He was talking off the top of his head. He had no idea how much Darcy had cost Franklin but it certainly seemed to impress Leo. His hunch was obviously right. Forced to take Leo on board, Darcy had nevertheless kept the true scale of his operation a secret from his partner in crime.

Leo was incensed.

'How much?' he demanded of Darcy. 'How much have you been holding back? If I find you've been lying . . .'

'Nothing! I swear it!' Darcy was panicking. 'He's just trying to stir you up. Can't you see? He's playing for time.'

Leo was silent for a moment. 'Maybe you're right at that,' he said shrewdly. 'And then again, maybe there's some truth in it. I think I'd like to find out, but not here. We'll take the car and you, Yank, will drive it.'

This was not what Ross wanted at all. If he were

to get in that car, he would very soon leave all chance of help from McKinnon's men far behind him. He must play for more time. Surely help wouldn't be much longer in coming?

Or would it? There were several miles of lanes round the Oakley Manor land. How many men had McKinnon got? He slipped Darcy's flick knife from his pocket and released the blade.

'How did you know where we were?' Ross asked Leo, pushing Darcy a step closer to him.

'I didn't. I was coming to see what had happened to the Land-Rover. Darcy was expecting to hear that you'd had a nasty accident but nobody called and he wanted me to find out what had gone wrong. I should have told him to do his own fuckin' dirty work,' Leo added sourly, reflecting on what he had just learned.

Darcy was getting fidgety. 'He's playing for time, Leo!' he repeated urgently. 'There are others coming. McKinnon's men. They set me up but I got away. They could be here any minute. We must go!'

'We *will* go,' Leo assured him.

'Okay, but now!' Darcy said, frantic. 'Look, I'll let you have your share of the money – it's only fair, after all. Get rid of Wakelin and let's go.'

Ross tightened his grip on Darcy and squinted into the light. 'Looks like a stalemate, doesn't it, Leo? You can't have the money without Darcy and I have him as my insurance. If you try to take him from me, I'll stick this in him.' He raised his right hand, in which he held the knife. It gleamed as it caught the light. 'On the other hand,' he continued, 'you could forget the money and try for me anyway.'

'I don't think you'll use that,' Leo said, taking a step closer.

Ross didn't think he would either. At least, not on Darcy. That wouldn't gain him much, except a bullet from Leo's gun an instant later.

'You bet I will,' he lied, with as much savage conviction as he could muster.

From the way Darcy was shaking, he at least believed it.

'Leo! Be careful! He'll bloody do it!' he said in desperation.

Leo stepped closer. 'No, he won't,' he countered confidently. 'He hasn't got the guts. And besides, he knows he'll be dead if he does.'

Barely three feet away now, Ross could see the faint gleam of Leo's teeth as he smiled. Oh, hell! he thought and shoved Darcy towards him as hard as he could.

Out of the corner of his eye, as he dived towards the darkness of the hedge, he saw the two men stagger back and fall in an untidy heap against the radiator of the car. With a sharp crack the gun fired as Ross completed his roll and fetched up in the nettles and brambles beneath the hawthorn.

The car had been a temptation but Ross was by no means confident he could make a three-point turn in the narrow lane before Leo recovered his wits.

For a moment, after the gunshot, there was no

sound from the two men. Then, 'Shit! You fucking idiot!'

Ross heard the sound of boots scraping on the tarmac and then saw Leo's wiry form stand up. Darcy, he supposed, was lying in the deep shadow below the range of the car's lights. Had he been shot?

After a moment, Ross dismissed that idea. The gun had gone off after Darcy had cannoned into Leo. If the gun had been between them the report would surely have been muffled.

Leo by this time had made his way round to the side of the car, which looked, now Ross could see it more clearly, like some kind of four-wheel-drive vehicle. He opened the door and reached inside. Seconds later a beam of light sprang from his right hand as he swung round towards the verge where Ross lay holding his breath. It was clearly time to move.

He lunged to his feet, hoping Leo wasn't ambidextrous or, even better, that he had lost the gun when he fell.

He hadn't. Two shots in quick succession whined over Ross' head as his knee gave way and reduced his intended sprint to an undignified scuttle. He reached the gate and scrambled over, landing on his backside in the wet grass of the field. He heard Leo curse again and scurried, crabwise, into the shelter of the hedge once more. Here, inspiration unfortunately ran out.

The field was three or four acres in size and the hedge he was presently pressed against ran for a hundred yards or so in a straight line, all neatly cut and laid, and as impossible to penetrate as a stone wall. There was nowhere to run. Even supposing, Ross thought with weary despair, that running was an option.

Leo was climbing the gate now, doubtless having first sorted the gun and the torch into the appropriate hands. He swung the torch in a rapid and inefficient arc, which blessedly failed to pick the American out, pressed as he was into longer grass at the base of the hedge. Then he turned away from Ross and began to search the far side of the gate first.

The wind had dropped substantially now but not enough, Ross hoped, for Leo to hear the swishing of his body snaking through the grass. In a vain attempt at a bluff, he moved in a commando-style slither, away from the shadow of the hawthorn and out into the open grass.

He forced himself to keep moving when, after twenty feet or so, he was sure that Leo must soon turn and see him.

He kept his head low, resisting the temptation of looking behind to see where Leo was, and when he was perhaps fifty feet from the hedge, turned and collapsed with gasping, heart-thudding relief into the wet grass.

He felt horribly vulnerable. The grass had not been grazed for several weeks, the Colonel hoping to get a second crop of hay off it, but because of the hot spell it was barely eight inches long and by no means thick. Ross could only hope that if Leo shone the torch his way, he would, head on as he was, pass for one of the several molehills in the vicinity.

Leo had moved to the near side of the gate now, and was searching the area where Ross had until recently lain. Surely when he failed to find him close by, he would abandon the search and leave before McKinnon's men arrived.

Indeed, it seemed that was what he was going to do. From his lowly position, Ross saw him make his way back to the gate and pause, swinging the torch once more in a wide arc. It passed over Ross about three feet above his head, went on, stopped and came back. Almost instantaneously, Ross heard a swishing in the grass behind him.

Darcy! he thought with a sick sense of failure.

Somehow, while he was concentrating on Leo, Darcy must have got round behind him. Just *how* he had managed it in the time, Ross didn't have leisure to consider. He tensed himself to try and turn and come to his feet in one movement, aware as he did so that he still held the knife in his hand. This time he knew that he would use it if he had to. His situation was desperate and the survival instinct was strong.

Just as he began his move he felt something brush his back and warm breath huffed in his ear.

Definitely not Darcy!

Telamon, who had wandered over curiously to see why his master was full-length in the grass, threw up his head in alarm as Ross surged up suddenly, right under his nose.

His situation already betrayed, Ross grabbed at the lead rope, which had come unknotted, and flung himself, for the second time that day, at the horse's back.

The stallion, understandably unnerved by the violence of Ross' actions, plunged forward, and his arm was nearly pulled out of its socket as he clutched a handful of chestnut mane and hung on, landing sprawled across the horse's loins.

Something buzzed past his left ear as he struggled to pull himself to a more secure position and he realised with desperation that Leo was shooting at him again.

Telamon was galloping blindly towards the gun, probably heading for the gate, and Ross was completely powerless to stop him. He couldn't remember how many times Leo had fired and even if he could, he thought numbly, this wasn't a western; modern guns almost certainly held more than six shots at a time.

He felt the horse flinch momentarily as the crack of a second shot sounded. The gap between Leo and the horse was only a matter of feet when he stopped aiming at Ross and aimed at the horse.

Sick with fear for both of them, Ross dug his heels into the stallion's chestnut flanks and rode him hard at the man ahead.

With any other horse in the stables, Ross knew it wouldn't have worked. Horses almost invariably avoid hitting human beings if it is within their power to do so. Racehorses twist desperately to keep from trampling fallen jockeys.

Telamon was bold. He perhaps sensed by his stance that Leo was aggressive, and he had in a comparatively short time developed an uncommon bond with Ross. Without hesitation, the horse galloped the last few strides towards Leo and half-leapt as he reached him, his knees and chest cannoning into the man's upper body and flinging him to the ground. Ross caught a glimpse of Leo below him, arms upflung, eyes wide in terror, and then he fell away behind as the stallion plunged on.

Just as they reached the gate, three or four strides later, both Ross and the stallion were blinded by the glare of a car's headlights as it turned into the field gateway.

Ross involuntarily threw up an arm to shield his eyes, and Telamon, having no such resource, shied abruptly away, dumping him without ceremony on to the grass. He tucked and rolled like a jockey, fetching up by the far gatepost, which he used to pull himself painfully to his feet. From there, partially in the shadow of the hedge, he squinted to try and see beyond the light.

His one comfort was that if it was Darcy, then at least he was unarmed, though in his own present state of mental and physical exhaustion, Ross doubted if he could put up much of a fight. He was just at the stage of wondering why, if it *was* Darcy, he didn't just turn the car round and go, when a metallic click sounded close to his left ear and something cold touched his temple. He froze.

'Hold very still,' a voice warned. 'You are just a millimetre away from the final mystery.'

23

Ross practically stopped breathing.

Roland! Who'd been listening in the hall; who was never, it seemed, far behind when there was trouble. Now where exactly did he fit into all this?

A torch was flashed in Ross' face and the familiar, well-bred voice exclaimed: 'Good God, it's our American friend! Sorry, old boy. You should have said something.'

The gun barrel dropped and Ross almost fainted with relief. He managed a shaky grin.

'For a moment, I couldn't seem to think of anything appropriate,' he said.

'You could have asked if I had a licence for this,' Roland said seriously, holding up the gun. 'Awfully important to have a licence.'

'Why didn't I think of that?' Ross remarked dryly. 'Dreadfully bad form to get shot by an unlicensed gun.'

Somehow after all that had gone before, this ridiculous conversation with Roland had a strangely calming effect. How and why he came to be there and what business he had carrying a gun seemed for the moment largely unimportant, although Ross was beginning to suspect that he knew.

'Where's Leo?' Roland asked.

'Somewhere back there.' Ross waved a hand. 'Telamon knocked him down. I don't know how badly he's hurt.'

Another two vehicles drew up in the lane and disgorged their loads of passengers, and suddenly the night was full of noise and bustle.

Roland opened the gate to let Ross back through and then followed his torchlight across to where Leo lay. Ross didn't look, resolutely keeping his back turned.

'Ross!' Franklin hurried forward, deeply concerned. 'Are you all right? We could hear bits of what was going on but we just couldn't get to you. There are trees down all over the place. We were praying we wouldn't be too late.'

'Not half as much as I was,' Ross assured him. 'Yes, apart from having aged ten years, I'm fine. You knew where I was then? I wasn't sure if you did.'

Somebody switched on a spotlight on top of one of the newly arrived vehicles and it blazed out, illuminating the scene.

McKinnon approached. He was smaller than Ross had remembered him; such was the authority of the man, subconsciously Ross had allowed his increasing respect for him to influence his memory of the physical person.

'I incorporated a tracking device in that wire you're wearing,' he said in answer to Ross' remark. 'It's a good job I did, though I can't claim to have foreseen having to chase you half across the county.'

Ross grinned. 'I didn't foresee it myself but I couldn't face seeing him get away when we had him – confession and all.' Belatedly, he remembered Franklin's presence. 'I'm sorry,' he said, awkwardly. 'I was hoping we'd be proved wrong, right up to the moment he admitted it.'

Franklin shook his head, the forthright courage that had sustained him for so long not deserting him now.

'No. I knew you must be right as soon as McKinnon put it to me. Looking back, I can see there have been pointers I should have spotted. I think I was wilfully blind.'

'It's understandable,' McKinnon observed. 'No one likes to think that their friends, let alone their family, could be criminally inclined, but the sad fact is that all too often crimes are committed by someone the victim knows. The difficulty in this case was to recognise the motive.'

'Where's Darcy now?' Ross asked, looking round.

'Wearing a pair of particularly attractive matching bracelets,' Roland said, coming back from the field to join the others in the lane. Then, like Ross, he remembered whom he was addressing. 'Sorry, Franklin.'

The businessman shook his head. 'No, you forget, I heard the things he said. I feel little for him except pity. Like Ross said, he had every chance but he threw it back in my face.'

Ross was slightly taken aback. After telling Darcy about the wire, he had more or less forgotten it himself. He wondered what else he might have said.

McKinnon glanced at Roland and raised his eyebrows.

He shook his head significantly.

With a shock, Ross remembered Leo. 'Is Leo . . .?' he began and then tailed off as he read the answer in Roland's face.

'He's dead,' he said, matter-of-factly. 'Broken neck, I should think, and it couldn't have happened to a nicer bloke. You've done the world a favour, old chap.'

Ross turned and stared blindly at the figure lying beyond the gate, now respectfully shrouded in a coat, presumably Roland's. Heaven knew he had no reason to regret the man's passing, but to have been the direct cause of it . . . That was something else.

McKinnon stepped up behind him. 'We heard the shots, Ross. You had no choice. Don't let him spoil your life even after he's dead. He's not worth it.'

Ross shook his head. 'I know. It just takes a bit of getting used to, that's all.'

McKinnon patted him on the shoulder, comforting by his presence; not wasting words.

Ross forced his thoughts in another direction. 'Roland works for you, doesn't he? Did you recruit him like you did me?'

McKinnon smiled. 'Good gracious, no. He came to us straight from the army, five or six years ago now. He was looking for an interesting career without all the restrictions of army life, and an army contact put us in touch. We suited him and he suited us. Very well, as a matter of fact.' He shook Ross' shoulder gently. 'Come on. We should be getting back to the house. The Colonel will be wondering what the hell has happened. He thinks a lot of you, you know. Don't worry about this. My men will clear up here. One of them will phone the police when they're ready. A shocked passer-by, you know the sort of thing.'

Ross glanced at him. 'What about . . .?' He inclined his head towards the field. 'Won't there be trouble?'

McKinnon tutted. 'Nasty accident. Trying to catch a loose horse that's been frightened by the wind. Always a risky business . . .'

With a shock, Ross remembered Telamon. 'You'd better tell your men to keep that gate shut, there's several thousand pounds' worth of show-jumper somewhere in this field. And, while I think of it, I dropped Darcy's knife. Over there somewhere, about forty or fifty feet out.'

'Right.' McKinnon gave instructions to his men. 'We'll find the knife, and we'll catch the horse, if we can. Now, let's get going. You're wet through.'

Ross felt his clothing, surprised to find that he was indeed wet through. He hadn't even noticed. It had stopped raining somewhere along the line but crawling through the grass hadn't helped.

In due course Darcy, nursing a sore head courtesy of the bull-bars on Leo's vehicle, McKinnon and one of his men travelled back to the Manor in one vehicle, while Franklin, Roland and Ross took another.

Franklin, who was understandably subdued, sat in the back to allow Ross to sit in the front where he could stretch out his leg. His antics on and finally off Telamon had just about finished it. It would still just bear his weight, if painfully, but it would not bend at all. Sighing, he contemplated the tiresome round of consultations and operations and therapy that would now become unavoidable.

To take his mind off that dismal prospect he thought instead about Roland. What he'd learned that evening explained a lot that had been puzzling him but there was still much that didn't mesh.

'It was you, wasn't it, that night in the yard?' he said finally, looking across at the Colonel's son, who was driving with what, for him, was remarkable restraint. 'You did some sort of judo on me, dumped me on the ground and lit out! Why didn't you tell me you were one of the good guys? You knew who *I* was.'

'I was under orders,' Roland said smugly. 'And I always do as I am told. There *was* an intruder that

569

night, though. Darcy, I suppose. I think your dog chased him off.'

'But why shouldn't I have been told?' Ross asked. 'I wasted a lot of time wondering what you were up to.'

'Because, old boy, to be blunt, we didn't know you. We only had Lindsay's word for a character reference; that and what we could find out by asking around, and to be frank, some of your references weren't exactly glowing. Under stress you might have given us both away for all we knew. Edward felt it was an unnecessary risk.'

Ross had to allow that that made sense but it was ironic that on the night he was picked up for drink-driving he had worked so hard to lose Roland. If he had only known . . . He said as much.

Roland laughed and shrugged. 'I've followed you all over the place these last few weeks. I was supposed to be watching your back. McKinnon felt you were attracting rather a lot of attention from our friend. Sod's law you had to spot me that night. By the way, what *were* you in such a hurry to tell Franklin that night?'

Ross was half-embarrassed. 'I'm not sure exactly. It was something your father said that set me thinking. He warned me that Darcy was pretty ticked off with me because of the way Peter was behaving, and the more I thought about it, the more I wondered about their relationship.

'God knows how I would have put it to you, Franklin!' he added, over his shoulder. 'I was dreading it! So you see, I can't claim any brilliant deduction. I had nothing to tie Darcy in to the blackmail. It just seemed to be a loose end and I thought I should speak to you before McKinnon. Give you a chance to shout me down.'

'I wouldn't have shouted,' Franklin said soberly. 'You know, there have been times when I've wondered, seeing how Darcy is with Peter, but my comfort comes from the boy himself. He's a far stronger character than Darcy or my brother ever were. I think that's good enough for me.'

'I said as much to Darcy,' Ross agreed. 'He wasn't too impressed.'

'I can imagine,' Roland said. 'Oh, and by the way, I think you'll find your drink-driving charge will be dropped. I persuaded our boys in blue to take a look at the bottle after all, and I think they'll be contacting you shortly to examine your finger-tips, so to speak. If you're sure you didn't touch that bottle, you should be in the clear.'

'You phoned them on the way back,' Ross said, remembering. 'I wish I'd known. You let me suffer!'

'Suffering is good for the soul,' Roland said lightly. 'Besides, I didn't want you falling on me in gratitude. Ruins a decent suit, being fallen upon.'

Within fifteen minutes, having circumnavigated the Oakley Manor estate to avoid various fallen trees, both parties, minus Darcy, were ensconced in the Colonel's study.

The gathering was lit by paraffin lamps as the electricity supply had been an early casualty of the storm. The gale largely seemed to have blown itself out now and the comparative quiet was a relief. The Colonel, his son, Franklin, McKinnon and Ross all sat or sprawled on the leather chairs and gratefully accepted mugs of Irish coffee from Masters.

Peter and Danny were, they were informed, at the Scotts' cottage, consuming a large supper under Maggie's indulgent eye, and Darcy was securely locked in an upstairs room, handcuffs still in place. Bill had been sent to recover Telamon, well primed to lend credence to the loose horse story.

The atmosphere in the study was strange, half-triumphant and half-subdued. Nobody, least of all Franklin, could be sorry that it was all over but neither could anyone be completely satisfied with the outcome. The personal involvement saw to that.

Ross lounged in one of the armchairs, his leg propped up on a footstool, regarding the gathering drowsily over the rim of his mug. Unable to hide his disability any longer, he had been forced to admit that he needed help. A temporary lay-off was obviously on the cards but the disappointment was tempered by the assurances of the three owners present that their horses would be saved for him. They would be kept fit but their competitive careers placed on hold. It was more than Ross had dared hope for.

'Leo Jackson, or rather Lewis Roach, was a nasty piece of work,' McKinnon said presently into the thoughtful silence. 'Quite apart from the suspicion of assault in Ireland, we finally traced him back to London, where he's wanted by the Metropolitan Police for GBH. Apparently he worked for a building contractor until his foreman caught him stealing. The poor man got in the way of a fork-lift truck that Lewis happened to be driving and never worked again.'

'Stealing? That's not like Leo,' Ross observed with ironic surprise. 'But seriously, if it hadn't been for that crazy stallion of Roland's, I'd probably never have worked again, either!'

'I told you he was a battle charger,' Roland put in smugly.

McKinnon laughed.

'And what about Darcy?' the Colonel asked, carefully avoiding Franklin's eyes. 'I suppose he'll have to go to prison?'

'Well . . .' McKinnon hesitated. 'Franklin and I discussed that this afternoon while we were waiting for things to get underway, and we agreed that it would be better for all concerned if we can keep this business out of the courts. The injured parties are all in this room – with the exception of Peter, that is – and it isn't pleasant to have one's personal affairs dragged out under the public gaze. Of course, the decision rests partly with Ross, but if he agrees not to press charges at this point, Darcy will be asked to sign a detailed statement of his activities, witnessed by those present, and the family solicitor with whom it will then be lodged. In return for which, Darcy will go free, on the understanding that he returns all the proceeds of his crime and leaves the country on a one-way ticket – the further away, the better. I think for the boy's sake he will do so.'

Ross thought it far more generous than Darcy deserved.

'Ross?' Franklin was watching him anxiously.

'Oh, sure,' he said. 'That's fine by me. I don't think I want that kind of publicity any more than you do. To be honest, I've had a bellyful of publicity of any kind.'

Franklin's look held a wealth of gratitude. 'I don't know how to thank you,' he began earnestly.

'Please, don't. If I made any useful contribution it was as a catalyst. I think I charged round like a bull in a china shop until Darcy was sure I'd uncover him by accident, if nothing else! I mean, for a long time I had Roland down as the villain, for Chrissakes!'

'Roland?' the Colonel exclaimed through the general amusement. 'Good Lord! Why ever? He hasn't enough energy to be a criminal.'

Ross caught Roland's eye across the room and he winked. Ross had asked him on the way home why he had never told his father what his real profession was. 'Oh, I don't know. I expect I will one day. It's just . . . well, I think an excess of fatherly pride would be a little tiresome, don't you?' Roland had said. 'He's quite fond of me as I am, you know.'

After a few more minutes, McKinnon took his leave.

'I would imagine it won't be long before the police appear to inform you of the tragic "accident" that has happened on your land, involving one Leo Jackson lately in your employ,' he told the Colonel. 'I think it would be better if I have Darcy out of the way before they do.'

On his way out, he shook hands with each of them, pausing for a moment by Ross.

'If you ever grow tired of playing with horses, young man,' he said, 'you could always come and work for me.'

'Uh, thanks but no thanks, as they say,' Ross declined politely. 'I prefer problem horses to problem people.'

McKinnon shook his head, apparently not understanding how anyone could, and went on his way.

As he left, Lindsay arrived.

She came into the room unconscious of the preceding drama and it was clear that the atmosphere struck her almost immediately.

'I couldn't get through to the yard, there's a tree down, so I came round . . . Goodness, this is quite a crowd! What's been going on? Have I missed something?' she asked of no one in particular.

For some reason everyone looked at Roland.

He looked astounded.

'Why me?' he exclaimed in aggrieved tones.

Lindsay shrugged. 'Well, if it's some great secret . . . Ross will tell me later, won't you, Ross?' She moved across to sit on the arm of his chair, draping her arm round his neck.

Significant glances were exchanged around the room but Ross didn't care. His aches and pains began to feel more bearable by the moment.

'By the way,' Lindsay said, dismissing the mystery as of no importance, 'I've had an idea. I was wondering – do you think if we clubbed together we could buy Bishop for Ross to ride? I've got some money put by.'

Ross made a movement of protest, the Colonel and Roland looked thoughtful, and Franklin looked at his toes.

'I'm afraid,' he said in quiet apology, 'that this particular Yorkshire farmer has no wish to sell.'

Read on for a taste of
Lyndon Stacey's new thriller

BLINDFOLD

Available now in Hutchinson

1

The light bulb had blown.

With a resigned sigh Gideon stepped into the darkness of his hallway and turned to close the front door against the cold night wind.

There were two men waiting unseen, one outside and one in. Neither of them took the trouble to introduce himself.

As Gideon reached for the handle, the first man kicked the front door viciously from the outside, smashing it into his face and shoulder and sending him stumbling back into the waiting arms of the second. The arms wrapped around him without hesitation, enclosing his own in a hug of rib-cracking enthusiasm.

Pausing only long enough to regain some sort of footing, Gideon threw his head back hard, feeling it make contact with a satisfying crunch. There was a muffled curse and the owner of the arms fell away, freeing his captive as he clutched at his face in agony.

Gideon had little time to appreciate his freedom, for as he staggered upright he was first blinded by blazing torchlight, and then floored by an unseen fist which took him just below the ribs with all the force of a kick from an offended mule.

He found himself face down on the cold stone floor, his nose pressed to the uneven flags and one arm twisted up behind his back. There didn't seem to be anything he could usefully do about it, so he preserved what was left of his dignity and did nothing.

Something cold clicked on to his right wrist and the other one was pulled to join it.

Handcuffs! What the hell?

A hand pressed down none too gently on the back of his neck, forcing his face into even closer contact with the stone, and somewhere above his head a voice said conversationally, 'Be a good boy and lie still, and nobody will hurt you.'

A bit late for that, Gideon thought. He already felt steamrollered, and the left side of his face, which had taken the major part of the impact from the door, had begun to throb. He heard footsteps moving away and took the opportunity to roll on to his side to try and ease his painful breathing.

'You just try it!' a voice warned thickly from behind him. 'An' I'll put your lights out for good!'

Gideon had no intention of trying it, whatever *it* was. His head felt unpleasantly muzzy and he had a strong suspicion that for the time being he was probably best off horizontal.

A light clicked on across the hall in his sitting room.

'Leave him alone,' the first voice said from the doorway. 'Why don't you do something useful, like putting that bulb back in?' It was a strangely soft voice with strong undertones of some northern city, probably Liverpool. The other voice sounded similar but much rougher.

'He broke my fucking nose!' number two protested thickly, distinctly aggrieved.

'Well, I've felt like doin' it myself, more than once, so he's saved me the trouble,' the first voice remarked, further off now.

Gideon felt that had the circumstances been different, he could have liked this man.

In the shaft of light from the sitting-room doorway, he could see the heavy pair of work boots worn by assailant number two as they crossed and re-crossed his vision, three or four feet away. After a moment, the hall light came on once more.

He could hear the other man moving about in the next room and wondered what he was doing. If the object of the exercise were robbery, then they would find they had picked the wrong house. Gideon had little of value to this sort of thief: no television or video, no computer system or microwave, and very little cash about the place. His hi-fi was good but hardly state-of-the-art. Admittedly some of the furniture was antique – Gideon liked old, mellowed things – but its condition was unlikely to arouse much joy in the heart of a collector. Apart from his credit cards and the keys to the Norton, both of which were in his pockets, the only really valuable things in the house were the paintings, but none of them was particularly well known and his two visitors didn't strike him as connoisseurs.

The boots paused in their perambulations and came towards Gideon, abruptly banishing any thoughts of paintings to make room for more urgent considerations. A meaty fist descended and, hauling him to a sitting position, proceeded to drag him across the flagstones to the wall, where he leaned back gratefully and waited for the other walls and the ceiling to start behaving as walls and ceilings should.

Broken Nose hadn't finished with him. He crouched down to Gideon's level and, still holding him by the front of his leather biker jacket, pointed at his own heavy-featured, blood-streaked face, saying in a low but nonetheless menacing voice, 'I'll make you sorry you did this!'

Gideon was saved by the return of the other man, who was clearly in charge.

'Leave him alone! The Guv'nor wants him in one piece.' He pushed his injured colleague out of the way and bent down to hold a tumbler to Gideon's lips with a hand enclosed in a thin, black leather glove. 'Drink this.'

Gideon smelt brandy – his best Courvoisier – and obliged with no argument. The burning liquid did wonders.

'Thanks,' he said, and immediately felt stupid.

It was, after all, his own Cognac.

His jacket was grasped once more and he was
pulled to his feet, where he was surprised to find
himself standing face to face with his captor.
Surprised, because he himself stood six foot four
and was accustomed to looking down at most
people. This man was as tall or taller. He wore a
black woolly hat over very short fair hair, and a
cotton bandanna pulled up over his nose, bandit-
style, so that all Gideon could see was a pair of
uncompromising, ice blue eyes. Presumably the
other man had also worn his neckerchief in the
same way but it had since been removed and used
to mop his face. Both wore black jeans and black
leather jackets over dark roll-necks.

The tall one patted Gideon down in the manner
of one who had done it before and slickly removed
his mobile phone, wallet and keys from an inside
pocket.

'You won't be needing those,' he said, tossing
them on to a chair. 'Now, turn round.'

Gideon wasn't in a position to argue. He turned.
From behind, a thick, soft pad was placed over his
eyes and bound tightly in place with another piece
of material. Darkness was absolute. Firm hands
took hold of his shoulders and pushed him in the
direction of the front door.

'Right, let's get moving. We waited half an hour
for you, pal, and the Guv'nor doesn't like to be
kept waiting.'

'What the hell's going on?' Gideon protested.
'Where are you taking me?'

'The Guv'nor said to bring you, I don't ask why, I just do it.'

'I don't understand. Who is this Guv'nor?'

'Yeah, right. I'm really going to tell you.'

Gideon stumbled over his front doorstep and stopped. 'Are you sure you've got the right man?' he persisted, mystified. Less than an hour before he had been celebrating the completion of a commissioned racehorse portrait with some delighted clients. The situation was unreal.

'You *are* Gideon Blake and this *is* the Gatehouse to Graylings Priory?'

There seemed little point in denying it, since one look in his wallet would give the game away. Gideon nodded.

'Then we've got the right man. Now shut up and keep walking.'

Gideon did as he was told. There was nothing else he could do. Shouting for help would have been a fruitless exercise with his nearest neighbours the best part of half a mile away.

Moments later, he was shoved unceremoniously into the back of a van. A van which, on reflection, Gideon remembered seeing as he'd ridden past on his motorbike. Such things were notable in a country lane as quiet as this one. Broken Nose climbed in beside him, muttering darkly, the doors were slammed shut and with the tall man at the wheel, they moved off.

The bed of the van, on to which Gideon had been pushed, was completely devoid of any form of upholstery, leaving him lying on the bare metal ribs of the bodyshell. The pervading smell was of oil, and from the hollow sound of it, the vehicle was more or less empty.

With a sustained effort, Gideon managed to inch his way into an upright position by pushing his shoulders against the side of the vehicle and wriggling. Suddenly, just as he relaxed, the van turned and accelerated, throwing him against his companion, who swore and pushed him flat again.

'Cut it out!' the tall man said over his shoulder.

Gideon wriggled his way up once more and by bracing himself firmly with his feet, managed to stay there for the rest of the journey, which he judged was about twenty minutes. About halfway he began to shiver, due partly to the cold of the February night and partly to shock, but in the noisy darkness of the van his travelling companion didn't appear to notice, for which he was grateful.

Fear was pushing at the edges of his consciousness, but his overriding emotion at the moment was complete bewilderment. He was still half-convinced that it was all a case of mistaken identity. He was certainly not an obvious target for kidnapping, his family being no more than comfortably off, and he wasn't aware that he owed anybody any money. He was thirty-four, single, and a self-employed artist with a sideline in animal psychology, although sometimes it seemed to be the other way round. As far as he knew he had never stepped on anyone's toes.

What the hell were they playing at?

The van slowed, turned sharply and proceeded to bump violently over an extremely uneven surface for a few yards before coming to a halt. The engine rattled into silence and Gideon heard the tall man get out, then the back was opened and Broken Nose scrambled out, pulling Gideon after him. He landed awkwardly and would have fallen, had it not been for the hand grasping the collar of his jacket. His head was throbbing in earnest now and it took him a moment or two to regain his balance.

Footsteps could be heard approaching over the frosty ground and a new voice said, 'You certainly took your time. What happened?' The tone was terse and held no discernible accent.

'He was out,' the tall one replied. 'We had to wait half an hour.'

'Well, bring him in. We've been here too long as it is.'

They all began to move forward, Gideon stumbling between the two from the van.

'Did he give you any trouble?'

'A little,' the tall man admitted. 'He's a big bloke.' Then, with a chuckle, 'He bent Curly's nose for him.'

On the other side of Gideon, Curly swore viciously.

A door creaked open. It sounded like an outside door, Gideon thought, to a shed or a barn, not a house. They stepped inside. He was right. Under his feet the ground was soft like trodden earth.

He was propelled forward a few feet and then

stopped by a hand dragging on his leather jacket. The third man, who he assumed from his manner was the Guv'nor, spoke from his left side.

'We've got a little job for you to do, Mr Blake. If you co-operate you'll be out of here in no time and none the worse for it.'

He didn't say what would happen if Gideon didn't co-operate but somehow he didn't feel the need to enquire.

'You're an animal tamer, right? A – what do they call it – a horse whisperer?'

Gideon cringed inwardly. He hated the term, with its mystical connotations.

'I'm a behaviourist,' he amended, 'of sorts.'

'Well, whatever,' the Guv'nor said impatiently. 'But you sort out horses.'

'Sometimes.'

'Well, we need you to catch one. It's farting around in there and we can't get near it. Bloody mad it is! Kicked one of us already.'

Oh, cheers! Gideon thought. Aloud he asked, 'What's upset it?'

'I don't know!' the other man said testily. 'It's just like that. Maybe it's stressed. Maybe it's had a bad hair day. Just get on with it!'

'Well, I'll need something to catch it with and you'll have to undo my hands,' he observed practically.

'It's already got a bridle on. A headcollar or whatever you call it.'

'So how did it get loose?'

'What *is* this?' the man hissed, losing patience.

'Twenty fucking questions? You don't need to know what happened. Your job is to catch it. Right?'

Gideon took a steadying breath. The force of this man's personality made Curly's threats seem like those of a child.

'Okay,' he said, as calmly as he could. 'And my hands?'

'I can't let you free but you can have them in front,' the Guv'nor conceded.

'And the blindfold?' Gideon asked as one handcuff was undone and swiftly reapplied in front of him.

'No. That stays.'

'What's to stop me pulling it off myself?' he asked reasonably.

The Guv'nor leaned close. 'Nothing except the knowledge that if you do we won't be able to let you leave here.'

Gideon took his point.

'Useless to mention you're making my job almost impossible?' he suggested.

'Useless,' the other man agreed. 'Think of it as a challenge. Now get on with it!'

'And if I can't do it?'

'I don't think that's an option, do you?' he said softly.

Gideon was turned through ninety degrees and once again pushed forward.

'It'd be a help if I knew the horse's name,' he ventured hopefully.

'Tough.'

He took a deep, steadying breath and applied his mind to the problem. 'Okay, so how big is the area? How big is the horse? And where is it in relation to me at the moment?'

'About thirty feet by fifty. The horse is in the far corner, diagonally right from you. It's . . . I don't know, about average size. What does it bloody matter?'

From the rear another voice volunteered the opinion that the horse was about seventeen hands. Gideon assimilated the information, wondering at the same time just how many more people were standing silently around. It was almost eerie.

Anyway, one thing was clear. Whoever the Guv'nor was, he wasn't a horseman. Seventeen hands wasn't really average. Difficult to say what was. It just wasn't the sort of thing a horseman would say.

Trying to put his audience out of his mind, Gideon began to walk slowly in the direction of the animal, hoping that his way was unimpeded by obstacles. It was going to be difficult enough to gain the horse's confidence; doing a nosedive under its muzzle would seriously damage his chances of success.

The blindfold was a major hindrance. So much depended on body language with animals. Tiny changes of posture, movements of a horse's ears and eyes and the swishing of its tail, all gave away important information about the state of its mind. Normally, Gideon intuitively reacted to that information with his own body language; dominant posture when it was required, at other times submissive. Without it, it felt uncomfortably like a game of Russian roulette. He was frighteningly vulnerable.

This is crazy, he thought, I can't do it. And at the same time he knew he had no choice but to try.

Somewhere ahead and to the right of him, he heard the horse begin to shift restlessly, its feet thudding softly on the loose dirt underfoot. Gideon paused, reaching out with his mind to the animal. What came back was a powerful mix of emotions; anxiety and distrust, certainly, and fear, but laced through with an unmistakable vein of aggression, fairly unusual in a horse.

Gideon turned his head. 'He's a stallion?' he asked softly.

'Yeah. Get on with it.'

'Oh, shit!' he muttered under his breath. Concentrating hard, he reached out once more to the horse, trying to project an aura of calm and reassurance.

He could sense the stallion watching him.

Anxiety.

Indecision.

It wasn't sure whether to stand its ground or run. Fight or flight. Given the option, horses almost invariably choose the latter. Nature has equipped them with the means to escape and they make good use of it. Stallions, however, are often the exception. Fired with the instinct to protect their herd, they meet aggression with aggression, challenge with physical attack.

Gideon turned slightly sideways. He had no wish to appear challenging.

The horse was still.

Tense.

Watching him.

He would have given anything to be able to see it. Was it standing facing him, head high, defiant? Or had it lowered its head, considering the situation? The electricity in the air between them suggested the former.

Still trying to radiate reassurance, Gideon stepped closer, head slightly bowed, shoulders still angled away.

He'd moved too close, too soon.

With a flurry of hooves the stallion rushed him, its teeth closing with a painful snap on his shoulder before it backed away.

It hadn't gone far though. No more than a couple of paces. Gideon could feel the huffing of its breath on his face. He steeled himself to remain motionless, trying not to think of the damage those steel-sprung jaws could do; what havoc the immensely powerful legs could wreak on a soft, unprotected human body. Important not to think. He must be steady. Horses are strongly telepathic.

The stallion was unsure now. He could sense its bewilderment. It didn't know how to respond to somebody who neither fled nor tried to dominate. At least it hadn't run. If it started to race around he wouldn't have a chance, handicapped as he was. The signs were encouraging.

Gideon relaxed. He tried to project serenity,

picturing the horse in his mind, lowering its head and coming to him quietly. He was offering a refuge.

If the animal hadn't already been thoroughly unsettled by earlier, more direct attempts to catch it, the procedure wouldn't have worked, but after what seemed like a lifetime, he heard the stallion give a deep gusty sigh and smiled to himself. The horse was as good as his now. He took a step sideways, away from the animal, keeping his movements soft and slow.

The horse stepped warily closer, dropping its nose and blowing softly on Gideon's hands. The rope trailing from its headcollar flopped against his leg. He let the horse snuffle his hands, not allowing himself to think that it might suffer another flash of temper and take a couple of fingers off.

It didn't.

Much calmer now, it let Gideon rub its muzzle gently with his fingers and slowly, oh, so slowly, take hold of the rope. Hoping nobody would be stupid enough to call out, he turned away from the captive horse and took two or three experimental steps. There was a momentary resistance on the rope and then he heard the muffled hoofbeats of the stallion as it gave in and followed.

Strange, but when it came to it, most tame horses were glad to be caught again. Breaking free was instinctive but after the first wild exultation had ebbed they seemed almost relieved to have order restored.

Gideon told the horse quietly that it was a good boy.

Somewhere ahead and to his right, a low voice said 'Well done!' and he made his way towards it, slowing when the horse's hesitation told him he must be nearing the waiting group.

'He's very head-shy but I think he'll be all right now if you all stay calm and don't crowd him,' Gideon said, quietly. Then, almost surprising himself, 'He's in pain. Is he injured?'

'Shut up.' The Guv'nor again.

'Okay,' Gideon said, with a slight shrug. 'Well, who wants him?'

Somebody came quietly forward to take the rope from his grasp. He felt the horse's head go up a notch or two as control was transferred but it offered no further resistance as it was led past him and away.

Gideon heaved a deep sigh of release, aware for the first time that his shoulder was painfully bruised, and wishing he had his hands free to rub it. He was also aware that he only had the thickness of his padded leather motorcycle jacket to thank for the injury not being many times worse.

'Right.' The Guv'nor was speaking, back in charge. 'Fetch the other one and let's get it over with and get out of here! It's all taking far too bloody long!'

His task completed, Gideon stood still. Presumably someone would come for him before long. His knees felt shaky and he would have liked to have sat down but he could scarcely just collapse where he was. Ahead of him he heard a door open

593

and then the low whickering of a mare and the answering excitement of the stallion.

Why hadn't they used the mare to catch the stallion? he wondered wearily. Surely somebody could have caught hold of the rope while he was about his business, if that was what they'd intended him for anyway. Any horseman would have thought of it, surely? And if there wasn't a horseman amongst them, what the hell were they doing in possession of a stallion?

Feeling overlooked, he began to step cautiously forward.

'You! Blake! Stand still.'

Gideon obediently stood.

'You. Take him outside.'

Somebody grasped his arm and within moments he was out in the frosty night air again. His arm was released and the door shut behind him. Only the sighing of the bitingly cold wind disturbed the silence. Gideon stood where he'd been left.

Was everyone with the horses? he mused after a while. Was anybody actually watching him now or was he standing like a sucker with nobody near? He lifted his hands and rubbed experimentally at his cheekbone, just brushing the edge of the blindfold.

'It would be a shame if I thought you were trying to get that blindfold off, when all you had was an itch.'

Soft Liverpudlian accent. Curly's tall companion.

'That *would* be a shame,' Gideon agreed.

Nothing was said for a few moments then

Gideon broke the silence. 'Do this sort of thing often, do you?'

'Makes a change from the pubs and clubs,' his companion replied evenly.

'Been down south long?'

'Long enough to know my way around.'

'Yeah?' Gideon affected mild surprise. 'So, where would you say the nearest town would be to here?'

A low chuckle greeted this admittedly feeble attempt to draw him out.

'Listen, pal. I may have been born at night, but it wasn't *last* night. Now just shut up and wait.'

Gideon did as he was told.

He couldn't be sure how long he stood there in the bitter wind with his silent companion. Long before there was any sign of an end to his wait, he had begun to shiver violently and was in danger of losing all feeling in his hands and feet, but eventually the barn door creaked open and a horse was led past within a few feet of him. Shortly after, another followed and he heard the unmistakable hollow sound of hooves on wood, as they were loaded into a horsebox or boxes.

Footsteps approached, crunching on the frosty ground.

Gideon's heart began to thump uncomfortably. He hoped that his being blindfolded meant he was going to be freed as promised, but he was realist enough not to be sure of it.

The footsteps stopped in front of him.

'You know what to do,' the Guv'nor said quietly to Gideon's escort. 'Just give us all some breathing space and make sure no one sees you. And you,' he said, leaning close to Gideon. 'You'd do best just to think of this as a bad dream – one you were lucky enough to wake up from. Remember, we know where you live but you know nothing about us. Best let it stay that way. Understand?'

Gideon felt he probably did. At any rate, he wasn't about to argue.

There followed a journey which was essentially the same as the first, except – presumably – in the opposite direction. Gideon was seated next to the rear doors of the van, with Curly close beside him having an amusing time opening the door a crack occasionally and threatening to push him out. His tall friend had taken the precaution of cuffing Gideon's hands behind him again before they had set out, and with the road noise and the rushing of the wind, he felt desperately exposed in the open doorway.

After a while, Curly's companion caught sight of the baiting in his rear-view mirror and put a stop to it.

Gideon sent him a silent blessing.

Presently, after bumping for a hundred yards or so along an unmade track, the vehicle swung round in a semi-circle and stopped, engine still running.

'You've not far to walk,' the voice from the front informed him, 'but I'm afraid we can't take you any closer. We don't want you calling the boys in blue, do we?'

Gideon didn't see that an answer was called for, and he couldn't think of a polite one anyway.

'I've been admiring your boots,' the soft voice went on. 'I should think they'd fit me just fine, we're much of a size. Curly, would you do the honours?'

For a moment Gideon considered baling out voluntarily for the sake of keeping his boots but the idea died a death. He wouldn't exactly be able to sprint away, blindfolded and with his hands behind his back. He began to have second thoughts about the blessing so recently bestowed.

'I hope they pinch, you sonofabitch!' he muttered uncharitably.

'So, he does have feelings,' the tall one observed as Curly got to work.

Gideon simmered with helpless frustration. The boots were favourites of his, bought in America for a small fortune some six months before and now just nicely worn in. It wasn't only this, however, that depressed him, but the prospect of a hike of indefinite length over frosty, stony ground, with feet clad only in socks. It was ironic that half an hour ago he had been far from sure that he would be freed at all and now he was quibbling over the theft of his boots. It was a bit like being picked up at sea and then moaning because your rescuers weren't going your way, but the thought didn't appease him.

'Well, we'll be off, then,' the tall one said. 'It was a pleasure doing business with you.'

'Oh, the pleasure was all mine,' Gideon assured him sarcastically. Then, as Curly put a hand on his arm prior to pushing him out, 'What about the handcuffs?'

'Oh, you can keep them. We've got some more.'

Gideon's protest was cut short as Curly gave him an unnecessarily hard shove that pitched him helplessly out of the back of the van. He landed heavily on his shoulder and the side of his head on what felt like hard-packed gravel.

The van moved off promptly, as if they were afraid that he would somehow climb back in, but as Gideon rolled on to his back and sat up, he heard it stop again, a little way off. He felt a moment's sharp panic. Was Curly coming back to fulfil his earlier promise, after all?

'The key's in your back pocket, pal,' the soft voice called. 'Have a nice walk.'

Listening to the van pull away and breathing a choking lungful of exhaust fumes, Gideon nevertheless sent up a prayer of thanks to the stars.

His first impulse upon regaining his feet was to feel in his pocket for the key, but even as his fingers located it he realised he had little hope of using it successfully with his hands still behind his back, and stiff with cold into the bargain. It was more than likely that he'd drop it and, judging by the size of it, once dropped – in the dark and on an uneven gravel surface – it would stay dropped. Much better, if he could manage it, to get his hands in front of him, remove the blindfold and do the job properly. Carefully he palmed the key and closed his fist around it.

Bending forward, Gideon then attempted to slide his joined wrists down over his hips and buttocks, feeling the muscles in his back and chest strain with the effort. The pull of the metal bracelets on his wrists was intensely uncomfortable but he persevered and, with a groan of relief, made it.

His hands were now behind his knees. He knew he'd been able to step through his hands as a teenager but he was somewhat bulkier these days. After a pause to breathe he emptied his lungs, balanced on one socked foot and dragged the other through from front to back, his shoulders taking the strain this time. A sharper pain in his right shoulder bore witness to the damage the horse's teeth had done. The second foot was slightly easier and he stood up straight, feeling justifiably pleased with himself.

The irony was that if he'd been wearing his boots, with their inch or so of heel, he doubted very much if he would have succeeded in stepping through, and he would have found it exceedingly difficult, if not impossible, to have taken them off with his hands secured behind him. They weren't always easy at the best of times.

Lifting his joined hands, Gideon removed the blindfold, wincing as it pulled clear of his left eye where blood had run from the gash on his brow and done a painfully efficient job of sticking the material to his skin.

Blinking, he looked about him.

It was a fairly clear night with a moon that was a little more than half-full. Against the starry sky he could make out the shapes of trees surrounding him and see where the gravel track stretched away towards the road. There wasn't enough light to be of much help in undoing his handcuffs but twisting one hand to touch the other bracelet, he could feel the small hole that presumably accommodated the key. This done, it was a relatively simple task to release himself.

Feeling much happier, Gideon snapped each cuff shut once more and stowed them in his jacket pocket. The key he returned to the back pocket of his jeans, wondering as he did so just when the tall man had put it there.

A growing numbness in his feet reminded him that he had far more urgent concerns. The temperature was well below freezing and the ground frozen hard. He had at least a hundred yards to cover before he reached the road and no idea how much further after that. He thought he might possibly be in the lane that led to the old gravel pits just outside the village of Tarrant Grayling and, if so, his gatehouse home was going to be some three-quarters of a mile away. The spectre of frostbite reared its ugly head.

Peering at the lighted dial of his watch he discovered it was almost three in the morning; hardly the best time to try and hitch a lift on what was never a busy road.

With a heavy sigh, Gideon began his trek, trying to console himself with the fact that he had at least been left with his jacket, but in reality swearing bloody revenge every time his unprotected feet located a sharp stone.

The walk was a very long one.